CONTEMPORANEITY OF THE MAHABHARATA NARRATIVE

Notwithstanding its renowned comprehensive narrative encapsulation of the Indic culture, the Mahabharata keeps on posing a challenge to its contemporary readers: how do we relate to something over two-millennia old in today's context without freezing it in time? This volume looks at the problem from diverse periods and standpoints and shows us that this challenge is, in fact, a legacy of the Mahabharata and the responses to this challenge are what makes the text ever-contemporary to different readers of different times and positions.

It traces the evolution of the Mahabharata from its inception in the fifth century BCE to twenty-first century, spanning classical Sanskrit tradition, Persian and Bengali adaptations, the Mahabharata as a serialized TV show to more recent graphic narratives. By attempting to analyse this diversity, this volume further delves into how the issues in the Mahabharata resonate across time, from the world of ancient sages to contemporary struggles of women. The essays in this book adopt a dual perspective to appreciate both the Mahabharata's historical context, its exploration of war, heroes and heroines, gender, psychology, philosophy, and its implications for the future.

This book will be of interest to scholars and researchers of Indian literature, ancient literature and philosophy, English literature, cultural studies, visual studies, gender studies, and translation studies.

Anirban Bhattacharjee (PhD, CSSSC & JU, Kolkata) is an Assistant Professor of English at Santipur College and a visiting faculty at IISER, Kolkata. He has a sustained interest in the *Mahabharata* and is part of several international research groups on the text. He presented the opening plenary of the 2018 meeting of South Asian Literary Association. His recently edited volume is titled *Mahabharate Himsa* (2022).

Dhrubajyoti Sarkar teaches at the Department of English, University of Kalyani. His research interests are religious nationalism and religion-culture interface in the context of nineteenth-century South Asia.

CONTEMPORANEITY OF THE MAHABHARATA NARRATIVE

Epic of the Moment

Edited by Anirban Bhattacharjee and Dhrubajyoti Sarkar

Routledge
Taylor & Francis Group

LONDON AND NEW YORK

Designed cover image: Getty Images

First published 2025
by Routledge
4 Park Square, Milton Park, Abingdon, Oxon OX14 4RN

and by Routledge
605 Third Avenue, New York, NY 10158

Routledge is an imprint of the Taylor & Francis Group, an informa business

British Library Cataloguing-in-Publication Data
A catalogue record for this book is available from the British Library

ISBN: 978-1-032-38251-7 (hbk)
ISBN: 978-1-032-84956-0 (pbk)
ISBN: 978-1-003-51640-8 (ebk)

DOI: 10.4324/ 9781003516408

Typeset in Sabon
by Deanta Global Publishing Services, Chennai, India

The volume is dedicated to the respectful memory of
Alfred John Hiltebeitel (1942–2023)
who took a deep personal interest in the making of the volume
but could not give us a chance to deliver the volume in person

CONTENTS

Contributors   *ix*
Foreword   *xii*
Sibaji Bandyopadhyay

Preface and Acknowledgement   *xxiii*

Introduction   1
Anirban Bhattacharjee and Dhrubajyoti Sarkar

PART I

1   Asvamedhaparva: Jaimini and Vyasa   17
    Sekhar Kumar Sen

2   Nilakantha's Mahabharata and Presentist Objections to His Work   37
    Christopher Minkowski

3   Dramatic War, Fabulous Stories, and Legendary Kings: Persian
    Adaptation of Mahabharata as *Razmnama*   48
    Kashshaf Ghani

4   On Adaptation and Appropriation: Some Observations on
    the Sources of the *Mushalaparva* in Kashiramadasa's Bengali
    Mahabharata   66
    Soham Pain

5   Bankim Chandra Chattopadhyay's Lonely Middle Course: A
    Reading of the Mahabharata in *Krishnacharitra*   83
    Dhrubajyoti Sarkar

6 Relocating Mahabharatian Dystopia in Post-independent
India: Reading *Rangabharata* as a Political Caricature of the
Nehruvian Times 99
Pinak Sankar Bhattacharya

7 "Doomsday Epic"? P. Lal's *The Mahabharata of Vyasa* and the
Influence of European Modernism 110
Prayag Ray

8 Irreverent Readers, Worshipful Viewers: Post-emergency Epics
and Diverging Indian Nationalisms 121
Sucheta Kanjilal

9 Orality of "Then" and "Now": Narrating the Mahabharata on
Television 138
Sneha Roy Choudhury

10 Psychobiography and Authorial Subjectivity in the (Re)
presentation of Draupadi: Towards a Feminist Mythopoeia in
Select Retellings of the Mahabharata 153
Komal Agarwal

11 A World of Images: The Visual Identity of the Mahabharata 170
Sankha Banerjee

PART II

12 The "Avengers" in an *Itihasa:* Reading Revenge in the
Mahabharata 183
Kanad Sinha

13 Otherwise than Being: The Mahabharata, the Animal, and the
Eruption of the Ethical 202
Anirban Bhattacharjee

14 The Mahabharata War and Ambedkar's Critique of Violence
and Nationalism 212
Kalyan Kumar Das

Afterthoughts: In Search of the Antecedents to the
Mahabharata Concept and Ideal of *Anrisamsya*: Random
Reflections 224
Ranabir Chakravarti

Index 241

CONTRIBUTORS

Komal Agarwal is an Assistant Professor of English at Shaheed Bhagat Singh College. Her dissertation on select Modern Retellings of the Mahabharata has been awarded PhD by Jawaharlal Nehru University. Her research interests are the Mahabharata in its performative and popular versions. She is the founding coordinator of the Centre for Indian Knowledge Systems at her institution.

Sibaji Bandyopadhyay is a Distinguished Professor formerly affiliated with the Centre for Studies in Social Sciences, Kolkata, and the Department of Comparative Literature, Jadavpur University, renowned for his expertise in diverse branches of critical theory and cultural studies. With a prolific career spanning decades, inter alia, his long-standing interest in the academic discourse of the Mahabharata tradition has enriched the field of scholarship and inspired many generations of scholars and students. Some of his books are *Gopal-Rakhal Dvandasamas* (latest edition: 2023), *Sibaji Bandyopadhyay Reader* (2012), *Three Essays on the Mahabharata* (latest edition: 2017), *Alibabar Guptabhandar* (latest edition: 2024). He has jointly edited with Arindam Chakravarti *Mahabharata Now* (2014).

Sankha Banerjee is an Assistant Professor at St Xavier's College, Kolkata. His works have been collected by many art galleries, including the Museum of Contemporary Art, Lyon, France. He is currently working on the Indian epic the Mahabharata in a sequential art form, in collaboration with Sibaji Bandyopadhyay. The first two volumes, *Vyasa: The Beginning* and *Panchali: The Dice Game*, have been published by Penguin India.

Anirban Bhattacharjee (Ph.D., CSSSC & JU, Kolkata) is an Assistant Professor of English at Santipur College and a visiting faculty at IISER, Kolkata. He has a sustained interest in the Mahabharata and is part of several international research groups on the text. He presented the opening plenary of the 2018 meeting of the South Asian Literary Association. He has published articles in journals like *South Asian Review*, *Comparative Literature Studies*, *Journal of Dharma Studies* and *Sanglap: Journal of Literary and Cultural Enquiry*. His recently edited volume is titled *Mahabharate Himsa* (2022).

Pinak Sankar Bhattacharya is an Assistant Professor of English at Baneswar Sarathibala Mahavidyalaya, West Bengal. He completed his PhD from Banaras Hindu University on relocating the Mahabharata in Modern Indian English Drama. His research areas include Indian literature, performance studies, and cultural studies.

Ranabir Chakravarti, Professor, formerly, at the Centre for Historical Studies, Jawaharlal Nehru University, and an eminent expert in the social and economic history of early India, is known for his enduring interests in the Indian Ocean maritime trade during the pre-modern times. A regular contributor to peer-reviewed journals and edited academic volumes in India and abroad, he has authored/co-authored and edited/co-edited the following works: *Warfare for Wealth: Early Indian Perspectives* (1986); *A Sourcebook of Indian Civilization* (2000); *Indo-Judaic Studies in the Twenty-First Century: A View from the Margins* (2007); *Exploring Early India up to c. AD 1300* (2016); and *Trade and Traders in Early Indian Society* (2020).

Sneha Roy Choudhury is an Assistant Professor at IILM University, Gurugram. She earned her PhD at the Centre for Media Studies, Jawaharlal Nehru University, New Delhi. In her doctoral research, she studied the implications of a decaying culture of performativity through the analysis of region-specific ritual theatrical forms. Her research interests include theatre, culture, film and media, nationalism, and religion.

Kalyan Kumar Das is an Assistant Professor of English at Presidency University. His research publications in journals like *Critical Philosophy of Race*, *Economic and Political Weekly*, *Dewey Studies*, and *Contemporary Voice of Dalit* cover his areas of interest like critical theory, continental philosophy, critical caste studies, and race studies. His current research focusses on Dalit sartorial politics and Dalit aesthetics.

Kasshaf Ghani is an Assistant Professor of History at Nalanda University. His research interests focus on religion and cultural interactions in pre-modern South Asia through the history of Sufism. Starting off at the University of Calcutta, Ghani held research positions at the University of Sorbonne-Nouvelle and the Zentrum Moderner Orient. To his credit, Ghani has three books and edited volumes, and approximately fifty book chapters and articles published in a versatile fashion, ranging from specialist academic journals to magazines addressing an interested general audience.

Sucheta Kanjilal is an Assistant Professor of English and Writing at the University of Tampa. A scholar of South Asian studies, her work primarily interrogates colonialism, nationalism, and modern Hinduism. Her recent publications examine the impact of the Sanskrit epics and their adaptations on Indian politics. Her research on caste and the Mahabharata has been published in *Many Mahabharatas* (2021).

Christopher Minkowski is a Boden Professor of Sanskrit Emeritus at Oxford University, specializing in ancient Indian literature and textual studies. With expertise in Sanskrit and Pali languages, his research focusses on Mahabharata studies, manuscript traditions, and the intersection of oral and written traditions in South Asian literature.

Soham Pain is an Assistant Professor of English at Scottish Church College, Kolkata. A PhD from Jawaharlal Nehru University, and a Fulbright-Nehru Doctoral Fellow at the University of Texas at Austin, he specializes in Indian Knowledge Traditions. His current research focusses on medieval and modern retellings of the Mahabharata. His Bengali translation of Jacinta Kerketta's collection, *Jadon ki zameen,* was published in 2023.

Prayag Ray is an Assistant Professor of English at St. Xavier's University, Kolkata. His PhD, completed at Queen's University, Belfast, explored representations of Hinduism in British literature of the eighteenth century. He has published articles in Journals like *Postcolonial Studies*, *Poetry Ireland*, and the *Journal for Eighteenth-Century Studies*, as well as book chapters in edited volumes published by Springer, and Atlande.

Dhrubajyoti Sarkar teaches at the Department of English, University of Kalyani. His research interests are religious nationalism and religion-culture interface in the context of nineteenth-century South Asia.

Sekhar Kumar Sen is a retired Major General of the Indian Army. Sen is an independent scholar with deep and sustained interest in the textual tradition of early texts of the Mahabharata. He has edited and translated the text of *Jaimini Mahabharata* published by the Writers Workshop under the aegis of National Manuscript Mission.

Kanad Sinha teaches at the Department of Ancient Indian and World History, The Sanskrit College and University, Kolkata. His PhD dissertation at Jawaharlal Nehru University is entitled *From Dasarajna to Kurukshetra* (Oxford 2023). A number of his research papers on the Mahabharata have been published in various reputed journals. He won the V.K. Thakur Memorial Prize at the Indian History Congress.

FOREWORD

One

> The Mahabharata, known also as the *Itihasa*, cares not a whit for others' praise or plaudits.

Undergoing sporadic bouts of generation and elaboration for about eight hundred years, roughly between fourth century BCE and fourth century CE, the Mahabharata carries inputs from several contributors. The fiction-in-the-making, however, compresses its long-drawn production with the pretense that it was manufactured by a single person, namely, Krishna Dvaipayana Vyasa – he was the same "miracle-monger" of a compiler who had threaded together the four Vedas (*Mbh* 1.1.18, Buitenen 1973 20). We are informed in a few preliminary passages of Canto I or the "Adiparvan"/"The Book of the Beginning" of the *Mahabharata*: a) the full Vyasa-text was "repeated," and that too "truthfully," for the first time in a gathering by Vaisampayana, one of Vyasa's disciples; b) following the initial public recital, a professional minstrel called Sauti Ugrasravas communicated the "ancient lore" as it was "related" by Dvaipayana Vyasa to a band of seers – and, that counts as the second iteration of the publicly-performed *Mahabharata* (*Mbh* 1.1.9,18,15).

The *itihasa* assures us that both Vaisampayana and Sauti Ugrasravas represented to the letter whatever Vyasa had originally presented. Just the same, this affirmation of singular purpose ends up belying an unmanageable accretion. For, while the number of verses reeled off by Vyasa was paltry eight thousand, in Vaisampayana's recounting it got jacked up to twenty-four and in Sauti's case it reached the sky-high figure of eighty-four thousand. Contrary to the "Adiparvan's promise of flawless fidelity," the "sacred Account of the Bharatas" (*Mbh* 1.1.19, Buitenen 20) went on to expand with every retelling, becoming thereby open to the intrusion of numberless interpolations.

But the good news is, being large and containing multitudes, the *Mahabharata* can very well afford to be self-contradictory. The *Adiparvan* vouches for the two subsequent recitalists' unwavering adherence to the first-born *itihasa*. At the same moment, we hear in the same Book, Sauti – the galavanting versifier who made Vyasa's Collection 10.5 times bigger than it was at its inception – obliquely testifying to the *Mahabharata*'s cumulative growth at the hand of different meddlers: "Poets have told it before, poets are telling now, other poets shall tell this [*itihasa*]...in the future (*Mbh* 1.1. 24, Buitenen 21)." The putative suggestion is, neither the singular third-person pronoun "it" standing for the *itihasa* denotes a static entity nor are the poets "its" passive reciters. Rather, the *itihasa* keeps renewing "itself" by the grace of fresh storytellers.

Now, the fabricators, including the downright fabulists of yesterday have been as well as those of today and tomorrow must be of various stripes – some of them would be undeniably gifted, some lackluster mediocre, and the rest rank worthless. The increasingly massive chronicle could not but end up becoming a mixed bag. Yet, long back, placing the heaviest of premiums on the *Mahabharata*, Sauti had brazenly asserted that the Bharata-legend stands at the zenith of every conceivable poetry:

> From this supreme *itihasa* rise the inspirations of the poets...No story is found on earth that does not rest on this...Even as servants that strive for preferment live off a high-born master, so all the best poets live off this narrative. (*Mbh* 1.2.239-241, Buitenen 43)

Should we take seriously the *itihasa*'s declaration that while it does not require anybody's commendation or endorsement, every other text needs to be measured in terms of the unapproachable standard set by it? Or, should we dismiss the precious claim as mighty preposterous, as a piece of rude arrogance minted in the fevered brain of a loudmouth nomad?

Two

Thanks to many authorial participants, *itihasa* is rich in digression. Quirky in pattern, it often breaks off from continuing with a tale only to embark on another. Neither is there a clear-cut design, a distinctly discernible logic in the types of intercutting the *Mahabharata* seems to revel in. As a result, if this sub-episode is breezy, light-footed, even erotically naughty, then that sub-episode is weighty, heavy-going, even grimly moralistic. The best that can be said to explain the occasional preponderance of the sternly solemn at the expense of the playfully jocular – especially in Cantos XII and XIII, the *Santiparvan*/"The Book of Peace" and the *Anusasanaparvan*/"The Book of Laws" – is that with time there occurred a change of guard in relation to the shaping of the *Mahabharata* as we know it now.

During the initial phase, at the helm of the *Mahabharata*'s development was the Suta or itinerant bard – and, Sauti Ugrasravas, whose address to a group of seers inaugurates the *itihasa*, is the emblematic, prominent-most proxy for all those strolling rhapsodists. But slowly, as circumstances would have it, the importance of the creative wandering minstrels – said to be belonging to the despicable breed brought on by the union between a kshatriya or a man of the warrior class and a brahmin woman – began to fade. Eventually, the peddlers of yarns were toppled, almost wholly displaced by firmly-rooted, unbudging brahmins, specially by those affiliated to the clan of Bhrigu. And, the newcomers were single-mindedly committed to the task of construing as well as maintaining intricate webs of rites and rituals with a clear bias in favour of the uppermost caste. Scholars identify the process of usurpation of the role of the *Mahabharata*'s (chief) spokesperson from the "mixed-caste" Suta to the "pure-born" brahmin as *Bhargavayana* or "Bhargavification"(Chakravarti 2023 17–18).

The *Bhargavayana* resulted in a peculiar admixing of exciting intrigues centred on chivalry or amour with trying, ponderous explications on Laws mostly similar in kind to those churned out by Manu, a revered spearhead of Brahminical absolutism. But the appeal of shortish or longish storylines, neatly pinned or planted randomly, well-integrated or appearing out of the blue, is so strong that it remains undiminished no matter how many times strictures calculated to drive one towards the dreary desert of dead habit are delivered or the riot act read out. All said and done, the scriptural aspect of the *Mahabharata* falls far short of its narratorial achievement both in terms of edification and entertainment.

Marshalling many narratorial strategies, the Mahabharata succeeds in sculpting a plethora of inimitable characters. Despite being bogged down here and there by stodgy-stuffy lectures, the grand poem introduces personages who, reckless or otherwise, speak their minds fearlessly – holding their heads high, they puncture rounded discourses with great finesse.

Take for example: Pururava. He was a grandson of Manu the Lawmaker and a son of Ila who was a man and a woman in one body; he reigned over thirteen islands and was always surrounded by non-human creatures; he took a perverse delight in pillaging the gem-stacked hermitages in which pious brahmins, the ones forever busy in performing animal-sacrifices, dwelled; it was for the same lusty Pururava that Urvasi, the celestial courtesan, had fallen and they together had founded the lineage to which belonged the Pandavas and Kauravas, the two antagonistic groups of cousins for whose sake the "Great Mahabharata War" was staged; what is more mystifying is that Pururava, together with Urvasi, had brought to earth the Three Fires the lighting of which later became obligatory for all Brahminical sacrifices (*Mbh* 1.70.13-18; 1.70.21, Buitenen 174).

Pururava was deaf to all wisely counsel. Obviously, for his contempt for the sanctimonious hypocrites known to the world as "brahmins," he had to pay the ultimate price – infuriated by the Fire-procurer's audacity and haughty attitude, Sage Sanatkumar, Son of Brahma the four-faced creator, turned him to ashes (*Mbh* 1.70.19-20, Buitenen 174). But before his untimely as well as undeserved exit from the scene of the *Mahabharata*, it was Pururava who had restated the as-yet unsettled ethical paradox that has been ailing mankind since the beginning of Time. To make the matter more hilarious, Pururava the Aila or a scion of Ila the "freak," (Fitzerald 2004 354) is shown to have raised the disturbing question in the generally sermonic and soporific Canto XII or the "Santiparvan"/"The Book of Peace." Therein we learn, once upon a time, Pururava had asked of a reputed brahmin seer:

> If punishment affects someone entitled to reward - especially while evil is being done by others who are evil – then what reason would anyone have to do what is good? And what reason would anyone have not to do what is wrong? (*Mbh* 12.74.22, Fitzerald 354)

Three

Inescapable contradictions and yawning inconsistencies go a long way in turning the *Mahabharata* into a spectacular exhibit of split-characters. Ranging from the slippery scrupulous to the naively devious, from the ethically challenged to the artfully ethical, from the counterproductive moralist to the miscalculating schemer, from the self-exposing hypocrite to the guileless gambler and other such combination of contrarieties, its palette of personalities is overwhelming. And, in stark contrast to the wordy pontifications, it is the antics of these picturesque men and women which make the moral universe of the *Mahabharata* profoundly ambiguous. The *itihasa* resounds with questions both whose posing and mode of answering are still as relevant and problematic as when they were first articulated. A few dramatic examples:

- Canto V: "Udyogaparvan"/"The Book of Planning"

Sanjaya, the narrator of the "Great War" who was also an uncompromising pacifist, said to Yudhisthira, the Son of Dharma,

> A man's life is a brief deluge, permanently painful and changeable; ... If the wise cannot persuade his war-mongering ministers otherwise, he should leave the affairs of state in their hands and himself abdicate; ... It is better to live upon alms than to obtain sovereignty by war. (*Mbh* 5.27.3; 5.27.27; 5.27.2, De 1940 93, 97, 93)

To this wholescale attack on the very ideology of militarism, Krishna, perhaps the most war-mongering counsellor of Yudhisthira, retorted angrily: any talk that decries *karma* ought to be dismissed as mindless ramblings of foolish weak men; *karma*, though pre-assigned to individuals according to his *varna*, i.e., to his allotted standing in society, constitutes an inviolable Categorical Imperative, both in its particular and universal aspects; and Yudhisthira belongs to the *kshatriya* or warrior-community; hence, he has no other option but to fulfil his *karmic* incumbency of remaining forever enlisted in the army. (*Mbh* 5.29.7; 5.29.19-20, De 1940 101-102, 103-104)

• Canto VI: "Bhismaparvan":

Equating *karma* with *dharma*, Krishna reiterated the same principle – "You should attend to your own dharma; there exists no greater good for a *kshatriya* than a righteous battle" – when Arjuna, reflecting on the devastating consequences of war such as the slaying of one's elders, had become despondent and said, "It is better for one to live on alms than to kill his Gurus or preceptors." (*Mbh* 6.24.31, 6.24.25, Belvalkar 1947, 122, 121; Bandyopadhyay 2016, 193-263)

• Canto II: "Sabhaparvan"/"The Book of the Assembly Hall"

Brain befogged by the enticing game of dice, Yudhisthira lost every particle of his wealth to his avaricious cousin Duryodhana. Next, he betted on his four brothers one after another. After turning them into Duryodhana's slaves, Yudhisthira, at the nineteenth bid, signed himself up; and predictably, forfeited himself to his overjoyed cousin. Still in the thrall of the dancing dice, still mesmerized by the sight of brown nuts rolling down and springing up over and over again on the furrowed board, Yudhisthira went for the twentieth throw: the Son of Dharma made of Draupadi, his and his brothers' common wife, his final wager.

But Draupadi was not just a woman of peerless beauty, she was also possessed of extraordinary grit and intelligence. After she was dragged to the Gambling Hall, red with fury, Draupadi raised one of the most complex questions revolving round the concept of "private possession." She inquired of the elders present in the court, does one who has surrendered his own independence have the authority to surrender someone else's (*Mbh* 2.60.8, Buitenen 1975 140)? Failing to untangle the riddle – can a man bereft of I-ness denude others of their I-ness? – Bhisma, the celibate grandfather of the Pandavas and Kauravas, fell back upon the hackneyed patriarchal assumption of ownership. He granted, "A man without property cannot stake another's"; but then, he argued, there was an exception to this Law; for, since "wives [were] the husband's chattels," their personhood was forever chained to the male spouse's being (*Mbh* 2.60.40, Buitenen 1975 143). The implication was not having selfhood independent of Yudhisthira's, Draupadi had no business in framing the question vis-a-vis "possession" in the first place.

Should one participate in righteous war-campaigns which by the very dint of their nobility of purpose, automatically absolves the actors of the guilt of committing carnage; or, should one, no matter how serious the provocation, steadfastly avoid getting drenched in blood-rain; is there any one objective, unassailable standard which lends to the accurate determination of "righteousness"; does not every armed flare-up which appears to be just and honorable at the beginning, inevitably turns upon itself in the course of its unfolding and finishes up heaping one collateral damage upon another; can the sprightly exhortations of war-enthusiasts in the name of Duty, patriotic or otherwise be wholly outweighed by the arguments of conscientious objectors wary of non-antagonistic, i.e., secondary contradictions; the hawk or the dove, who, if at all, gets the last word; if the strict strictures of class-gender-caste-bound societies turn the idea of I-ness of dispossessed slaves into an unthinkable proposition, how come at certain strategic junctures those same "chattels," playing upon antagonistic, i.e., primary contradictions, think-out the fundamentals of the grammar of prohibitions – these are some of the practically innumerable intellectual teasers that the *Mahabharata* confronts its listeners or readers; no doubt, a few of those paradoxical constructions are, in the ultimate analysis, amenable to reasonable solutions; nonetheless, there are many, particularly those related to the text's principal thematic of War and Peace, that remain stubbornly irresoluble.

Four

The *Mahabharata* literally teems with *aporias*, meaning, the spots that, offering no gateways, only lead to blank holes. What is more, these impossible-to-navigate impasses have had the staying power to retain their relevance across centuries and continents – they still speak with the urgency of Nowness. The *itihasa* thus, on its own initiative, invites us to examine its entanglement with *history*.

An amalgam of three words, "iti" or "thus," "ha" or "it," and "asa" or "was," the Sanskrit *itihasa* implies on the surface, "thus-it-was." On the other hand, the genealogy of English *history* is rather long and twisted. Its Old English form was *istoria*, a transmuted form of classical Latin *historia*, which meant, investigation/research/description/written account of past events/story etc.; Latin *historia* in turn was lifted straight from Greek *historia*, which connoted, inquiry/knowledge from inquiry/judge; and behind Greek *historia* stood Greek *histor*, meaning, learned/wise. It is *histor* that ties firmly the Greek/Latin *historia* with the Sanskrit *itihasa*. For, the truth-value of the claim of "thus-it-was" could only be ascertained or guaranteed by someone whose judgment was sound. That the appellation *itihasa* has stuck to the *Mahabharata* is because it bears the authorial signature of Vyasa the Wise, the mighty learned man who was believed to have had edited the four Vedas; it is also because Vyasa's immense prestige was further fortified when Vaisampayana and Sauti were said to have successively parroted to the last syllable the "knowledge" which the foremost *histor* had gathered from his "inquiry" into the fratricidal strife between the Pandavas and Kauravas. It surely is not just a happenstance that the Greek *histor* shares the same Indo-European root with *wit*, which in archaic vocabulary signifies "(to) have knowledge," along with the Latin *videro*, meaning "see," and the Sanskrit Veda, implying, "knowledge."

Broadly put, the English *history* today stands for the practice of chronicling yesteryears on the basis of scientifically verifiable evidences, i.e., on hard facts which are simultaneously open to being shattered to pieces at a later date. Unlike the merrymakers dabbling in legends or make-believe, fantastical stories, no New Age historian can afford to be cocky, smugly confident about the conclusions s/he puts forward. But given the background of having a tangential link between the Greek-Latin *historia* and (reliable versions of) "thus-it-was" and an inter-knotting of the Greek *histor* with the Sanskrit *Veda* via *wit*, it is least bit surprising that *itihasa* has been adopted as a good enough equivalent for history in its present sense in Bangla and many more modern Indian languages without much fuss.

Nevertheless, the *Mahabharata* as *itihasa* has a special function in terms of evoking, at places distinctly, at others indistinctly, a profound ideological tussle which took place years and years back, a fracas that is yet to reach its point of culmination. For all we know, it is because the *Mahabharata*, in conjunction with its exciting, often breathtaking main narrative, provides a refracted and fractured portrayal of an ongoing struggle that Sauti had the temerity to brag, "No story is found on earth that does not rest on [the *itihasa*]." Well, even if we temper the uppity utterance by replacing "earth" with "India," it is still a tall claim.

Five

This happened twenty-five centuries ago in the eastern Indo-Gangetic plain – the then rulers, priests as well as householders residing in that region watched, watched to their utter bafflement, the sudden appearance of one band after another of people who had renounced the comforts of their hearth and home; always on the move, those outlandish drifters set up temporary tents only to engage in esoteric practices and interminable debates; just as they were dispersed in variously opposing camps so did their somatically exhausting exercises and cerebrally stressful positions differ. But in spite of the internal divisions in respect to backbreaking and mind-bending exertions, all of them were united in criticizing, even downright condemning, the premises of the then existing dominant ideology, the mainstays of priest-centric Brahminism. Collectively known as the Sramana, the nonconformist dissenters, spread between the virulently radical and the middle-path abiding moderate, included groups as variegated as the "Jain," the "Buddhist," the "Ajivika," the "Carvaka," or the "Lokayata," and many, many more.

Despite many unmitigable differences between themselves, the *Sramana* of all factions stood united against the brahmin class's favourite pastime of sacrificing animals in the name of appeasing the meat-loving gods. The *Sramana*s were full-throated in decrying the brahmins' consumption of beasts of the forest, cattle of the hills, fowls of the mountains after cooking them in the presumably holy sacrificial-fire for them, the eyewash of turning the supposed offering for gods into a proxy for self-feeding abetted with the hocus-pocus of mantras was the surefire proof of Brahminical hypocrisy. Reacting with might and main to the ostensibly pious but in truth the callous performance of *himsa* towards non-humans, the *Sramana*s raised the notion of *ahimsa* or nonviolence to a full-blown moral category. That, however, did not lead every *Sramana* to give up on partaking non-vegetarian meals. The creeds of nonviolence and vegetarianism developing along two separate vectors, the Jains and the Buddhists, for instance, followed different dietary courses. The former sect's rejection of "flesh" was so iron-tight as to allow for no exception from the very start; in contrast, the latter's attitude towards meat or fish, particularly, at its early stage, was more relaxed. Nevertheless, members of heterodox schools – be he a Jain, a Buddhist, an Ajivika, a Lokayata, or an adherent of some other *Sramana* persuasion – each of them deployed the genus of ahimsa to denounce the human's animalistic propensity to settle differences, not by the force of argument, but by the force of physical collision. In his battle of words against the varna-based Brahminical orthodoxy, every Sramana, whether the proponent of the "middle path-," the moderate Buddhist or the metaphysics-mocking, the radical Carvaka/'Lokayata" constantly disparaged the violence generated by the exchange of arms; simultaneously, the *Sramanic* concern for the mass-destruction of non-humans underscored a sensitiveness to the damage that the periodic massacres wrought by senseless bigots may do to the planet earth's eco-system.

In the *Mahabharata*'s "Adiparvan" there is that notorious episode in which Arjuna and his bosom-pal Krishna go about gleefully rampaging the Khandava forest. For the very fun of it, the duo organizes a bloodsport of enormous magnitude – putting the woodland to the fire, they together kill the bears, deer, snakes, hyenas, elephants, turtles, tigers, buffalos, lions, birds, practically, all the breathing-beings inhabiting it; with the Khandava all-ablaze, what only remains are burning wings, burning mane, burning paws, burning...*(Mbh* 1.217.1-15). The sky beginning to get scorched, seeking protection, the gods run to Indra, their king; shocked beyond belief by the Krishnarjuna carnage, the immortal residents of heaven shriek in unison, "Why are these people being burned by the Fire? Has perchance the end of the worlds arrived?" (*Mbh* 1.217.14-15, 1.217.16)

It is more likely than not that just as pacifist Sanjaya's stern admonition of militarist Krishna in the "Udyogaparva" so also the dire premonition of absolute annihilation which seizes the divinities on seeing the Khandava-inferno in the "Adiparvan" are both tinged with the *Sramanic* conception of *ahimsa.* This much has to be granted that the *Mahabharata* passages which bespeak of "Bhargavification" bear the stamp of, as S. Radhakrishnan, the translator of principal Upanisads, put it, "readjustments" initiated by Brahminism to process some of the objections raised by diverse Sramanic "systems of revolt (Radhakrishnan 1999 477–478)." As a result, again according to Radhakrishnan, (even the "Bhargavified") *Mahabharata* at places echoes the *Sramanic* maxim, "Thou shalt not do to others what is disagreeable to thyself (Radhakrishnan 1999 506)."

Six

As a means of illustrating "antagonistic compound," Patanjali of second century BCE, the celebrated author of the *Mahabhasya* or "Great Commentary" on Panini's grammar, had spoken of the "eternal conflict" between Brahmins and *Sramana*s. Furthermore, expanding on the Brahmin-Sramana antipathy, the same linguist had taken resort to the snake-mongoose enmity, the mutually reciprocal malice held by the two organisms which, by all account, defies termination. Similar is the case with the clash between Sanjaya's plea for abdicating the so-termed normative, pre-settled ordinances and Krishna's warm embrace of the mechanically determined, fore-packaged *karmic* credos. Also, there is no way by which the arguments that Krishna presented in a section of the second chapter of the *Gita* can be squared with crestfallen Arjuna's heart-felt remonstrations about liquidating near and dear ones on the battlefield. Krishna's reasoning therein was dismissed as vacuous and specious by Shankara, the formidable logician and the fountainhead of the vedanta school of Nondualism; it received the same treatment at the hand of Bankimchandra Chattopadhyay, the diehard anti-Shankara intellectual who, among others, in his bid to make the *Gita* relevant to the modern times turned the closed-unto-itself idea of *karma* into an open-ended idea of any *action*. The assurance voiced by Krishna in *Gita* II.37, that if a warrior dies fighting, he obtains the heaven and if he wins, he rules over the world, does not have the requisite punch to compel a warrior on the verge of renunciation to again pick up the cudgels on behalf of *karma* calling for *himsa*, violence.

There is no question, none, that in contrast to the *himsa* conducted for a worthy cause or otherwise, uncompromising *ahimsa* fosters fellow-feeling, *karuna* or compassion, encourages *anukrosh* or co-suffering, the tendency for crying out following someone else's cry and many such humane emotions. And, the *Mahabharata* providing as it does, a constellation of constantly wavering characters, a tapestry of ridiculous obsessions, intermittent but full-throated conflicts between the ideologies of *ahimsa*-centric detachment and *himsa*-centric enlisting which promise that the coming war would end all wars, brings us back to the question of Pururava. Ironically or cynically, we cannot be sure, he had raised this prickly existential issue involving *Justice* thousands of years ago, "If punishment affects someone entitled to reward – especially while evil is being done by others who are evil – then what reason would anyone have to do what is good?" It is this terrible enigma which rests inscribed at the heart of the Mahabharata – the enigma that both foregrounds the questions regarding desirability of and the irreconcilability between *himsa* and *ahimsa* and takes them far beyond the confines of the narrative and the constraints of immediate context.

Seven

Even while accepting that "in politics, there are no wholly good options, only shades of evil,"(Stone 2016 225) George Orwell, the author of the hopelessly dystopian but at the same time hopefully anti-authoritarian novel *Nineteen Eighty-Four*, rejected pacifism as "sheer sentimentality" at the dark hour of Nazism and advocated for the "prosecution of total war" against the forces led by the "criminal lunatic" Adolf Hitler. Seen in the light of the positive spin given to the term *karma* by Krishna in the *Mahabharata* or in the light of *action*, the modern extension of *karma* proposed by Bankimchandra Chattopadhyay, Orwell's stance does seem justified. But it is also distressing to learn in hindsight that it was the same total war directed at totalitarianism which quickened the birth and the calculated deployment of the potentially all-annihilating atom bomb.

What with the continuous pounding of Ukraine by Russia, the mutual bombarding by Hamas and Israel, what with the proliferation of killing-fields like Gaza, the exponentially increasing collateral damages and the ever-strengthening of malevolent regimes run by criminal lunatics, there is very little doubt that the Third World War, though formally unannounced, is upon mankind today. And, as the theoretical basis for *Justice*, the intensely debated topic in the Mahabharata, gets to be more and more problematic, the entanglement of *itihasa* with *history* becomes increasingly pronounced.

With death-for-all-at-the-same-moment emerging as a concrete possibility, a sense of futility cannot but overtake the human psyche. Running the risk of being a-historical but remaining faithful to the spirit of *itihasa*, the storehouse of grandly memorable legends, we conclude provisionally by formulating an absurd submission. Is it unlikely that ages ago the brahmin-baiting, animal-loving ruler of thirteen islands, himself a bundle of contradictions, Pururava, the consort of Urvasi, had unconsciously anticipated the present sorry state when he had archly asked of a seer, "What reason would anyone have not to do what is wrong?"

Sibaji Bandyopadhyay

Works Cited

Bandyopadhyay, Sibaji. "Seeing and Saying: A Reflection on the Mahābhārata's War-reportage", *Three Essays on the Mahābhārata: Exercises in Literary Hermeneutics*. Hyderabad: Orient Blackswan, 2016.

Chakravarti. Ranabir. 'Kathamukh' ['Preface']. *Bharate Mahabharate* ['In Bharat, In Mahabharata' in Bangla] by Sibaji Bandyopadhyay. Kolkata: Charvak and Ranaghat: Harappa, 2023.

Patañjalī. The *Vyākaraṇa Mahābhāṣya of Patañjalī* (volume 1), Edited by F. Kielhorn, Bombay: Government Central Book Depot under the aegis of The Department of Public Instruction, 1892.

Radhakrishnan, S. *Indian Philosophy* (volume 1), New Delhi: Oxford University Press, 1999.

Stone, John. "George Orwell on Politics and War", *Review of International Studies* (volume 43, Part II), London: British International Studies Association, 2016.

The Mahābhārata. (volume 1). 'The Book of the Beginning', Translated by J. A. B. Buitenen, Chicago: University of Chicago Press, 1973.

The Mahābhārata. (volume 2). 'The Book of the Assembly Hall', Translated by J. A. B. Buitenen, Chicago: University of Chicago Press, 1975.

The Mahābhārata. (volume 6). 'The Udyogaparvan', Edited by Sushil Kumar De. Poona: Bhandarkar Oriental Research Institute, 1940.

The Mahābhārata. (volume 7). 'The Bhīṣhmaparvan', Edited by Shripad Krishna Belvalkar. Poona: Bhandarkar Oriental Research Institute, 1947.

The Mahābhārata. 'The Book of Peace [Part I]', Translated by James L. Fitzerald. Chicago: University of Chicago Press, 2004.

PREFACE AND ACKNOWLEDGEMENT

This volume had a long journey in its making. In this journey, we learnt a lot about the Mahabharata, which had a transformative effect on us in many other ways. We will try to record some of them in the rest of this write-up but set out by apologizing to those whom we inadvertently fail to mention in this justifiably long list.

Factually speaking, it all started with the First Spring School on the Mahabharata, convened by Professors Sibaji Bandyopadhyay and Sanjay Palshikar in April 2010 at the Indian Institute of Advanced Studies (IIAS), Shimla. As early-stage (read, immature) research scholars, we spent a fortnight experiencing the opening of the magic portals to many maha-bharatas, in all of the following three levels. Intellectually, the convenors and the host of leading scholars in the field invited by them prodded us to fascinating new directions. Being in the company of young minds, in stages similar to us and chosen from across the country, allowed us to experience the diverse thought-world of our country on an everyday basis. Finally, the majestic Dhauladhar in spring and the material sublime of the IIAS campus and its generous hospitality became perpetually physically entangled in the memory of those days of expansion. Apart from the convenors mentioned above, Professors Arindam Chakrabarti, Vrinda Dalmiya, Nrisingha Prasad Bhaduri, and Ganesh Devy also spent a considerable time connecting with the participants in an encouraging way by listening patiently to their ideas and providing regular feedback to their tottering steps to make sense of it all. Hence, we take this opportunity to put our heartfelt gratitude in place to all the above. In a way, Professor Sibaji Bandyopadhyay's "Foreword" to this volume is a fitting drop of the curtain on an action that he himself set in motion in 2010. We are grateful to Professor Ranabir Chakravarti for writing an insightful and scholarly "Afterthoughts" and for providing intellectual support and constant encouraging nudges.

Almost a decade later, some of us gathered around our interest in the Mahabharata in April 2018 when Professor Sandip Kumar Mandal of Presidency University, Dr. Shamim Ahmed of Ramakrishna Mission Vidyamandira, and Dr. Anirban Bhattacharjee of Santipur College organized a national seminar titled *Epic of the Moment* at Presidency University. This event was made possible by the organizational and financial support from Dr. Arjun Choudhuri of Gurucharan College and The Northeast India Company. We also acknowledge the help and support from all the speakers and participants in that seminar who influenced our understanding of the traditions of the Mahabharata narrative.

Moreover, we gratefully acknowledge the help of Malvika Singh, publisher of *Seminar* magazine, in granting us permission to include Christopher Minkowski's "Nilkantha's Mahabharata" in this volume. Similarly, an earlier version of Kalyan Kumar Das's "The Mahabharata War and Ambedkar's Critique of Violence and Nationalism" was published in *Dewey Studies*. We also acknowledge the openness of the office bearers of the journal in allowing us to include a modified version of the paper in this volume. We acknowledge the help and support received from Dr. Kalyan Kumar Das and Dr. Suranjana Choudhury of North Eastern Hill University especially at the initial stage of conceptualizing the volume. Our students Gourab Singha, Arindam Biswas and Abhik Pal provided us with key support at crucial moments of the development of this volume. We acknowledge their efficient and selfless support.

Further, the volume would not take the present shape without the sharp criticism and necessary feedback received from the anonymous reviewers engaged by Routledge India; the failings remain our shortcomings, but all the advances made are due to their effort. In the same vein, we must record our gratitude to the staff of Routledge India, in particular to our commissioning editor Shoma Choudhury who patiently steered us through a long journey of making this volume a reality.

Finally, we acknowledge the support and patience of the contributors, all of whom have stood by us for more than three years in the making of this volume and responded with utmost alacrity to all our requests. This volume like all other edited volumes could not ever exist without the contributors.

Thank you all!

Anirban Bhattacharjee and Dhrubajyoti Sarkar

INTRODUCTION

Anirban Bhattacharjee and Dhrubajyoti Sarkar

Part I: Allegory of Writing and the Logic of Everyday

In the *Santi-Parva* of the *Mahabharata*, Ugrasravas, attempting to tie up or string together the lexias and the meanderings of the text, repeats to Saunaka that

> Vyasa made a *sandarbham* of the Bharata out of desire for dharma, that Vaisampayana sang it to the mortals, Narada to gods, Asita Devala to the Fathers, Vyasa's son Shuka to the Yaksas and Raksasas, and it is equal to the Vedas.
>
> *(Hiltebeitel 278)*

Conceiving the text as a classic plural is, in a certain way, listening to the shimmering exchange of multiple voices posed on different discernments. The tenacity of the text trickles from its gaps. The moments of (complete) closure(s) are constantly in retreat. A number of quiet words or concepts are stitched into or appear as wounds upon the body of the narrative – narrative that travels in revelation from expectation to truth(s). The act of narration becomes a sort of interweaving (*verwebung* in German, *texere* in Latin), in a Derridean sense, of experience and representation, screening and framing, simultaneity and recounting, engaging one another in a radically undecidable manner. *The Mahabharata* is fascinated with the act of re-reading – pleasurable and productive in its commitment to difference – something that Roland Barthes visualized as a "lisible" space, where the ultimate and the conclusive are kept at a desirable distance by the iterative structure of

DOI: 10.4324/9781003516408-1

language. Instead of promising a decisive and coherent movement, the narrative through its snares, secrets, and enigmas provokes an untameable migration of meanings and offers us an inexhaustive potential for repeated entry into an eerie sensation of discovery of its spectrum of concerns. A spectrum that includes moral and ethical dilemmas, logical paradoxes, and unavoidable impasses that constructively baffle the entrant into its experiential *jouissance*.

The narrative structure is severally layered, sometimes engrafted or embedded, combining subsequent and simultaneous narration. Alfred Hiltebeitel in his *Rethinking the Mahabharata* (2002) sees the narrative emboxed in a series of frames: the authorial frame outermost, letting Vyasa move in and out of the spatio-temporal limits of the text; the inner genealogical frame tracing a dynastic story, with authorial interventions, through seven generations; and the middle cosmological frame in the *Naimisha* forest, fusing the epic's spatio-temporal indicators. The book engages with and examines how the act of narration, tellings and retellings, involves several notions of temporality, "anachronies," and iterations (Gennett 1980 23). The present moment shuffles past and future events and carnivalizes one's normative sense of chronicities as discussed by Arvind Sharma first in his 1974 article "The Notion of Cyclical Time in Hinduism." In its intersection of "rhizomic" sites and temporal orders, the Mahabharata narrative sparks up a polyphonic battle-royal – a multiplicity of voices, points of views, subject-positions, and different kinds of realities, constantly clashing and coalescing. The act of narration exemplifies the problem of how to translate knowing into telling. Interestingly, the word "narrate" originates from the Latin word *gnarus*, meaning knowing or to get acquainted with, which is again associated with the Sanskrit root *gna*, meaning "to know." The gigantic multiform narrative underlies the problem of fashioning human experience into a form assimilable to structures of meaning that are generally human rather than culture-specific.

It is the textual plural where every interest, every social institution, every ritual practice is transformed into a narrative that straddles and disturbs the frontier between the religious and the political. For instance, in the *Nakula-upakhyan* that appears towards the end of what Renard Gennete in his 1979 book calls an "Architext" after the great and destructive battle, the victorious king Yudhisthira is encouraged to perform a grand sacrifice, *ashvamedha*, as a means of expiating the sins of battle and of underscoring the imperial sovereignty of the Pandavas. The *nakula* with the golden flank (*rukma-parsva*), addressing the king in a voice like thunder and lightning, apprises: "Ye kings, this great sacrifice is not equal to a *prastha* of powdered barley given away by a liberal Brahmana of Kurukshetra who was observing the *Unccha* vow" (Ganguli 1925 172). He asserts that the gleaner possesses more merit than those who engage in costly, showy, and public sacrifices;

the "liberal inhabitant" gave the total mass of barley gleaned to a voracious guest, though this meant death and starvation for him and his family. The golden flank occurred to the mongoose when he ate a paltry amount of lefto-ver barley; but this grand *ashvamedha* sacrifice is something of a failure, as his other flank has not turned into gold during the ritual. Nakula's recounts call into question the value of the Vedic sacrifices and the act of war.[1] The Mahabharata narratives have the potential of undoing what is sanctioned and legitimized – an interruption of/in the Vedic politico-religious establish-ment. The book attempts to spotlight how the hegemonic structures con-stantly invent tricks and strategies to counter, assuage, and check the forces of denial. It deals or dabbles with the ontology of the surplus and the excess. The book specifically focusses on how the act of narration/retelling happens through a kind of self-reflexivity and a persistent auto-critique – a perfor-mance "under erasure" (Derrida 1978 60).

In "The Epic of the Bharatas," it is pointed out that

> The *Mahabharata* calls itself *itihasam-puratanam* – thus indeed it was in times past. This is not a Rankean statement and there are no defini-tive claims to historicity of persons and events in the narrative. However, there is a hint that some of the narrative may have been an attempt to cull from the remembered tradition that which may have happened, even if what is culled is disordered in the retelling.
>
> *(Thapar 2010)*

The Mahabharata as *itihasa* speaks of a lost time, seeking to integrate it into the present, but aware of the insufficiency of its own cry in the wilder-ness, it also speaks of the future. Retelling, in this mode of conceptualizing, is always performative. The prefix "re" in "retelling" underlies a genera-tive capacity, singular and free brilliance, and the production of the "new." Romila Thapar attempts to understand and grasp the being and time of the *Mahabharata* in the interspersing of the two kinds of societies, both par-tially sequential and partially concurrent – the tradition of a later society remembering and reconstructing what it believes to be the earlier one, where the reconstruction becomes the perceived past. Although, by staying close to the ambience of the Vedic/Brahmanic culture, the *Mahabharata* acquires a well-defined historical basis, the volume would take into consideration how the whole oeuvre of the *Mahabharata*, the southern recensions included, has taken shape over a period of time and assumed authenticity of the tradition, reflecting as well as moulding it through millennia. Sukumari Bhattacharjee alleges that one significant moment of its discursive composition was when the Shramanic religions, the philosophy of the Upanishads, the rise of vari-ous monastic orders as well as repeated foreign invasions broke like giant waves on the intellectual life of India.[2] Irawati Karve in her *Yuganta: The*

End of an Epoch (1991) observes that the Mahabharata is the story of "the quarrel between cousins for the possession of property and status" (Karve 2007 162). Though this theme is "universal" to a patriarchal society, this particular epic is about a Kshatriya family; with the rise of Buddhism and Jainism, the Vaishyas, however, as the rich supporters of these two monastic religions, gained in importance; the *Sutas* and the *Nagas* and the peoples with clan-names of birds and beasts remained in existence against a blurred background of a caste-society. The book, in particular, analyses how the contrasting theories of time and history, myth and signification, in oriental and western discourses, foreground "the clash of chronologies" projected, doubted, dismissed, or hyper-magnified during and after the colonial moment (Trautmann 2009 xxvii). Frame, singulative or iterative narration, or re-telling creates and disrupts the space of omni-temporality in which newness/nowness often flares up in disguise and through displacements. The narrating or performing agent, enmeshed or dipped in the logic of repetition, practice, or ritual habit, has to cope with "unforeseen and ever-changing situations" (Bourdieu 1977 72). It is the very act of repeating the daily rites, the re-taking and re-versing of the "same" that purports to the continuous production of the "new." Ritual acts, hitherto maintained and camouflaged by means of symbolic forms and patterns of action, suspend any temporal order of before and after. The *Karmic* structure in the *Mahabharata* and Brahmanic texts ritualizes the social routine, making everyday performance distinctly non-everyday. The daily performing of the *grihya* rites or *nitya* (regular) sacrifices for a householder inheres a structural need marked by a kind of "newness" and "nowness." The logic of rites thus installs now as its impetus of existence and becoming its movement too. It captures the paradoxical movement of "repetition" and "recollection," conforming to the conjecture presented in Plato's dialogues in Parmenides: "this strange instantaneous nature, this something patched between movement and standstill and that does not exist in any time" (qtd. in Melberg 1990 75). The book addresses this logic of omni-temporality and omni-contemporaneity of the text, the logic of practice that has slipped into the nooks and spacings of the everydayness of today. We re-read and interrogate: if ritual-routine is so "constitutive," how do we approach "getting over" it?

The polyphonic epic narrative exposes that "political command" is persistently forged as an assertion against woman's "domestic government," alongside the substitution of "moral for physical love," to "protect man from his destruction through the fury of woman" (Derrida 1978 175–176). The narrative arc exemplifies that Draupadi, the Kshatriya woman, deprived of her prior rank and status, absorbs onto her body the symbols of political fraudulence perpetrated on the Pandavas. As Sairandhri (meaning, an expert maid), as mother and as a volatile body-subject, Draupadi seems to have had a profound awareness that she has been an instrument to the annihilation of a dying era and an ancient dharma, taking up, at times, agential initiatives in her repeated entries into the space of the public. In the *Sabhaparva*, we see an outraged Draupadi chastising the usher Pratikami for his temerity to speak to her, as he does, as if she were already and indisputably now a "slave" and she demands to know if there was nothing else left for the king to stake. Geared with the information about the sequence of the stakes, Draupadi forwards a specific question to Yudhisthira "Whom did you lose first, yourself or me?" that raises the legality of the stake and the lawfulness of the act (qtd. in Chakravarti 2017 137). We join Chakravarty in asking "is there any deeper level of meaning in terms of power and agency being wagered in the game of dice, in the loss of the kingdom and of the loss of the self" (146)? The book attempts to understand how the woman performs the act(s) of resistance by remaining within the limiting frame of immanence.

The volume particularly focusses on the narrative networks involving those inside the epic, translations and adaptations of the epic, re-imagined fictional and performative forms based on the *Mahabharata*, and popular cultural manifestations that are centred around the epic. In doing so, individually the chapters and collectively the volume would attempt to approach the "moment." Of course, the "moment" mentioned above will have a bidirectional latitude. The contemporaneous moment or "now" when placed in the cyclical epic timeframe of "now" of the epic gains the additional vantage perspective of making the very notion of "now" denser. This allows the present iteration to not only interrogate the constitution of "now" and "everyday" but at the same token offers depth and solidity to the sense of nowness by removing the constraints of fragility and ephemerality. The book further proposes to read the liaison between the Mahabharata and contemporaneity as being symptomatic of a "time-loop" and binds together diverse readings, interventions, and inquiries into the logic of synchrony and simultaneity.

The Mahabharata stands out as a "cultural paradigm" that, in a way, inaugurates the history of a community (Arditi 1994 602). We encounter the "thingy" materiality of the text in its constitutive collection of relations that reciprocally project and determine a world, a (symbolic) "habitus" with its historical contingencies and precariousness (Bourdieu 1977 17). The book attempts to examine and re-read the "present-at-hand" thingness of the text in terms of its relationship to lived experience or its possible relationship with the co-occurrent subject of the moment (Heidegger 1967 5). The essays in the book are, in a way, united/connected in their effort to situate the Mahabharata(s), the written oeuvre, the Ur-text and its multiple recensions, translations, and adaptations, popular cultural manifestations and media reproductions within the fatal fabric of everydayness of today, where the materiality of the text has been sought, sensed, and gathered through the re-reading of the Sanskrit mnemotexts, one of them most recently discovered and translated, the poetics and politics of retelling and their hermeneutic re-adjustments in the colonial and postcolonial moment(s), the exercises and engagements with literary and philosophical hermeneutics, adaptations and appropriations in major/minor performing arts, and cultural trans-creations across diverse Indic spaces; and the singularity of the collective particularly lies in its theoretical and representational engagements with contemporary social, cultural, religious and political concerns.

The *Mahabharata*'s theme of internecine conflict and violence is deeply unsettling to a culture that considers itself grounded in tolerance and strongly valorizes the ethical propriety of *ahimsa*, social interaction, and the preservation of harmony among different callings and castes. The central event of the epic narrative is the exterminatory *Bharata* war that ends in, as Sheldon Pollock notes, "anomie, ascetic suicides and apocalypse" (Pollock 1986 71). With its hyper-focus on the themes of murderous rage and collective punishment, beginning from Ugrasrava's account of Janmejaya's sacrifice to the genocidal rampage, to mass extermination of plants and non-human creatures in the form of burning of Khandava forest, to Aswathama's revenge unleashing the fearsome Brahmashira directed towards the embryo in Uttara's womb, the Ur-text with its various recensions mirrors and anticipates the cosmic destruction of the world (*pralaya*), the great apocalypse, inaugurating the *Kaliyuga*. As a storehouse of information, the Mahabharata furnishes ample materials for its authors and translators keen on spinning new versions of them and producing new narrative channels out of tributary streams. While the Sanskrit *mahakavyas* or court-epics are generally presumed to have been closely connected to the affirmation of royal power, Magha's seventh-century epic *Shishupalavadha*, an ornate re-creation of a presumptive sourcetext in the *Sabhaparvan* of the *Mahabharata*, surprisingly goes out to emphasize the non-royal status of the hero, Krishna, and his hostility towards royalty and court power. In contrast, Bharavi's *Kiratarjuniyam*, a sixth-century court-epic, describing in eighteen cantos the combat between Arjuna and Shiva in the guise of Kirata, is almost obsessed with the nature and dynamics of kingship. With hundreds of written and oral accounts, as Wendy Doniger writes, the Sanskrit epic demonstrates that it "flickers back and forth between Sanskrit manuscripts and village storytellers, each adding new gemstones to the old mosaic, constantly reinterpreting it" (Doniger 2009 264). Also, there are some fragment verses like Nitivarman's *Kichakavadha* and Bhatta Narayana's *Venisamhara* that depict events from the epic in alternating perspectives. Nell Shapiro Hawley directs our attention in her "The Remembered Self: Arjuna as Bṛhannalā in the Pañcarātra" (2021) to six Mahabharata-inspired plays that were recovered in Kerala, initially attributed to one of the earliest and most celebrated Sanskrit playwrights, Bhasa (b. third century CE), predating Kalidasa: *Pancharatra*, *Karnabhara*, *Dutavakya*, *Madhyamavayoga*, and *Uruvanga* demonstrate a strong commitment to representing both the ethos of disintegration and the aesthetics of mirroring and repetition that characterize the Sanskrit epic itself.

Now the question is: what would contemporizing entail? Is it but an articulation of the intermediateness, the conflict between the universal and the particular time, the past has gone by and the future arriving, in Vyasa's own word: "Poets have told it before, poets are telling it now, other poets shall tell this history on earth in the future" (Buitenen 21).[3] The central concern of the *Mahabharata* text is the disintegration of the family lines. Serious attempts have been made to keep the line(s) intact. Even Bhisma's lifelong practice of celibacy could not sustain it. He implored Karna to reveal the secret of his birth, which could certainly end the war of succession between two groups of princely cousins. These two conflicting sections are mentioned in the narrative in the form of immoral Duryodhana and righteous Yudhisthira and his allies. Once the Kurukshetra War was over, nothingness loomed large. Then again, the same note of wailing, victory and defeat, and genocide.

In Buddhadev Bose's modern retelling of the Mahabharata (1974), we find Yudhiṣṭhira, a hero who conforms to the narrative demand for perfection: his blemishes make his character more credible and human. But, despite his tendency to agonize interminably about actual or intended action, his subtlety of reflection helps him reach ethical truths. Analysing the principal protagonists in the text most concisely, Bose has pointed out: "Yudhiṣ ṭhira is not as celebrated as Arjuna, but he is the hero and the central figure of the Mahabharata" (Mukherjee 1986 148). The book constantly makes us confront some ethical-philosophical moments, subtly underscoring that there are deeper destructions that cannot be fought only with the skill at arms.

In contrast to Pratibha Ray's or Chitra Banerjee Divakaruni's Draupadi, which are discussed at length in the volume, *Bheel Bharath*, a non-Sanskrit variant of Vyasa's *Jaya*, narrated by the Doongri Bhils of Gujarat, presents Draupadi as a woman of exceptional beauty with golden hair and milk-white complexion, who willingly and repeatedly mates with the serpent-king Visuka when her consort and the mighty warrior Arjhan is defeated by him in a duel. The women characters in the text are fiercely independent and adapt bravely to the constantly changing circumstances as the Kaliyuga insidiously impacts the narrative. In *Parva* (1979), a Kannada retelling of the epic, Bhyrappa's men, however, are not semi-divine heroes but weak and hesitant humanized beings slowed by regret for their wasted life. The text narrated through the personal reflections of the principal characters reserves sympathy only for Krishna, not a divine incarnate but a cunning strategist, willing to question the blind courage or the constant impregnation of Dasis. Bhyrappa is relentless in exposing the hollowness of *Aryadharma* as nothing but drinking, hunting, adultery, gambling, and fighting wars. He demythologizes the whole of the Mahabharata and makes it a story of a clash between two kingdoms. In the final episode, we see a huge crowd of women pregnant from being raped by the soldiers during the war turning up and asking Yudhisthira in court who would be their father. The new king sitting on the throne confronts the crowd, absolutely catatonic, looking at the rain pouring down outside with no answer to give them. The strategies of contemporizing the epic are enacted and re-enacted by humanizing and secularizing the text, with a complex presentation of characters moving through moral puzzles, sometimes going against the received philosophical wisdom of separating epistemology and ethics. As we remember Yudhisthira's famous saying: "Wise men disagree, traditions conflict, the real nature of Dharma is hidden in the cave" (*Aranyakaparva* 313.17) – elements of uncertainty and self-doubt persist in the Mahabharata text, pointing towards the impossibility of any theoretical closure with ever-shifting horizons of meaning(s).

Part II: Narrating the Narration

Following the above-mentioned schema, this volume is broadly divided into two sections. Each section addresses a specific narrative concern. The chapters in the volume are organized on the chronological order of the primary text they discuss. However, this is done with the awareness that there are fundamental problems with following such a chronoligical order. For an epic that talks to various ages in a complex temporal matrix, a linear chronological model is not just inadequate but also self-defeating by implication. Hence, in spite of such a chronological arrangement, the sections are not chronologically connected and can be read independently and randomly. Following such a methodological caveat, the sections are entitled: narrative engagements and critical thematic engagements. Again, the categories are neither absolute nor adequate for various other purposes. For example, a rigorous questioning of the notion of "contemporary" in these sections can often raise more fundamental questions regarding the notion as adapted and encoded in the text itself. The arrangement is acutely aware of such ambiguities too and offers it only for the sake of a rather contingent categorization that can only create further questions to augment the possibilities indicated in the chapters themselves. The narrative engagements discussed in this section stretch across close to millennia of Indic narrative traditions, from the times of Jaimini of tenth century CE to B.R. Chopra of 1980s! Needless to say, they are not part of a hoary monolithic "ancient" world. This sectionalization is done with the awareness that there is a prevailing tendency to telescope earlier times into a single category from the current vantage point; a tendency that often fails to distinguish between the functional conveniences of such categorization and the concomitant cognitive ossification that comes with such telescoping. It should serve more as a reminder that there is no single Sanskrit tradition which in itself can be seen as a complementary parallel to the diverse Mahabharata tradition. Further, the chapter on a recently discovered and once-thought-to-be-lost manuscript of Jaimini also draws our attention to the fact that the Sanskrit tradition is not a stable and static one. Rather this is a tradition that too is open for change, incorporation, and expansion. The second chapter in this section shows how the medieval Sanskrit scholar Nilakantha (seventeenth century CE) adapted his exegetic text to speak to his own time rather than to an eternal timeless time. The following chapter on *Razamnama* discusses the chequered history of production and transmission of India's most famous Indo-Persian adaptation of the Mahabharata narrative. Though this is a near-contemporary text of Nilakantha, their dissimilarities and differences could not be wider. The next group of essays on Bengali engagements with the Mahabharata narrative has a similar diversity of temporal distribution. However, both the temporal spread and the cultural geography are comparatively smaller for these essays. That does not in any way diminish the diversity and counter-intuitive nature of the narratives the sections discuss. The chapter analysing the genesis and evolution of *Mushalparva* of Kasiramdas's, who was also near-contemporary of Nilakantha, adapting the Mahabharata for a Bengali audience, also shades new lights through recent archaeological as well as textual discoveries. Following chapter takes us on a temporal leap to nineteenth-century colonial Bengal. They analyse Bankimchandra Chattopadhyay's "reformation" of the Mahabharata narrative in his *Krishnacharita*, in search of an authentic nationalist history. The project of textual criticism for Bankim Chandra Chattopadhyay is, however, deeply related to his understanding of the Mahabharata as history. *Krishnacharita* marks the beginning of a clear philological method for Bankim. Two important books that declare the *Krishnacharita* as a crucial moment in the conceptualizing of historicity in colonial Bengal are Partha Chatterjee's *Nationalist Thought and Colonial World: A Derivative Discourse* (1986), and Sudipta Kaviraj's *The Unhappy Consciousness: Bankimchandra Chattopadhyay and the Formation of Nationalist Discourse in India* (1995). While Chatterjee finds that historicizing Krishna was important for Bankim within a scientific and rationalist framework in order to legitimize his larger political philosophy, Kaviraj speaks of a classicization of Krishna in which Bankim constructs a rational theology through an exegesis of the Mahabharata for a new national-popular mobilization. As we go back to Tagore's 1895 review of the *Krishnacharitra*, we see it begins with a comment on the nature of colonial society that, deprived of actual political agency, has fallen into a state of uncritical navel-gazing. Tagore appreciates Bankim's attempt completely to change the way in which religious belief functions in the Indian context, which encourages an inflexible and blind attachment to scriptural knowledge and to established customary rituals in the matter of worship. Tagore argues that in breaking out of that mould, Bankim invigorates a critical understanding of *Dharma* in its breathtaking complexity. Following four essays in this section move to the twentieth-century independent India. Though they are specifically concerned with comparatively recent ways of responding to the *Mahabharata*, there is no rigid category to delimit the applicability of the term "contemporary." For convenience, the term is applied to post-structuralist thinking on the section on critical approaches and postcolonial India in these chapters. These are no stable or rigorous categories, but we hope these will be easier for the readers of this volume to identify with. This is not a statement made with clarity and certainty and is made even more steadfast in its uncertainty by the very first critical engagement before the first section itself. In this extended discussion on the changing nature of contemporaneity itself and its variants informing the Mahabharata, many of the major concerns return to enrich the chapters analysing "un-certain" richness in the narrative traditions of the Mahabharata. All four of the following chapters focus on various recent adaptations of the Mahabharata narrative. The Kannada theatrical adaptation *Rangabharata* offered a trenchant critique of the mainstream national political climate of the Nehruvian era of independent India. In a similar way, the following chapter on one of the most extensive and magisterial transcreative essays on the Mahabharata by P. Lal shows how the claims of the eternal epical time and sensibility are still circumscribed by a doomsday vision of the contemporary, which in itself is only contemporary but not eternal. Moreover, this chapter specifically places such a doomsday vision within the early-twentieth-century European Modernism. Thus, this chapter contends that P. Lal's transcreation in the latter half of the twentieth century of the Mahabharata narrative is actually embedded within the Modernist sensibilities.

On the contrary, the following two chapters offer an analysis of the televised narratives to show that even if such productions originally intended to offer a unified national narrative, they ended up kickstarting a recent tendency to present a hegemonic nation that might in the long run end up weakening the national consciousness. First of these chapters align the national political course of post-Emergency India to its gradual evolution of the eighties' ethos. The chapter by reading the novelistic engagement in Shashi Tharoor's *The Great Indian Novel* (1993) and the early televised adaptations respectively show how the narrative of the Mahabharata is adapted to two contradictory ideological tractions. Moreover, these chapters not only bring interesting findings regarding individual adaptations but also show how these adaptations too working "anachronistically" make the epical chronicity ever-contemporary in the most unexpected ways. This brings us to the end of the first section containing chapters on specific engagements with the narrative of the Mahabharata across a diverse temporal spectrum.

The body of revisionist literature that retellings of myths comprise is indeed topical, born out of the author's own spatio-temporal context, reflections, and subjectivity. Employing a feminist myth-critical lens, one of the chapters in the section undertakes a study of the politics of narration in the (re)presentation of Draupadi in select retellings of the Mahabharata, namely in Pratibha Ray's *Yajnaseni* (1984) and Chitra Banerjee Divakaruni's *The Palace of Illusions* (2008). It scrutinizes the role that the authorial subjectivity of the authors of retellings – Ray and Divakaruni – plays in their retelling of a popular character and familiar trope, and also the distinct creative shades they add to the psychobiography of the central hero(ine) of the epical story, simultaneously humanizing the feminist Draupadi of the epic and transforming her into a contemporary feminist character that the readers find more relatable. The final essay in the first section studies the complex panelling of *Vyasa: The Beginning* (2017), a comic book written by Sibaji Bandyopadhyay which attempts to trace the subaltern roots of the Mahabharata from within its social and cultural milieu. One of the most interesting features of the book is the way the graphic narrative spirals out in space and time. Behind a conventional facade of a regular layout, the artist Sankha Banerjee leaves behind some "wounds" within the panels that open up the text both literally and metaphorically. These wounds and scars foreground, in the somewhat autobiographical self-(reflexive) writing, the debate regarding the ingenious ways a narrative can be mapped within a page of a comic book: the phantasmagoria of lust, violence, and subterfuge in an epic tale of war, revenge, and peace breathes alive within the "boxes" that contain the visuals.

In the second, comparatively leaner – but no lesser in gravitas – section, this volume presents three chapters which are concerned with specific critical thematic engagements. Thus, these chapters are usually concerned either with a particular aspect of the narrative that has been repeatedly highlighted and returned to by various narrators or are focussed on the themes that need our attention as a concern that is quickly gaining ground due to a contemporary view or attitude. This section thus straddles across both the temporal categories mentioned above to delimit the use of "contemporary" in these chapters. The first one in the section addresses the concept of the "avenger" in the Mahabharata while the second one addresses the issues of animality in the narrative. The figure of the "avenger" though is often associated with the epic stories of battle and confrontations and hence extended widely to the battlefield of the Mahabharata is brought into the central question of this chapter. This question subsequently leads to challenging, if not negating, the very trope of the avenger usually applied to the epic heroes. This chapter thus presents the contemporary popular culture validation of the avenger figure as an epic hero vis-à-vis the presentation and questioning of this idea in the Mahabharata narrative. The moot point whether there is continuity or divergence between the representation in a historic sense and its contemporary version is the principal thesis of this chapter. In the following chapter, we find a discussion on the representation of animality in the Mahabharata narrative as a manifestation of some of the most entrenched ethical questions that are raised and attempted. Animals do appear for diverse reasons in the Mahabharata, but among them probably the most fundamental one is in the figure of human alterity. The question of being human in exception to being animal is analysed in this philosophically dense chapter. Finally, the reference to the cruelty and animality in this chapter, in a way, paves the logical transition to the next chapter in which B.R. Ambedkar's questioning the ethicality of the violence embedded within the war narrative of the Mahabharata, and by extension to the Indian nationalist discourse, is extensively discussed. Ambedkar's Buddhist non-violent critique is further extended and contemporized by the subtle recontextualization within the Pragmatism as elaborated by John Dewey. In particular, by reminding us of the philosophical complexity and breadth offered by Ambedkar's invocation of the Dharmavyadh in the Mahabharata narrative, this chapter allows an imaginary reconfiguration of Ambedkar as our contemporary Dharmavyadh. While the organizing principle of this work is not guided by any other principle than the fact that the narrative of the Mahabharata has been responded and adapted by various narrative and recipient cultures of the Indian subcontinent, one may hopefully emerge if the chapters in this volume eventually start talking to each other across their temporal and contextual concerns. Further, though the geographical spread of the narrative traditions is not a focus of this volume, it too may eventually become a model that may be replicated with adequate linguistic, regional, and sub-national specificities. Whether such possibilities become realities is something that remains to be tested only once the perusal of this volume is completed. The text of the *Mahabharata* inhabits an irreducible plurality in its structure and content that interrupts the presence. A genuine response to the critique of "nowness" and presence intractably underlies an ethic of responsibility from within towards the singular and the other, and without this exigency, no ethico-political question has any chance of being opened up and awakened at the (present) moment.

Notes

1 For more discussion on the subject Hegarty, James, *Religion, Narrative and Public Imagination in South Asia: Past and Place in the Sanskrit Mahabharata* (Routledge Hindu Studies Series), London, 2011.
2 For more details, see Bhattacharjee, "The Epic Mahabharata," *Women and Society in Ancient India*, Basumati Corporation Ltd, 1994.
3 Further quotations from the text of *Mahabharata*, if not mentioned otherwise, is from this (J. A. B. van Buitenen's) translation.

Works Cited

Arditi, Jorge. "Geertz, Kuhn and the Idea of a Cultural Paradigm." *The British Journal of Sociology*, Vol. 45, No. 4, Dec. 1994, pp. 597–617. JSTOR, www.jstor

Bourdieu, Pierre. *Outline of a Theory of Practice.* Translated by Richard Nice, Cambridge University Press, 1977.

Buitenen, J. A. B. van., trans. *The Mahabharata*, vol. 1, The *Book of the Beginning.* University of Chicago Press, 1973.

Chakravarti, Uma. "Who Speaks for Whom?" *Mahabharata Now: Narration, Aesthetics, Ethics.* Edited by Arindam Chakrabarti and Sibaji Bandyopadhyay (2017): 132–152.

Derrida, Jacques. *Writing and Difference.* Translated by Alian Bass, University of Chicago Press, 1978.

Divakaruni, Chitra Banerjee. *The Palace of Illusions: A Novel.* Doubleday, 2008.

Doniger, Wendy. *The Hindus: An Alternative History.* Penguin, 2009.

Doniger, Wendy. The Hindus: An Alternative History, Oxford University Press, 2009.

Ganguli, Kisari Mohan. *The Mahabharata of Krishna-Dwaipayana Vyasa.* Vol.11. Revised by Pratap Chandra Ray, new ed. D. Bose, 1925.

Hawley, N. S."The Remembered Self: Arjuna as Bṛhannalā in the Pañcarātra", in Nell Shapiro Hawley and Sohini Sarah Pillai Ed.), *Many Mahabharatas*, State University of New York Press, Albany, 2021.

Heidegger, Martin. *What is a Thing?* Translated by W. B. Barton, Jr. and Vera Deutsch, Gateway Editions, 1967.

Hiltebeitel, Alf. *Rethinking the Mahabharata: A Reader's Guide to the Education of the Dharma King.* University of Chicago Press, 2002.

Karve, Irawati. *Yuganta: The End of an Epoch.* 1991. Translated by Karve, Orient Longman, 2007.

Melberg, Arne. "Repetition (in the Kierkegaardian sense of the term)." *diacritics* 20.3 (1990): 71–87.

Mukherjee, Sujit. *The Book of Yudhisthir: A Study of the Mahabharat of Vyas.* Sangam Books, 1986.

Pollock, Sheldon. "Introduction" to The Rāmāyaṇa of Vālmīki: An Epic of Ancient India, vol. 2, Ayodhyākāṇ ḍa, trans. Sheldon Pollock. Princeton University Press, 1986.

Thapar, Romila. "The Epic of the Bharatas." *Seminar*, no. 608, Apr. 2010, www.india-seminar.com/2010/608/608_romila_thapar.htm.

Trautmann, Thomas R. *The Clash of Chronologies: Ancient India in the Modern World.* Yoda Press, 2009.

PART I

1

ASVAMEDHAPARVA

Jaimini and Vyasa

Sekhar Kumar Sen

Who Is Jaimini?

The Mahabharata says that Maharshi Krishna Dvaipayana Veda Vyasa had four disciples: Sumantu, Vaishampayana, Jaimini, and Paila. Shuka, Vyasa's son, Shukracharya, was the fifth. It is further stated in the Mahabharata that Jaimini was one of the *udgatas* (one of the four principal priests at a sacrifice who chants the hymns of the *Sama* Veda) at the *Sarpasattra* sacrifice of Janamejaya. Also, he came to Indraprastha to receive Yudhishthira and visited Bhishma on his bed of arrows.

That is all the information we get from the epic on Jaimini. Who then is this Jaimini? As in the case of all self-effacing authors of extant Sanskrit literature, barring a negligible few, not much is known about him except a few legends and that he was a seer-philosopher of great eminence, the founder of the *Purva Mimamsa* school of thought. Several of the *Puranas* are in the form of addresses to Jaimini. In *Markandeya Purana*, Jaimini asked Maharshi Markandeya four pertinent questions about the Mahabharata. Markandeya did not have time and directed Jaimini to the sons of sage Drona (the fourth son of Mandapala, not the guru of the Pandavas and the Kauravas) for the answers. The four sons of Drona had become birds due to a curse and lived on the Vindhya Mountains. Their names were Pingakhya, Vibodha, Suputra, and Sumukha.[1] Jaimini went to them and got his doubts clarified. The birds also told him many other stories and narrated some didactic principles, mostly as spoken by Markandeya, and these form the entire content of the Purana. Similarly, the *Mahabhagavata Purana* is narrated to Jaimini by Vyasa. Jamini appears in conversation with sages in the *Purushottamakshetra Mahatmya* of the *Vishnukhanda* of the *Skanda Purana*. In the *Kurma Purana* (chapter 13),

DOI: 10.4324/9781003516408-3

Jaimini puts some questions to Vyasa. According to the *Panchatantra*, Jaimini was crushed to death by an elephant.[2]

Works of Jaimini

Jaimini, as mentioned earlier, authored the *Purva Mimamsa* and is one of the earliest major interpreters of the Vedic thought. *Purva Mimamsa*, also known as *Karma Mimamsa*, is considered to be one of the oldest treatises available in ancient Indian literature (c. 300 BC).[3] In his exposition of the *Mimamsa Sutra*, he laid emphasis on the ritualistic parts, the *Brahmana* portion of the Vedas, not the philosophical aspect.

Bhagavata (I.6.53) and *Vishnu Purana* (III.4.9) have credited him with being a contributor to the *Sama* Veda. Veda Vyasa is said to have taught the four Vedas to four of his disciples: the *Rik* to Paila, the *Yajuh* to Vaishampayana, the *Atharva* to Sumantu, and the *Sama* to Jaimini. There is a *Jaiminiya* branch of the *Sama Veda* extant in Kerala to this day. He wrote the *Jaiminiya Grihya Sutra* too. "The *Jaiminiya Grihya Sutra* which is divided into one part of twenty-four *khandas* and another of nine *khandas*, seems to presuppose the *Jaiminiya Samhita* of the *Sama-veda*," says Dr. R.N. Dandekar.[4] Monier-Williams confirms it in his dictionary. A *Jaiminiya Shrauta Sutra* also exists, which is dated to the pre-Panini period (sixth or fifth century BC).[5] Jaimini's treatise on astrology, *Jaiminiyasutram* or *Upadesha Sutras*, is well-known. The *Jaimini Sutras* is a unique classic, rated by many as next only to the *Brihat Parashara Hora Shastra*.

> Several of the "The Jaimini System" principles were mentioned by Parashara in his *Brihat Parashara Hora Shastra*. While Parashara mentioned them briefly, Jaimini expounded them fully. Hence it is known as the "Jaimini system of astrology." It is quite a unique predictive system. While using a lot of basics of the Parashara system, it also employs a different set of aspects and *Karakas* and some different type of *lagnas*. It is very popular in Andhra Pradesh.[6]

Another work named *Upakarmanga-Paddhati* is also attributed to him. Interestingly, Monier-Williams mentions that Jaimini had also authored a *Jaiminiya Kosha Sutra* and the *Jaiminiya Bhagavata*, "name of a modern version of the *Bhagavata* Purana."[7] *Jaiminiya Brahmana Upanishad*, also called *Talavakara Aranyaka*, is a philosophical discourse of the *Sama* Veda dealing with death, passage to other worlds, and reincarnation. There is also a *Jaiminiya Arsheya Brahmana*. In addition to these, a hand-written copy of *Abhimanyu Upakhyanam* is preserved in the museum of the Baroda Oriental Institute. The pundits hold that this must have been a part of the *Drona Parva* of Jaimini's Mahabharata.[8]

Petteri Koskikallio and Christophe Vielle have discussed the various works that are either written by or attributed to Jaimini, or claim to be a part of *Jaimini Bharata*[9]: Following is a brief summary of their findings. Jaimini is credited with composing several texts, although some of them are yet to be discovered. One such work is the *Jaimini Bharata*, a version of the Mahabharata believed to be authored by Jaimini. Although this particular version remains elusive, some parts of it are known to exist. One existing section of the above is the *Jaiminiyashvamedha*, which differs significantly from Vyasa's version of the same event in the Mahabharata. Printed in 1863 in Bombay, this section focusses on Yudhishthira's Ashvamedha sacrifice and is considered the standard edition. Sita's victory over the thousand-headed Ravana is narrated in *Sitavijaya*, a part of the Ashramavasaparvan of Jaimini's work. This tale is absent in Valmiki's Ramayana but has a variant in the *Adbhutaramayana*. Similarly, the *Mairavanacaritam*, or *Hanumadvijaya*, recounts Hanuman's defeat of Mahiravana to rescue Rama and Lakshmana. While not found in Valmiki's Ramayana, it is claimed to be a part of *Jaimini Bharata*. *Setumahatmya* discusses the significance of the Rameshvaram Setu and is linked to the *Aranyakaparvam* of *Jaimini Bharata*. The legend of Harishchandra is detailed in *Harishchandropakhyana*, supposedly part of the Harivamsha section of *Jaimini Bharata*. The Harivamshaparvam presents a version of Harivamsha as part of *Jaimini Bharata*. *Jaiminiramayana* focusses on the Ramakatha, featuring various episodes not commonly found in other versions. *Jaiminibhagavata* contains selected tales of Krishna's Vrindavana adventures from the *Bhagavata Purana*. Finally, there are several miscellaneous puranic tracts attributed to Jaimini, including *Jaiminipurana*, *Jyesthamahatmya*, and *Jaiminiyasamhita* of the *Brahmandapurana*. These cover diverse topics like the significance of the month of Jyestha, dialogues between Jaimini and various kings, and genealogies intertwined with mythical narratives.

In the course of conducting research for editing the first English translation of *Jaiminiya Ashvamedha Parva*, an exciting discovery was that the Government Oriental Manuscripts Library and Research Centre, a unit of the Tamil Nadu State Department of Archaeology, possesses palm-leaf manuscripts in Grantha script claiming to be parts of the missing *Jaimini Bharata*. Details were made available, thanks to the kindness of Shri T. S. Sridhar, IAS, Principal Secretary Tourism and Culture and Commissioner of Museums, Government of Tamil Nadu. The details are as follows:

- *Mairavavanacharitam* (Grantha script): Complete
- *Sahasramukharavanacharitam* (Grantha): Complete
- *Setumahatmyam* (Grantha): Incomplete
- *Jaimini Itihasa* (Grantha): Complete
- *Jaimini Bharata* (Grantha): Incomplete

- *Kusha-Lavopakhyana* (Grantha): Complete
- *Jaimini Bhagavata* (Odiya): Ends with *Ashtavakrasapa*
- *Jaimini Ramayanam*: *Ramanamamahatmye Vyadhasya Saptarshi*
- *Sandarshanamnama* (Grantha): Incomplete
- *Jaimini Grihyamantravritti* (Devnagari): Incomplete
- *Jaimini Grihyaprayogaratnamala* (Grantha): Incomplete
- *Jaiminisutra/Upadesasutra* (Telugu): Incomplete

Jaimini Bharata – An Enigma?

Did it exist or not? One keeps asking this over and over again. Many learned scholars have held that there was no such work as the *Jaimini Bharata* but it keeps peeping through the obscurity of antiquity, creating confusion and debate. Dinesh Chandra Sen mentioned more than a hundred years ago that only *Ashvamedha Parva* of the *Jaimini Bharata* has been found. In the opinion of modern historians, Jaimini had composed only the *Ashvamedha Parva*. Sen opines, "But till the search for ancient Indian books is not over, this opinion cannot be accepted as infallible truth."[10] The situation has not changed since then. Koskikallio and Vielle too write,

> The form *Jaimini Bharata* tends to stress the point that there existed an independent version of the whole *Bharata* epic composed by Jaimini. The usual conception is that only the *Ashvamedha* book has survived from Jaimini's variant epic...the epic connection of the JA (*Jaiminiyashvamedha*) is most probably an artificial one.[11]

However, they immediately add, "But this does not necessarily mean that the JA cannot be a part of a larger project." With the passage of time, the belief that Jaimini never wrote a complete *Bharata* is becoming stronger as it has not been found yet. At the same time, one can hardly ignore the evidence, however weak, which indicates that there was such a variant epic penned by Jaimini. All the books mentioned above which claim connection with the various *Parvas* of that elusive composition of Jaimini and the evidence available in the *Jaiminiyashvamedha* itself cannot just be brushed aside as irrelevant and inconsequential. After all, there are so many books that remain undiscovered which we know of from references in other works. An examination of some of the evidence will be useful here.

The claim of the other compositions mentioned above, such as *Sitavijaya*, *Setumahatmya*, *Abhimanyu Upakhyanam*, etc. has already been noted. Let us now see the evidence available in the *Jaiminiyashvamedha* itself.

In the first place, the last *shloka* of the book is the strongest evidence. It clearly says: (Jaimini said to Janamejaya,) "O Lord of the earth, I have narrated fourteen *Parvas* to you. Now, O king, listen to the *Parva* named

Ashramavasa." There can be no doubt that there were thirteen *Parvas* preceding this one and definitely the *Ashramavasika* after it (which has been mentioned in the verse) and presumably the *Mausala*, *Mahaprasthana*, and *Svargarohana* thereafter. One does not need to go beyond this *shloka* in search of proof.

Secondly, the second *shloka* of the *Parva* (the first being an invocation) containing a question from Janamejaya, clearly indicates that the *Parva* comes in the middle of a narrative. It is part of a book, not the first verse of a new work. Moreover, as K.N. Shastri and N. Ranganatha Sharma point out, "It is not proper tradition to begin a book without a proper context. One can guess that there might be other *Parvas* preceding this text."[12]

Thirdly, at the end of chapter 36 (the story of Kusha and Lava), a new character, Suta, appears, following the Vyasan tradition with precision. He addresses a group of sages, whom we have not met till now, and tells them that he has so far narrated to them what Jaimini had described to King Janamejaya at his royal court. He further tells them of the merits that accrue from listening to this story of the battle between a father and his sons which unfortunately was not narrated by Valmiki. Here we see that Jaimini adhered to the basic structure of Vyasa where Vaishampayana narrates the story to Janamejaya and Sauti repeats it to the sages at Naimisha forest with one little difference: in Jaimini's Mahabharata, Jaimini narrates the story, not Vaishampayana, and Suta repeats it, not Sauti. It is interesting to note that he has retained the family appellative of Sauti. The ascetic Ugrashrava belonged to the suta family and was, therefore, called Sauti. Jaimini has directly named him Suta. This sudden appearance of Suta in the narrative again confirms that there must have been previous sections of the book where this Suta made other periodic appearances. He might even have begun the narrative as Sauti did in Vyasa's version! All these reasons lead us to believe that the complete Jaimini Mahabharata did exist at some point in time as Monier-Williams' dictionary declares.[13]

Fourthly, in chapter 43, Tāmradhvaja suddenly becomes Suchitra without any explanation. This indicates that the reader already knows who Suchitra is. Why Tāmradhvaja is also called Suchitra must have been explained in some previous *Parva*.

With this entire evidence, one can reasonably suppose that there did exist a larger composition, perhaps named *Jaimini Bharata*. But the question is: why did Jaimini write a Mahabharata when his preceptor had already written one and that too not very long ago?

At this point, it may perhaps be useful to jog the memory regarding the composition of the Mahabharata. In the fifth chapter of the *Anukramanika* section of the *Adi Parva*, it is mentioned that Vyasa first wrote a *Bharata Samhita* consisting of twenty-four thousand *shlokas* (I.1.61).[14] Then he improved it by adding the *Anukramanika* section consisting of one hundred and fifty *shlokas*. He first made his son, Shuka, learn this *Samhita* (collection) and then gave it to his other disciples. Thereafter, he authored a *Samhita* of sixty lakh *shlokas*. Out of that, thirty lakh *shlokas* were meant for the abode of the gods, fifteen lakh for the world of the manes, fourteen lakh for the world of the *Gandharvas*, and only one hundred thousand *shlokas* for the world of the humans. Narada disseminated the *Samhita* in the world of the gods, Asita Devala in the world of the manes, Shuka narrated it to the *Gandharvas*, the *Yakshas*, and the *Rakshasas*, and Vaishampayana to the humans. Vaishampayana narrated the composition to Janamejaya during the intervals of the snake sacrifice under the instructions of Vyasa who sat and listened to his recitation. Ugrashrava, son of the *suta* (bard) Lomaharshana, generally addressed as Sauti, heard Vaishampayana's narration at the court of Janamejaya and then repeated it to sage Shaunaka and others in the Naimisha forest in the intervals of the sacrifice they were performing. Thence it has come down to us.

The reason for Jaimini's effort has been recorded in the very beginning of the Mahabharata.[15] Vyasa taught the Mahabharata to his four disciples and his son Shuka. They then proceeded to publish their own versions. Here Mahabharata ends and legend begins: Vyasa asked them to write their own versions and narrate those to him. Apparently, he approved the text of Vaishampayana and liked the *Ashvamedhaparva* of Jaimini. He asked Jaimini to retain this *Parva* and drop the rest of the text since those sections portrayed the *Pandavas* in quite an unfavourable light. Sridhara in his *Pandavapratapa* (a seventeenth-century Marathi abridgement of the Mahabharata) says that Vyasa had condemned Jaimini for having added his own matter to the original.[16] Hence, but for the *Ashvamedhaparva*, the rest were condemned (which makes no sense). The legend says that the obedient Jaimini obliged and so today we have only the *Ashvamedhaparva* of Jaimini's *Bharata Samhita*.

A.K. Bandyopadhyay refers to another legend according to which Jaimini's composition, being superior in poetic qualities and variety of events, was prohibited by Vyasa from being broadcast.[17]

From all indications, however, it appears that Jaimini did not really drop the rest of his composition. If he had, he would have suitably modified the text of his *Ashvamedhaparva*. I do believe that there is every probability that the complete *Jaimini Bharata* was extant at some point in time.

Of the versions rendered by the other disciples, there is no sign, not even the version of Vaishampayana which Vyasa had supposedly approved. Nevertheless, most probably those too existed, because *shlokas* I.57.73–75 of the *Adi Parva* of Vyasa's Mahabharata state that Vyasa made his disciples and his son study the Vedas and the Mahabharata and *they composed separate Samhitas of their own*. This confirms at least the first part of the legend narrated earlier that they authored their own versions of the

Mahabharata. It must be kept in mind though that what Vaishampayana narrated to Janamejaya under Vyasa's supervision was Vyasa's *Samhita* and not his own version.

Dating Jaimini

This leads us to a very pertinent question. Is this Jaimini, the disciple of Vyasa who wrote a version of the Mahabharata, the same as the one who wrote the *Jaiminiyashvamedhaparva?* Is this the same Jaimini who authored *Purva Mimamsa* which is dated around fifth–third century BC? It is not likely because the time difference between the two appears to be too much. From the evidence emerging from the *Jaiminiyashvamedhaparva* itself, it is seen that it could not have been written before the tenth century CE. The scholars who have done research on *Purva Mimamsa* hold that this work of Jaimini is one of the earliest works of the Indian system of philosophy and was written around the beginning of the Christian era. So the same Jaimini could hardly have written both the books. There are, however, some pointers available in the *Ashvamedhaparva* itself which provide some information regarding the period when it was composed. Let us first examine the information available in the book.

In chapter 2 verse 28, Jaimini writes, "In the past was the stone not redeemed on being touched by the feet of Rama?" This refers to the Ahalya episode of the *Ramayana*. But in Valmiki's *Ramayana* she is neither petrified nor does Rama touch her with his feet. Actually, he and Lakshmana touch her feet. This is the *Kathasaritsagara* version of the incident.[18] In Valmiki, her husband Gautama, on finding out her indiscretion, curses her that she would become *"durnirikshya"* – invisible – to everyone and repent for thousands of years in this *ashrama* lying on a bed of ashes and subsisting only on air till Rama came and accepted her hospitality. In the later *Uttarakanda*, the story is slightly different. There Gautama curses her with loss of her uniqueness as the only beautiful female and that other lovely woman would be born. He also prescribed that the curse would end when Vishnu came as Rama and accepted her hospitality. In the Mahabharata version of the story, the furious Gautama asks his son Chirakari to kill his polluted mother but later regrets his rash command. In *Brahma Purana*, Gautama turns Ahalya into a dry stream. She would be redeemed on mingling with the Gautami River. Only in Somadeva's *Kathasaritsagara* we find that Gautama turns Ahalya into stone. Jaimini must have taken this reference from *Kathasaritsagara* and, therefore, would have written after Somadeva (1070 CE).[19]

In chapter 11, we find that Krishna, en route Hastinapura with Bhima, passes through Vrindavana where the *gopis* run to meet him. There is no sign of Radha here which indicates that this text predates her introduction into the Krishna myth in the *Brahmavaivarta Purana*.[20]

In 53.5, we see that paper is being used, so he could not be coterminous with Vyasa. In 68.4.5, the word *pustaka* (book) is mentioned, which proves that Jaimini is at least post-*Harivamsha* where the word occurs possibly for the first time[21] (first–third century CE).[22]

There are many instances when Jaimini refers to idol worship. For example, in 53.13, Dhrishtabuddhi tells Chandrahasa, "If you break my seal, the sin of destroying two idols of Shiva will be yours." This indicates a period later than Vyasa (fourth–second century BC) when idol worship (puja) was added and gradually replaced yajna under the mounting influence of indigenous culture.

In 53.43, Jamini writes, "When one *Hastini* girl went forward to see the flowers." This has an obvious reference to Vatsyayana's classification of women into four categories of which *Hastini* is the fourth. It is argued that this establishes that Vatsyayana's *Kamasutra* (second century CE) predates Jaimini. However, Vatsyayana was compiling previous works on the erotic, just as Kautilya did with earlier treatises on political science. Therefore, a reference to *Hastini* does not necessarily mean that it is Vatsyayana's contribution. It could certainly be taken from tradition.

In chapter 55, verse 7–7.5, the astrologers say to Madana, "Varaha and others have said that today's splendid and flawless twilight moment (*godhulika*) is fruitful for human beings." Jaimini must be referring to Varaha-Mihira, a famous astrologer-astronomer and author of the *Panchasiddhantika* (575 CE) and the *Vrihat Samhita* who died in 587 CE. Some authors have expressed doubt whether the Varaha Jaimini is referring to is Varaha-Mihira or not.[23] But no astrologer of that name other than Varaha-Mihira is known to us. This places Jaimini after the sixth century CE.

In chapter 58, verse 27, there is mention of the *linga* being broken in Kashmir by non-believers. The reference is to the soldiers of Bengal going to Kashmir and breaking the image of Ramasvamin there in revenge for the treacherous murder of their king by Lalitaditya Muktapida (699–736 CE), the king of Kashmir. This incident took place somewhere in the eighth century CE and was recorded by Kalhana in *Rajatarangini*, which he completed writing around 1150 CE. In any case, if Jaimini is referring to this incident, then the earliest that he would have written *Ashvamedhaparva* is after the incident. It does not matter whether he knew about it independently (Kalhana says that this story of great loyalty and sacrifice became known all over the country) or read about it in *Rajatarangini*. Unless this verse is an interpolation, or it refers to some other incident, it indicates that Jaimini composed *Ashvamedhaparva* after either the eighth century CE when the incident occurred or 1150 CE when Kalhana completed writing *Rajatarangini*.

In addition to this, in Jaimini's 58.95–97, there are references to the Mahabharata, the *Harivamsha,* and the *Bhagavata Purana*, and in 16.28 and 50.17–17.5 to the *Gita.* There is controversy regarding the date of *Bhagavata Purana* too. A.K. Bandyopadhyay places on record the opinions of different authors, such as Burnouf, Colebrook, Wilson, Anandatirtha Madhvacharya, Ramanuja, Ballalasena, Alberuni, Winternitz, Bhandarkar, Pargiter, and Farquhar in his comprehensive work and concludes, "Modern researchers (he mentions the work of Dr. Rajendra Hazra) conclude after analysing facts and evidences that the *Bhagavata Purana* cannot be later than the eighth century."[24]

So, if the *Bhagavata Purana* is dated around the eighth or even the tenth century CE, Jaimini could not have written the *Jaiminiyashvamedha* before that date. In Jaimini, there are two references to the attempted disrobing of Draupadi and Krishna saving her from public ignominy in response to her prayers. In the Critical Edition of the Mahabharata, all this is absent. There, as Duhshashana pulls at her clothes another garment appears each time. There is great clamour in the assembly and Bhima utters his famous vow against Duhshashana who sits down, tired and ashamed. Draupadi's prayer and Krishna's immediate response in providing her with an unending supply of clothes, quoted in the footnotes of the Critical Edition, was interpolated in the later versions of the episode. This helps in dating Jaimini's work. Pradip Bhattacharya writes, "In later recensions, Draupadi calls out to Govinda, Krishna and "Gopijanapriya", the last epithet indicating a post-*Harivamsha* addition."[25] Jaimini's inclusion of this episode establishes its period as post-*Harivamsha* which is sometime by the first–second century CE.

W.L. Smith writes,

> Opinions on the date of *Jaimini Bharata,* which might be connected with early *Panchatantra* texts, especially the *Narayaniparvan* of the Mahabharata, vary. Winternitz writes, "it is not earlier than the later sections of the Purana literature", and in any case later than the *Bhagavata Purana* which it quotes (Winternitz 1972: 586). Karmarkar (1960: xxiv) assigns it to the time around the beginning of the present era but gives no reason for doing so. Derrett (1970:24, 27) suggests 1100–1200, a date which seems reasonable.[26]

Ganesh and Shastri believe that Jaimini's *Ashvamedhaparva* cannot be very old since its language is not ancient. Dr. Ganesh says that modern scholars opine that it is not older than the tenth century CE. Dr. Shastri says, "It is difficult to maintain that the ancient Jaimini (author of *Purva Mimamsa)* is the author of this text (*Ashvamedhikaparva*)."[27]

Then, is Jaimini of *Mimamsa Sutra* the same as the Jaimini of *Ashvamedhaparva*? Is Vyasa of Mahabharata the same as Badarayana of

Uttara Mimamsa? Is he the guru of Jaimini? We are inclined to think that he must have written *Ashvamedhaparva* after Somadeva's *Kathasaritsagara* and Kalhana's *Rajatarangini* and agree with Derrett's view, referred to by W.L. Smith, that Jaimini wrote it in the twelfth century CE.

Another idea may be examined. Jaimini, the author of the *Purva Mimamsa*, and Jaimini, the author of the *Ashvamedhaparva*, cannot be coterminous. The *Jaiminisamhita* has been dated by Vielle to the second half of the sixth century CE.[28] Kalidasa's *Raghuvamsha* (18.33) too refers to Jaimini as a yoga guru of Pushya. These give us other Jaiminis. Is it possible that an earlier Jaimini, Vyasa's disciple, composed the *Ashvamedhaparva* and, following the *guru-shishya-parampara* (preceptor-disciple tradition), a later Jaimini, the present redactor, gave it the current form after updating it with interpolations of his own, including contemporary references and using contemporary language? The intervening Jaiminis too could have added their own contributions. What happened to Vyasa's epic could easily have happened to *Jaimini Bharata*. In verses 26–29, *Mumukshukanda*, Section 3 of the *Yoga-Vashishtha Ramayana*, Vashishtha mentions ten incarnations of Vyasa and predicts that he will be born eight more times. In the *Vishnu Purana* (III.3), we find that there were as many as twenty-eight Vyasas. Why not a series of Jaiminis as well?

Vernaculars

Jaimini's *Bharata*, or what was available of it, the *Ashvamedhaparva*, was popular throughout India, perhaps because of its inherent entertainment value. It has all the trappings that capture the public imagination. So, it left quite an impression on the early vernacular literature of many regions of the country. However, the vernacular versions have mostly been selective. The translators have not included all the sections of the original and some added their own stories to the text.

It was in Bengal that the influence was felt most powerfully. It is interesting to note what Dinesh Chandra Sen has to say about it, "Sanjay, Kabindra (Paramesvar), Srikaran Nandi and almost all later translators have written that they translated (the Mahabharata) following the Jaimini-*Samhita*. They have very little connection with Vyasa, except a few references here and there and that is all...."

The oldest translation of Mahabharata in Bengali, according to Dinesh Chandra Sen, was perhaps the one which was done at the instance of Sultan Nusrat Khan or Nasir Khan (1285?–1325), named *Bharat Panchali*. He admits that it has not been found but mentions that it is referred to in Kabindra Parameshvar's Mahabharata. This composition in all probability never existed. It is possible that the reference he found really referred to Nusrat Khan, son of Sultan Hussain Shah of Bengal, who went to Chattagram with Paragal Khan as the king's representative.

The earliest available translation is Kavi Sanjay's Mahabharata. His date cannot be determined conclusively but most probably he was a contemporary of Krittibas (not later than the fifteenth century CE), according to Dinesh Chandra Sen and Munindra Kumar Ghosh.[29] On the basis of Ghosh's comprehensive and convincing research, we shall continue with the view that Kavi Sanjay was the first translator.

Kavi Sanjay has based his narrative on Vyasa's Mahabharata except for the *Ashvamedhaparva* which he took entirely from Jaimini, replacing Vyasa's *Ashvamedhikaparva*. He has avoided all didactic and philosophical material and unconnected stories while including many folktales to cater to the public interest. I would like to mention here that very recently Dr. Pradip Bhattacharya has translated Kavi Sanjay's Mahabharata into English.[30] This is the first English translation of Sanjay's composition.

Thereafter, in the early sixteenth century CE, Kabindra Parameshvar translated the Mahabharata (up to *Stree Parva* according to Dinesh Chandra Sen, but according to Munindra Kumar Ghosh, up to *Ashvamedhaparva*, the later *Parvas* being interpolations) under the patronage of Paragal Khan, a commander of the troops of Nawab Hussain Shah (1493/4–1519)[31] at Chattagram. This came to be known as the *Paragali* Mahabharata.[32] Asit Kumar Bandyopadhyay indicates that this composition was known as *Pandavavijaya* because "Parameshvar has named his poem everywhere as *Pandavavijaya*...Kabindra Parameshvar composed the Mahabharata in brief which became known as *Vijaya Pandava* or *Pandava Vijaya*."[33] This Mahabharata is very short (one that could be heard in one day, according to Kabindra) and includes basically the battle accounts, especially in the *Ashvamedhaparva* which, as in the case of Sanjay's work, is from Jaimini.

After Paragal's death, his son Chhuti Khan became the commander and governor at Chattagram and got Jaimini's *Ashvamedhaparva* translated by Srikara or Srikaran Nandi (the poet calls himself "Srikaran" in his verses). This came to be known as *Chhuti Khaner* Mahabharata. A version of it was included in Kashiram Das's Mahabharata.

Thereafter we have a fairly long crop of translations, some of which are Dvija Abhiram's *Ashvamedhaparva*, Ananta Mishra's *Ashvamedhaparva*, Nityananda Ghosh's Mahabharata, Dvija Ramchandra Khan's *Ashvamedhaparva*, Kabichandra's *Mahabharata*, Shashthibar Sen's *Bharata*, Gangadas Sen's *Adi* and *Ashvamedhaparva*, Rameshvar Nandi's *Mahabharata*, etc., and nearly all of them followed Jaimini while translating the *Ashvamedhaparva*.

Jaimini's book is popular in southern India too, and in Kannada and Telugu, there are complete renderings of the book. The remarkable works of Lakshmisha of Karnataka (Kannada seventeenth–eighteenth century CE) and Pillalmarri Pinaveerabhadriah of Andhra Pradesh (Telugu fifteenth century CE), like most of the other vernacular versions, are original compositions based entirely on Jaimini.

In Assamese, Haribara Bipra (thirteenth or sixteenth century CE) wrote *Lava–Kusar Yuddha Babhruvahanar Yuddha*, and most probably *Tamradhvajar Yuddha* based on Jaimini. He is known to be one of the earliest authors to translate Jaimini in any vernacular. The Kuch king Naranarayana (1540–1584) ordered Ramasarasvati or Aniruddha to edit the Assamese Mahabharata. He composed up to twelve *parvas* and then the *Ashvamedhaparva* was written by Gangadas, Bhabanidas, and Subuddhi Ray (sixteenth or seventeenth century CE) and inserted into this Mahabharata. Gangadhar (of uncertain date) wrote *Sitar Banabas* based on Jaimini.

In Oriya, Nilambara Das translated Jaimini *Mahabharata* in the fifteenth century CE, and Indramani Sahu wrote *Brihat Jaimini Bharata* in two volumes.

In Marathi the story appears in *Bhavartha Ramayana* (based on *Ananda Ramayana*) and in *Srijaimini-Ashvamedha: Mula va Marathi Bhashantara* (Wai Damodara Lakshmana Lele Press, 1913).

In Gujarati, Premananda wrote *Chandrahasakhyana* in 1671 CE. There is also the *Atha Gurjarabhashasamanvitam Srijaiminiyashvamedhaparvan Prarabhyate* of Suryanarayana Press, Ahmedabad, 1965.

In Hindi, Tulsidas wrote *Lavakusakanda* in the *Ramcharitamanasa*. Pandit Ramadhar Shukla Shastri has translated the complete *Jaiminiyashvamedhaparva* published by the Gita Press, Gorakhpur, in 1961. *Atha Srijaiminiyashvamedhaparvaprarambhya* of the Venkatesvara Press of Bombay, V.S. 1989 (1932 CE), contains a Hindi translation. Bhanubhakta (1814–1889) included it in his Nepali *Ramayana* as a separate chapter named *Ramashvamedhakanda*. The story is also included in the Kashmiri *Ramayana* of Divakara Prakasa Bhatta (end of eighteenth century). There are Tibetan, Thai, and Malay versions too, but the stories there are very different.

Razmnama

The most exciting version is the *Razmnama* (The Book of War), the Persian abridgement of the Mahabharata, prepared at the behest of Akbar, the great Mughal emperor (1542–1605). He invited some erudite Sanskrit scholars to assist the Persian scholars of his court to prepare an authentic version of the epic. The names of only some of the Sanskrit scholars are available, viz. Debi Misra, Satavadana, Madhusudana Misra, Rudra Bhattacaraj, Chaturbhuja, and Sheikh Bhawan (originally a Dakhini Brahmin). They assisted Naqib Khan, Shaikh Sultan (Haji) Thanesari, Mulla Sheri, and Abdul Qadir Badauni who wrote the text in Persian. Dr. J.J. Modi states that most of the Persian translation was done by Haji Sultan Thanessari in four years. The Haji said, "I render into modern language the knowledge of ten thousand years." Abul Fazl provided a lengthy introduction. In the next chapter of this book, we will read an extensive analysis of *Razmnama* with a particular focus on its narrative quality.[34]

What interests us is the section on *Ashvamedhaparva*. This particular *Parva* is taken from Jaimini, not Vyasa. The episodes depicted in the Birla *Razmnama* are those of Babhruvahana, Yudhishthira's yajna, Anushalva, Hamsadhvaja, and Bhishana. One big problem with the Birla *Razmnama* is that this version of the *Parva* cannot be taken as representative of the original *Razmnama*, since, in the words of Das, "The exploits of the sacrificial horse – related in the *Ashvamedhika parva* –are shown in 47 illustrations in the Jaipur copy, 22 in the 1598–99 copy against only four in the Birla copy."[35] (In fact, there are five illustrations, not four. Das has missed the fifth one – plate 79 – while editing.) Even then it does give us a glimpse of what must be there in Akbar's *Razmnama*.

These pictures are very exciting for two reasons. One, they create a comic book ambience. If the text accompanying the pictures was available, it would have been fascinating. Secondly, it is interesting to see the characters clad in Mughal attire and presented in an unfamiliar ambience.

The existence of so many vernacular versions in so many Indian languages proves the extreme popularity of Jaimini at one time. Jaimini pervades not only the vernacular literature but also the performing arts, traditions, folklore, and culture. To quote a few examples, we have temples dedicated to Vrishaketu in Himachal Pradesh. The story of Vrishaketu is narrated in the *patas* of Bengal; stories of Chandrahasa, Yauvanashva, Anushalva, Tamradhvaja, etc. are played out in *Yakshagana* performances of South India.

Ashvamedhaparva – Jaimini and Vyasa

Jaimini's work is essentially different from Vyasa's. While the basic structure of the *Parva* is the same as Vyasa's – both begin with Yudhishthira's lament and go on to narrate the decision to perform the horse sacrifice, the tour of conquest under the leadership of Arjuna, the performance of the sacrifice, and the story of the golden mongoose–the details are different. There are, of course, a few similarities but most of the episodes are different. Some of the important points of similarity and difference including those outlined by R.D. Karmarkar in his introduction to the *Parva* in the *Critical Edition of the Mahabharata* (1958) will be discussed here. But before that, it is pertinent to give a brief description of Jaimini's text for the convenience of understanding.

The *Jaiminiyashvamedhaparva* has sixty-eight chapters. The first fourteen chapters deal with Yudhishthira's decision to perform *Ashvamedha yajna* on Vyasa's advice, the description of the horse, the fetching of the horse from King Yauvanashva of Bhadravatipuri by Bhimasena, Vrishaketu, and Meghavarna after a great battle, Anushalva's attack on Krishna and his defeat at the hands of Vrishaketu, the inauguration of the yajna, and commencement of the horse's tour under the protection of Arjuna. The tour continues till the sixty-second chapter. There are thirteen episodes that occur during the journey.

Chapters 62–68 deal with the return of the horse, a very detailed description of the performance of the sacrifice and all the rituals, stories of the quarrelling Brahmins, the golden mongoose, and, finally, the merits of listening to the story of the sacrifice.

The only major stories common to both the texts are those of the Arjuna–Babruvahana conflict, the Arjuna–Duhshala encounter, and the story of the mongoose and the Brahman family, with major differences in the details of the first two. The main structure of the Babruvahana story, once again, is the same – Arjuna reaches Manipura,[36] berates Babruvahana, a battle takes place, Arjuna dies, and is revived by Ulupi (Krishna in Jaimini) with the help of the jewel. But then, the details of the story are quite different. In the Vyasa text, Arjuna goes to Manipura after he visits Duhshala at Sindhudesha. In the Jaimini text, he goes to the city of Jayadratha (the kingdom un-named) much after his visit to Manipura. In Jaimini, Chitrangada is the daughter of a Gandharva king, instead of Chitravahana as in Vyasa's. In Jaimini, Chitrangada misses a beat while dancing and her father curses her to be a crocodile, later to be redeemed by Arjuna. How she is redeemed is not told but, after the birth of a son, she goes away to Yudhishthira (!) and Babruvahana is raised by Ulupi. In Vyasa, there is no such story.

In Vyasa, the story of Barga and four other *apsara*s turned into crocodiles by a curse and redeemed by Arjuna after he leaves Manipura is unrelated to the Babruvahana story. In Jaimini, Arjuna meets both Ulupi and Chitrangada at a pilgrimage place and marries, saving Ulupi from her guru's curse. In Vyasa, Arjuna marries Ulupi at a pilgrimage centre (there is no curse but only the satisfaction of Ulupi's lust) and Chitrangada in her father's kingdom. In Jaimini, Arjuna dies because the vengeful Jvala instigates Ganga to curse Arjuna and she herself becomes the death-arrow for Arjuna and enters Babruvahana's quiver. In Vyasa, Ganga does not curse but the Vasus do with Ganga's approval. Ulupi comes to know about the curse and appeals to the Vasus through her father Vasuki to withdraw the curse. The Vasus assure Vasuki that when Arjuna dies at the hands of his son, he will be free of the sin of killing Bhishma unfairly. So Ulupi "arranges" the death of Arjuna so that he is free of the sin and revives him with the life-giving jewel which appears as she remembers it. In Jaimini, however, the story goes through various twists and turns, covering a space of six chapters, after Arjuna's death. Ulupi sends an envoy to bring the life-giving jewel from the snake kingdom. When he fails due to court intrigue, an enraged Babruvahana invades the *Naga* kingdom in Patala and, after a great battle, snatches *amrita* and the *Sanjivani* jewel from the *Naga*s to revive Arjuna. It does not work as Arjuna's severed head is stolen. So Krishna has to appear and, with his divine power, bring the head back and revive Arjuna with the jewel. Ulupi has no role here. Jaimini's Babruvahana story is long and involved but Vyasa's is simple, straightforward, and bereft of complications. There is no Krishna, no Naga court, no battle with the *Naga*s, no boon of the *Naga*s, and no curse by Ganga. This episode also includes the *Ramakatha*, which Vyasa tells in the *Vana Parva*, which will be discussed later.

The second similar story is that of Duhshala. In the version of Vyasa, there is a battle between the Sindhu army and Arjuna. Duhshala's son, the boy-king Suratha, dies of fright. Duhshala goes with her grandson and appeals to Arjuna to have mercy and stop the battle. Arjuna is embarrassed and takes her home but does not invite her to the sacrificial ceremony. In Jaimini, there is no battle, the boy-king (unnamed) dies, Duhshala berates Arjuna in no uncertain terms, and appeals to Krishna (there is no Krishna in Vyasa) who is present. There is no grandson. Arjuna here is defensive, "I have not caused any distress to your son. Even then, forgive me for all the deeds I have committed in the past...O sinless one, conquering all the enemies I shall give the entire kingdom to you." In Vyasa, he is much more intense and solemn, "We have fought like dogs over a piece of meat and the meat has lost its savour." In Jaimini, Krishna revives the son and Arjuna invites Duhshala to the yajna.

The mongoose story is the same, except that Vyasa's *Krodha* (anger) is Dharma in disguise whereas Jaimini's *Krodha* is *Krodha* himself. One notices a rather interesting situation in this episode. On comparing the narration of this episode in the *Critical Edition* and the Jaimini version, one finds that twenty of twenty-two *shloka*s of 14.92 and nine *shloka*s of the first ten of 14.93 of the *Critical Edition* are repeated verbatim in the first twenty-nine *shloka*s of chapter 66 of Jaimini's work. Jaimini just lifted these *shloka*s from his guru's Mahabharata, without changing a word, and inserted them in his own work! If one searches diligently, other such similarities would surely be found in other parts of the two books. Unless Jaimini was a disciple of Vyasa, he would not have plagiarized with such impunity. In the *guru–shishya parampara* (preceptor–disciple tradition), the disciple has every right over the guru's creation. Since such a symbiotic relationship does exist between the two, as proved by this example, one is tempted to believe the tradition that Vyasa did ask his disciples to write a *Bharata* and they did so.

The points of similarity end here. For the rest, these two works are entirely different from each other. Jaimini's book is substantially larger than Vyasa's *Ashvamedhikaparva*. Jaimini's is completed in sixty-eight chapters and contains 5,147 verses, whereas Vyasa's has 3,320 verses in 133 chapters.

Most of Jaimini's characters find a place in vernacular literature, oral traditions, and performing arts. They are not known to Vyasa. For example, Anushalva, Chandrahasa, Sudhanva, Yauvanashva, Tamradhvaja, Viravarma, etc. are found in the *Yakshagana* of Karnataka. Jana (Jwala), Chandrahasa, Nilaketu, Pramila, Tamradhvaja, and Mayuradhvaja have been mentioned in the *jatra* or folk theatre traditions of Bengal. Some characters who play a peripheral role in Vyasa become larger than life in some local traditions of South India; for example, Iravan/Aravan, the son of Arjuna-Ulupi. Some characters that are important in Vyasa, such as Abhimanyu, are assigned different roles in local traditions. Abhimanyu desires to marry Sundari, daughter of Krishna–Satyabhama, according to the Malayalam tradition, or Sasirekha, daughter of Balarama-Revati, according to Telugu and Kannada traditions. He is helped by Ghatotkacha and Iravan in achieving his objective.

These episodes are not mentioned in Jaimini because *Ashvamedhaparva* is not the right place for them. Is it not possible that these occur elsewhere in the larger *Jaimini Bharata*?

Finally, the most significant and unique contribution of Jaimini to the genre of ancient Indian literature, perhaps, is the *Ramakatha* – the Kusha-Lava story. Even though this episode is irrelevant to the central theme of the text, this is the longest story in Jaimini *Ashvamedha Parva*. This particular story of Jaimini, not narrated by either Valmiki or Vyasa, has caught the attention of the people and has become an extremely popular ballad sung in the villages. Vyasa ends his *Ramakatha* with the conquest of Lanka, and in Valmiki, if the *Uttarakanda* is not considered to be an interpolation, Lava–Kusha just appear at the yajna site with Valmiki and sing the story of Rama. Jaimini begins his story from the point where Vyasa ends. Why did Jaimini begin this completely unprovoked story? Was it merely to draw a parallel to another story of father–son conflict – the Arjuna–Babruvahana encounter? Or, was it because he felt the need to have his own *Ramakatha* since Vyasa had one, beginning from where Vyasa left off? And if the incident does not occur either in the *Ramayana* or in the Mahabharata, then where did he get the story? It is not even found in Kalidasa's *Raghuvamsham*, another storehouse of the story of the *Raghavas*. The idea of a conflict between Rama and the twins is first seen in Bhavabhuti's *Uttararamacharita* (seventh century CE), in which Chandraketu, Lakshmana's son, escorts the horse of Rama's *Ashvamedha*. Lava seizes it and a battle starts between the two. Rama arrives to end the battle. Kusha arrives and meets Rama and then, through a play staged by Valmiki, Rama and Sita are happily united. Although this text could not have been the source for Jaimini as it differs substantially from the latter's more elaborate and dramatic content, it does give the impression that by 600 CE, the idea of a confrontation between Rama and his sons existed. It is also possible to think of Bhavabhuti as the originator of the idea. Even though there is a *Kushalavopakhyana* in Vimalasuri's *Paumacariyam*, a Jaina *Ramayana* in Maharashtrian *Prakrit* (c. 473), where Ankusha and Lavana, sons of Pauma (Rama) and Siya (Sita), venture into a tour of conquest and fight with Pauma and Lakkana at Saketa (Ayodhya), it is drastically different from Jaimini and Bhavabhuti. Ravisena's *Padmacharitra* (a Jaina version in Sanskrit; c.700) narrates the same story with peripheral differences. Similar is the case of Somadeva's *Kathasaritsagara* tale of Rama's *Naramedha* Yajna (c. 1070), in which Lakshmana captures Lava, the elder brother in this case, and takes him to Ayodhya to be slain in sacrifice. Kusha, having heard of Lava's capture, fights with Rama and Lakshmana, defeats them, frees Lava, and finally gets acquainted with Rama. This too therefore does not pass muster.

That brings us to the *Padma Purana* (*Patalakhanda*) which Koskikallio and Vielle describe as a "contemporaneous text."[37] The story jells beautifully with that of Jaimini. Here, Shatrughna's troops encounter numerous adventures and confrontations, and this covers a substantial part of the book as compared to Jaimini's three-and-a-half *shloka*s. He finally reaches Valmiki's hermitage and Lava captures the horse. In the ensuing terrible battle, the twins get the better of Shatrughna who is rendered unconscious. They tie up Sugriva and Hanumana and drag them home as battle trophies. Sita releases them and by her grace all the dead soldiers and commanders regain their lives. Shatrughna returns and on hearing the story Rama sends for the sons and Sita. The sons come but Sita refuses. Lakshmana goes again and this time Sita relents and Rama and she are united. Meanwhile, the twins sing the *Ramayana* for Rama. In Jaimini's story, after Shatrughna falls unconscious, Lakshmana, Bharata, and Rama come, one after the other, to fight the twins and are defeated. Valmiki arrives and revives everyone by sprinkling nectareous water.

The two stories are essentially similar in spite of some differences. There are many stories narrated in the *Padma Purana*; for example, Sita's curse, Bhrigu-Chyavana-Sukanya, and Yagini episode, which are absent in Jaimini. The main difference is the battle sequence which is much longer and varied in Jaimini. In fact, this battle sequence is a brilliant product of Jaimini's creativity, which later authors, especially the vernacular, adopted happily. However, the similarities are overwhelming. Not only the Lava–Kusha story, but many of the other episodes of the *Padma Purana* have been narrated in chapters other than the *Ramakatha* by Jaimini. The abundance of such similarities leaves us without any doubt that one of these texts must have been the source for the other. If we consider *Padma Purana* to be the source for Jaimini, the variety and length that Jaimini introduces in the text, especially in the battle sequence, clearly establish him as a poet with a creativity of higher order. On the other hand, if we consider that Jaimini preceded the *Padma Purana*, then it is Jaimini all the way – the story is entirely his invention with seeds of the idea taken from stories like the *Uttararamacharitam* and *Kathasaritsagara*.

These and many other small differences, not discussed here, make the reading of this text uniquely intriguing. Going through the text generates a distinct feeling that it was to emphasize two basic points that Jaimini embarked upon in this stupendous project. Firstly, he felt a need to create a next generation of heroes more powerful than the previous ones. We have already seen some of the heroes of the next generation in action in *Ashvamedhaparva* – Vrishaketu, Meghavarna, Anushalva, Suvega, Sudhanva, Suratha, Bhishana, Pravira, Babruvahana, Tamradhvaja, Lava, Kusha, among others. In addition, we have Mairavana, Birbahu, Taranisen – all Ravana's sons, Makaradhvaja – Hanuman's son, on the evidence of tales told in folk plays and cinema. Secondly, his core interest lies in the propagation of a particular version of Vaishnava *bhakti*. In Jaimini, it is not merely *bhakti*; it is *bhakti* in enmity – you worship the Lord as an enemy. When your deity appears as an enemy, the battlefield becomes your temple and you worship him by fighting him following your *svadharma* as a true Kshatriya, sincerely and without giving or asking for quarter. Jaimini needed to show that the next generation was very heroic as well and that they also had *bhakti*, which was steadfast even when they confronted their deity as an enemy. This strengthens the feeling that Jaimini must have written the controversial *Bharata*, and one can only hope that one day the other chapters of *Jaimini Bharata*, which promise to be equally captivating as the *Ashvamedhaparva*, will be found for our edification.

Notes

1 In the *Adi Parva* of the Mahabharata, the names of the four sons of Mandapala are: Jaritari, Sarisrikka, Stambamitra, and Drona. In *Markandeya Purana*, only Jaritari and Drona are mentioned.
2 http://www.mimamsa.org/authors/jaimini.html.
3 "Introduction Part 1: A Short History of the *Purva Mimamsa* Shastra" in *Tattvabindu* of Vachaspati Mishra with *Tattvavibhavana* of Rishiputra Parameshvara by R.A. Ramaswami Shastri, 1936, Annamalai University Sanskrit Series No. 3, reprinted 1991, Navrang Booksellers and Publishers, New Delhi.
4 R.N. Dandekar, "Literature of Brahminism in Sanskrit," *The Cultural History of India*, Vol. V, ed. Suniti Kumar Chatterji, Ramakrishna Mission Cultural Institute, Kolkata, 1978, p. 34.
5 http://en.wikipedia.org/wiki/Shrautasutra.
6 http://www.astrojyoti.com/jaiminisutrasmainpage.htm.
7 M. Monier-Williams, *A Sanskrit-English Dictionary*, Motilal Banarsidass, Delhi, reprint 2005, p. 425.
8 Sharma, Janakinath, Introduction, *Jaiminiyashvamedhaparva*, Gita Press, Gorakhpur, 2nd edition, no date.
9 Petteri Koskikallio and Christophe Vielle, "Epic and Puranic Texts Attributed to Jaimini," *Indologica Taurinensia*, Vol. xxvii, Edizioni A.I.T., Torino, 2001, p. 67–93.

10 Dinesh Chandra Sen, *Bangabhasha O Sahitya,* Gurudas Chattopadhyaya & Sons, Kolkata, 7th edition, no date, the first edition of his book came out in 1896, p. 155.

11 Koskikallio and Vielle, *op.cit.* p. 69.

12 Kadaba Nanjunda Shastri and N. Ranganatha Sharma, Preface to the Kannada translation of *Jaiminiyashvamedhaparva.* An English translation of the Kannada version was very kindly sent by Dr. T.S. Bhanumurthy of Chennai in 2005, received courtesy Dr. T.V. Seshachala Shastri.

13 Monier-Williams *ibid.*

14 All references to the Mahabharata are to the BORI edition of Pune, 1960 ff.

15 *Adi Parva*, 1.1.63; 1.57.73–75.

16 R.D. Karmarkar, Introduction to the Critical Edition, *Ashvamedhaparva*, BORI, p. xxiv and R.G. Harshe, "Vestiges of Sanskrit Influence on Early French Literature," *Dr. C. Kunhan Raja Presentation Volume*, ed. M. Natesan and M.G. Manohar, Adyar Library, Madras, 1946, p. 245, fn.2.

17 A.K. Bandyopadhyaya, *Bangla Sahityer Itibritta*, Modern Book Agency, Calcutta, 2006, vol.1, p. 434.

18 Pradip Bhattacharya, *Panchakanya: The Five Virgins of Indian Epics*, Writers Workshop, Kolkata, 2005, p. 22–23.

19 Bhattacharya, *op. cit.,* p. 21.

20 Earliest eighth century CE, then tenth century, finally fifteenth century. http:// www.boi-mela.com/Banglapedia/ViewArticle.asp? TopicRef=4309.

21 Monier-Williams *op. cit.* p. 640.

22 Catherine Ludvik, "A Harivamsa Hymn in Yijing's Chinese translation," Journal of the American Oriental Society, 10.1.2004 and M. Winternitz, *History of Indian Literature,* Vol. 1, Motilal Banarsidass, Delhi, 1st edition, reprint 2003.

23 Koskikallio and Vielle, *op. cit.* p. 73.

24 Bandyopadhyay *op.cit.* p. 466.

25 Pradip Bhattacharya, "Was Draupadi ever sought to be stripped?" ABORI vol.86 2005.

26 W.L. Smith, "The Jaimini Bharata and its eastern vernacular versions," *Studia Orientalia*, ed. The Finnish Oriental Society, vol.85, Helsinki, 1999, p. 391.

27 Personal communication.

28 Vielle, *op. cit.* p. 347.

29 Munindra Kumar Ghosh, Introduction to *Kabi Sanjay birachita Mahabharata,* Calcutta University, 1969, p. 153.

30 Bhattacharya, Pradip, *The Mahabharata of Kavi Sanjay*, Dasgupta & Sons, Kolkata, 2019.

31 Sen, *ibid,* p. 116.

32 Interestingly, another translation is found during this time, known as *Bijoy Panditer Mahabharat.* D.C. Sen writes, "We know these two books (*Paragali Mahabharat* and *Bijoy Panditer Mahabharat*) as the same book. There is a phrase in the *bhanita* (opening or closing lines of a poem containing the poet's name) of Kabindra, '*Bijoy pandaba katha amritalahari* – The story of the Pandavas' victory is like waves of nectar'. Some stupid copyist has made it '*Bijoy-Pandit katha amritalahari* – Bijoy Pandit's story is like waves of nectar.'" (*op. cit.* footnote in p. 455).

33 Bandyopadhyay, *op. cit.* p. 441–442.

34 Modi, Dr. J.J., "King Akbar and His Persian Translation of Sanskrit Books," ABORI, Vol. 6, Pune, 1925, p. 95–96.

35 Asok Kumar Das, *op. cit.,* p. 19.

36 In Vyasa's *Adi Parva*, the kingdom is named Manilura where Arjuna weds Chitrangada, is in South India, and explains the presence of the Pandya king (Chitrangada's father) on the Pandava side in the war. Interestingly, Alli, the

heroic queen of Tamil folklore, also belongs to the Pandya kingdom and we see shades of Alli in Chitrangada and Jaimini's Pramila.

37 Koskikallio and Vielle, *op. cit.,* p. 332.

Works Cited

Bandyopadhyay, Asit Kumar. *Bangla Sahityer Itivritta.* 3 vols., Modern Book Agency, Kolkata, 6th edition. 2006.

Bhattacharya, Pradip. *Panchakanya: The Five Virgins of Indian Epics.* Writers Workshop. 2005.

Das, Asok Kumar, *Paintings of the Razmnama,* The Book of War, Mapin, Ahmedabad, India, 2005.

Ghosh, Munindra Kumar, ed. *Kabi Sanjay Birachita Mahabharata,* University of Calcutta, Calcutta, 1969.

Karmarkar, R. D., ed. *The Āśvamedhikaparvan: Being the Fourteenth Book of the Mahābhārata the Great Epic of India.* Bhandarkar Oriental Research Institute, 1958.

Koskikallio, Petteri and Christophe Vielle, *"Epic and Puranic Texts Attributed to Jaimini,"* Indologica Taurinensia. Vol. Xxvii, Edizioni A.I.T., Torino, 2001.

Lal, P., *The Complete Virataparva, The Mahabharata of Vyasa,* Writers Workshop, 2006.

Modi, Dr. J.J., "King Akbar and His Persian Translation of Sanskrit Books", *ABORI,* Vol. 6, 1925, pp. 95–96.

Monier-Williams, M., *A Sanskrit-English Dictionary,* Motilal Banarsidass, Delhi, rpt. 2005.

Smith, W.L. "The Jaimini Bharata and its Eastern Vernacular Versions", Studia Orientalia, ed. *The Finnish Oriental Society,* Vol. 85, Helsinki, 1999, p. 391.

Sen, Dinesh Chandra, *Bangabhasha O Sahitya,* Gurudas Chattopadhyaya & Sons, Kolkata, 7th ed. (first edition 1896).

Sharma, Janakinath, *Introduction, Jaiminiyashvamedhaparva,* Gita Press, Gorakhpur, 2nd edition, n.d.

2

NILAKANTHA'S MAHABHARATA AND PRESENTIST OBJECTIONS TO HIS WORK

Christopher Minkowski

Readers of the Mahabharata today might find in its stories and lessons something more than the welcome diversion that reading them provides. This is what the authors intended, and they tell us so.[1] In composing the Mahabharata, the authors created an account of those events of the past that had given their present its shape. The authors considered their present to be removed from the time of the Mahabharata. They saw that as a different age, one that had come to an end by and with those epic events. Nevertheless, it was an age not wholly disconnected from their own. For them, the behaviour of the epic's characters in the face of the changes that overtook the world was still relevant to thought and conduct.

In turn, the authors' present is removed from our own. For us, it appears to be a different age, one that has come to an end, but perhaps not wholly disconnected. How, then, might a reader today set about finding in the Mahabharata something more than diversion? The ancient Sanskrit text is vast and sprawling; indeed, it is proud that it covers everything. It describes a form of society and a way of life very different from our own, and in places gives advice that does not appear to be relevant now. Can the Mahabharata be as universal as its opening passages claim? Or is its destiny today only to serve as a vehicle for antiquarianism or atavism, exoticism, or nostalgia?

Here it would be useful to remember that readers looking into the Mahabharata for its cultural resources would not be the first to do so. In their search they could perhaps take guidance from the example of earlier readers, even if they might not make the same use of the text as their predecessors. Such earlier readings are most accessible to us in the form of the commentaries on the Mahabharata. From the eleventh century on, Sanskrit authors produced commentaries on the epic, as a whole or in part, and

DOI: 10.4324/9781003516408-4

produced shorter essays on the text's significance. Those authors lived and wrote in particular times and places, and their readings of the epic reflect their situation. What they made of the Mahabharata has been preserved for us in their commentaries, mostly in unpublished manuscripts.

Here I wish to discuss the work of Nilakantha Caturdhara, a Sanskrit intellectual who wrote a commentary during the second half of the seventeenth century. This commentary, the *Bharata-bhava-dipa*, or "Light on the Inner Significance of the (Maha)bharata" became an influential one among readers in Nilakantha's day, and has remained so ever since. In it, Nilakantha consciously sought to make the text relevant to his own world. For that, he later received criticism from modern scholars, who found his approach anachronistic, in the parlance of modern historicist-philological research. It is some features of this anachronism, or here let us instead call it presentism, that I wish to discuss, as they seem to be relevant to the ambitions of the collection in which this essay appears.

Nilakantha was a desastha Brahmin from Karpuragrama, or Kopargaon, a temple town on the banks of the Godavari river in what is now the Ahmadnagar district of Maharashtra[2] (Gode 1942 and Printz 1911). He moved to Banaras, as many hundreds of other learnt Deccani Brahmins had done in that period, for his further education and career. Banaras was then at the height of an efflorescence of Sanskrit learning, and, after a period of dormancy, had once again become the central node in the subcontinent-wide network of communication for the Sanskritic knowledge systems.

Intellectuals based in Banaras at this time attracted patronage and support from all over India. There were even nobles at the Mughal court who supported the intellectual flowering, as did some of the Mughals themselves, and we know that Nilakantha composed one of his works at the request of the Maharaja of Bikaner, Anupasimha, who served the Mughal emperor, and was a celebrated bibliophile. The sastris in Banaras were sought after especially for their expertise in the knowledge systems of dharmasastra, mimamsa, vedanta, *jyotisa*, literary theory, and for their contributions to literature.[3] In addition to their individual opinions, they were called on for collective ones. The sastris would on certain occasions assemble at the Mukti Mandapa, a pavilion in the Visvanatha temple, the principal temple in the city to Siva as Lord of All, to make collective decisions about difficult points of dharma that had been referred to them by local and regional pandit assemblies (Pollock 2001).

Nilakantha wrote a dozen or so other works, but he is best remembered for his commentary on the Mahabharata, including its long "appendix" (*khila*), the Harivamsa. His commentary was well received in its own day and circulated to many parts of India fairly rapidly. There are extant manuscripts, both of Nilakantha's commentary and of Nilakantha's edition of the epic text, that date from Nilakantha's lifetime and from the decades that follow. These extant manuscripts are now held in collections in many parts of India.[4] The entire commentary has been in print since the mid-nineteenth century, and it remains the only Sanskrit commentary on the whole of the Mahabharata that is available in its entirety in published form.[5] For this reason, it is still widely used by readers of the Sanskrit text, much more so than any other commentary.

Nilakantha often relied on earlier commentaries, especially the commentaries of Devabodha, the earliest known (eleventh-century North India or Kashmir), and Arjunamisra (sixteenth-century Bengal). Commentaries before Nilakantha's usually took the form of localized glosses of difficult words as well as of annotations of particularly thorny verses, known collectively as the *kutaslokas*. The commentators also had to concern themselves with establishing just what the text of the Bharata was, as there had come to be different versions in different parts of the subcontinent. The commentators knew this from consulting the manuscripts available in their day.

Among his other contributions, Nilakantha created a fresh "cosmopolitan" edition, based on collecting manuscripts from different parts of India.[6] Even more important, however, was that Nilakantha proposed an interpretation of the significance of the Mahabharata as a whole, which he then attempted to elucidate both in his explanations of the arrangement of the epic's hundred sections (*parvan*), and in his localized comments on particular stories and verses.

While this was something no previous commentator had done, the Mahabharata had already attracted synthetic interpretations of its significance and value. The Mahabharata was, after all, a principal work in the Sanskrit literary and intellectual tradition and served as the basis for many poetic and dramatic versions, of both particular episodes and its main story.

The intellectuals were just as interested as the poets. Sastris in the Vedic tradition, especially the *mimamsaka* theorists of interpretation beginning with Kumarila Bhatta (early eighth century), considered the Mahabharata to be a dharmasastra and had devoted some consideration to how it was to be read as such (Fitzgerald). This was the general approach of the commentators who preceded Nilakantha: to read the Mahabharata as an instruction in the four ends of man (*purusartha*).

Meanwhile, literary theorists in medieval Kashmir, especially Anandavardhana (ninth century) and Kuntaka (late tenth century), considered the Mahabharata a model of literary expression, an example of a poem that successfully produced the aesthetic sentiment of tranquillity (*santarasa*) in an experienced reader, largely because of the way in which it heaped up in the reader's mind the impact of life's tribulations, losses, and disappointments, even in the lives of exemplary people (Tubb 1991).

Just as significant for understanding the intellectual and cultural context of Nilakantha's commentary, however, are the "sectarian" readings of the

Mahabharata that had been advanced in independent essays by promoters of distinct forms of Vedantic theology. An early and prominent example was the *Mahabharata-tatparya-nirnaya*, the Determination of the Meaning of the Mahabharata, of Madhvacarya (thirteenth-century Karnataka). This essay of nearly 5,000 verses proposed a Vaisnavite reading for both the Mahabharata and the Ramayana, and in effect made both of the epics into treatises in Madhva's version of dualist theology.

Closer to Nilakantha's own day was the work of Appayya Diksita (sixteenth-century Vellore), whose *Bharata-tatparya-samgraha-stotra* "Song of Praise that Gathers the Meanings of the [Maha]bharata" proposed an ingenious reading of the Mahabharata that made it into a text of Sivadvaita, that is, of a soft or qualified version of non-dualism, in which Siva was the ultimate, abstract Being (brahman).[7]

It was probably in response to these works and other similar ones that Nilakantha designed his commentary as a properly non-dualist or Advaitin reading of the text, but a reading in which the ultimate, abstract Being was embodied as Vishnu in the form of Krishna, as an aid to the understanding of the spiritually undeveloped.

What could be "presentist" in this sort of metaphysics? Modern philological scholars, who have been principally concerned with attempting to reconstruct the meaning of the Mahabharata "as it was" for the period in which it was composed, considered all of the sectarian essayists to be anachronistic in their approach, in that the sectarian works attempted to read back into the text an overall meaning for the work that modern scholars determined it not to have had originally. The views of Nilakantha, whose commentary was in print, and on the same page as the epic text consulted by the moderns, came in for special notice, and for special disapproval.[8]

It can certainly be shown that Nilakantha was a presentist in his approach to the Mahabharata, that is, that he thought of the epic in terms of the cultural setting of his own day. In his commentary, he famously identified some of the weapons of the epic warriors with the military technology that was rather new in his time. For him, the kshatriyas in the Mahabharata were fighting with muskets and cannons, and building fortresses that were designed both to use and to defend against those weapons. Nilakantha, furthermore, used words from the spoken languages of the seventeenth-century India, including vocabulary from Arabic and Persian, to explain the epic's weaponry and other elements of its material culture.

Other new things were brought into the commentary as well: in one of his philosophical passages, he updated the old Advaitin analogy of the snake and the rope, which was used to explain the workings of maya, by introducing the example of eyeglasses (*upanetra*), which make letters that are illegibly small large enough to read.[9] Furthermore, Nilakantha signalled his adherence to a view generally held by the sastris in Banaras in his time, though not by all others elsewhere, when he indicated that the long chapter of the Santiparvan about the dharma of kings applied to all those who were in power, whether they were kshatriyas by birth or not.[10]

For anything other than historicist scholarship, there is nothing terribly reprehensible in these contemporary touches. Something like it is probably the norm rather than the exception for the way readers make use of classics. I think of Nilakantha's use of new things as being something like the details in the work of Italian painters in the Mannerist school during the Renaissance. Painters like Veronese draped the figures in their depictions of Biblical stories in the rich fabrics that were newly available from merchants in Venice (some shipped there from India, of course).

It is, however, Nilakantha's concern with the present in his philosophizing about the ultimate that is more significant, and to which I turn for the remainder of this essay. Elsewhere I have argued that, although it might now strike us as "business as usual" in a Sanskrit commentary to advocate a philosophical reading of the epic as a whole, and to be more specific, a non-dualist one, complete with Vedantic allegories and invocations of support from rarely cited Vedic texts, nevertheless this was something unusual and fresh in the period in which Nilakantha produced it, and the reason for its success. His sustained discussions of fine points of philosophy were about something that mattered to his contemporary readers.

Nilakantha's discussions, which can seem to the casual reader to be well off the point of the epic verse to which they are appended, are better understood against the intellectual-cultural background of the period, in which a fierce contest was being waged by authors writing from within various movements, and by non-allied authors as well. Some of them were aligned with Madhva's movement of Vaishnava theistic dualism, and its numerous intellectual descendants; others with Ramanuja's movement of theistic "qualified" or soft non-dualism. There were also realist logicians (*naiyayikas*) and arch-conservative Vedists (generally *mimamsakas*) who had views on these matters, mostly hostile to Vedanta, and especially non-dualist forms of it. The opinions of these authors, writing from the cultural centre, had a bearing on the daily religious and spiritual practice of many people, and on their views of how society was to be arranged.

Nilakantha brought the terms of this debate into his Bharata commentary. It is always clear what his own affiliation was. He was a partisan of the strict version of non-dualism that derived from the writings of Sankaracarya. He cited the works of Sankara, Suresvara, Vacaspatimisra, Vidyaranya, Sadananda, Sarvajnatman, and other figures in the Advaita school as sources of authority.

In the seventeenth century, the Advaita version of Vedanta ruled in Banaras. Advaita had become the establishment position, as it were, but there were challenger movements and sampradayas, as mentioned. The challengers had exerted pressure: intellectual, institutional, and social, on the centre in Banaras, and there had been developments in response, even in the thinking of the Advaitins, and new attempts at hybrid solutions. Appayya Diksita, mentioned above, an influential figure in this period, wrote treatises advocating both the strong form of Sankara's Advaita (in works like the *Siddhantalesasamgraha*) and also his own version of a qualified Saiva non-dualism, Sivadvaita (in the *Sivarkamanidipika*).[11]

Even more influential in Banaras was the work of Madhusudana Sarasvati, who had lived in the city a century earlier and had written works of two kinds, some that argued with great philosophical sophistication for the most exacting form of Advaita (in his *Advaitasiddhi*) and others, intellectually formidable as well, in which emotional devotion (bhakti) to a personal deity, viz. Krishna, was explored as an alternative path, one as valid as the Vedantic one (in his *Bhaktirasayana*). In some places, Madhusudana argued that the goal of this path, union with the personal God, was several steps above and beyond ordinary Vedantic enlightenment (*jivanmukta*). Madhusudana's Advaitin works were circulated, cited, and given commentaries by the mainstream Advaitins. His philosophical formulation of the emotional devotional turn was followed by some of them.

Nilakantha was clearly influenced by Madhusudana's writings on Advaita, and he too engaged himself with developing a form of theology of a personal deity that could be accommodated to the non-dualist position. However, he seems not to have accepted the superiority or independence of the bhakti path, and to have sought to shift the balance back in favour of abstract non-dualism and away from emotional devotionalism.

What was the bearing of all of this rather abstruse theologizing on life in the real world? The meaning and significance of Nilakantha's reading can be seen in his attempts at a sort of pluralism, or advocacy of religious ecumenism. I end with the discussion of two passages from Nilakantha's Mahabharata commentary that show his attention to the social and cultural practices of his day, and that reflect an interest in influencing them.

The first is found in the introductory essay (*adivakya*) that precedes his comments on the first verse of the Adiparvan. Here Nilakantha got onto the subject of the varieties of marks worn on the forehead, the *tripundra*, *urdhvapundra,* and so on. The forehead mark was a way of displaying one's affiliation to one or another tradition of worshipping one or another supreme deity. The proper conduct associated with wearing a forehead mark had become a topic of some concern in this period, as a result of rivalries between movements.[12]

Nilakantha brought the subject up in the course of his discussion of the value of reading the Mahabharata. In response to the possible objection that the Mahabharata was not, after all, one of the revealed Vedic texts (*shruti*), and therefore not reliable as a source of knowing about dharma, Nilakantha argued that the entire genre of literature to which the Mahabharata belonged, the *smrti*, should be understood to be based on some passage of the Vedas, whether that basis is evident or not. This was a position that the theorists of interpretation, the *mimamsakas,* had worked out long ago.[13] Nilakantha here followed the line of argument of the *mimamsakas*, and mentioned two of their canonical examples of behavioural commands from the *smrti* literature and their *shruti* basis.

But then Nilakantha introduced something new, another behavioural command from the *smrti*, i.e. "One should make one's forehead mark from earth."[14] He then set about finding the basis for this command in the extant Veda, and claimed to find it in two verses in the Rgveda about the triad of artisanal deities, the Rbhus. This might strike the unbiased reader of the Rgveda as an unlikely source, as the two verses appear to be about how the Rbhus fashioned four Soma cups out of one, and how they drove a lame cow to the water and carved up its flesh and carried away its dung.[15]

Nevertheless, Nilakantha applied his commentarial arts to the words of these verses, and found in them something extraordinary. The verses turned out, in Nilakantha's reading, to describe three different ways in which people might become the divinity: by pilgrimage, by fire-rituals, and by showing mercy. Furthermore, the verses taught the substances to use for making forehead marks, in order to indicate the form of the deity with which one might choose to unite.[16]

As the verses of the Rgveda were not complete in themselves in these instructions, Nilakantha showed that they also taught how we are to complete them by appealing to other texts. Which texts depended on one's choice of deity: either Vaishnava texts, or Saiva texts, or tantric texts associated with Ganesa, Devi, or Surya. He also found in the verse provision of a sort of non-aligned, Vedas-only (kevala-vaidika), option.

The reason that Nilakantha had begun this discussion was to show that the Mahabharata was a reliable source of instruction for readers. That point, however, had already been made in works of the past, using arguments that Nilakantha knew and referred to. The introduction of this additional, learnt, and lengthy discussion was for the purpose of making a larger claim about the Mahabharata and its allied tradition: that the received tradition of the classics provided instructions for how it was to be read in his own time, and that those instructions allowed for a variety of movements and practices, supported in different ways and by different textual sources.

Nilakantha turned to a related point a little later in his commentary on the Adiparvan, as part of an extensive discussion of the philosophical underpinnings of the nondualist theology that he thought the Mahabharata disclosed.[17] Given that the deity was one, a lesser mode of the ultimate, and not different from the worshipper in any deep way, he asserted, the partisan quarrelling about the hierarchy of particular forms of the deity was misguided and harmful. I cite some of the passage here as a way to conclude, as it gives a sense both of the content and of the tenor of the theological debates of the day, and of Nilakantha's awareness and view of them.[18]

Some people, unaware of the tradition that has been passed down, as described above, of a practice of meditation that brings the mind to the unmanifest (undifferentiated Being), think that liberation means attaining the heavenly world of some high deity, and that there is no other, more abstract essence of the deity. In doing so, they reject the view established by all of the sastras, that there is no experience of duality of any kind in the state of liberation.

The (mutual) criticism of the (Vaishnava) *Bhagavata Purana* or the [Saiva] *Sutasamhita* as being demonic forgeries is based on setting out a hierarchy of Vishnu and other deities, using the obstinate claims of worshippers that Vishnu is the ultimate while Siva is a mere unliberated soul or vice versa. This criticism results from not understanding the parameters of sastric inter- pretation. According to the principle of contingent utility, one simply relies on whatever form is expedient to enable the divine to descend into the mind.

As for the mutual defamation that one finds in passages of the Saiva and Vaishnava puranas of the texts and followers of the other sort, that is not really there to serve as defamation of something that deserves to be defamed. It is there, rather, to praise what it is that ought positively to be done (*vid- heya*), just in the same way that one finds in the Vedas passages that encour- age one positively to do the yajnas correctly, by pointing out the negative consequences of the erroneous practice. The point cannot be criticism per se, as then worship of both gods would have to be abandoned. We could rather think that, as in the case of comparable Vedic passages, the passages we see in the Saiva and Vaishnava puranas are there to indicate an optional choice of one or the other, or perhaps a combination of both, for specified results.

In fact, though, passages of this sort should be understood as being about two forms of brahman, the causal and the caused, in which certain terms of praise and rebuke, respectively, are used according to an especially created convention. As an example, we might consider the inquisitive man who, in order to find out what will provoke his new, innocent young wife, shouts abuse at the family dog, while calling it by the name of her brother, his brother-in-law. She then (mistakenly) thinks that he means to insult her brother and becomes angry.

In this way, in the Saiva texts, the word Vishnu is used as a convention to express the caused (*karya*) brahman, and worship of him is taken for this purpose to lead merely to the highest good that the caused brahman can afford, that is the heavenly world of Brahma. Brahmaloka is designated hell in the Saiva texts, because it is, relatively speaking, a form of suffering, designed for men who have achieved an attainment that is inferior (by com- parison to the ultimate liberation brought about through a higher form of meditation on the causal brahman). And *mutatis mutandi,* the same thing goes for the Vaishnava texts.

> Those base, low-class Vaishnava and Saiva partisans do not understand the language of variety used in the puranas. They are unaware of the Vedic statements about non-difference which point out the fault that lies in seeing difference between Siva and Visnu and that are described in the Smrti literature as follows, "Those who have been misled by religious imposters are bewildered by the impression of difference when they see Brahma, Krsna and Rudra, and do not see them as one." They do not know the truth of the Sastra that the one root cause is to be distinguished from the final effects it produces, just as an actor only appears to be different characters. And accepting only one or other of the forms of God they criticize each other, making a great mutual ruckus, and hence as a result of the injury they do to the masters they are readying themselves only for hell. That is all I will say about that.[19]

There are elements here of a claim that one still encounters today, usually in a blander and less philosophically precise form, about the one god who may legitimately be worshipped in many forms. It used to be asserted that this sort of claim was paradigmatic of the Hindu tradition in all eras. Versions of that claim supported experiments with a variety of secularism in the Gandhian and Nehruvian era. On the other hand, it has been asserted more recently that this sort of claim is a modern development, one that emerged in the nineteenth century as part of the transformation of Hinduism into neo-Hinduism. I tend to think of it as a modern development, but in a modernity that started much earlier than is usually thought, one that was already underway in the seventeenth century. Modern readers of the Mahabharata may not wish to do with the text what Nilakantha did. Nevertheless, one can glimpse in his encounter with the epic some possibilities for modern multicultural India.

Notes

1 There is scholarly discussion about how many authors, enunciators, compilers, and editors the Sanskrit Mahabharata has had. That is not an argument I seek to provoke here. I have used the plural, since that is what I think is correct. If any reader is convinced, however, that the Mahabharata had only one author, e.g. Krsna Dvaipayana, then that reader should consider the use of the plural to be a Sanskritic form of respect.
2 His father, Govindasuri, was probably the adhyaksa of either the Sukresvara or Kacesvara temples on the island in the Godavari at its sangam in Kopargaon. The family name, Caturdhara is a Sanskritization of Chauduri.
3 See O'Hanlon 2010. We see the names of several of Nilakantha's teachers recorded in the documents produced by these assemblies in the 1650s and 1660s. The Visvanatha temple had been rebuilt in 1585 during the reign of Akbar and

was torn down again in 1669 during the reign of Aurangzeb. Nilakantha was probably in the city during the period both before and after this demolition.

4 On balance, the evidence suggests, furthermore, that for many of these manuscripts, the regions where they are now held are the same regions where they had been copied and read. See Gode 1951, Minkowski 2005.

5 There is still no text-critical edition of the commentary, and the published versions leave something to be desired.

6 Cf. the sixth verse in his opening of the commentary on the Adiparvan. bahun samahrtya vibhinnadesyan kosan viniscitya ca patham agryam | pracam gurunam anusrtya vacam arabhyate bharatabhavadipah ||

7 The *Bharatatatparyasamgrahasloka* is much shorter, consisting of only twenty ornate verses accompanied by Appayya's own commentary. For an analysis of how Appayya made a similar argument about the Ramayana in a companion work, see Bronner.

8 On Nilakantha's reception, see Minkowski 2005.

9 *Bharatabhavadipa* (henceforth *BhBhD*) on Moksadharmaparvan, Santiparvan, verse 1.

10 *BhBhD* on Rajadharmaparvan, verse 1. For more on the reasons why this view was of great relevance at the time, i.e. when the Maratha leader Shivaji was consecrated as a kshatriya king, see O'Hanlon, 2010, Deshpande.

11 Appayya organizes his work around the writings of a predecessor, Srikantha, but is nevertheless innovative in his approach. See McCrea 2014.

12 See Horstmann 2009, 325, where she cites a passage of the Vaidika-Vaishnava-sadacara, a work of the early eighteenth century, by Harekrsna Misra, which lays down the rules for one sectarian group. See also Clementin-Ojha 2000.

13 In the smrtyadhikarana of the Mimamsasutra (1.3.1–2). See Minkowski 2005 240–241, where I cite some of Nilakantha's remarks.

14 urdhvapundram mrda kuryat etc. *Brahmanda Purana* as cited in the Ahnikaprakasa, a dharmasastric text Kane 1968–1977, 2.1: 673.

15 What Nilakantha bases himself on in this passage seems to be that it records a difference of opinion among the three Rbhus, and describes the separate activities of each one.

16 As Nilakantha reads it, the Rgvedic verses are recommending gopicandana, i.e. white clay from pilgrimage places, ashes from cow dung that has been burnt as the fuel for a fire in a yajna, or a mixture of red clay and yellow orpiment.

17 BhBhD on Adiparvan 1.23, asac ca sadasac caiva … This is the most complete discussion of the topic to be found in the commentary.

18 In some of what follows, I provide a full translation; in other places, I condense. The whole passage can be found in *Kimjavadekara* 1929, 1:7.

19 tam imam pauranam bhasabhedam ajanantah pamarah saivaVaishnava pasada 'brahmanam kesavam rudram bhedabha-vena mohitah | pasyanty ekam na jananti pakhandopahata jana' iti tatraiva smarya-manam sivavisnvor bhedadarsane dosam udahrtyabhedasrutis capasyanto mulakaranam evantyat karyan nata iva tattadrupena bhasata iti sastratattvam ajananto 'nyatararupaparigrahenetaram nindantah parasparakalahayamanah svamidrohan narakayaiva sajjante ity alam. This is a revised version of a translation that appears in Minkowski 2010, 132.

Works Cited

Bronner, Yigal. "A Text with a Thesis", in Yigal Bronner (ed.), *Language, Culture and Power: New Directions in South Asian Studies*. Association of Asian Studies, 2011.

Clementin-Ojha, M.C. "Etre un Brahmane smarta aujourd'hui", *Bulletin de l'Ecole francaise d'Extreme-Orient,* 87, 2000, 317–339.

Deshpande, Madhav. "Ksatriyas in the Kali Age: Gagabhatta and His Opponents". *Indo-Iranian Journal,* 53:2, 2010, 95–120.

Fitzgerald, James. "India's Fifth Veda: The Mahabharata's Presentation of Itself", in Arvind Sharma (ed.), *Essays on the Mahabharata.* Leiden, 1991, 150–170.

Gode, P.K. "Nilakantha Caturdhara, the Commentator of the Mahabharata - His Geneaology and Descendants", *Annals of the Bhandarkar Oriental Research Institute,* 23, 1942, 146–161.

_____, "Some Contemporary Manuscripts of the Works of Nilakantha Caturdhara, the Commentator of the Mahabharata - Between A.D. 1687 and 1695". *Journal of the S.M. Library,* Tanjore 4.1, 1951. Reprinted in *Studies in Indian Literary History,* vol.2, 1954), 491–498.

Horstmann, Monika. *Der Zusammenhalt der Welt.* Harrassowitz Verlag, 2009.

Kane, P.V. *History of Dharmasastra.* 5 vols. 2nd ed. Bhandarkar Oriental Research Institute, Poona, 1968–1977.

Kimjavadekara, Ramachandrashastri. *Mahabharatam with the Commentary of Nilakantha.* Citrashala Press, 1929–1936.

McCrea, Lawrence. "Coloring Tradition: Appayyadiksita's Invention of Srikantha's Vedanta." *Journal of Indian Philosophy,* 44:1, 2014, 81–94.

Minkowski, Christopher. "Nilakantha's Instruments of War: Modern, Vernacular, Barbarous". *Indian Economic and Social History Review,* 41, 2004, 365–385.

_____. "On the Success of Nilakantha's Mahabharata Commentary", in F. Squarcini (ed.), *Boundaries, Dynamics and Construction of Traditions in South Asia.* Firenze University Press, 2005.

_____. "A Guide to Philological Argument in Early Modern Banaras", in Sheldon Pollock (ed.), *Epic and Argument in Sanskrit Literary History: Essays in Honor of Robert P. Goldman.* Manohar, 2010.

O'Hanlon, Rosalind. "Letters Home: Banaras Pandits and the Maratha Regions in Early Modern India". *Modern Asian Studies,* 44:2, 2010, 201–240.

Pollock, Sheldon. "'New Intellectuals in Seventeenth-Century India", *Indian Economic and Social History Review,* 38, 2001, 3–31.

Printz, W. "Bhasa-Worter in Nilakantha's *Bharatabhavadipa* und in Anderen Sanskrit-Kommentaren". *Zeitschrift fur vergleichende Sprachforschung* 44, 1911, 69–109.

Tubb, Gary. "Santarasa in the Mahabharata", in Arvind Sharma (ed.), *Essays on the Mahabharata.* Brill, 1991, 171–203.

3

DRAMATIC WAR, FABULOUS STORIES, AND LEGENDARY KINGS

Persian Adaptation of Mahabharata as *Razmnama*

Kashshaf Ghani

Modern-day understanding of South Asian cultural spheres as mutually self-contained, representing two immutable religious traditions of Hinduism and Islam – that coexisted for over a millennium in the South Asian subcontinent – obscures a historical understanding of these worlds driven by elite languages – Sanskrit, Arabic and Persian. Rather than being Janus-faced, as commonly believed, these cultural worlds reveal a history of long, varied and often complex interactions at multiple levels, hence enriched by each other. Among other things, the exchange of knowledge systems presents us with a tangible framework through which such a hypothesis is historically traceable.

The earliest reception of Indian sciences in the Islamic world can be traced to the Abbasid Caliphs of Baghdad, Harun al Rashid and his son Al-Mamun who patronized the translation of Sanskrit works, apart from those in Latin, Greek, Roman, and Pahlavi into Arabic, across fields of Philosophy, Metaphysics, Logic, Mathematics, Astronomy, Astrology, Medicine, Stories, and Fables (Ernst 175–177). The earliest stories and fables of the *Panchatantra*, written in Sanskrit by the sage Vishnuvarman around 300 CE, were translated into Pahlavi or Middle Persian during the reign of Sasanian monarch Khosrow Anushirvan (531 579 CE), from where Abdullah ibn Muqaffa (d. 760) translated them into Arabic. This classical work came to be known as the *Kalila wa Dimna* after the two central characters of the jackals, being the earliest example of stories borrowed from the Mahabharata. This Arabic version was thereafter again translated into New Persian with the title *Anwar-i Suhaili* (Lights of Canopus) by Husain Waiz

DOI: 10.4324/9781003516408-5

Kashifi in the court of the Timurid ruler of Herat, Muhammad Hussayn Bayqara in the early sixteenth century. Another Persian work, titled the *Majma ul Tawarikh,* also contains stories from the Mahabharata originally translated into Arabic by Abu Salih bin Shuaib bin Jami from Sanskrit. The Persian translation was undertaken by Abul Hasan al Jili in 1026 CE. Given the cultural reception of the Mahabharata epic, scholars have suggested that several prose and poetical works in Persian were influenced by this Sanskrit text. The primary of which could be the national epic of Persia, the *Shah Nama* (Book of Kings) written by the renowned poet Firdausi (Husain 267–268; Modi 85–87).

The earliest Muslim scholar to engage with the Indic world of Sanskrit was the Persian polymath Abu Rayhan al Beruni (d. 1048 CE). He took a keen interest in Sanskrit and Indian culture and travelled extensively in north India, leaving behind a comprehensive survey of Indian knowledge in his *Kitab al Hind* (Sachau xxxvii–xlviii). With the establishment of the Delhi Sultanate in the thirteenth century, combined with the rise of the regional vernaculars, the elite world of the Sanskrit cosmopolis came to be challenged. However, Sanskrit does not disappear from the realm of public knowledge production. Instead, Sanskrit scholars sought patronage in the courts of the regional Sultanates – like Gujarat and Bengal, where they were engaged in textual creation and translation. Between the late fifteenth and early sixteenth centuries, Srivara's *Kathakautakam,* Kalyana Malla's *Sulaimaccarita,* and Udayraja's *Rajavinoda* capture a Sanskrit literary culture in the sultanate of Gujarat (Obrock 58–59). Similarly in Bengal from the fourteenth century, the Sultanate courts engaged with the Ramayana and the Mahabharata, through multiple translations from the Sanskrit original into Bengali – a vernacular language which till then lacked an elite status to be a vehicle for great Sanskrit epics. Knowledge circulated through Sanskrit texts, particularly related to astronomy and sciences, appealed to the early Mughals like Babur and Humayun. It was, however, in the period of Akbar that we witness the engagement of Persian scholars of the Mughal court with Sanskrit works on a scale hitherto unseen. It is to this story that we turn.

I

Akbar's fame as a patron of art, culture, and scholarship followed close on the heels of his fame, even greater perhaps, as an empire builder. Within a decade of abolishing the *jiziya* in 1564, Akbar established the translation bureau (*maktab khana*) at his capital in Fatehpur Sikri. The task was cut out. An extremely efficient bench of scribes, secretaries, historians, linguists, and artists was given the responsibility of translating a range of Sanskrit texts starting from the *Rajatarangini* to the *Ramayana* into Persian. They were also asked to undertake Persian translations of Arabic encyclopaedias and histories and rework on older Persian classics, in the sense of giving those a new form with a revised content. The other important task was to translate the *Baburnama* – the memoirs of Zahiruddin Muhammad Babur – from Chaghtai Turkish to Persian (Rice 125; Ali 38–40).

Works selected for translation from Sanskrit to Persian were chosen from a wide cross-section of fields that included religious texts like *Atharva Veda* – the first project taken up for translation by Abdul Qadir Badauni with the help of Shaykh Bhavan, thereafter Faizi, then Haji Ibrahim Sirhindi, before finally being abandoned; historical treatises like the *Rajatarangini* by Maulana Imamuddin; romance stories like *Nala Damayanti*; and works on mathematics and astronomy like the *Lilavati* by Fayzi. Mughals had a strong affinity for stories and fables, being familiar with the production and circulation of wondrous stories (*ajaib dastans*) throughout the Perso-Arabic world. One of the first illustrated works commissioned by Akbar was the *Hamzanama*, constituting the imaginary accounts of travel and wonderful adventure around the personality of Amir Hamza, the uncle of Prophet Muhammad. Thereafter, in 1574, another important work of Indian origin, the *Singhasan Battisi* (Thirty-two Tales of the Throne), was chosen for translation. The original Sanskrit contains a series of thirty-two tales on Raja Bikramjit of Malwa. The translated work was known as *Nama i Khirad Afza* (Wisdom Enhancing Book). Flowing from this interest, the *Panchatantra* was once again picked up by Akbar's translators. In the first exercise, the *Anwar-i Suhaili* was rendered into simple Persian for wider reception in a new format titled as *Iyar-i Danish* (Touchstone of Intellect). The second version was a direct translation undertaken by Mustafa Khaliqdad Abbasi from the Sanskrit original titled *Pancakhyana*. Thereafter, the Sanskrit Ramayana was translated between 1585 and 1589 by Abdul Qadir Badauni (Badauni 183–184; Haider 116–117; Chaudhuri 29–32; Ali 173–174).

Apparently, the idea was to expand Mughal frontiers of knowledge through deeper engagement with the Indic intellectual world captured in Sanskrit. As a cultural project, it was aimed at opening windows of engagement between various communities that inhabited the Mughal world, adhering to Persianate and Sanskritic cultures. An overarching political dimension however dominated these projects, as discussed below, concerned directly with the ideas of kingship and authority within the Mughal Empire.

Looking closely, it is discernable that the *maktab khana* was meant to "translate" two imperial agendas into action: expanding the realm of Persian with the aim of making it the official language of the Mughal Empire across the court and the lower sections of the imperial bureaucracy. Towards this end, all office-holders, clerks, scribes, accountants, secretaries, were made to learn Persian, through madrasahs. To facilitate this programme, a multi-tiered language training curriculum was developed. It was meant to expand the realm of Persian as a prestige language, a position previously commanded by Sanskrit, thereby defining the imperial identity through a uniform set of Persian cultural traditions (Alam 317–349).

Satisfied with the progress of the translation bureau riding on the rapid spread of Persian throughout the empire, Akbar embarked on his second agenda – the ambitious project of translating Sanskrit epics for a Persianized audience. In 1582, the bureau was entrusted with the responsibility of translating the Mahabharata. Following imperial orders, scholars set out to translate all the eighteen books of the epic into Persian, including the Harivamsa, which details the life of Krishna as an incarnation of Vishnu. It took a team of scholars – Muslims and non-Muslims – from diverse backgrounds, years to finish the work, to be titled as *Razmnama* (Book of War) and remain one of the most extensive translation projects the Mughals undertook. The description of the initiative is as follows (Haider 119).

Among the remarkable events of this year (AH 990/ CE 1582) was the translation (*tarjuma*) of *Mahabharata*, which is one of the greatest books of India (*muazzam kutub i hind*). It comprises all sorts of stories (*qisas*), moral injunctions (*mawaiz*), advices (*masalib*), ethics (*akhlaq*), norms of good conduct and manners (*adab*), and religious knowledge (*ma'rif*), beliefs (*itiqadiyat*), and modes of worship (*tariq i ibadat*), all presented in the context of wars between the tribes of Kurus and Pandus. According to legend, the Kurus and the Pandus were the rulers of India more than 4,000 years ago. The Hindu unbelievers consider it a matter of great religious merit to read and make copies of the *Mahabharata*, but they keep it hidden from Muslims.

II

Mulla Abdul Qadir Badauni in his *Muntakhab ul Tawarikh* records (Badauni 319–321),

Collecting together the learned men of India (*danayan i hind*), His Majesty directed that the book Mahabharat should be explained (*ta'bir*). For two nights His Majesty personally had it explained to Naqib Khan, who wrote out the resultant text in Persian. On the third night His Majesty summoned me and ordered me to translate (*tarjuma*) it in collaboration with Naqib Khan. In three or four months out of the eighteen chapters (*fan*) of that stock of useless fables, at which eighteen worlds may remain in wonderment, I wrote out two chapters. And what censures I did not hear from Akbar, so that the accusations that I am an "unlawful earner" (*haramkhor*) or a "turnip eater" (*shalghamkhor*) meant as if my destiny from these books was just this. Destiny is destiny! Thereafter Mulla Shiri and Naqib Khan completed that section (*para*), and one section Sultan Haji Thanesari brought to completion. Shaykh Faizi was then appointed to write it in verse and prose (*nazm o nasr*) ... His Majesty named the work Razmnaama … Shaykh Abul Fazl wrote a preface of the length of two quires for that work.

The exercise was initiated under the supervision of Naqib Khan (historian), Mullah Shiri (poet), Sultan Thanisari (fiscal administrator), and Badauni (secretary) himself. It was then translated into elegant prose by Fayzi. Other members of the team included Amir Fathullah Shirazi, Haji Ibrahim Sirhindi, Mukammal Khan Gujarati, Shaykh Abul Fazl, Qasim Beg, Sayyid Ali Tabrizi, Khwaja Abdul Samad (Shirazi), Daswanth, Basawan, Keshav Das, Lal, Mukund, and Farrukh Beg. As mentioned in the colophons, this bench was assisted by Brahmans who could read Sanskrit: Deva Mishra, Shatavadhana, Madhusudana Mishra, Chaturbhuj, and Shaykh Bhavan.[1] Their deep involvement and collaboration was imperative for such a major translation project (Husain 280–281; Modi 95–96; Ali 41).

This pool of talent who were responsible for producing *Razmnama* across literary, linguistic and artistic traditions, were Central Asians and Persians attached to the Mughal court, descendants of families arriving in the preceding centuries from the greater Islamic world, local Indian Muslims, Hindus, and Jains. This created an intellectual environment with much scope for intercultural literary and artistic exchange, under the patronage of Emperor Akbar, who was repeatedly recognized as the driving force and the fountainhead of remarkable energy behind such projects (Adamjee and Truschke 141–142).

The *Razmnama* was not a word-by-word translation of the Mahabharata, as the exercise required interpretations across multiple languages, as will be discussed in this chapter. Yet the instructions to the translators were to translate the entire text, retaining the linguistic meaning and cultural essence as much as possible without imposing theological and cultural concepts externally. It was intended to be available to a wide readership of both Muslims and non-Muslims. Therefore, the idea was to keep the narration simple and clear as much as possible. Keeping this in mind perhaps the Persian book begins with an invocation to Lord Ganesha, rather than Allah through the use of the Quranic formula of *Bismillah*. The objective mentioned above was easier said than done. The two sets of scholars – Brahmans trained in Sanskrit and Muslims trained in Persian – had to communicate across two cultural and linguistic worlds, which now takes us into the strategy for translation (Haider 119–120).

Interestingly, none involved in translations of the Mahabharata had a strong command over both Persian and Sanskrit. Bi-lingualism was a rarity in those times. Only a few people proficient in both the languages would be attached to the courts of Akbar and Jahangir. Krishnadasa and Kavi Karnapura both authored bi-lingual Sanskrit-Persian grammars, and Siddhichandra claims to have known Persian. However, none of these individuals were directly involved in the translation of the Sanskrit materials. Translations therefore would take place through successive stages of interpretations from Sanskrit to Hindavi, a shared vernacular, and finally from Hindavi to Persian, in a process of collaboration where none of the participants knew both the languages. The Mughal *Razmnama* was not based on a single source, but combined at least two Sanskrit versions and some oral stories. The final selection of the text was a likely outcome of a discussion and debate among the Brahman translators. According to the lead translator Naqib Khan, the vernacular translations of the Sanskrit texts were communicated orally and not through intermediary written texts. This would be reinforced through a short note in one of the colophons of the 1584 *Razmnama* (Ali 41; Modi 102–103; Truschke 507).

Naqib Khan, son of Abdul Latif al Husayni, translated (the Mahabharata) from Sanskrit into Persian in one and a half years. Several of the Brahmans – such as Deva Mishra, Shatavadhana, Madhusudana Mishra, Caturbhuja, and Shaykh Bhavan – read this book and explained it in Hindvi to me, a poor wretched man, who wrote it in Persian.

The dominance of orality in the translation exercise also is attested by Abul Fazl Allami in his preface to the imperial edition of the *Razmnama*. The two groups of individuals, Sanskrit scholars and Persian translators, participating in this collaborative exercise are described by Abul Fazl as "learned people and linguists from both these communities who are distinguished by their impartiality and fair-mindedness" (Haider 120–121).

An illustration from the 1599 copy of the *Razmnama* is clearly indicative of this collaboration between scholars across communities. It depicts two seated groups of people reading, writing, and engaging in an animated discussion. The Muslim scholars are gathered in the upper portion sitting on a floral arabesque carpet, while Brahmans occupy the lower portion sitting on a floor with a checkered pattern. In costume and physiognomy, the two groups are largely indistinguishable as the majority of them are seen to wear the *jama* (Mughal robe) and the turban. Men in the upper portion of the painting have beard and are seen working with a pencil box and a wooden chest containing codices, a commonly used format for Islamic manuscripts. Individuals in the lower half of the painting have their foreheads adorned with *tilaks* and are seen working with scrolls written in the Devanagari script, from a cloth bag. Quills and an ink pot can also be identified.

The text at the top of the image mentions that scholars and linguists of both groups sat together in one place, with sources that were agreed upon as reliable, and working towards a common objective. Using their expert knowledge, they translated the epic into a common language. The marginal note in the bottom left explains that the linguists of both groups – Muslims and Brahmans – wrote out the Mahabharata together with Shaykh Abul Fazl (Adamjee and Truschke 145–146).

The Mughals, particularly Akbar, being the first to undertake such a translation project, most certainly on this scale, there was no top-down set of instructions that guided Mughal translations. Imperial histories never mention a manual in this regard nor offer a full-fledged theory of translation. Individuals working at every step shaped the texts and manuscripts that became the defining works of Mughal literary culture within the Indo-Persian tradition. Individuals with a mix of imperial, vocational, and cultural affiliations along with diverse religious backgrounds had various roles to play where one's religion hardly ever determined his contribution.

III

For Mughal translators, the interpretation of the Sanskrit Mahabharata closely followed the original storyline spread over eighteen sections, including the Harivamsa. Frequent use of phrases like "narrators" and "Indian storytellers" in the opening lines of the various sections in the *Razmnama* indicates how Mughal translators approached their work – narrating a long, fascinating story (*ajaib dastan*) on India's historical and cultural past made intelligible to them by the interpretations of their Sanskrit interlocutors (Truschke 508).

That the Mughals used multiple source texts for the *Razmnama* project and had a keen eye for fantastic stories is reaffirmed when we find that both groups of scholars, rather consciously, chose an altogether new and starkly different Sanskrit recension of the *Aswamedha Parva*, the fourteenth book of the Mahabharata, based on the *Jaimini Ashwamedha*, an anonymous twelfth-century manuscript. This is the section where the great horse sacrifice is performed by Yudhisthira, the eldest among the Pandava brothers, on the advice of sage Vyasa, to announce his supreme authority as the sole ruler of Hastinapura. Compared to the Sanskrit original, the Mughal translators were readily attracted by the vivid and enjoyable storyline in the *Jaimini Ashwamedha*. Interestingly, of all the books in the imperial copy, this is the best documented and most heavily illustrated. In the first chapter of this volume an extensive discussion on this text can be found.

In the original Mahabharata text, the pace of the narration is arrested as Krishna delivers a long discourse on philosophical ideas. The *Jaimini Ashwamedha* on the other hand deletes Krishna's speech altogether. Instead, it details Arjuna's adventures as he followed the white horse wherever it wandered in the year before the sacrifice. His fantastic experiences take place in a kingdom where only women live, and in a place where all men are born and die within the same day. In one such episode, the horse gets inadvertently captured in the kingdom of Babhruvahana, Arjuna's son from Chitrangada. Refusing to fight through a gesture of obeisance, he offered gifts and his service instead. This incited the wrath of Arjuna who kicked his son's face into the dirt, refusing to recognize him as his son (Truschke 509).

This episode is picked up by Mughal painters Dasavanta and Miskina for a vivid portrayal in the imperial *Razmnama*. It shows dismayed followers and retainers look on as Arjuna knocks Babhruvahana's crown to the ground with the force of his heels. The painting corresponds to the text which commences with Babhruvahana's offer of peace and concludes with "Arjuna reacted violently in his heart and grew angry at the nobles' speech. He struck his foot on Babhruvahana's head" (Seyller 46–49).

The 1599 *Razmnama* composition by Khema follows the imperial version, with subtle changes. Babhruvahana's crown is still in place, he clasps his hands together in submission, and the painting shows much less density and sprawl as in the imperial counterpart.

In the 1616–1617 *Razmnama*, Qasim brings in Brahmans and grooms to accompany Babhruvahana who meets his father underneath a large tree. Arjuna retains his dark complexion, his crown, and the Gandiva. The painting again draws its cue from the text that begins with an account of the gifts presented to Arjuna and his entourage and moves on to Babhruvahana's first speech and Arjuna's violent response. It concludes with, "He struck his foot on Babhruvahana's head with such force that the youth's face tasted the earth. Babhruvahana lifted his head from the ground and said, 'O father, what is my crime that you strike me?" Arjuna replied "I hit you because you are not my son."

Understandably, therefore, the focus of the painting, in contrast to the previous ones, was not on the act of Arjuna striking his son to the ground, but rather on the conversation that followed in the aftermath of the strike.

It is no surprise therefore that Mughal scholars and artists devoted more energy to the *Aswamedha Parva,* where they consciously perhaps chose to move away from reliable Sanskrit sources to ones like the *Jaimini Ashwamedha* that met the Mughal taste to draw on the Persian *ajaib* literary traditions for the *Razmnama* project. Such lively and bizarre narratives were more in place with the Persian literary genre of the *dastan* (narrative literature) that was full of fantastic elements (*ajaib*) rather than a heavy religious vocabulary.

For those who argue that the Mughal interest in the Mahabharata arose from their religious inquisitiveness about a "Hindu"/Indian culture, it needs to be reiterated that translators at the time of Akbar would seldom consider the Mahabharata as primarily a "Hindu" religious text.

A browse through the Persian Shahnama perhaps affirms the hypothesis. Against the backdrop of an epic face-off between the Persians and the Tartars, the Shahnama narrates the tragic duel between the Persian legend Rustam, and his son Sohrab fighting from the side of the Tartars. Till the very end of their duel, both would be unaware of their biological connections, unlike the *Razmnama,* but the defeat and death of the valiant Sohrab in the hands of his father, the great Rustam, would not be lost on the Mughal scholars. The parallels across literary genres are unmistakable.

On the lighter side, Mughal engagement with the *ajaib* genre had its origins much before the *Razmnama* was put to pen. In a project which would be the first of its kind, Akbar's court laboured on the *Hamzanama,* mentioned above. Abul Fazl compares the two works, remarking that the Indian epic remains more fantastic and unbelievable than the Arab counterpart – "In this book such extraordinary things are on every page, every section, and every chapter." This is probably evident from the fact that the imperial *Razmnama* carried maximum illustrations for this section, as referred to in Arjuna's episode above; and the *Jaimini Ashwamedha* was probably introduced to the Mughals by the Sanskrit scholars who must have been aware of its existence and the suitability of its narrative style to the strong preference of Mughal scholars for wondrous stories and fables, which could also be an indirect reason for their choice of the Mahabharata as a translation project (Truschke 509–10).

IV

Claims of linguistic compartmentalization hold little ground when we look into the translation processes that characterized the *Razmnama.* First was the practice of transliteration, rather than translation of the Sanskrit words – *gandharva, naraka,* and *purana* – that allowed the Mughals to retain a large amount of Sanskrit vocabulary in a Persian text, even when Persian equivalents were available in some cases, like *dozakh* for *naraka.* On other occasions, words that have already entered the Indo-Persian usage like Brahman for someone who undertakes idol worship were also retained without translation. The *Razmnama* often carries full Sanskrit quotations from the Mahabharata transliterated in Persian, without translation or interpretation. Along with this, the *Razmnama* also incorporates long lists of Sanskrit names, of individuals, kings, and sages, with a careful emphasis on pronunciation. Such practices are meant to preserve the essence of the original text in an attempt to preserve continuity as well as initiate understanding between the Indic and the Islamicate. Once more, this allows us to understand the *Razmnama* project as a cross-cultural exercise rather than a literal translation of a religious epic (Truschke 511).

Secondly, we may be curious to know and understand what sense did Mughal translators make of the idea of divinity and divine characters in the Mahabharata. The answer is complex as the translators chose to retain the larger religious framework using terminologies like *devata* and *bhagawan,* but at times did include the Islamic idea of divinity. For example, in the beginning of the translation, Brahma is addressed as *khudavand* (the God), and his "Great Glory and Magnificent Bounty" is expressed through the common phraseology – *jalla jalaluhu wa amma nawaluhu*. Allah seems to comfortably exist with Hindu polytheistic counterparts. In the story of Nala and Damayanti, the latter appeals to the God for help in choosing Nala. In these translations, a ready reference to the Quranic vocabulary is evident.

God, May He be Exalted and Glorified!
Khuda-yi ʿazz wa jall
O Solver of Obstacles and Leader of the Lost
ay gushayandah-i karha-yi bastah wa ay rahnama-yi gumshudigan

The bulk of translators in Akbar's court who worked on the Mahabharata condensed the Bhagavad Gita to a basic sketch finding it difficult to situate, but also offering no reason for this abbreviation. It could be assumed that they were little interested in theological content and the dense philosophical discussion of the Bhagavad Gita, and that their idea of religious texts in Hinduism was more about the Vedas. However, several scholars from the court of Akbar translated the Bhagavad Gita as a standalone text. Three most famous renditions were by Abul Fazl, Fayzi, and Abdur Rahman Chishti. Later, the Mughal prince Dara Shukoh also actively participated in one of the translations, primarily with an agenda to bring out the commonalities between Hindu and Islamic ideas. But his interest lay more in Yoga Vasishtha and the Upanishads (*Sirr i Akbar*). In the *Razmnama*, Krishna is portrayed as speaking to Arjuna not as a divine incarnation of Vishnu, but as a "teacher of truth" and the messenger of the God (*Allah*), and elsewhere Krishna is also portrayed as a *deva* and placed alongside *khuda*, the Islamic concept of the Divine (Truschke 512–514).

V

Did ideas of religion, rather than historical and literary values of these texts, draw the Mughals towards Indian epics? The characterization of the *Razmnama* as a Hindu religious text with theological orientation commissioned by Akbar for translation, primarily to promote mutual understanding between Hindus and Muslims of his realm, is a thesis by scholars that rests on the preface by Abul Fazl[2] (Badauni 319–320),

It was desired [by the king] that the Mahabharata which is replete with the most valuable things connected with religion be translated into diverse tongues so that those who display hostility [Hindu and Muslim] may refrain from doing so and may seek after the truth ... Having become aware of each other's virtues and vices, they should make laudable efforts to rectify their own states ... the books of the two communities [Hindu and Muslim] were translated into the common language ... the simple minded folks having thus realized the truth and thereby rescued from the clutches of the ignorant ones who show themselves as learned, would be in a position to achieve their goal in life.

In total, Abul Fazl mentions five major objectives for translating the Sanskrit Mahabharata into Persian and disseminating it for wider consumption – to reduce sectarian animosity among Hindus and Muslims, curtailing the control of religious leaders over the masses, exposing questionable Hindu doctrines thereby checking their bigotry towards Muslims, checking the narrow perspectives of Muslims by introducing them to cosmologies beyond sacred history, and finally, allowing greater accessibility of the past history for guidance of rulers. It may be noted that after the translation was complete, "the Amirs had orders to take copies of it, with the blessing and favor of God" (Badauni 319–321).

In the preface to the imperial edition, Abul Fazl further observes that the Mahabharata contains valuable philosophical and cosmological knowledge, and that thirteen different schools of Indian thought are represented in the text. He points out that the text is made up of 100,000 verses of which a large portion is devoted to the great war between the clans of the Kaurava and Pandava. Later, in the preface, Abul Fazl points out more directly to the nature of the Mahabharata as the Mughals understood it, describing it as a text of "advice, guidance, stories, and descriptions of war and feasting (*razm wa bazm*)." Abul Fazl and historian Badauni would categorize the *Razmnama* also as a historical work (*tarikh*) of pre-Islamic India, focused on the practice of kingship. The court of Akbar understood the book as an epic work on India's long history of kingship focused on warfare/*razm*, hence the naming of the Persian edition as *Razmnama*/Book of War (Ernst 180).

Akbar and also his court were more interested in knowing about ancient Indian history and concepts of kingship through the pages of the Mahabharata. This had its precedence with the preoccupation of Akbar's court with historical chronicles like *Chingiznama* and *Tarikh i Khandan i Timuriyya* which strategically situated the Mughal dynasty within ruling lineages like the great Chinggis Khan and the House of Tamerlane. In a similar manner, adapting the Mahabharata for a Persianate audience under the aegis of the Mughal emperor presented Mughal kings in a long and glorious line of pre-Islamic Indian kingship. The closest parallel to this would be the patronage of Muslim political dynasties of Persia, particularly the Safavids, towards the production of the Shahnama – which in turn placed such Muslim ruling houses from tenth century onwards within an extended genealogy of Persian kingship predating the arrival of Islam in Iran.

Abul Fazl, when describing the Mahabharata with reference to Persian genres of literature, compares it to the histories (*tarikh*) and accounts (*tabaqat*), but not to any Islamic religious text – *speech of this extent and breadth, with these strange things and wonders, is not present in the other various histories (tawarikh) of the world. There is no trace of this amazing speech in the accounts (tabaqat) of the world.* As mentioned above, and reaffirmed here, the words of Abul Fazl clearly identify the *Razmnama* as a work of fantastical stories (*ajaib*) which are narrated to Mughal translators by Indian storytellers (Sanskrit scholars) without any explicit characterization of the text as a religious account (Truschke 515).

Though the Mughals freely used Islamic terminologies throughout the *Razmnama*, and framed the Bhagavad Gita even in its truncated form within a known idea of monotheism, they were perhaps wary of inserting any Islamic theological concept to facilitate the translation. In a rare account by Badauni describing the translation process where he explains as to why he was accused as *haramkhor* and *shalghamkhor,* we get a clearer sense of the careful approach adopted by the Mughals. In the private and public audience hall, Akbar summoned Badauni, and said to Abul Fazl, "We imagined that this person was a young, unworldly adherent of Sufism, but he has turned out to be such a fanatical theologian (*faqih-i mutassib*) of Islamic law that no sword can slice the jugular vein of his bigotry."

The Emperor's strident remark was regarding Badauni's usage of a verse from the Persian poet Hafiz – "Every action has its reward and every deed its recompense." This was with reference to an episode from the Mahabharata where a dying sage advises his disciples to recognize the God as the supreme creator and pursue the path of knowledge, and to combine the latter with good deeds as all actions are accountable. As mentioned, Persian verses were freely used in the *Razmnama* as an accepted translation strategy in the Persianate world. However, the Emperor understood the verse as a reference to the Islamic Day of Judgment along with the two angels who account for human deeds as good and bad. Badauni had to defend himself by arguing that the Sanskrit Mahabharata too carried concepts of reward and punishment through one's afterlife in heaven and hell. Badauni could eventually convince the Emperor that the verse is in accordance with Indic concepts of individual deeds and their fallout (Badauni 398–401; Modi 100–101; Truschke 516).

VI

Mughal engagement with the *Razmnama* as a text primarily about political authority and exercise of kingship has been hinted at above. Moving away from the readily deployable idea of tolerance practised by the Mughal Emperor Akbar and hence his engagement with the non-Muslim cultural world of literary practice as a means to seek legitimacy, scholars have strongly suggested a revisit. In the absence of modern-day ideas of "Hindu," and *religion* as a field of academic study, scholars argued for the Mughal translation of Mahabharata to be led by "historical and political considerations," in line with earlier translations of *Panchatantra* and *Singhasan Battisi* (Truschke 514–515; Ernst 179–180). Abul Fazl saw the *Razmnama* primarily as a historical account of ancient India, with major biographical additions like the Bhagavad Gita on the life and discourses of Krishna. We again refer to his remarks from the preface of the *Razmnama* (Truschke 121, 130),

> Therefore the beneficent mind (of Akbar) decided that this book, which contains the explanation of the antiquity of the universe and its beings, and is even totally occupied with the eternity of the world and its inhabitants, should be translated into a quickly understood language ... Likewise the minds of most people, especially the great kings, love to listen to histories, for the wisdom that is contained in the divine makes the science of history attractive to their hearts, for it supplies admonition to the wise. Taking counsel from the past and counting it as a bounty for the present time, they may expend their precious hours in that which is pleasing to God. Therefore kings are most in need of listening to the tales of their predecessors.

In the process of identifying the *Razmnama* as a text with distinct political overtones, Mughal translators single out the fifth section of *Udyoga Parva* and the twelfth section of *Santi Parva*, which addresses topics like political power (*rajya*) and appropriate kingly behaviour (*rajdharma*). While the former is on the issue of negotiations to avoid civil war, the latter discusses the reconstruction of a kingdom after war. These two sections on political authority and kingly rule directly address the Mughal concern with concepts of kingship. And the Mughals are not unique in this regard. Throughout the Perso-Islamic world, there has been historically a keen interest in practices and expressions of kingship through literary productions which often borrowed from Indic traditions like the Panchatantra, as well as later-day European mirror-for-princes literature. Mughal translators approached the *Razmnama* as a discourse on political kingship, with Akbar's rule situated at its centre, where the translation of political concept *swadharma* is drawn from the Persianate and Islamicate traditions of Divine beneficence *rahmat-i Ilahi* (Truschke 518).

In an episode where Manu is described as an exemplar of just rule by Bhishma, Mughal translators redirect the narrative focussing on the kingly virtues of their own Emperor,

> (Manu) showed compassion and mercy to the entire world and spoke to everyone with visible joy ... It is hoped, according to the magnificence of

God, Praised and Exalted, that the shadow of justice and the compassion of his most exalted majesty, king Akbar – under whose justice, compassion, and grace all people in the world rest – would be perpetual and everlasting so long as the world exists.

By praising Akbar as a just and worthy Indian king in a narrative frame that extols the virtues of the legendary ruler Manu, the Mughal translators celebrate their Emperor through a clear political approach that justifies Akbar's supreme authority in all of India through his presence in the narrative of the *Razmnama*. In the Turco-Mongol imagination of kingship, the Mughals saw themselves as world conquerors, and Akbar's rule is likewise seen as eclectic dispensation where all religions recognized his *just* authority. The *Razmnama* through multiple indications and references in this direction effectively uses both Indic and Persianate cultures towards framing imperial authority through the persona of Akbar, who in the Preface is praised as "the most perfect person of the time" – a clear reference to the Sufi doctrine of the Perfect Man (*insan-i kamil*) embedded within a Hindu epic (Truschke 518–519).

VII

Finally, the *Razmnama* is also unique as an exercise not only in literal translation but opens up a rich and complex visual world to its readers through the miniature illustrations that adorn the text, indicating its unique attempt to translate an ancient Indian epic not only in the textual format but through visual representations as well. The latter is a standard feature for works produced in the Perso-Islamic world under courtly patronage. Though an in-depth analysis of these images as visual texts remains beyond the scope of this essay, it is relevant however to discuss the strategies through which scholars and illustrators worked on a single body of text towards very different outcomes (Seyller 37–66).

Once the initial translation of the text was finished, the emperor and other patrons would commission illustrated copies of the text during the late sixteenth and early seventeenth centuries. The paintings incorporated an array of Indian and Persianate visual traditions and, by building upon the textual translation, communicated key aspects of the narrative to a Persian-speaking audience. The extensively illustrated imperial manuscript completed between 1584 and 1586 is currently preserved in the City Palace Museum in Jaipur. The second oldest known illustrated copy of the *Razmnama*, completed between 1598 and 1599 is better known to scholars. The third important copy was produced in 1616–1617 for the personal collection of Abdul Rahim Khan i Khanan.

The imperial painters were trained either in Safavid-Timurid, or Indian painting styles, or both. Their religious and ethnic background was never a consideration when assessing their stylistic contributions to a painting or manuscript. A skilled Hindu artist like Keshav Das exhibited creativity and versatility in masterfully executing Persianate scenes, Indian images, and even the earliest known Mughal depiction of Christ's crucifixion, from European drawings. His talent rather than his Hindu background accounted for him being one of the seventeen artists singled out for praise by Abul Fazl in the *Ain i Akbari* from among "more than one hundred artists who have become famous masters," and also among those who "approach perfection" or "are middling." Though Keshav Das typically represented himself as a humble and lowly artisan, simply dressed and barefooted, a mere servant to his king, in reality his brushstrokes played a crucial role in the formation of Mughal imperial culture (Adamjee and Truschke 141–142).

Persian translations of Sanskrit works like the Mahabharata were often accompanied by extensive illustrations where Mughal artists would draw freely from an array of visual, textual, and oral traditions when approaching Indian stories. Hindu and Jain images in the imperial collection provided access to a range of Indian imagery, which, combined with temple figurines, provided familiar representations to Mughal painters and artists of the Hindu deity Vishnu, and his incarnations, especially Krishna and Rama. For depicting particular events, cues would be taken from the first and last lines of the narration, where several narrations can be incorporated in layers within a single image (Adamjee and Truschke 148).

The practical problem that challenged Mughal painters in such projects was the lack of a codified tradition of illustrations for Mahabharata manuscripts in South Asia, as a result of which paintings – both in style and content – would differ, at times quite sharply in manuscript copies, even where same subjects are depicted. For *Razmnama* paintings, Mughal artists would from time to time fall back on Persianate models whenever they could come across a thematic similarity – as in the illustration of battlefields. Artists would freely borrow ideas not only from Timurid illustrated copies of the Shahnamah and other Persian epics, they would also readily use the imperial copies of Baburnama and Akbarnama for ideas when illustrating Indian epics. In a generalized illustration, only the Persian inscriptions in the bottom margins of the page would provide crucial information depicting the battle and the key actors involved (Seyller 40–41; Rice 127–128).

Conclusion

During the fifty years of Akbar's reign, scribes, authors, translators, and artists flourished under the Mughal patronage. The emperor himself, members of the royal family, and court elites commissioned new works and lavish manuscripts. Between the 1570s and 1590s, dozens of illustrated manuscripts were produced at the imperial atelier on subjects such as history, philosophy, and literature. These manuscripts included original poetry and prose compositions, fresh translations of texts from other languages, and copies of Persian literary classics. The majority of the nobility, as well as scholars and translators, worked within Persianate literate, artistic, and cultural traditions. Close to one dozen texts were rendered from Sanskrit to Persian in the period of Akbar alone, of which the most important ones would be the Mahabharata and the Ramayana.

Mughals also inherited textual and visual traditions of imagining Indian culture. Historical chronicles accessed by the Mughal elite incorporated abridgements of Hindu and Buddhist narratives. These works were illustrated both before and during Mughal rule. Sanskrit texts had been rendered into Persian and Arabic in India even before the advent of the Mughals, during the Delhi Sultanate. Mughal translators and artists built upon this rich history and heritage of imagining the Indian subcontinent, as well as pursuing new directions in creating some of the finest illustrated manuscripts in understanding cross-cultural encounters in early modern India.

Mughal engagement with Sanskrit scholars and texts introduces us to an imperial process that led to an active cross-cultural engagement, involving intellectuals, scholars, scribes, and poets who carried out hundreds of translations and adaptations of Sanskrit stories, knowledge systems, and texts into the Persianate world. What this resulted in was a distinct form of Persianate culture in the Indian subcontinent through an influx of Sanskrit ideas, narratives, words, and phrases leading to the rise of an Indo-Persian cultural tradition. This rich literary and cultural heritage forged by the coming together of different elite linguistic and cultural worlds has been disregarded for a system of understanding where religious denominations are readily attached to cultural determinants, like language.

The latter becomes the primary reason why Persian translations of Sanskrit texts as a rich body of creative knowledge is largely wiped off from modern India's intellectual memory. A particularly flawed colonial approach for studying ancient civilizations saw Sanskrit as a Hindu language, while Persian was identified as an Islamic language having Middle Eastern origin. Such a mindset clearly outlives India's colonial past into the modern and everyday lives. The acceptance of *Razmnama*, or for that matter the Persian translation of the Ramayana, presents a conundrum as modern-day understandings of religion and linguistic worlds are conveniently projected backwards onto the historical past. Such a skewed perspective refuses to see how Sanskrit scholars across India were eager to accept the patronage of Muslim courts; and how the Indo-Persian world encompassed a diverse and rich group of multi-religious scholars – largely non-Muslims – who "wrote in Persian, worked in Persian language courts and read texts in Persian." Continued disregard of this rich literary and cultural heritage in favour of narrow religious binaries dooms complex composite projects like the *Razmnama*.

Lastly, while reading this essay, many might learn for the first time how the Mughals combined a politico-cultural heritage that included Central Asian, Persianate, Muslim, and non-Muslim Indian traditions. Though such projects of translation would primarily address the Persianate world of the Mughal audience, it was not beyond the aesthetic and linguistic horizon of resident non-Muslims, as seen above, particularly with the spread of Persian as the language of the Empire. The fusion of Indic and Persianate approaches created manuscripts where the text and images worked in tandem to define the contours of an Indo-Persian, rather than Indic or Persian, aesthetic culture. Such creativities that spanned across multiple textual and visual worlds continued to leave their impact long after the actual process of translation was completed by scribes and copyists.

Notes

1 For a brief account of the translators, see (Modi 96–99)
2 For a complete translation, see Husain 275–280; Ernst 180–182

References

Adamjee, Audrey Truschke. "Reimagining the 'Idol Temple of Hindustan': Textual and Visual Translation of Sanskrit Texts in Mughal India." *Pearls on a String: Artists, Patrons and Poets at the Great Islamic Courts*. Ed. Amy S. Landau, Seattle and London: University of Washington Press, 2015. 141–65

Alam, Muzaffar. "The Pursuit of Persian: Language in Mughal Politics" *Modern Asian Studies* 32.2 (1998): 317–49

Ali, M. Athar. "Translations of Sanskrit Works at Akbar's Court" *Social Scientist* 20.9–10 (Sept–Oct 1992): 38–45

———. "Translations of Sanskrit Works at Akbar's Court" *Mughal India: Studies in Polity, Ideas, Society and Culture*. Ed. M. Athar Ali, Delhi: Oxford University Press, 2014. 173–82

Badauni, Abdul Qadir. *Muntakhab al Tawarikh*. Eds. Captain W.N. Lees and Munshi Ahmad Ali, Vol. 2. Calcutta: College Press, 1865

———. *Muntakhab al Tawarikh*. Trans. George Ranking, Sir W. Haig and W. H. Lowe, Vol. 2. Calcutta: Asiatic Society of Bengal, 1884–1925

Chaudhuri, Jatindra Bimal. "Muslim Patronage to Sanskrit Learning" *Modern Review* 73.1–6 (January 1943): 29–32

Ernst, Carl. "Muslim Studies of Hinduism? A Reconsideration of Arabic and Persian Translations from Indian Languages" *Iranian Studies* 36.2 (June 2003): 173–195.

Haider, Najaf. "Translating Texts and Straddling Worlds: Intercultural Communication in Mughal India." *The Varied Facets of History: Essays in Honour of Aniruddha Ray*. Eds. Ishrat Alam and Syed Ejaz Hussain, Delhi: Primus Books, 2011. 115–24

Husain, Shaikh Chand. "Translations of the Mahabharata into Arabic and Persian" *Bulletin of the Deccan College Research Institute* 5 (1943–44): 267–80.

Modi, Jivanji J. "King Akbar and the Persian Translations of Sanskrit Books" *Annals of the Bhandarkar Oriental Research Institute* 6.2 (1925): 83–107.

Obrock, Luther. "Muslim Mahakavyas: Sanskrit and Translation in the Sultanates." *Text and Tradition in Early Modern North India.* Eds. Tyler Williams, Anshu Malhotra and John Stratton Hawley. New Delhi: Oxford University Press, 2018. 58–76.

Rice, Yael. "A Persian Mahabharata: The 1598–1599 Razmnama" *Manoa* 22.1 (2010): 125–31.

Sachau, Edward. *Alberuni's India.* New Delhi: Rupa, 2005. Preface.

Seyller, John. "Model and Copy: The Illustration of Three 'Razmnama' Manuscripts" *Archives of Asian Art* 38 (1985): 37–66.

Truschke, Audrey. "The Mughal Book of War: A Persian Translation of the Sanskrit Mahabharata" *Comparative Studies of South Asia, Africa and the Middle East* 31.2 (2011): 506–20.

_____. *Culture of Encounters: Sanskrit at the Mughal Court.* New Delhi: Penguin, 2017.

4

ON ADAPTATION AND APPROPRIATION

Some Observations on the Sources of
the *Mushalaparva*[1] in Kashiramadasa's
Bengali *Mahabharata*

Soham Pain

Introduction: Kashiramadasa and His *Mahabharata*

Kashiramadasa, or Kashirama dasa, is a celebrated seventeenth-century Bengali poet whose verse translation of the *Mahabharata*, called the *Kashidashi Mahabharata* after his name, stands out as the best among all mediaeval Bengali renditions of the epic in literary excellence and popularity. The poet was born in a Vaishnava Kayastha family, and his *Mahabharata* is permeated by a Vaishnava sensibility, and the composition is orientated towards a glorification of Krishna. Kashirama's diction and style betray formidable knowledge of Sanskrit and first-hand familiarity with the source text. However, much of his material has also been drawn from popular oral traditions, *Saraladasa*'s Oriya and Kavindraparameshvara's Bengali translations of the *Mahabharata*, and the *Purana*s.

Scholars generally agree that Kashirama himself could finish only the first three *parva*s and at best the fourth. A manuscript of the *Dronaparva* mentions that Gadadhara's son Nandarama undertook the unfinished task in response to his dying uncle's last wish. However, besides Nandarama, Asitkumar Bandyopadhyay (1980: 470–471) mentions Bhriguramadasa, Dvija Raghunatha, Gadadharadasa, (Kashiramadasa's brother?), Nityananda Ghosha (an elder contemporary of Kashiramadasa whose own translation of the Mahabharata exists as a text separate from Kashiramadasa's), Gangadasa Sena, Rajendradasa, Gopinatha Dutta, and Kashiramadasa's own son (anonymous) as the possible contributors to the completed text. By common consent, poetic merit is at its height in the sections attributed to Kashiramadasa himself.

DOI: 10.4324/9781003516408-6

As we have mentioned already, the *parva*s following the *Virata* in Kashiramadasa's text are not his own composition, and this applies to the *Mushalaparva* as well. However, having said that, it is also true that the entire work betrays a remarkable coherence, and indeed, over the centuries, the general reader has taken the entire text to be an organized whole. Thus, the life of the text and the history of its non-academic and pre-colonial reception have nothing to obstruct a study which treats the *Mushalaparva* as an integral part of the larger work. Moreover, all the hands that contributed to the completion of the text having been of Vaishnava background, the undertone of *bhakti* and the theme of glorification of Krishna, remain pretty much consistent throughout all the *parva*s. It would be interesting to analyse how these Vaishnava poets of mediaeval Bengal, individually or as a group, approached the epic material, and what methodology they followed while adapting it to their own sensibility and to the taste of their target audience.

The Maushalaparvan in the Mahabharata

The *Maushalaparvan* is the eighteenth *parvan* in Vyasa's Sanskrit *Mahabharata*. One of the shortest, this *parvan* delineates the story of the demise of the clan of the Vrishni-Andhakas, in the thirty-sixth year of Yudhishthira's reign. The main incidents may be summarized as follows:

I.   I.15–22: The Vrishnis disguise Krishna's son Samba as a pregnant woman and take him to the *rishis* Vishvamitra, Kanva, and Narada. The latter are then cryptically asked whether the pregnant woman that they see would produce a male or a female offspring. The *rishis* see through the trick and curse that Samba would give birth to a *mushala* (pestle) and that would bring about the complete destruction of the Vrishni clan, barring Krishna and Balarama.

II. I.23–31: Krishna is informed of the curse but he declines to help his kinsmen. At King Ahuka-Ugrasena's command, the pestle is ground and the powder, along with one small remaining piece, is cast into the ocean. Liquor is banned in the land.

III. II.4–16: Dvaraka is struck by ill omens.

IV. II.18–22: Krishna recognizes the horrifying omens as having been the same during the Bharata battle.

V.   II.23–24: Krishna decides to fulfil Gandhariis curse (in the *Striparvan*) and announces that the Yadavas should undertake a pilgrimage to the holy site of Prabhasa.

VI. III.1: Ladies sight a terrible and mysterious dark woman in their dreams, who is reported to have snatched the *mangalasutras* of the ladies.

VII. III.2–6: Ill omens are described once again. Krishna's (and Balarama's) divine possessions disappear.

VIII. III.7–10: The preparation and the journey to Prabhasa are narrated.

IX. III.11–13: Uddhava meets Krishna and leaves his mortal self.

X. III.13–16: The Vrishnis start drinking.

XI. III.17–34: Satyaki, inebriated, reminds everyone of Kritavarman's heinous act of assisting Ashvattaman in the night massacre of the sleeping warriors of the Pandava army. Kritavarman retaliates by accusing Satyaki of having killed the helpless Bhurishravas. This sparks the brawl, and in the process, both Satyaki and Kritavarman are killed. Krishna's son Pradyumna also dies.

XII. III.35–45: Pradyumna's death angers Krishna who then uproots a handful of eraka reeds, which immediately turn into a mushala. Krishna then starts killing the people around him with this mushala. The people around follow his example and uproot the reeds, and each time the reeds turn into pestles. The Vrishnis kill one another and die, Krishna himself having taken part in the brawl.

XIII. III.46–47–IV.1: Krishna, Daruka, and Babhru go in search of Balarama and find him reclining under a tree.

XIV. IV.2–3: At Krishna's command, Daruka sets out to bring Arjuna to Dvaraka.

XV. IV.4–5: Babhru is killed by a stray pestle from a hunter.

XVI. IV.6–11: Krishna goes to Dvaraka, informs the ladies and his father Vasudeva of the calamity, and returns to Prabhasa.

XVII. IV.12–16: As Balarama resorts to yoga, his spirit leaves his body in the divine form of the cosmic serpent Shesha emerging from Balarama's mouth.

XVIII. IV.17–20: Krishna remembers the past incidents and realizes that it is time for him to leave the world. He resorts to yoga.

XIX. IV.21–23: He is shot in his heel by the hunter Jara, who, however, realizes his folly and asks for forgiveness.

XX. IV.23–28: Krishna comforts Jara and ascends to heaven, welcomed by the gods.

XXI. V.1–15–VI.1–28: Arjuna arrives at Dvaraka and meets the bereaved ladies and Vasudeva. Vasudeva laments the calamity.

XXII. VII.1–14: Arjuna comforts Vasudeva and declares that, as commanded by Krishna, he would escort the women and remaining survivors out of the city, as a deluge was impending.

XXIII. VII.15–27: Vasudeva's death and funeral described.

XXIV. VII.28–31: Arjuna reaches the spot of the carnage and performs the funeral rites of the dead, including those of Krishna and Balarama. (The epic thus implies that Krishna did leave behind his mortal body.)

XXV.   VII.32–45: Arjuna escorts the ladies out of Dvaraka as the ocean gradually engulfs the city.

XXVI.   VII.46–66: A band of robbers attacks the people and abducts many of the women as Arjuna's strength and powers miraculously fail him.

XXVII.   VII.67–72: Arjuna crowns Vajra as the king of Indraprastha.

XXVIII.   VII.73–77: Krishna's wives Rukmini and Jambavati (and three others) ascend the funeral pyre, while Satyabama and the rest retire to the forest. Arjuna decides to meet the sage Vyasa.

XXIX.   VIII.78: Vyasa explains that Krishna's demise was the play of cosmic Time and it heralded the departure of the Pandavas themselves.

A close scrutiny of the above points can lead us to certain conclusions. The most intriguing is the character and role of Krishna in this context. First of all, before the *rishis* curse the Vrishnis, Krishna has no conscious or unconscious role to play. Secondly, when he learns about the curse, Krishna takes a stoic stand. Even when the verbal abuse starts, Krishna initially remains a silent onlooker, without any attempt to either prevent it or aggravate the situation. However, he *does feel* aggrieved once his firstborn is killed, and takes up arms. Moreover, there is a clear indication that Balarama is upset, and the way he retires from the world is evidence enough that he has little feelings left for his younger brother.[2] However, despite being unequivocal about the human frailties in Krishna's behaviour, the epic repeatedly reminds the reader of the divine side of his character. Thus, he is said to have been competent in thwarting the calamity, but he did not intend to intervene in the course of events. Krishna, even while taking part in the skirmish, "is only fulfilling his role as nemesis, making truthful each and every vow and curse made previously that pointed to the ineluctable destruction of the warriors and the Yuganta, the end of an Era" (Benjamin Preciado-Solis, 2005:244).

Once again, Jara is reported to have witnessed him in his divine four-handed form, and there can hardly be any doubt that the wound that he incurs from the arrow is of little consequence in the course of his departure from the earth. But earlier in the *Anushasanaparvan*, there appears the story of the sage Durvasas putting Krishna to a test. By the end of this story, death is predicted to enter into Krishna's body through the soles of his feet (159.43–44). Finally, curiously enough, the grand description of Krishna's ascent to heaven is contradicted by the statement that Arjuna burnt his mortal remains.

Apart from Krishna, the other major character in the *Maushalaparvan* is Krishna's son, Samba. His role is pivotal in the sense that it is his masquerade which invites the curse and brings about the destruction of the Vrishnis. Georg von Simon (2007:235–6) has drawn our attention to *Anushasanaparvan* (XV.3–4) where Shiva, and more specifically his spouse

Uma, respond to Krishna's prayers and grant him "a son named Samba." Drawing on this link, Simon points out that "Samba" is no more than an epithet of Shiva as it is a compound (sa+amba) which means "with Amba." Thus, in the *Maushalaparvan*, Samba, a transvestite and an agent of destruction, is evocative of Shiva in his aspects as Ardhanarishvara and Rudra the destroyer. Simon's research (2007:236–7) also takes into account the possible sacrificial metaphors that run implicitly throughout the text:

> The annihilating battle of the *Maushalaparvan* could hint at the ritual of *soma*-pressing. The *mushala* to which Samba gives birth may then be interpreted as a development of the upper, pestle-shaped press-stone (*gravan*) in the so-called *ulukhala* type of *soma*-pressing device... the *mushala* is first pulverized and thrown into the ocean. But from the ocean it apparently reappears in the form of a certain rush or reed (*Eraka*)... [which] are miraculously reconverted in Krishna's hands into an iron club... It is thus Krishna himself who becomes instrumental for the disaster. Krishna is Vishnu incarnate, the god who from the late Vedic period is identified with the sacrifice (*Yajna*).

Simon (2007:238) also points out that the disguised Samba is said to be the spouse of the hero Babhru, and "*Babhru*," "the brown one" in Vedic texts, is also used as a designation of the *soma* juice. Finally, Simon (2007:239) sees the "drinking bout as a kind of perverted *soma*-pressing and *soma*-drinking ritual."

An interesting aspect of Samba's masquerade and its repercussions is the theme of male pregnancy, a very popular motif in Hindu mythology. Preciado-Solis (2005:243) suggests that if the *rishi*s are assumed to answer Samba's mockery in his own coin, then the *mushala* can be taken to be a euphemism for the penis. Indeed, the epic leaves no doubt that no external piece of iron was inserted into Samba's robes. The text (I.25–26) runs as follows:

> When the next day came Samba actually produced an iron bolt through which all the individuals in the family of the Vṛṣṇis and the Andhakas became reduced to ashes. Indeed, for the destruction of the Vrishnis and the Andhakas, Samba brought forth, through that curse, a dreadful iron bolt, that looked like a huge messenger of death. The fact was duly reported to the king.

If Preciado-Solis's observation is correct, then the *mushala* can be taken to be representative of Shiva's emblem, the *lingam*, thus reinforcing the connection between Samba and Rudra-Shiva.

Finally, the link between the Bharata war and the episode of the pestle can hardly be ignored. The brawl happens at this point of the story, but its seed is sown immediately after the Kurukshetra war when the bereaved queen Gandhari holds Krishna responsible for the devastation, and curses that the latter's own kinsmen would die in a "lowly manner" (*kutsitenabhyupayena*, XXV.45). Even in the present *parvan*, the omens which serve as premonition are described to be similar to those that heralded the war. In this context, we may also note the two mysterious figures mentioned in II.1–3 and III.1. One is Kala embodied as a dark man and another is an unspecified dark lady, both of terrible appearance. It is indeed tempting to identify the male figure with Rudra-Shiva and the dark lady with Kali/Kalaratri, both of whom appear in the *Sauptikaparvan* and preside over the night massacre at the Pandava camp. Thus, the episode of the pestle is also a sequel or a replay of the cosmic game of dissolution in which the deities (including Vishnu and Shiva) play out their respective roles. (For a fuller discussion, see Hiltebeitel, 1990; Ruth Katz, 2007).

Vishnu Purana *(V.37–38) and* Shrimadbhagavatam *(XI. 1, 6, 30–31)*

Two other Classical Sanskrit sources for the *Maushala* episode are the *Vishnu Purana* and *Shrimadbhagavatam*. These are sectarian Vaishnava texts, and while retaining the major storyline, they add, delete, or alter small but significant details.

While the epic never made the connection between the pestle born of Samba and the reeds which turn into pestles during the brawl explicitly, this text mentions the reeds as having been issued from the powder of the pulverized pestle. Also, the text narrates how the remaining part of the pestle was swallowed by a fish, how it went into the hands of the hunter Jara, and how he fixed it in his arrow, the very arrow which pierced through Krishna's heel (V.37.9–14). After the initial description of the curse and the birth and pulverization of the pestle, the author of the *Vishnu Purana* (Goswami 1896) inserts a conversation between Krishna and a messenger from the gods (V.37.15–26). The messenger informs Krishna that the gods want Krishna back in heaven in his divine form, and Krishna assures the latter that he would retire from the human world after bringing about the destruction of his own kinsmen, the Yadavas. Unlike the *Mahabharata*, this text does not make Krishna's devotee Uddhava ascend to the heavens, who, instead, is said to leave for Badarikashrama.

The most important innovation, however, is to make Krishna himself command the Vrishnis to drink (*chakrustatra surapanam vasudevanumodi-tah*, V.37.37). Secondly, in this text, Krishna is not the silent onlooker he seemed to be in the epic, but actively tries to stop the brawl. Only when the inebriated Vrishnis mistake him for an enemy and attack him, is Krishna seen to uproot the reeds and participate in the carnage (V.37.43–45). It is interesting to note that Krishna's divine possessions are said to disappear only at this point and not before the brawl (V.46–47). The text does not mention Babhru, and glowingly describes the hunter Jara's ascension to the heavenly abode in a celestial vehicle (V.37.62–69). Krishna's own mansion is reported to have been spared by the sea (V.38.9–10). When Arjuna asks Vyasa the reason behind the calamity and also behind his own failure to resist the robbers, the latter, among other things, specifically mentions Krishna as having been the source of his power (*Krishnasyaiva tadbalam*, V.38.25). This is a far cry from Vyasa's emphasis on the cosmic game of time in response to Arjuna's query in the *Mahabharata*. Finally, the author of the *Vishnu Purana* seems to have been pretty uncomfortable with the fact that the honourable Yadava ladies were abducted by the robbers, and therefore, as a mythological explanation, adds the story of Ashtavakra's curse upon the divine damsels. The story goes that the sage was initially pleased with them and granted them a boon that they would get "the best of men" as their husband. But soon they insulted the sage and he uttered a curse that they would be abducted. However, upon being propitiated, he once again blessed them saying that they would attain the celestial abode afterwards (V.38.70–84).

Now we may turn to the version of the episode as recorded in *Shrimadbhagavatam*. The *Krishnacharitra* in this text is modelled, on the whole, upon the *Vishnu Purana*, but is much more elaborate, innovative, and has a greater devotional touch. The *Maushala* episode in this text is narrated in four chapters (XI.1. 6. 30–31). It is interesting to note that in this text, the narration commences with Krishna pondering on the evil ways of the Vrishnis and the possible means of their destruction (XI.1.3–4). Having thought of the Brahmana's curse as the appropriate way, he then sends the *rishis* to the holy site of Pindaraka, where their encounter with Samba takes place (XI.1.5, 11–12). While uttering the curse, the Brahmanas do not mention Krishna and Balarama as exceptions (XI.1.5,11–12). *Shrimadbhagavatam* (XI.6) replaces the divine messenger with the entire multitude of gods, led by Brahma himself (Tagare 2007). Moreover, the text seizes the occasion of meeting between Krishna and Uddhava to insert a book-length conversation between the two, running through twenty-four chapters, popularly known as the *Uddhavagita*. The narration resumes in chapter 30, and the brawl is described. In this description, Krishna and Balarama are both said to have been attacked by their drunken kinsmen, and both are seen retaliating (XI.30.21–22). There are other innovations as well, but the most captivating passage is the one which describes Krishna's last moment. In a tone far removed from that of the *Mahabharata*, *Shrimadbhagavatam* (XI.3.6) declares:

By the technical *Yogic* process called *agneyi* whereby the *Yogi* concentrates his mind on fire and burns down his body, the Lord did not consume with fire his world-enchanting form which was very auspicious for concentration and meditation (and was the support of the world) but entered with his body his own realm.

Thus, there are no mortal remains of Krishna to be wept over by his wives, and evidently while mounting the pyre, the ladies have only their "hearts fixed on him" (XI.31.20).

What deductions can we draw from these two versions then? It is clear that to the authors of these texts the *Mausala* episode is important not as a sequel to the Bharata war or as a necessary prelude to the demise of the Pandavas, but in its own right. The focus of the texts is Krishna himself, God incarnate and the sustainer of the world, and it is from this perspective that the episode finds entry into both of them.

However, there is a subtle difference between the ways in which these two texts see Krishna. Freda Matchett (2008) points out that in the *Vishnu Purana*, Krishna is conceived of primarily as an *avatara* of Vishnu. Though certainly he is the greatest of all *avatara*s, and more fully evocative of Viṣṇu's supreme form than any of them, simultaneously, for the *Vishnu Purana*, he is only a part of *Vishnu* as "no *avatara* can be thought to rival Vishnu as Supreme God" (Matchett 2008:93). In *Shrimadbhagavatam*, however, Krishna is not one of the many *avatara*s and not even the foremost of all of them, but is the "Lord Himself" (*bhagavan svayam*), and the source of all the *avatara*s. To quote Matchett (2008:187):

the *Bhagavata* ensures even more that no reader/hearer could mistake him [Krishna] for just one more *avatara* figure. Krishna here is not only acting out the human roles of cowherd boy, householder and warrior chief. He is even playing at being an *avatara*, allowing himself to be listed among the many and varied forms which he brings into being.

Both the texts thus uphold the *Maushala* episode as yet another instance of Krishna's greatness. There is a bid in both these texts to attribute Krishna's role in the massacre primarily to his divine responsibility to rid the earth of grief and evil as either God or God incarnate, and not to his being a representative of Cosmic Time. Again, both these texts refrain from mentioning Krishna's personal grief at the death of Pradyumna, and make him take up arms only when attacked. Krishna is even seen in an attempt to stop the massacre. Similarly, there seems to exist a strong bond between him and Balarama, something which can be attributed to their being *avatara*s of Viṣ ṇu. Moreover, it does not require the *rishi*s to specifically mention the two brothers as exceptions to their curse, as it is implicitly understood that mundane deaths are not for God or his *avatara*. Thus, even while both the texts describe the biography of the pestle in some detail, the texts leave no room for any doubt that the very incident of Jara's shooting of Krishna is merely an excuse on the part of the divine Lord to grant Jara salvation. Last but not the least, it seems that by not mentioning Babhru, by not laying much emphasis on Samba, and by making Balarama and Krishna fight shoulder-to-shoulder, *Shrimadbhagavatam* clearly strips the narrative of the complex ritualistic subtext of which the *Mahabharata* is so particular.

Early Bengali Poetry, Bengal Vaishnavism, and the Maushala Episode

With this framework in mind, we may now proceed to analyse how the Bengali poets of the mediaeval period engaged with the *Maushala* episode. Kashiramadasa's is not the first Bengali version of the *Mahabharata*, and is preceded by the versions of Kavindra Parameshvara, Shrikara Nandi, and Sanjaya, to name only a few (Sen 1940:257–79). The number is legion, and not each of these poets came up with a complete version, and therefore we may stick to Kavindra's, the first complete one in the Bengali language. However, almost a century before Kavindra, poet Maladhara Vasu composed *Shrikrishnavijaya*, a biography of Krishna in Bengali verse, adapted from the tenth and eleventh *skandha*s of *Shrimadbhagavatam* (Sen 1940:89–96). Thus, the first rendering of the *Maushala* episode in the Bengali language comes through the *Bhagavata* and sets the tone for future renderings.

The first major innovation on Maladhara's part was to add that Krishna is concerned not just about the fact of his own progeny being evil but also about the huge number of the Vrishnis (Mitra 1944:590, 640). Thus, the issue of population explosion becomes significant. Secondly, in an act of departure from all the three Sanskrit sources mentioned above, the *mushala* is said to have been inserted into Samba's robes in order to give him the appearance of a pregnant woman, and the *mushala* drops (apparently due to its weight) the moment the *rishi*s utter that Samba is going to give birth to it "immediately" (*eikhane prasaviba dekhibe sarvajana*, Mitra 1944:593). Moreover, the *rishi* cursing here is Durvasa (Durvasas), and not the ones mentioned in the Sanskrit sources. This may either be because of the popular reputation of Durvasa being irascible or because of the epic association of durvasa's prediction of Krishna's death with the *Maushala* episode (Mitra, 1944:593).

Maladhara's originality also lies in making Krishna reveal his plan to his parents and grandfather, and most importantly to Balarama. Krishna instructs the former to forget earthly relations and concentrate on the supreme *Brahman*, and makes the latter a party in his grand scheme of wiping out the Vrishnis. The two brothers, as they lead the Vrishnis to the

Prabhasa, are described as escorting the entire family to their doom (Mitra 1944:640–41). The description of the carnage is brief but follows the one in *Shrimadbhagavatam* closely. However, it's unusual that while describing Balarama's demise, the poet reverts to the description in the *Mahabharata* and ornately narrates the grand scene of *Shesha* emerging from the latter's mouth (Mitra 1944:642–43). The rest of the narration is on the whole loyal to the Sanskrit source, but unlike the latter, Maladhara's text mentions Krishna's wives mounting the pyre grasping Krishna's lifeless body (Mitra 1944:648). It is also significant to notice that Arjuna's failure in protecting the ladies is attributed not to the loss of his power but to the ineffectiveness of his missiles when hurled at the *Daitya*s, who have replaced the robbers in Maladhara's work (Mitra 1944:650–51). This unexpected turn of events is then described to be an eye-opener for Arjuna, who realizes that all the victories he had won in the past were because of Krishna's powers (*ekhane janilo gosain-er maya saba*, Mitra 1944:652). One last innovation on the poet's part is to mention that the abducted ladies turned into stone at the touch of the *Daitya*s, and their honour was not violated in any way (Mitra 1944:658).

In contrast to Maladhara's text, Kavindra's *Mahabharata* devotes only two *shloka*s to narrate the episode and that too in the form of a dialogue between Yudhishthira and a messenger from Dvaraka (Bhowmik, 1949:636). There is no mention of the exodus of the remaining Vrishnis under Arjuna. Given the fact that Kavindra's patron Paragal Khan was interested in a summary of the main narrative and instructed him to compose his version to meet this specific requirement, it is understandable that Kavindra had little choice. Moreover, neither Kavindra nor his patron was a Vaishnava, and therefore the episode of Krishna's demise was not of any particular interest to them.

Following the Chaitanya movement, however, there was an efflorescence of Krishnaite literature in Bengal. While most of these writings focused on the lover aspect of Krishna, the *Mahabharata* renderings were not altogether shunned. Most of the Bengali *Mahabharata*s from this period came from the pen of poets who were officially initiated followers of Vaishnavism. Kashiramadasa was a Vaishnava, and so were his kins who completed his incomplete text, and so was his contemporary Nityananda Ghosa, lots of passages from whose independent work have found entry into Kashiramadasa's text, thanks to compilers and plagiarizers. For the present purpose, it would suffice to emphasize two or three dogmas of Bengal Vaishnavism, which would be helpful in order to grasp how the *Maushala* episode was viewed in this tradition.

(i) Krishna is God himself, and not an *ansha* or *avatara*. His two-handed human form represents the Supreme divinity, higher than all other forms, including the four-handed form of Vishnu. "The historical Krishna is the descent of the eternal Krishna, in whom are embodied supreme puissance, supreme love, and supreme bliss" (Kapoor 1977:107).

(ii) Krishna and Balarama are inseparable, and the duo is characterized by *equal luminosity* (*samaprakashatvam*, Goswami 2014:143).

(iii) Yadavas are eternal "attendants" (*parikara*) of Krishna. Their relationship with Krishna is not determined by mundane acts of birth or adoption or marriage, but by the *bhava* (particular emotion) they have for the latter.

(iv) *Lila* (divine play) is of two types: perceptible (*prakata*) and imperceptible (*aprakata*). The Death of the Yadavas belongs to the first type. God's *parikara*s being manifestations of his integral *svarupashakti*, they are beyond Time and Space, and therefore it is absurd to talk of their death: "the Yadavas were not actually destroyed, nor was Arjuna actually defeated, but the occurrences were arranged as an illusion by the Bhagavat... to demonstrate that the curse of a Brahmana can never remain unfulfilled" (de 1961:338).

The Mushalaparva *in Kashiramadasa's* Mahabharata

Given the lineage of Kashiramadasa and his followers, it is expected that his rendering would be permeated by a Vaishnava sensibility. However, there is also awareness on the part of the poet that he is composing the *Mahabharata* and the glorification of Krishna is not his sole purpose. Thus the epic begins with a eulogy of Ganesha, followed by a hymn addressed to Vyasa. A brief introduction to the *Mahabharata* and a few verses describing its significance and centrality among the scriptures follow. Then the narrative commences following the structure of the original: the conversation between *Ugrashrava* (*Ugrashravas*) and the *munis*. Thus, there is no acknowledgement in the beginning parts of the text that it is being written specifically to glorify Krishna. But very soon legends from Krishna's life independent of his association with the Kuru-Pandavas find entry into the main narrative. Thus, the story of Krishna's attack on *svarga* in order to keep Satyabhama's request to bring the Parijata is given in much detail. Similarly, in the *Sabhaparva*, Vibhishana is said to have visited Yudhishthira's *rajasuya* sacrifice as he had learnt that Krishna, the reincarnation of Rama, would be present at the venue. When he was barred from entry, Krishna takes offence and shows his *vishvarupa* to overwhelm the people there and make everyone realize that a *bhakta* is not to be mistreated. Again, the *Ramopakhyana* in Kashiramadasa's text, following *Shrimadbhagavatam*, acknowledges that Jaya and Vijaya, the doorkeepers of Vaikuntha, were born thrice on earth as Hiranyaksha–Hiranyakashipu, Ravana–Kumbhakarna, and Shishupala–Dantavakra, each time destined to be killed by an *avatara* of Vishnu.

Kashiramadasa and his flowers, however, tried to stick mostly to the narrative portions of the epic, and did away with complicated and philosophical passages. Therefore, the *Bhagavadgita*, such a poignant and central portion of the epic, is given only 121 *shloka*s. It is understandable that the target reader of Kashiramadasa was the layman and therefore he had to draw a balance between his Vaishnava theological ideas, stories of Krishna's life, the Sanskrit *Mahabharata*, existing Bengali versions, and the local legends.

A reading of the *Mushalaparva* in his *Mahabharata* betrays his debt mainly to *Shrimadbhagavatam* and its Bengali version by Maladhara. Krishna's concern about the sheer number of his own progeny is echoed in this text. In this text, too, Krishna privately speaks to Balarama and reveals his plan of destroying the entire clan. Then Krishna requests his father to organize a *yajna* where Brahmanas should be invited and propitiated. This was an excuse to bring the Brahmanas to Dvaraka. Once they arrive, Krishna requests them to go and meet his children who were recreating themselves. While this is more or less in line with the *Bhagavata* version of the story, the use of the backdrop of the *yajna* is interesting. Is the Bengali poet then aware of the sacrificial symbolism used in Vyasa's text? The tradition of *yajna* had certainly declined in Bengal, and had little relevance for Kashiramadasa's target readers. But the poet was well-versed in Sanskrit, and it was not unusual on his part to have been aware of the subtexts running through the Sanskrit epic.

Having said that, it must also be acknowledged that Kashiramadasa's Samba is not evocative of Rudra-Shiva in any way and it would appear too far-fetched to read into the description any ritualistic meaning. As already mentioned, if all the events in the *Mahabharata* were conceived of as instances of Krishna's own *prakatalila* in Bengal Vaiṣṇavism, there was apparently no need to see the narrative as a cosmic game where each deity plays out his assigned role. Therefore, for the uninitiated, Samba here is a mortal human figure, but for the Vaishnava, he emerges as a *parikara* who is participating in *Krishna*'s *lila*. Unlike his precursors, Kashiramadasa is more interested in describing Samba's cross-dressing and make-up, apparently motivated by the desire to entertain the groundlings. He devotes no less than six *shloka*s to describe Samba's feminine disguise (Sil 2017:1149). The *mushala* which issues from Samba is, as described in Maladhara's version as well, an external one, and it falls down when the *rishi*s utter the curse. What motivated these poets to do away with the original version? Did mediaeval Bengali society find the story of male pregnancy absurd and scandalous? Or, were the poets themselves uncomfortable with it? Or, did they just want to be realistic? These are points to ponder.

The narrative then reverts to following Maladhara's version. Here, too, Krishna advises his parents to resort to spirituality. However, while in Maladhara, the brawl was briefly described, and its immediate occasion was not mentioned, Kashiramadasa devotes three large sections to narrate the heated debate and the carnage following it. Kashiramadasa's originality is evident particularly in the way he manipulates the plot here. In Vyasa's text, the debate commences when Satyaki accuses Kritavarman of having assisted Ashvatthaman in killing the sleeping warriors in the Pandava camp. Here the context is different. Krishna here acts as the supreme manipulator of events and the main catalyst in the brawl.

The Yadavas are described as enjoying themselves. After some sports in the water, the people sit together and start drinking, conversing casually among themselves. In the course of the conversation, they start talking about the Bharata war, and Krishna requests Satyaki to describe the exploits the latter performed in the battlefield. This draws from Satyaki a proud and exaggerated account of his deeds, and Krishna seizes the opportunity to taunt him and remind him how he was defeated by Karna and Drona, and also by Bhurishrava (Bhurishravas), who almost killed Satyaki but for the fact that his hand was chopped off by Arjuna at the last moment. Satyaki, Krishna reminds, had then released himself from Bhurishrava's clutch, and beheaded the helpless, wounded king. The people around are rather surprised to see Krishna criticizing his dear friend Satyaki. Satyaki is angered by Krishna's taunts and defends his action. Additionally, he accuses Krishna of having deliberately advised the Pandavas to stay away from the camp on the fateful night when Ashvatthama had launched his attack, thereby making the sleeping warriors an easy prey for the attacker. Kritavarma is enraged at Satyaki's insulting remarks about Krishna and picks up a quarrel. This triggers off the brawl, and Kritavarma and Satyaki are killed. The weapons are soon exhausted, and miraculously, they prove ineffective on the Yadavas. Then Krishna cunningly draws the attention of the inebriated fighters to the reeds that have grown from the powder of the *mushala*. The reeds turn into *mushala*s in the hands of the fighters, and surprisingly enough, those very people who were impenetrable to the weapons start falling down lifeless at the very touch of these *mushala*s.

A careful study of the entire description leaves no doubt that the episode is constructed in a way as to glorify Krishna and his *lila*. Krishna is cunning; he inspires the brawl, and also points out the reeds. But he himself does not participate in the carnage, even after his children die in front of his eyes. As a silent onlooker, he is playing the role of God the manipulator, and enjoying the drama he himself has directed. There is also an implicit acknowledgement of the fact that the Yadavas being *parikara*s are not dead in reality. Similarly, Krishna's taunts at his close friend, and Satyaki's retaliation, are also illusory at best. Thus, while in Vyasa, Krishna seems to favour Satyaki, and his relation with Kritavarman is certainly not warm, in Kashiramadasa, these issues are absurd, as the bond between Krishna and the Yadavas is eternal.[3]

Two other passages in the *Mushalaparva* which merit critical attention are the scenes of Balarama's and Krishna's own demise. Unlike the Sanskrit epic, where Balarama is cold towards Krishna and adopts a stoic silence and leaves his mortal body in the form of the divine serpent *Shesha*, the scene in the Bengali text is replete with undertones of *bhakti*. Balarama and Krishna are seen embracing each other in full faith, and their fraternal bond seems to be as strong as ever. The passage can be translated as follows:

> The slayer of Madhu came close to Rama, and the two brothers embraced each other. Rama then sat in *yogasana* in the coast of Prabhasa, and thinking of *paramabrahma* in his heart, kept doing *japa*. Beholding Krishna's face with his pair of eyes, Rohini's son left his body by the power of *yoga*.[4]

It is more than evident from such a description that here Balarama is conceived of as an aspect of Krishna, and certainly subordinate to him. Balarama's demise is more in line with that of an ideal *bhakta* of Krishna than that of an epic hero or even a deity in his own right.

The scene of Krishna's own demise is more or less faithful to the descriptions found in *Shrimadbhagavatam* and *Shrikrishnavijaya*, but has a rare twist. While in both these sources, the conversation between Krishna and Jara ends in Jara's triumphant ascent to heaven, in the *Kashidashi Mahabharata*, we see an attempt to explain the incident with the help of a myth. Krishna, apart from assuring and blessing Jara, is also made to remind Jara of a past birth in which he was angada, the son of the monkey king Vali (Valin), killed by Vishnu's *avatara* Rama. Later, Rama was pleased with Angada's loyalty towards him in his war against Ravana, and wanted to grant him a boon. Angada had taken this opportunity to ask for a chance to kill his father's slayer. Jara only fulfilled the boon that was granted to him by shooting the arrow. This certainly is not mentioned in any of the sources that we have studied so far. The present author would argue that this is a part of the local Eastern Indian *Ramayana* tradition and was borrowed by Kashiramadasa from the famous and hugely popular Bengali *Ramayana* by the poet Krittivasa.[5] However, in the *Krittivasi Ramayana*, Jara is not the reincarnation of Vali's son Angada but of Vali himself. Vali's wife Tara is made to utter the following words:

> My lord was quite gentle and therefore did not curse you. But I shall pronounce a curse on you... The way you have killed my innocent husband, he will kill you similarly in the next birth. The words of [a] chaste lady cannot be otherwise.

> *(Nagar and Nagar 1997:204)*

Finally, the relation between the *Maushala* episode and the Bharata war is not obvious in Kashirama's text. That the destruction of the Vrishnis is a fulfilment of Gandhari's curse is acknowledged, but the ill omens are not said to be similar to those that preceded the Kurukshetra war. The brawl is sparked off by discussions about the war, but there is no indication that it is a replay of the same, except for the fact that Krishna is the manipulator in either case. In Vyasa's text, the link was reinforced by the sightings of Kala and Kali, but these two figures are conveniently absent in Kashiramadasa's version of the story.

The rest of the *Mushalaparva* in the *Kashidashi Mahabharata* seems to follow *Shrikrishnavijaya* closely but simultaneously inverts the conception of the *parva*s in Kavindra's *Mahabharata*. In Kavindra's text, there is no separate *Mushalaparva*, and the episode is reported very briefly towards the end of the *Ashramikaparva* itself. Kashiramadasa's *Mahabharata*, on the other hand, does not have a separate *Mahaprasthanikaparva*. The exodus of the Yadavas under Arjuna is followed by Arjuna's conversation with Vyasa, and immediately after that there are lengthy passages where the Pandavas lament the demise of Krishna and the destruction of the Yadavas. These lamentations end with the Pandavas' decision to quit the world. The journey proper is clubbed together with Yudhishthira's ascent to heaven in the *Svargarohanaparva*.

Conclusion

In conclusion, we may say that Kashiramadasa's *Mushalaparva* is a mediaeval Vaishnava rendering of the original episode, suited to a Bengali lay audience. Kashiramadasa and his followers had been judicious enough in their choice of sources, and prioritized poetry and popular appeal over loyalty to the Sanskrit version. It must be noted that the *bhakti* elements in the narrative were also part of the mass culture in Kashiramadasa's days.

Like Vyasa's *Mahabharata*, the *Kashidashi Mahabharata* is also endowed with two levels of meaning, one explicit and the other symbolic, but unlike the former, the latter's symbolism is drawn from Bengal Vaishnavism instead of Vedic sacrificial rites and Puranic cosmogony.

Notes

1 Sanskrit *Maushalaparvan*. For this chapter, the Bengali spelling of nouns has been followed while referring to the names of Bengali poets, texts written in Bengali, and the characters appearing in them. In most cases, the nominative singular for a Sanskrit name is considered to be the standard form in Bengali. Thus, the standard form for the Sanskrit "Ashvatthaman" in Bengali is "Ashvatthama." The present author has retained the Sanskrit form while referring to the character in Vyasa's text, but followed the Bengali spelling with reference to Kashirama's

text. The same applies to "Kritavarman" (Kritavarma) and a few others. It is acknowledged that this method may be confusing to some extent.

2 For an overview of the troubled relationship between the brothers, see Bhaduri, 2010.

3 For an analysis of Krishna's relationship with Kritavarman, see Bhaduri, 2010.

4 *ramera nikata asi shrimadhusudana/*
bhai bhai miliya karena alingana//
prabhasera tire rama yogasana kari/
hridaye paramabrahma jape mana kari//
yugala nayane heri krishnera vadana/
yoge tanu tyajilena rohininandana//
(Sil 2017:1159) [Translation mine]

5 A variant of the story appears in Saraladasa's celebrated Oriya *Mahabharata* as well. The Oriya poet makes a grief-stricken Arjuna battle with Jara in order to avenge the death of Krishna (Mishra 2007).

Works Cited

Primary Texts and Translations

Bhowmik, Kalpana, ed. *Kavindra Mahabharata: Lipitattvika-Bhashatattvika Samiksha o Samskrita Mahabharatera Sange Tulana*. Bangla Academy, 1999, Dhaka.

Kashidashi Mahabharata. Edited by Benimadhab Sil. Akshoy Library, 2015 rprnt, Kolkata.

Krittivasi Ramayana. Edited by Benimadhab Sil. Akshoy Library, 2017 rprnt, Kolkata.

Krittivasi Ramayana. 2 vols. Translated by Shantilal Nagar and Suriti Nagar. Eastern Book Linkers, 1997, Delhi.

Shri Shri Krishnasandarbha. Edited and translated by Prangopal Goswami. Sanskrita Pustak Bhandar, 2014, Kolkata.

The Bhagavata Purana. Part V. Translated by G. V. Tagare. Motilal Banarsidass Publishers Private Limited, 1978, 2007 rprnt, New Delhi.

Vishnupuranam. Calcutta H. C. Dass. Edited and translated by Prangopal Goswami. H. C. Dass. 1896, Calcutta.

Secondary Sources

Bandypadhyay, Asit Kumar. *Bangla Sahityer Itivritta*, Vol. 3, Part 1(Bengali). Modern Book Agency, 1980, Kolkata.

Bhaduri, Nrisingha Prasad. *Mahabharatera Pratinayaka* (Bengali). Ananda Publishers, 2010, Kolkata.

De, S. K. *Early History of the Vaishnava Faith and Movement in Bengal*. Firma K. L. Mukhopadhyay, 1961, Kolkata.

Hiltebeitel, Alf. *Krishna in the Mahabharata*. State University of New York Press, 1990, New York City.

Kapoor, O. B. L. *The Philosophy and Religion of Shri Chaitanya*. Munshiram Manoharlal Publishers Private Limited, 1977, Delhi.

Katz, Ruth. "The Sauptika Episode in the Structure of the Mahabharata" in Sharma, Arvind, Ed. *Essays on the Mahabharata*, New Delhi: Motilal Banarasidass, 2007.

Matchett, Freda. *Krishna: Lord or avatara? The Relationship between Krishna and Viṣṇu*. Routledge, 2008, London.

Mishra, Bijoy M. "Shri Krishna Jagannatha: The Mushali-parva from Sarala's Mahabharata" in *Krishna: A Sourcebook*, Edited by Edwin F. Bryant. Oxford University Press, 2007, pp. 139–62.

Mitra, Khagendranath (Ed.), *Maladhar Basur Srikrishnabijay*, Calcutta: Calcutta University Press, 1944.

Preciado-Solis, Benjamin. "The Episode of the Mauṣalaparvan" in *The Mahabharata: What is not Here is Nowhere Else (Yannehasti na Tadkvacit)*, Edited by T. S. Rukmani, pp. 239–44, Munshiram Manoharlal Publishers Private Limited, 2005, Delhi.

Sen, Dinesh Chandra. *Vrihat Vanga*. Vol. 2. Dey's Publishing, 1993, Kolkata.

Sen, Sukumar. *Bangla Sahityera Itihasa*. Modern Book Agency, 1940, Kolkata.

Sheridan, Daniel P. *The Advaitic Theism of the Bhagavata Purana*. Motilal Banarsidass, 1986, Delhi.

Simon, Georg von. "Krishna's Son Samba: Faked Gender and Other ambiguities on the Background of Lunar and Solar Myth" in *Gender and Narrative in the Mahabharata*, Edited by Simon Brodbeck and Brian Black, pp. 230–57, Routledge, 2007, London.

5

BANKIM CHANDRA CHATTOPADHYAY'S LONELY MIDDLE COURSE

A Reading of the Mahabharata in *Krishnacharitra*

Dhrubajyoti Sarkar

> In fact, the difficult task of rescuing the *itihasa* from our shastra could only
> be taken up by Bankim. On the one hand, the inability of the Europeans
> to understand the true spirit of the Hindu shastras; on the contrary, the
> hesitation of the Hindus to test the shatric truths with objectivity and
> logic ... The need of the hour is to rescue the true history from this crisis.
> – Rabindranath Tagore. "*Krishnacharitra*." 460

This chapter[1] argues that Bankim Chandra Chattopadhyay's *Krishnacharitra*
is a representative reading of the Mahabharata narrative in nineteenth-
century Bengal by consciously following a middle course. Such a proposition itself might sound rather untenable, particularly since Rabindranath
Tagore's complete refutation of Bankim's search for a historical Krishna
in the Mahabharata, in his 1895 review of the essay that later reappeared
in the book *Adhunik Sahitya* [lit. Modern Literature 1907]. In contemporary understanding, Bankim's choice of reading the life of Krishna in the
Mahabharata as a historical method is decidedly a redundant, if not regres-
sive, action. Having said that, we must take note of the fact that, as evidenced
in the epigraph to this chapter, Tagore too lauds Bankim's sagacity and
boldness to test the truth of the shastras by allowing them to pass through
contemporary critical tools. This statement becomes particularly relevant
within the context of their contemporary revivalist broad brush strokes to
make everything acceptable by dint of their shastric sanction, nullifying any
space for human rationality[2] (Tagore 447). However, moving away from that
particular debate, this chapter situates Bankim's work within the context in
which it was originally conceived and presented; the context Tagore hints
at in the above quotation. Accordingly, this chapter contends that Bankim's

DOI: 10.4324/9781003516408-7

conscious choice of this middle course is elaborated in at least three specific aspects of the reading and presentation strategies as adopted by Bankim. Further, Bankim's choices of readership and genre are discussed in this chapter with particular focus on his elaborate discussion of his scholarly method adopted in this project. While attempting to do the above, this chapter also situates it within the larger context of Bankim's own works.

Bankim published his first popular Bangla novel *Durgeshnandini* (one of the early translations was titled *The Chieftain's Daughter*) in 1865 before dabbling in an English serialization of *Rajmohun's Wife*, a text that went almost unnoticed by the contemporary readership. *Durgeshnandini* is not a unanimous choice for the first Indian, or even Bangla, novel. However, it certainly marks the beginning of the illustrious career of Bankim as a writer. Between 1865 and 1882, Bankim rose through the ranks of bureaucracy of Bengal Provincial Service at a frustratingly slow pace and was repeatedly transferred throughout the erstwhile British-ruled Bengal. Starting from *Durgeshnandini* all the way to *Anandamath* (1882), he picked up the local legends of his official stations like Jehanabad in *Durgeshnandini* (now Arambagh), Midnapore, Rangpur, and Lalgola, to allow them the full imaginative flowering in his one after another immensely popular novels based on both historical times and his contemporary Bengali Hindu society. However, even if the publication of *Anandamath* in 1882 has a similar genesis from the legend and visit to the local Kali temple at Lalgola, it marks the beginning of a distinct phase in Bankim's writing.

In spite of major revisions included in the later editions, the main narrative of worshipping the spirit of the nation as the mother goddess and the sacrifice of the countrymen considering themselves as the children of that mother to ameliorate the suffering of the mother has overtaken all other aspects of Bankim in the popular and scholarly discussion of Bankim for more than a century. This has been reinforced by translation and espousal of the life model by the early twentieth-century nationalists like Aurobindo Ghosh, and subsequently inspired by his example by an entire cult of pan-Indian revolutionaries. Around the time of Aurobindo's adaptation of Bankim's narrative presentation of the nation as the mother-goddess *Bharatmata*, in early twentieth century pictorial representation by Abanindranath Tagore reinforced this idea further into popular nationalist imaginary. In contemporary times, the visual imagery of *Bharatmata* has sometimes undergone further closer identification with more popular canonical goddesses of north Indian theistic Hindu iconographical traditions. On the one hand, this has led to a kind of recognition of Bankim as a pioneering nationalist thinker that is sometimes forgotten by the invocation of a much earlier, almost racist-coercive nationalist reading stretching back to any and every anti-British antagonism in the Indian subcontinent. On the contrary, this recognition of Bankim as an original thinker of a particular brand of Hindu-theistic nationalism has led to a drastic erasure of the complexity of Bankim's thought. In particular, post-independence Indian Marxists have traced the roots of ultra-nationalist, Hindu supremacist, Hindu nationalism in this particular narrative of Bankim's mother goddess. This particular view of Bankim propagating a rightist ultra-nationalist, Hindu supremacist Indian nationalism has been ossified further by the adoption of this particular imaginative narrative by such forces working in contemporary India. In consequence, while there have been a number of serious engagements with Bankim's subtle and innovative conception of a non-derivative Indian nationalism, most notably in Chatterjee (*Nationalist Thought and the Colonial World* 1986), and the complex treatment of his artistic condition beyond the simplified binary relation between his subject position and the colonial authority, most notably in Tapan Roychoudhury (*Europe Reconsidered* 1988) and Sudipta Kaviraj (*The Unhappy Consciousness* 1995), the gibe against the historical sensibility of the Subaltern Collective as the "Bankim and Bhadralok studies" echoes the general lack of acceptance of the unique contribution of Bankim in many areas of late nineteenth-century Bengali thought (Guha 495). In particular, with reference to the concerns of this volume, whenever someone takes note of the fact that Bankim had a sustained engagement with the Mahabharata that stretches over a period of approximately two decades, due to the above two extreme receptions of Bankim as a Hindu revivalist, this particular engagement with the Mahabharata is also similarly clubbed with these extreme positions. He is sometimes hailed as one of the pioneering nationalist thinkers responsible for resurrecting the prestige of the ancient text and salvaging the primacy of its hero Krishna against the anti-national objections raised by detractors of Hinduism, Christian missionaries, and the Brahmos. Alternatively, he is condemned for feeding the sentiments mentioned in the previous sentence.

Many scholars of Bankim have often noted a distinct schism in Bankim's thought as manifested in his writings during the 1880s. We have already mentioned the publication of *Anandamath* in 1882. His subsequent novels *Devi Chaudhurani* and *Rajsingha* within the same decade are often clubbed together with *Anandamath* to form a thematic trilogy, labelled as *Anusilan trilogy*. In particular, *Devi Chaudhurani* very consciously invokes the theme of *nishkam karma*, a concept adapted from Srimadhbhagavadgita, to be applied to one's role in the public sphere of political import. As a clear textual record of its sympathetic reception among a section of Bengali readership, we find a relevant section of the novel is being read and discussed by Mahendranath Gupta on 27 December 1884 in Sri Ramakrishna's room at Dakshineswar, soon after its publication (Gupta 719–723).

Ramakrishna's earlier meeting with Bankim at the house of Bankim's colleague Adhar Sen on 6 December 1884 led to moments of disappointment in the confrontation between earnest enthusiasm that marks the former to be such an otherworldly saint and Bankim's self-deprecating cynicism about the human condition that mark him as such a modern mind (Gupta 1118–1119). Though Ramakrishna's anti-intellectual fervour is clearly evidenced in both these incidents, it is also indicative of the fact that a puritanical section of the Bengali society that previously for a long time avoided Bankim's *biliti* (foreign) romances now deems him fit to admit his writing in solemn company.

This schism or division in Bankim's work around the 1880s is usually premised on an event quite external to the development of Bankim's personality and thought world. In 1882, William Hastie wrote a letter to *The Statesman* heavily criticizing the extravagant *shraddha* ceremony conducted at Sovabajar Rajbari. Incidentally, around the same time, Hastie was also instrumental in directing Narendranath Dutta, one of his students at Scottish Church College, to Sri Ramakrishna at Dakshineswar to witness the ecstasy mentioned in William Wordsworth's *Excursions*. Needless to recall, the visit to Sri Ramakrishna on Hastie's suggestion proved momentous in the making of Ramakrishna's most famous disciple in the future Swami Vivekananda. In spite of their many similarities in representing the vision of a reformed Hindu society, Bankim and Vivekananda differed significantly in their response to the ritualistic extravaganza of contemporary Hindu religious practices. In fact, Vivekananda's numerous harangues against the material extravaganza of Hindu ritual practices use some of the arguments of Hastie in a much more vitriolic manifestation. However, in this case, Hastie's letter prodded Bankim in a different way and Bankim anonymously engaged in an epistolary duel with Hastie over many issues of *The Statesman* defending Hindu ritualistic practices and counterattacking the Christian missionary position against it.

Nabin Chandra Sen, a close friend of Bankim, discouraged (461) him from dissipating his energy by engaging in a public controversy like this and instead asked him to write something of more enduring value to serve the same purpose. This led to Bankim giving up on the controversy and instead publishing a discursive tract in English, also modelled like a series of letters, but now addressed to an English-educated Bengali young man, titled *Letters on Hinduism*. Though historians like Amiya Sen disagree with placing so much importance on the idea of a schism in Bankim's work in the 1880s by prioritizing an external event to such a degree, this idea has remained a popular choice.[3] Thus, Bankim's *anusilan* trilogy of novels is placed parallel to his nonfictional works like *Letters on Hinduism*, *Dharmatattwa*, *Krishnacharitra*, *Devtattwa*, and his incomplete (at his death) commentary on Srimadbhagavadgita. Whatever conceptual convenience may be derived from such chronological and thematic categorization of Bankim's works, at least with reference to *Krishnacharitra* and Bankim's desire to seriously engage with the Mahabharata narrative, we find a continuity of preoccupation stretching all the way to 1874, almost a decade prior to the Hastie controversy and its purported influence on the making of later Bankim.

While reviewing Akshay Chandra Sarkar's *Prachin kabya samagra* [lit. a collection of ancient poetry] – a work somewhat similar to the scope of Percy's *Reliques* with a clear emphasis on religious verses – Bankim categorically discusses the need to discuss the nature of the diverse representation of Krishna in ancient literature. Particularly, he touches upon the difference and mutual contradiction between the representation of Krishna in the Mahabharata and in other major devotional works like Bhagavatam. The review essay was collected in the volume titled *Bibidh Samalochana* [lit. miscellaneous review] in 1876 but was soon discarded from the expanded *Bibidh Prabandha* [lit. miscellaneous essays]. While he resumed serializing a similar work discussing the nature of representation of Krishna, now called *Krishnacharitra* in the newly-founded *Prochar* [lit. ministry]. Incidentally, the same Akshay Kumar Sarkar, while reviewing whose work Bankim first forayed into the issue of discussing the representation of Krishna in the Mahabharata, was the editor of *Nabajeeban* where Bankim started serializing his *Dharmatattwa*. Between 1884 and 1886, after serializing eighteen chapters, Bankim published the hitherto serialized material in the book form as the first part of *Krishnacharitra* in 1886. Thus, as mentioned above, Bankim's interest in a serious engagement with *Krishnacharitra* with reference to the Mahabharata was not something that was suddenly triggered by the Hastie controversy. Having said that, it must be recognized that by Bankim's own admission, the nature of that engagement with *Krishnacharitra* and the Mahabharata significantly changes between these two periods. In the preface to the final edition of *Krishnacharitra* published towards the end of his life, Bankim categorically states that the difference between what he wrote in *Bangadarshan* in 1874 is as different as darkness to light from his present opinions, almost two decades later.

Even if Bankim resumed serialization with two subsequent chapters in 1887, the serialization suddenly stopped at that point. For the early phase of the *anusilan* trilogy, it is possible to draw a set of concentric circles of thematic concerns starting with the concern and techniques of the self in which the path of sublimation of one's faculties can be aligned with the *deshbhakti* – service and devotion – to the larger national community, even if Bankim's own ambivalence between the Bengali provincialism and pan-Indian nationalism remains unresolved. These concentric circles are further neatly aligned between his discursive texts and the fictional narratives produced at the same time. However, Bankim's last original novel *Sitaram* was also published around the same time in 1886, but in this novel a similar alignment cannot be drawn anymore. Moreover, even in the earlier alignment, there are clear problems of theoretical application to narratives. For example, if we accept that the theoretical discussion of the *anusilan* model was first clearly adopted for explication in *Dharmatattwa* and it was narrativized in *Devi Chaudhurani*, then we should see it to be supplemented by the concrete manifestation of those theoretical formulation. However, while the *Dharmatattwa* was still being serialized, we find a rushed publication of the first part of the *Krishnacharitra* as a book and a subsequent attempt to proceed with the second part of the same. By the end of 1887, the serialization of *Krishnacharitra* was abandoned, and by 1888, Bankim published *Dharmatattwa*. Moreover, in the opening sections of the *Dharmatattwa,* it is clearly mentioned that the volume is intended to fill in the void that exists in the absence of any such systematic book with a similar title. The reality is quite the opposite as there are certainly more than one important publication before this volume with a similar title and similar concerns; first is Keshub Chunder Sen's magazine called *Dharamatattwa* and Rajnarain Basu's *Dharamatattwa Dipika*. If we dispense the highly unlikely idea that Bankim was not aware of such publications, and thus does not end up highlighting his ignorance of the contemporary textual scenario of the similar subject, might we hazard that he was drawing attention to the originality of his formulation? If that is the case, then the whole *anusilan* schema becomes an imposition or claim on the present for a conceptual reality in the idealized future. However, what about the present that draws on the past of the community? Certainly, there is something quite abrupt and contingent in this apparently haphazard series of publications, unless we see the above chronology of the theoretical followed by the exemplary is replaced by the exemplary necessity of the past being succeeded by the ideational possibility of the future. In effect, the ideal of the past reality in *Krishnacharitra* was succeeded by the ideal of the future reality in *Dharmatattwa*.

Bankim's writing came to a halt after the 1888 publication of *Dharmatattwa*. Apart from enlarging and revising *Rajsingha* we do not find him working on any original novel. Even if he might have been working on *Krishnacharitra* on his own, we do not find any manifestation of that. Apparently, the work-life balance and the failing health were working in disfavour, as he took voluntary retirement in 1891 at the age of 53, after putting in 34 years of public service, with a clear intent to devote his wholehearted attention to writing. However, as mentioned above, for the final three years of his life dedicated entirely to the pursuit of writing, he did not write or conceptualize a single new novel. Instead, we find him completing the remaining half of *Krishnacharitra*. There was a subsequent second edition, published immediately after his death, with further elaboration and incorporation of newer material. He also started working on his ambitious serialization of *sloka-by-sloka* commentary of *Srimadbhagavdgita* which remained unfinished at his premature death in 1894. That clearly indicates that he was preparing for a much larger project than anything else, including his previous tentative attempts to gain foothold in the textual interpretive space of the Sanskrit texts in Bangla. And thereby, this was not a textual foray into the uncharted territory by an established author, but in reality, this is an altogether different knowledge project based on the Mahabharata that Bankim was preparing himself to be immersed in.

This chapter claims to show that the specific contextualization of this preparation takes us to the heart of the context within which Bankim was undergoing the serious preparation mentioned above. By the 1860s, the Missionary zeal of the various branches of the Brahmo Samaj movement systematically contended and offered a polemic repartee to the Christian missionary condemnation of Hinduism. However, by the 1880s the Brahmo Samaj movement itself lost much of its zeal and energy due to its own fractious and fissiparous entropy caused by internal moral complexities and contradictions. This, in turn, led to the serious worsening of the attitudes between the Hindus and Brahmos to further detriment of the latter. At the turn of the century, a group of Brahmos, like Rajnarain Basu, even openly declared themselves as Brahmos and Hindus. This situation in the 1880s created a perfect vacuum to be filled by the zealous revivalists with their own Hindu missionary position. Around the same time when Bankim was formulating his model of application of the *nishkam karma* in *Devi Chaudhurani* and was clarifying his ideas in *Letters on Hinduism*, an entire group of thinkers and activists of Hindu missionary mould were making their presence felt in Calcutta as well as in smaller mofussil towns across Bengal. In this context, in particular, we must mention Krishna Prasanna Sen, Sasadhar Tarkachudamani, and the *Bangabasi* publication house.

Krishna Prasanna can be arguably considered to be the first recognizable Hindu missionary speaking to public gatherings across Bengal, arousing revivalist Hindu pride and rebutting both the Christian missionary and Brahmo criticism of traditional Hinduism. Sen was almost a decade ahead of Vivekananda's oratorial tour from "Colombo to Almora." Many sensible observers of the time like Bipin Chandra Pal found him "sentimental, vulgar and abusive." However, they were quick to note that "this very sentimentality, vulgarity and abuse went down with a generation of half-educated Bengalees who had been wounded ... by the vulgarities of the Anglo-Indian political of the type of Branson" (Pal 335). To some extent, Sen's organizational model and enterprise freely adapted the Brahmo missionaries or organizers of the Hindu Mela in urban centres before him, but the success of the Arya Dharma Procharini Sabha and the Dharma Mandali, the organizations that backed him and similar causes of revival of Hinduism, were unparalleled in their reach. Specifically, the ability of all three abovementioned agents to reach out beyond the confines of urbane, educated, and sophisticated parts of Hindu society in an earthy diction easily understood by their audience created their larger bases beyond cities of Calcutta and

Dacca to reach the smaller towns and mofussils of Bengal. This allowed an easy identification by the listeners by avoiding the usual problem of the condescending distance often ingrained in all reforming rhetoric. Like his Brahmo counterparts, making the best of the expanding railway network, Krishna Prasanna too travelled to places like Benares and Lahore to spread the idea of an all-India Hindu identity. Moreover, like Brahmo missionaries, he was not constrained by his linguistic resources to be confined within a particular class of English-educated audience and showed a fairly good command of Hindi to acquire a sizeable Hindi-speaking clientele.

The *Bangabasi* also achieved a similar success as promised right from the beginning of its publication. Within a few months of its publication, its subscription numbers in the mofussils stood at 7,000, thus swiftly overtaking the 5,000 subscribers within the city limits of Calcutta. Not complacent with their success in the provincial Bengal, like *Dharmaprocharok,* the mouthpiece of the Arya Dharma Procharini Sabha, *Bangabasi* too recognized the potential to reach out to an all-India Hindu audience by often publishing bilingually in Bangla and Hindi. Among the major authors identified as the *Bangabasi* group, Chandranath Basu's *Shakuntala Tattwa* (1881) offered a major example of the potential of reading an earlier narrative to fit contemporary concerns. Though Chandranath was solely concerned with Kalidasa's work and not its place in the Mahabharata, he was in a completely different way from his German Idealist predecessors long before him, making the narrative to bear upon his concerns with laws and customs of Hindu marriage.

Sasadhar Tarkachudamani (1851–1928) was a noted Sanskrit pandit but with no formal knowledge of English. Hailing from a poor but respectable family of Vedic scholars, he suffered early setbacks primarily due to the premature death of his father when Sasadhar was a young boy. While working as the family pandit of Annada Prasad Gupta of Qasimbazar, Sasadhar made the best use of the large scriptural collection of his patron. It is reported that on Annada Prasad's patronage, he visited Benares to expand his Sanskrit scholarship. Annada Prasad was also the first president of *Arya Dharma Pracharini Sabha*, of which Krishna Prasanna was the most important minister. In Calcutta, Sasadhar was initially received well by the weekend gathering at Bankim's place by Bankim and his friends.

Sasadhar does not figure prominently in the popular imagination any more, but his major contributions are widely felt in many aspects of revivalist Hindu thought even now. For his contemporary audience, and even for a later generation, Sasadhar's most lasting contribution seems to be the habit of explaining seemingly purely ritualistic aspects of Hindu practices on the basis of 'scientific' tenets. However, on record, it must be accepted that this too has been preceded by the activities of the Theosophists. However novel or sensational his public addresses in this mode were, they were eventually rejected by all three possible groups of his audience. Though both Bankim

and Rabindranath held Sasadhar in admiration, yet in spite of their initial admiration, Western-educated *bhadralok* quite soon rejected Sasadhar's
methods and axioms as rather unconvincing. Though Bankim sounds not
much prescient in this respect, in *Devtattwa* he comments that Sasadhar's
version of Hinduism will not find any taker in the long run. For the mofussil
audience, the references too quickly became unattractive, if not tedious.
For both the orthodox Sanskrit scholars and the spiritually earnest-minded
(again, Sri Ramakrishna is dismissive of Sasadhar in conversation with his
Western-educated disciple Mahendranath), Sasadhar's use of Western methods to interpret the superiority of Hinduism seemed to be rather unbecom-
ing of such a Sanskrit scholar (Amiya P Sen 219).

By 1885 Sasadhar was in the middle of a public argument with Bankim
and his friend Akshay, the editor of *Nabajeeban,* over the publication of a
rejoinder of Sasadhar's, against one of Bankim's articles. Matters worsened
when Sasadhar and his followers like Bhudhar Chattopadhyay, editor of
Vedvyas, made noisy protests against the serial publication of Bangla translation of *Rgveda* by R.C. Dutt in *Nabajeeban*. Sasadhar was rather antagonistic to the idea of cheap translations of the authoritative Hindu texts being
available in translation – in spite of his inclusion in the group of editors at
Bangabasi to produce such texts. He was not only suspicious that such a
move would erode the authority of the Sanskritist Brahmins as custodians
and interpreters of the *Shastras*, but he also worried that Western-educated
interpreters and translators, like R.C. Dutt, could bring in quite radical and
unprecedented viewpoints to traditional texts, of course Sasadhar did this
without reflecting on his own interpretive overtures of explaining traditional
texts through dubious but fashionable scientific vocabulary circulating in his
own time (qtd. in Amiya P Sen 234).

Both Sasadhar and Krishna Prasanna, either individually or jointly or as
representatives of the particular organizations they championed at various
points, gained steady popularity among the literate population in the cities
through 1884–1886. It lost its momentum after that phase but was revital-
ized after the passing of the Age of Consent Bill in 1890, reaching another
peak in 1891–1892. This chapter's contention is that it is not a mere numerical coincidence that Bankim's rushed publication of the first volume long
before its logical appearance after the completion of *Dharmatattwa*, and
again his complete first publication in 1892 plots favourably against exactly
the same two periods in which Sasadhar and Krishna Prasanna hogged the
limelight of revivalist movement originating in Bengal. He was presenting
his books not just as an alternative to the orthodox camp, but he was, in
fact, writing in refutation of their position. His decision to refuse to toe the
line of ultra-orthodox defence of every contemporary Hindu practice as a
form of nationalist commitment leads us to steer clear of the radical condemnation of every aspect of Hindu life, as has been in practice for a long

time in reform movements. Incidentally for all three groups, their decisions were also connected to their own ideas of nationalist commitments.

The complete *Krishnacharitra* (1892) has seven parts. Of these seven parts, from the second section titled "Brindaban" to the seventh, titled "Prabhas," Bankim offers us a retelling of the life of Krishna. However, the first section "Preliminaries" is not as such part of the life of Krishna. Instead, like any formal discursive text, it states the purpose and methodology of the text in seventeen chapters. The sixteenth chapter "Harivamsa" was left out of consideration in the first partial publication, as that concerned Krishna only as found in the Mahabharata. Even without that chapter, the section occupied almost one-third of the 198-page first part as published in 1886. For the rest of this chapter, we will mostly engage with this part of the text to substantiate the previously stated position that Bankim consciously placed his work in the middle course by steering clear of both the pro-West radicals and chauvinist orthodox groups resisting any reform of Hindu society. Moreover, in this attempt of forging the middle course through his version of the life of Krishna, Bankim engaged in a textual clarification, if not purgation, of the Mahabharata narrative to suit his purpose. But, what was his stated purpose?

In the first chapter of this section titled "Rationale," Bankim encapsulates the breadth of the problem that necessitates the writing of his own life of Krishna. In contemporary practice, he finds that Krishna has an abiding presence in every aspect of Indian and Bengali Hindu life. A large section of these people also considers Krishna to be a living incarnate of the Godhead. However, the question as to which Krishna they are referring to creates a serious problem. Since they consider Krishna to be a living divine incarnate, his life must also be a representation of the highest moral principles that human beings can conceptualize. However, the details of his life as it is part of the common parlance does not in any way stand up to that ideal state. According to the popular legends of Krishna, he was a thief in infancy who used to steal butter; as an adolescent he led a number of Gopa women astray by indulging in sexual permissiveness; as an adult he is a fraud who tricks people like Drona to their death (*Krishnacharitra* 1).[4] Bankim accedes that the conception of the ideal human manifestation is not compatible with such a figure of unacceptable attributes. He further states that this led him to search for the true nature of Krishna's life, and this volume is going to be the presentation of his findings. But to begin with, he clearly states that his findings have led him to conviction that indeed the life and character of Krishna is of exemplary nature. In fact, he places Krishna even above Buddha and Christ because the life of Krishna touches upon many more aspects than the ascetic lives of the former demonstrated (*Kc* 3).

Further, he categorically asks the reader to set aside his own convictions regarding the divinity of Krishna and asks them to follow his arguments to understand Krishna as an ideal human being. In this same section, Bankim categorically refers to the contemporary agitation of Hindu reform movements [*tabe ekhan hindudharmmer andolan kichu prabalata labh kariyache Kc 2*] with its two extreme camps of the reform agitations of the Hindu society: the radicals in favour of overhauling of the Hindu society by discarding everything of the past and their opponents in favour of retaining everything in toto. Bankim's argument is that the decision regarding retaining the old or discarding it essentially involves the moral question of Krishna's character, since based on the argument in the previous paragraph, Krishna is the ideal human representation of the ancient Hindu thought. To arrive at their own conclusions regarding the moral character of Krishna, and by extension ancient Hindu worldview, the contemporary readers need to set aside their own belief positions and replace them with a method of derivation.

As he sets out to resolve the apparent maze of conflicting narratives of Krishna, Bankim clearly mentions the methodological problem of propositional intolerance raised by both the above-mentioned groups. According to the local custom, one group considers anything written in Sanskrit – "anything ending with the distinctive end-nasal" ["*jaha kichhute anuswar ache*"] – to be infallible and authentic. This also leads to their corollary belief that a single person has divided the *Vedas* into four parts, written the Mahabharata in a hundred thousand verses, *Harivamsa* and eighteen puranas, and accomplished everything five thousand years ago. Moreover, everything has remained unaltered as Veda Vyas accomplished them five thousand years ago. They are not only not ready to test their opinions, but also consider any such activity to be sinful and cause a national disaster (*Kc* 4–5). On the other end, Bankim finds a group of Euro-American scholars who have acquired a smattering of Sanskrit and resolved on establishing the inferiority of the Hindu scriptures. According to Bankim, for scholars of a politically superior race, the achievements of the ancestors of their subject race of the Hindus is not something easy to accept. Not only scriptures are dismissed summarily, but all other areas of ancient achievements like numerical theories, astronomy, lunar calendar, and writing system too are declared by them to be derivative and borrowed from other cultures. This does not end in an indirect barrage of invectives; but Bankim goes on to name Max Weber, James Ferguson, and William Dwight Whitney to be faulty of such an attitude (*Kc* 5). Having categorically mentioned the fact that he is not interested in engaging with such 'famous' scholars who are out there to vilify the Hindu, Bankim further laments that there are blind followers of such Euro-American opinions among his countrymen. In his typical satirical vein, he says,

> Those who are so dedicated to the service of everything foreign, starting from such foreign scholars to the foreign dogs that they do not even give

alms to the native beggars, to say nothing of reading native books, are not my intended audience.

(Kc 6)

But he still hopes that a section of his educated countrymen who love the truth and their own country will read his work with due attention and an open mind. This is the numerically small group of readers in the middle course to whom Bankim addresses his work.

Bankim entitled the third chapter "The Historicity of the Mahabharata." Though this is primarily focused on using the historical validity of the Mahabharata to salvage a stable historic narrative of the life of Krishna, the arguments in this chapter certainly return to Bankim's long-standing concern with a "national" history of Bengal. In his numerous essays, for example, a series of essays in the second part of *Bibidh Prabandha* with indicative tiles like "Bangalar Itihas" [history of Bengal], "Bangalar Kalamka" [blot on Bengal], "Bangalar Itihas Sambandhe Kayekti Katha" [some notes on the history of Bengal], and "Bangalar Itihaser Bhagnamsha" [fragments of history of Bengal], Bankim repeatedly returns to the need of a sense of history for the self-identity of Bengalis as a distinct community. Chronologically speaking, as a non-fiction, this was the volume Bankim published immediately before *Krishnacharitra*. In spite of the usual criticism of Bankim's identification with a purely Hindu view of Bengali history, he was in fact more concerned with the cultural specificity and flourishing of Bengali culture, which he was quite aware often occurred during the Pathan and Afghan rule of Bengal. In this chapter, Bankim is insistent in taking us to the old Sanskrit nomenclature of *itihasa* to represent ancient Indian historical sensibility. Since the term *itihasa* has been traditionally used specifically in the Ramayana and the Mahabharata, Bankim finds these two to contain a historic core. Conversely in calling these epics like their Greek counterparts, he sees a dismissive stand of the Euro-American critical strategy to deny historicity to these texts. Defending the charges of supernaturalism and fantastic against these two *itihasa* texts, Bankim contends that the celebrated historic texts from the Western tradition, like Herodotus and Livy, too contain plenty of fantastic and supernatural elements in them. If this does not invalidate their claim to a historic method, neither should it happen in the case of the Mahabharata *(Kc 8)*. In fact, it becomes the responsibility of a modern scholar to salvage the historic core of the Mahabharata to restore it to its original appellation of the *itihasa*.

In chapters 4 to 6, Bankim attempts the dating of the war of the Mahabharata because even the detractors of the historicity of the text of the Mahabharata, accept that war mentioned in the text is a historical reality. By a close application of the astronomical methods to similar temporal and astral phenomena mentioned in the text of the Mahabharata, Bankim arrives at a date around 1430 BCE (*Kc* 15). On the way to arriving at this date, Bankim discards the opinions of both the Indians who places the war in the beginning of the *Kali* era at c. 4992 BCE and the Western scholars like Max Weber and John Bentley who places the war as late as fifth century BCE. Once he establishes the chronology of the war narrated in the Mahabharata, in chapters 6 to 8 Bankim proceeds to discard the scholarly opinion of Lawson, Max Weber, Monier Williams and R.C. Dutt, all of whom think that the historic war was a Kuru-Panchal war and the Pandavas were later extrapolated into the narrative. By the same logic, he also tries to establish an incontrovertible argument in favour of the centrality of the existence of the Pandavas and Krishna as their main advisor in the war of the Mahabharata. In the subsequent chapter, he accepts that there is a large section that has been attributed to the Mahabharata through blatant accretion and that needs to be excised to reclaim the historically authentic core of the narrative.

In the tenth chapter titled "Method to exclude extrapolations" (*Kc* 32–34), Bankim places his own methods of scholarship to find out the historical core of Krishna narrative within a diverse domain of technical methodologies. For example, he offers a hierarchical system of methodologies in which methods of everyday conclusions are superseded by the ratiocinations of the jurisprudence, which in turn is superseded by the inductive reasoning as adopted in the philosophical and scientific derivation. He offers an extensive structured argumentative flow in seven successive logical statements to decide whether something in the circulated text of the Mahabharata is part of the original historical core or a later interpolation. Following this, Bankim clearly enunciates the three successive elements in the existing Mahabharat narrative and directs his exercise to reclaiming the first circle of the narrative that will serve his purpose of writing the historically accurate life of Krishna. Developing his methodology in the same line of argument, he clearly states three postulates that will guide the rest of his search: (a) anything that can be proven to be an extrapolation will be discarded, (b) any supernatural will be discarded, and (c) anything which is neither an extrapolation nor supernatural but is blatantly falsified too will be discarded.

Whether his conclusions are methodologically rigorous or whether there is scope of a fallacious loophole in their application in the rest of the narrative is not the prime concern of this discussion. Instead, what is an undeniable fact is that Bankim is allowing a narrative that is often considered sacrosanct in its available shape to be subjected to the methods of logical reasoning and the methods adopted by the scholars in the tradition of the Higher Criticism of his own century. This particular orientation in finding the *sitz-em-Leben* or the dynamic nature of the contemporary state of the text (as opposed to the "dogmatic" view of the eternity of a text) is very clear in Bankim's attempt to trace the textual transmission of the contemporary texts of Mahabharata, Puranas, and the Harivamsa in his analysis of chapters 12 to 14. Just as this volume has its first Chapter devoted to the surviving *Asvmedhaparvan* of Jaimini, Bankim too acknowledges the purported importance of Jaimini's lost text in the making of the extant text of the Mahabharata narrative (*Kc* 36).

That he was reacting to two extreme positions in many issues related to the scriptural and historical revival and reform is most apparent in the first part of the *Krishnacharitra* itself. This also gives us a possible answer to why the publication of this volume, even in an incomplete state, was such an urgent decision for Bankim in 1886. It was not the content or the confirmation of Krishna's ideal state that was the urgent necessity of Bankim's textual intervention at that stage in the commotion of the reform movements of the 1880s. Instead, the methods and the concomitant attitudes inherent in such methodological positions were the most important aspects with which Bankim wanted to forge into fresh territories.

We should also take note that Bankim's methodological explication is also closely connected with his positions related to intended readership and the position within the old Anglicist vs Orientalist debate. By repeatedly making a choice in favour of writing in Bangla for issues that he considered most important for his Bengali readership, his contemporaries and friends like Nabin Chandra Sen often felt that he was missing out the opportunity to address a Pan-Hindu national audience that exists beyond the Bengali linguistic boundaries. In fact, Nabin Chandra indicated this specifically with respect to Bankim's choice of writing "Bande Mataram" in an alternate linguistic register by mixing Sanskrit and Bengali. This reads rather prescient in hindsight looking at the broader issues involved in the controversy surrounding the song, including its use of language. Further, he clearly acknowledges his debt to many Western scholars of Indology, like Horace Wilson, Goldstucker, Max Weber, and Edwin Muir, even if he refutes some of their opinions. In the same breath he also acknowledges Indian scholars like R.C. Dutt, Satyabrata Samashrami, and Akshay Kumar Dutta. Thus, he consciously works against allowing a possible racial-locational bias to creep into his position in terms of accepting or rejecting the scholarly positions in the course of his own study.

Finally, though it is beyond the scope of this chapter, a cursory comparison of all three aspects of Bankim's reading of the Mahabharata – scholarly methodology, choice of genre, and expected outcome – stands out against two other near-contemporary works that also attempted to offer a reading of the life and works of Krishna. Sasadhar Tarkachudamni's "Amar Krishna" takes a clearly personal faith-based approach in which Krishna is the divine incarnate who appears every time the Hindu dharma is in decline. On the contrary, Nabin Chandra Sen's quartet based on the mythical biographical outline of the lives of Krishna and Balaram ultimately takes the form of speculative fiction encompassing a large arena, even touching Greek mythology and comparative religion. Bankim's work steers clear of these possibilities to focus on the human ideal within a historically conscious context, in spite of the declaration of his personal devotional position. However, Tagore, in the previously mentioned review, considers Bankim's attempts in such a direction to be a failure and a particular disservice to the resuscitation of the ideal in Krishna. In particular, Tagore thinks that Bankim's angry retort to various real and imaginary opponents actually demeans the stature of Krishna; and all these happen because of Bankim's attempt to foist a predetermined "theory" [in original] of Krishna's divinity (Tagore 462). Whatever hindrance it might have created for this scholarly project, Bankim was at least conscious of the possible interference of this personal belief in his pursuit.

This chapter concludes with a reminder that like many other milieus before and after it, the nineteenth-century Bengal too responded to the Mahabharata narrative in diverse ways. However, for Bankim Chandra Chattopadhyay, it yielded a reading specifically meant for English-educated Bengali readers that the author expected, on the one hand, to address the personal individual quests of self-development and, on the other hand, allowed a reification of the identarian community based on the reclamation of its historical sense through Krishna as its hero of the history.

Notes

1 A shorter version of this chapter was presented at a seminar on the Mahabharata organized by the Department of Bengali, Presidency University, Kolkata on 3 April 2018.
2 For a good understanding of the precepts of Tagore's criticism of Bankim's fallacies, see Ahona Panda's "How to Be Political without Being Polemical." Though we do not have Bankim's rejoinder to Tagore's criticism of Bankim's fallacious formulations – Bankim died in 1894 – to call it a debate proper.
3 For the categorization of Bankim within the group of thinkers opposed to the orthodox revivalist group and some of the major drifts of argument, this essay is indebted to Amiya P Sen's *Hindu Revivalism in Bengal* (2001). However, due to the focus of this volume, this chapter is specifically concerned with Bankim's use of the Mahabharata narrative for charting the middle course in Hindu revivalist thought.
4 The title of the text is abbreviated to *Kc* for parenthetical citations in the rest of this chapter.

Works Cited

Chattopadhyay, Bankim Chandra. *Krishnacharitra.* 1892 edn. Kalikata: Bangiya Sahitya Parishad, 1941.
Guha, Ramachandra. "Beyond Bhadralok and Bankim Studies." *Economic and Political Weekly* 31.8 (1996): 495–96.
Gupta, Mahendranath (Sri M). *SriSri Ramakrishnakathamrita.* 2 Vols. 1886 chronological edn. Kolkata: Udbodhan, 2008.

Pal, Bipin Chandra. *Memories of My Life and Times*. Vol. II. Calcutta: Bipin Chandra Pal Institute, 1973.

Panda, Ahona. "How to Be Political without Being Polemical: The Debate between Bankimchandra Chattopadhyay and Rabindranath Tagore over the Kṛṣṇacaritra". *Many Mahābhāratas* edited by Nell Shapiro Hawley and Sohini Sarah Pillai. New York: State University of New York Press, 2021. pp. 279–323.

Sen, Amiya P. *Hindu Revivalism in Bengal 1872–1905: Some Essays in Interpretation*. Delhi: OUP, 1993.

Sen, Nabin Chandra. *Nabin Chandra Rachanabali*. Vol. II. Kolkata: Bangiya Sahitya Parishad, 1959.

Tagore, Rabindranath. "Krishancharitra". *Rabindra Rachanabali*, Vol. 9. Kalikata: Visvabharati, 1941. pp. 446–462.

6

RELOCATING MAHABHARATIAN DYSTOPIA IN POST-INDEPENDENT INDIA

Reading *Rangabharata* as a Political
Caricature of the Nehruvian Times

Pinak Sankar Bhattacharya

Adaptation as a technique in the field of storytelling gained prominence in the 1950s of post-independent India. Earlier the nature of the adaptation in Indian literature aimed to magnify the works of the classical doyens, but in a nation fraught with the famine of 1943, the riots and partitions, an expensive Independence, and the political assassination of Mahatma Gandhi, the context of adaptation changed to a drastic level. Such a complex decade deserves a complex meta-text, and Vyasa's *Mahabharata* with its struggle for power, illusory politics, situational ethics, and divisions and discriminations serves as the best inspiration to the adapters. It also resulted in the pronouncement of a new diction, a new content, and a new performativity to promote Indianness in theatre as declared in the Manifesto of the Progressive Writers' Association (1936). Inspired by the Manifesto, a new group of dramatists tried to create a heterotopic (Foucault 25) Indian theatre where the rank and the low together promote indigenousness in theatre. Theatre practitioners like Habib Tanvir, Ebrahim Alkazi, and others sought at times to mould and adapt classical literature into a new dimension. Written in 1965, Adya Rangacharya's Kannada play, *Rangabharata* offers a commentary on the Nehruvian era thereby reiterating the importance of both textual politics and political texts. In this paper, the illusory politics and compromises of the state apparatuses in the Nehruvian era with respect to Rangacharya's *Rangabharata* shall be analysed by a textual analysis. The text shall also be read as a political caricature transcending the bounds of the meta-text. This paper on its way will take up certain episodes of the *Mahabharata* as depicted in the play and refer to them as the reflection of the political scenario of the Nehruvian era.

DOI: 10.4324/9781003516408-8

Adya Rangacharya's *Rangabharata* presents contemporary socio-political and cultural problems. The two characters of the play switch their identities at regular intervals. In the play, Dhritarashtra of the epic regularly alternates with an aged rustic, Dharteppa. While another character initially represented as Sanjaya of the epic becomes the rustic Sanjappa in the very next moment. This switching of the roles from the ancient epic to the contemporary rural scenario is a basic component in Rangacharya's contemporizing the *Mahabharata* in his play. *Rangabharata* presents several episodes of the *Mahabharata* through the conversations of Dhritarashtra-Sanjaya alias Dharteppa-Sanjappa. Amongst them, some have originally been part of the epic, while others are improvisations for the play. Commenting on this play, U.R. Ananthamurthy says:

In one of his plays *Ranga Bharata*, the timeless mythological world and the contemporary social reality are telescoped – each shedding light on the other. Dharthappa, a village elder is also the Dhritarashtra of the epic Mahabharata, the blind father of the Kauravas. But he is now blind, *with eyes*. Sanjaya, the visionary of the Mahabharata, who acted as commentator to the blind Dhritarashtra, is also Sanjappa of the present.

(228)

In the introduction of the play, G.S. Amur states:

The scenes from the *Mahabharata* are transformed by the subtle infusion of contemporary experience and these are followed by the dialogues between Dhritarashtra – Dharteppa and Sanjaya-Sanjappa which seek to clarify the meaning of the scenes presented and raise fundamental human issues.

(xxiii)

He also quotes Rangacharya and reveals his purpose of writing the play where the five human passions – desire (*Kama*), greed (*Lobha*), pride (*Mada*), error (*Moha*), and anger (*Krodha*) – are symbolically synchronized with the contemporary social situation for a comparative temporal unification (xxiii).

Through the different incidents chosen from the *Mahabharata*, *Rangabharata* portrays the short-sightedness of the policymakers, ideological jeopardy, continuously increasing corruption, and the delusion of citizens of newly formed independent India. The *Mahabharata* is a tale of a society that breaks the ancient customs, thereby moving towards a chaotic world. In his famous essay, "The Socio-cultural Milieu of the Mahābhārata: an Age of Change" (1990), G.C. Pande describes the society of the *Mahabharata* in the following words: "It reflects the contradictions of an age of transition when an old aristocratic and ritual order was yielding place to a new order in which lawless tyranny, social miscegenation, religious scepticism, and heterodoxy were emerging as significant features" (123). Likewise, the *Mahabharata* narrates the defunct situation of a society without a definite ideology through the "unnatural events." While describing the desolate situation of Hastinapur prior to the *Dharmayuddha*, Vyasa opines,

> Asses are taking birth in kine. Some are having sexual pleasure with mothers. The trees in the forests are exhibiting unseasonable flowers and fruits. Women quick with child, and even those that are not so, are giving birth to monsters.... Infants, as if urged by death, are drawing armed images, and are running against one another, armed with clubs, and desirous of battle are also breaking down the towns (they erect in sport).
>
> *(Ganguli Vol. II* Bhishma Parva *5)*

Such a society reflects a frightening and undesirable dystopian situation. The *Dharmayuddha* was imagined as the symbolic victory of law and order and freedom from tyranny. However, such expectations are quickly shattered as social degeneration manifests itself in the *Mausala Parva* after *Dharmayuddha* has been concluded. Similarly, the dream of a new nation seemed to wither away as historical events like partition, famine, and bureaucratic corruption hovered upon the Nehruvian era. This suggested that the ideal opportunity for the nation was always threatened by the inevitability of dystopia. Adya Rangacharya's *Rangabharata* deliberately and satirically exaggerates different episodes of the epic in order to display the concurrent political caricature, thereby presenting the contemporary crises of the nation through the *Mahabharata*. W.A. Coupe in his article "Observations on a Theory of Political Caricature" (1969) quotes the opinions of the German poet-philosopher Friedrich Schiller. Schiller primarily divides satire into two categories: "an emotional and serious" satire, which he terms as "punitive" satire and a satire of "humorous and jesting fashion" which he labels as "laughing or playful" satire (89). Rangacharya's *Rangabharata* seems to follow the punitive satire, of the categories indicated by Schiller, to describe the political crisis of the Nehruvian era.

The Lacanian Mirror Stage of post-independence Indian politics begins with a handful of politicians and bureaucrats trying to assemble the newly formed indigenous power. The state apparatus born of the British Raj nurtured the free generation through the Ideological State Apparatus (ISA) and incarcerated through the Repressive State Apparatus (RSA). Therefore, on one hand, the mediums of ISA manipulate the ideology of common mass heavily, and on the other, courts and police handle political upheavals with an iron hand. In *Rangabharata,* episodes like one where Duryodhana tries to brainwash Bhishma saying, "... those who have greater strength alone are entitled to rule (Rangacharya 266)," and the other like Yudhishthira's idea of situational friendship with Duryodhana as spoken to Bheema and Arjuna: "When all is said and done, Duryodhana is, after all, one of ours ... No matter what he does, he is one of ours! (286)," are worth mentioning as the function of ISA. Duryodhana's words bear the characteristics of modern-day State, and the situational friendship is the symbol of modern-day political alliance. The strict and unjust nature of RSA is portrayed by the plight of Draupadi during the Vastraharana episode who retorts by saying: "You are merely the wicked ones who think they can do anything simply because they have authority on their side! (275)."

Rangacharya attempts to look into the historical progress of the nation from the stage of the ideal to that of reality. This observation concerns every abstraction, human agency, and institutions involved. To draw attention to the significance of the ideal, the playwright presents the episode where Yudhishthira (Dharma) and Yaksha (The Voice) discuss certain principles or foundations of this society. Rangacharya employs ingeniously dark humour to allow the scene to comment on contemporary reality. In the play, Yaksha (The Voice) asks Yudhishthira (Dharma): "You are not interested in answering my questions. Yet you have agreed to answer. What do they call this behaviour in the age of Kali?" (291). In response, Yudhishthira says: "You Spirit, doing harmful things for self-benefit is called the supreme moral principle able of bribe-taking, corruption" (291). Large part of the rest of the conversation too comments on the contemporary state of degradation of the society. Some of the salient ones are:

THE VOICE. *By giving up of what can we attain a better state?*
DHARMA. *Shame*
THE VOICE. *What should be given up if no harm is to result?*
DHARMA. *Truth*
THE VOICE. *What should one give up to acquire wealth?*
DHARMA. *Integrity and honesty.*
THE VOICE. *What is the nature of penance?*
DHARMA. *Doing anything to keep intact your position of power.*
THE VOICE. *What is self-control?*
DHARMA. *To thrash those soundly who dare to criticize us.*
THE VOICE. *What is forgiveness?*
DHARMA. *To protect one's folk no matter what they do.*
THE VOICE. *What is called shame?*
DHARMA. *The act of others opposing us.*
THE VOICE. *Who is a good man?*
DHARMA. *One who can do nothing.*
THE VOICE. *Who is a bad man?*
DHARMA. *One who insists on doing good deeds. (294)*

By portraying Yudhishthira and the Yaksha episode from the *Mahabharata*, Rangacharya tries to demonstrate the influence of "State Apparatuses" in the collective unconscious of the people of the state. In the play, we find Yaksha trying to empower the ideological mindset of the ruling class in a dialogue with Yudhishthira. While the Yaksha plays the role of the Educational ISA, Yudhishthira, in return, emphasizes the need for the RSA in a newly formed nation devoid of a proper ideology and policy making.

After India's Independence, it seems that the power of the common mass has withered owing to the fear and the trauma of the genocide during partition, refugee problem, assassination of Mahatma Gandhi, Kashmir issue, Sino-Indian war, food crisis, etc. This fear-generating phenomenon is what Yudhishthira prophesied about while answering Yaksha. Criticizing the common mass in the play, Dharteppa-Dhritarashtra says, "I represented the present citizens who are blind despite their eyes!" (Rangacharya 299). The apathetic common mass somehow tries to live out their lives in the survivor series of the world as sycophants of the rich or powerful people. However, they do not show any loyalty to their patrons. Diverting from the storyline of the epic, Dharteppa condemns Sanjappa for disloyalty and being unethical. Sanjappa has compromised with his ideals and maintained his favour to the existing power structure. Dhritarashtra accuses Sanjaya of being the ancestor of the contemporary common mass who serves as sycophants to the political leaders of the ruling parties in the present nation of democracy. Dhritarashtra says:

> Today's Sanjappa is yesterday's Sanjaya. He is at his old game. Then he first praised Kauravas and switched later to praising Pandavas, and today he is a sycophant showering praise on ministers. Next, he will change sides to shower praise on others.
>
> *(304)*

However, Dharteppa-Dhritarashtra fails to comprehend that innumerable Sanjappas of contemporary Indian society tremble in the fear of oppression and they end up in endless compromises.

Not only the proletariats but also the State compromised at times. One of the episodes from the *Vana Parva* performed before Dharteppa-Dhritarashtra and Sanjappa-Sanjaya is when Duryodhana is captured by the Gandharva king Chitrasena and is eventually released by the four Pandavas. Yudhishthira counts Duryodhana as one of the family members and says: "When all is said and done, Duryodhana is, after all, one of ours" (Rangacharya 286). After the performance of Yudhishthira-Chitrasena episode, Dharteppa concludes that by helping Duryodhana, Yudhishthira has destroyed the opposing polarities of ideology represented by them, and as such a compromise between opposite poles is subject to condemnation.

According to Dharteppa, Yudhishthira's support of Duryodhana "is a new style of ruling a kingdom. For the love of their party, to lose one's humour. To support their side even if it is wrong" (Rangacharya 289). Dharteppa draws parallels between the event and contemporary opportunistic politics. In contemporary opportunistic politics, political parties ignore their ideological standpoints in order to enjoy authority by any means, fair or foul.

In the post-independence Indian political scenario, many such opportunistic alliances abound. The 1962 Sino-Indian War caused a rift within the Communist Party which led to the formation of CPI (M). The difference was between the followers of universal ethics who criticized both the Chinese government and the Indian government, and the followers of situational ethics who as Indians felt that though the Indian government was filled with bourgeois capitalists, it was their patriotic duty to support the Indian government against Chinese aggression.

These situational compromises in the hierarchy, temporary solutions as they are, result in extensive categorization in the substructures owing to clashes of interests. In this regard, Dharteppa-Dhritarashtra's comments regarding the rivalry between Pandavas and Kauravas for the throne become quite significant. Criticizing the Pandavas, Dharteppa holds them responsible for introducing the idea of divide and rule among men. He says: "Fortunately, the Pandavas did not demand their own rivers, hills and forests! Otherwise, the people of today would have demanded them also. They would have said, 'We want a Ganga for ourselves, a Varanasi for ourselves, we want one'" (Rangacharya 271). If the contemporary socio-political scenario is observed, then one can easily detect the logic in Dharteppa-Dhritarashtra's comment. The division of states owing to lingual unity is the beginning of ruling by dividing independent India. In 1948, the Constituent Assembly appointed a Linguistic Provinces Commission under Justice S.K. Dar to analyse the possibility of a linguistic reorganization. However, the commission opined that the linguistic reorganization would paralyse national unity. In spite of that, another committee led by Jawaharlal Nehru, Sardar Vallabhbhai Patel, and Pattavi Sitaramayya was set up in December 1948. This committee favoured the linguistic reorganization. On 19 October 1952, freedom fighter Patti Sriramulu's death demanding an Andhra state for Telugu speaking intensified such demands for linguistic states. Not only on the basis of lingual diversity, but in the post-independent India, the separatist forces try to gain their own separate rule on the basis of caste, religion, and even for the sake of industrial areas.

The different political parties consider the common citizen of the country as their lab rats. The common people have no other alternative but to comply with the governmental decisions which are derived on the basis of majority. Duryodhana neglects Bhishma's opinion of the division of the kingdom and says that the kingdom is not gained by rules and ethics, rather it is gained through the display of power. Duryodhana tells Vidur:

> To rule a kingdom, you need prowess, uncle. You who have been always giving lessons of morality to everyone will have to do it to yourself, for a change! It means those who have greater strength alone are entitled to rule.
>
> *(266)*

To emphasize his opinion that the right to rule should rest with the Kauravas and not with the Pandavas, he says:

> If you want to know what I mean, I'll tell you in one word. My party has one hundred in addition to me. But they are just five all put together! That's what I mean – our numerical strength is overwhelming. That is why sovereignty should come to me.
>
> *(267)*

The fact that the majority in number justifies the right to rule is actually a portrayal of the RSA getting authentication by the dictums of ISA. This claim of Duryodhana is a political mockery of the educational ISA of Dronacharya's Gurukul. The post-independence era until 1965 when this play was written bears testimony to Indian history where a single political party had gained power on the basis of majority.

If such policies (as Duryodhana speaks about in the context of division of power) are fructified by the State, it results in gradual corruption at the bureaucratic level. Just like the ideal authority of the state is employed by Duryodhana, the outcome results in a deterioration of the bureaucracy. Tragedy lies in the fact that the seriousness of the old is appropriated and remodelled as the new to reap personal gains. The episode of molestation of Draupadi could have been avoided had the administrative machinery opposed the abuse of *Rajdharma*. Neither the Kauravas nor the Pandavas were willing to do so. Instead, Draupadi's remark summarizes the aberration: "You think you are running a kingdom! Listen then. You listen to me. I am the masculinity that all men have lost in your kingdom" (275). By stating words like "male" and "masculinity" Draupadi challenges the unethical assertion of *Rajdharma* that treats her modesty as a commodity. Commenting on Draupadi's claim, Dharteppa nods in agreement by saying: "You need qualification to exercise authority... Authority is needed to do good to others, not for snatching from others what belongs to them" (280–281).

The seventieth section of the *Santi Parva* of the *Mahabharata* (Ganguli Vol. III 156) outlines the king's righteous use of authority among all the thirty-six forms of ideal duties. Though a king possesses authority, he cannot monopolize and manipulate it according to his own will. He has always been instructed to think about the well-being of his subjects. He is also instructed to seek the advice of his council of ministers. The molestation of Draupadi indicates the failure of the Kauravas to learn and implement such tenets of ideals of kingship and the degenerate state of the royal court. The message that comes out of this whole episode belies people's trust in the efficiency of the administration. The duty of the royal court is to protect and serve. For this, people pay taxes. If a princess has no security and dignity within a royal precinct, it is impossible for the ordinary people to avail that. In the play, Draupadi also points out this fact by saying, "When the bodies of countless women in your kingdom lack the protection of clothes to preserve their honour, I feel myself ashamed to wear them and go about" (Rangacharya 276). The rulers have collectively failed to employ their authority in the right way.

Dharteppa's views regarding authority are equally applicable to the Nehruvian era. In Prime Minister Jawaharlal Nehru's famous speech, *A Tryst with Destiny*, delivered on 15 August 1947, the hopes, aspirations, and optimism for a new-born nation are reflected. He said:

A moment comes, which comes but rarely in history, when we step out from the old to the new, when an age ends, and when the soul of a nation, long suppressed, finds utterance. It is fitting that at this solemn moment we take the pledge of dedication to the service of India and her people and to the still larger cause of humanity.

(Nehru. Selected Works of Jawaharlal Nehru.
Second Series Vol 3. 135)

Nehru's hopes were not realized soon as the bureaucratic structure of the colonial times could not be dispensed with and therefore a gradual decline in the public administration system occurred. He was aware of the fact that public administration fell into the clutches of bureaucracy. It seems as if the state has compromised with its colonial past and hence is unwilling to develop an alternative administrative structure.

The apocalyptic moment in the socio-political sphere does not occur unless an illusion is built on a large scale. While from time to time the masses are fed with aspirational dreams like *Garibi Hathao*, India Shining, *Achhe Din, Swachh Bharat,* and so forth, the political and public administration keeps on fooling them with such virtual realities. Rangacharya paints Maya in a unique manner by transforming him from the status of the demon in the source text to Mayappa, a representative of the capitalist class in his play. In the play, Mayappa seems to be a master of illusion and an agent of capitalism who conjures a pond with good investment and fills up an empty space with water in no time. Regarding this activity, Dharteppa tells Sanjappa:

"Why shouldn't I tell you the story of how that fellow Mayappa who estimated its expenditure at Rs. 30,000, actually spent Rs. 50,000, got it filled with water carried to it by coolies two days earlier and hoodwinked us into believing that the pond had ground water?

(Rangacharya 295)

Dharteppa adds how his sons have secretly been maintaining trade relations with Mayappa:

I scolded my boys about the way they were ruling their kingdom .... I advised them countless times to smoke out these cheats like Mayappa! Do you know what my boys say? They say, "Let it be, father!" They must have slipped up somewhere, but he is a good man, Mayappa! You know he has paid Rs. 65,000 to our party fund?

(296)

The issue of Maya donating Rs. 65,000 to Dhritarashtra's sons' party fund is a contemptuous act in the ethics of the *Mahabharata*. The seventy-first section of the *Santi Parva* of the *Mahabharata* (Ganguli Vol. III 157) has strictly instructed a king to collect revenue from three sources: one-sixth of the total harvest, money collected in the form of fines, and security taxes collected from traders and merchants for their respective protection.

In the colonial period, capitalist families like the Birlas, Tatas, Singhanias, and Dalmia-Jains competed with the British capitalists in trade, banking, transport, industry, and other sectors. Although the outflow of wealth was prevented by these indigenous capitalists, individuals, like Mayappa, evolved from petty industrialists to financiers of the Indian National Congress and subsequently influenced the political affairs of the party. The Bombay Plan, or the Plan of Economic Development for India, in 1945, outlined the need for India's building up of an indigenous capitalist goods industry instead of depending on advanced nations (Lockwood 618–631). After Independence, the Central government began to develop the industrial sector in public ownership. Besides Nehru and the Left nationalists, even the Indian capitalists contributed to the cause. In order to develop good chemistry with the ruling class, the capitalists decided to support the government despite incurring losses. For many capitalists, another aim for many capitalists was to derive future illegal benefits by donating large sums of money to the party fund during elections. This practice became a widespread and continues even today. During the first and second Fifth Year Plan, the government issued numerous large contracts for construction. To secure these contracts, capitalists heavily influenced the political parties. Mayappa's artificially filling up ponds and bribing Dhritarashtra's sons with Rs. 65,000 is a mockery of the political structure. Dharteppa-Dhritarashtra informs Sanjappa-Sanjaya that even opium withers away and brings the addict back to consciousness:

> I said that they not only "clapped" but also "laughed". It is the laughing that is crucial. Do you know why? The spectators know that the beauty of Surpanakha in the religious narratives and the water-filled pond in your play are equally illusory, not true! That's why they laugh.
>
> *(Rangacharya 297)*

"Today, tragedy is collective" (Camus 267). Albert Camus indicates the irredeemability of the working class, and it seems unfortunate that the oppressed section could react in the same manner in the political dystopia that India has "evolved" into with the illegitimate alliances in the state apparatuses. In the play, Sanjaya is that unchangeable colonial order of bureaucracy who succeeds in fooling Dhritarashtra all along. As the former declares: "I am the leader who goes forward and you are the dog following me. If I reach heaven it is as good as your reaching it" (Rangacharya 309). This statement is clearly indicative of the relation between the "haves" and "have-nots." The play suggests that the "gains" of the "haves" are presented so tactfully to the "have-nots" that the latter is made to believe that the "gain" is theirs too. Dhritarashtra, realizing his defeat, marvels:

> Even if I don't reach it is as if I have reached! Bravo! Possessing without possessing! Bravo! Bravo! Sanjappa, this is indeed a novelty! Bravo! Making the have-nots feel happy that they have what they really do not have! Sanjappa, this is the crown you have put on the story of Bharata!
>
> *(310)*

Set against the backdrop of the epic, the play *Rangabharata* shows how the deceits, false hopes, forgery, and other vices transcend the epic time and still remain relevant in independent India. Dhritarashtra and Sanjaya are still existent in the forms of Dharteppa and Sanjappa, and their stories still unfold the underbelly of corruption of the ruling classes that led to the famous *Dharmayuddha* of Kurukshetra many years ago. The gap between an ideal society and its rulers as described by Bhishma remained constant in the epic itself; *Rangabharata* only reiterates how that gap has ever increased even after the euphoric Independence of 1947.

Works Cited

Althusser, Louis. *Lenin and Philosophy and Other Essays*. Trans. Ben Brewster. Monthly Review Press, 1971.

Amur, G. S. Introduction. *Listen Janmejaya and Other Plays by Adya Rangacharya.* Ed. G. S. Amur. Sahitya Akademi, 2005. ix–xxvi.

Ananthamurthy, U. R. "Kannada Drama." *Indian Writing Today* 14 (1970): 228–233.

Camus, Albert. *Camus at Combat: Writing 1944–1947.* Princeton University Press, 2006.

Coupe, W. A. "Observations on a Theory of Political Caricature." *Comparative Studies in Society and History* 11.1 (1969): 79–95.

Foucault, Michel, and Jay Miskowiec. "Of Other Spaces." *Diacritics* 16.1 (1986): 22–27.

Ganguli, Kisari Mohan., Trans. *The Mahabharata. Vols. I–IV.* Munshiram Manoharlal, 2008.

Lockwood, David. "Was the Bombay Plan a Capitalist Plot." *Proceedings of the Indian History Congress* 72.1 (2011): 618–631.

Nehru, Jawaharlal. *Selected Works of Jawaharlal Nehru.* Second Series Vol. 3. Ed. S. Gopal. Jawaharlal Nehru Memorial Fund, 1985.

Pande, G. C. "The Socio-cultural Milieu of the Mahābhārata: an Age of Change." *The Mahābhārata Revisited.* Ed. R. N. Dandekar. Sahitya Akademi, 1990. 121–137.

Rangacharya, Adya. *Rangabharata.* Trans. K. Raghavendra Rao. *Listen Janmejaya and Other Plays.* Ed. and Intro. G. S. Amur. Sahitya Akademi, 2005. 251–310.

7

"DOOMSDAY EPIC"? P. LAL'S *THE MAHABHARATA OF VYASA* AND THE INFLUENCE OF EUROPEAN MODERNISM

Prayag Ray

Introduction

Purushottama Lal (1929–2010) was an Indian professor of English, as well as a poet, translator, and publisher. Perhaps his greatest literary achievement is his sloka-by-sloka translation of the Mahabharata into English, considered one of the most complete editions of the epic. Before beginning this project, in 1980, he published a highly condensed prose retelling of the epic, which he published as *The Mahabharata of Vyasa*. It may be considered a prefatory keynote struck before the unveiling of a magnum opus, and contains the essence of his vision of the epic in a condensed and crystallized form.[1]

This essay attempts to outline and evaluate how P. Lal interprets the Mahabharata in this condensed transcreation, and to assess the strengths and weaknesses of Lal's approach. Lal's book condenses all eighteen parvas of the Mahabharata into a 400-page prose retelling prefaced by an informative Introduction aimed to enrich the understanding of both the lay reader and the academic. In brief, Lal attempts to modernize the epic, while trying to retain what he believes is its core "message." Two passages from his Introduction make his intent clear. On the one hand, he argues: "it is imperative for a translator to bow to the culture of the age in which, or for which, he is writing" (53). On the other hand, he also claims: "What matters is not so much the language as the values enshrined in the epic; I have tried to put across these values ... adopting an intelligently genuflecting attitude to the vast culture that Vyasa so richly documents" (54).

While claiming close fidelity to a supposed ur-text – which Lal, following tradition, attributes to "Vyasa" – he has nevertheless inflected the retelling with assumptions drawing on the disciplinary parameters within which he

DOI: 10.4324/9781003516408-9

was positioned. As a professor of English in Kolkata at a time when English studies in India was still dominated by the study of the national literature of Britain and the liberal-humanist model of pedagogy was yet to face the onslaught brought on by the institutionalization of cultural studies and "theory" in the 1980s – described by Rajeswari Sunder Rajan as the "crisis in English Studies in India" ("English Literary Studies" 67) – his work is deeply influenced by certain humanist and modernist paradigms. What I seek to assess in this paper is how applicable such paradigms are to the Mahabharata. I also compare and contrast Lal's interpretation of the epic as marking the end of an age with Iravati Karve's discussion of the same, in her *Yuganta* (1969).

Content: Lal and the Legacy of Indology

Lal declares in his Preface – and the text bears this out – that his focus has been on narrative: "I have selected only such slokas as formed a continuous narrative, leaving out the large clutch of sub-stories, legends, peripheral digressions and other tangential material that is fascinating in itself but not absolutely relevant to the tale" ("Preface"). Thus, it is clear that like several Indologists, such as Herman Oldenburg – who described the epic as a work that "began its existence as a simple epic narrative" but "became, in the course of centuries, the most monstrous chaos" (quoted in Dandekar, *Revisited* 71) – Lal perceives a lack of artistic unity in the text, and attempts to redress this. Tales such as those of Damayanti and Savitri thus do not make it into Lal's condensed retelling; his version concentrates on what he calls the "hard core narrative" (7). Lal has also consciously made an attempt to de-Brahminize the epic. He defends at length his decision to omit the Bhargava additions to the text, which he feels amounts to "an often embarrassing glorification of everything Brahminical" (13).

Despite Lal's omission of what he feels is superfluous, a problem that arises with his bare "hard core narrative" is that drastic compression leads to it reading as a dizzying sequence of events following one another in such rapid succession that the affective impact of the narrative is dulled. Perhaps attempting to mitigate this, Lal develops the post-Kurukshetra parvas (10–18) in some detail, treating them expansively enough to emphasize the pity of war. His central contention is that the book highlights the difficulties inherent in following *dharma*. The Kurukshetra war and its fallout, to him, highlight the failure of dharma. Despite the subtlety of dharma, the epic enjoins us to be compassionate: "without compassion all is lost." This is what Lal calls "the essential structure and message" of the epic (51). While a focus on the complexity of dharma is by no means an unusual reading of the epic, I will argue that Lal's understanding of this issue is specifically inflected by Modernist literature and its articulation of the Western crisis of faith in the late nineteenth and early twentieth century.

Both in his decision to omit interpolations and digressions from the main narrative, and in his desire to distil a certain zeitgeist or "essential" message out of the core text, Lal embodies the legacy of Orientalist mediators of Indian religious texts. Robert and Sally Sutherland Goldman describe two dominant tendencies in the work of the Indologists on the Mahabharata:

> The first has sought to strip the poems of those sections, which appeared to early philologists to be suspect, that is not to belong to the earliest form of the works ... The second project was that of reducing the seeming jumble of stories, prescriptions, descriptions, sentential, etc. to some single, central "meaning".
>
> *(9)*

Both these tendencies – informed by "the values of the European enlightenment [sic] viz., reason, and a sense of order, a particular sense of form and aesthetic value and the tools of scientific philology" – are strongly felt in Lal's reading (R. Goldman and S.S. Goldman 9).

It is to be noted, however, that a certain reverence for the epic more in line with the traditional Indian reception of the text is also markedly present, as evident when Lal admits to an "intelligently genuflecting" regard for Vyasa (54). The Goldmans write that for indigenous scholars, both Hindu epics were essentially "histories that have been skilfully wrought into moving verse and infused with a rich moral texture at the hands of inspired poet-sages" (6). This reverence for the inspired poet-sages who told a tale with lasting moral value is evident both in Lal's retelling and in, for instance, the early writings of R.N. Dandekar on the epic. The latter, for instance, writes that "the appeal of the *Mahābhārata* is not merely Indian or national; it is essentially human or universal" (67). Such sweeping claims are couched in grand narratives – increasingly shied away from in critical writings since the post-structural turn in the Humanities – informed both by these authors' Indian identity, and by the legacy of European Humanism within the English-studies fraternity in Indian universities at their time of writing.

Language and Translation

Let us briefly examine the style and language that Lal employs in his retelling. In his Preface, Lal claims that his "aim has been to re-tell the story ... always in Vyasa's own words, without simplifying, interpreting, or elaborating" ("Preface"). Whether there ever was an ur-text of the epic written by a historical personage called Vyasa is doubtful. V.S. Sukthankar, editor of the Poona critical edition of the epic, reminds us that "we have a text with about a dozen, more or less independent versions, whose extreme types differ, in extent, by about 13,000 stanzas or 26,000 lines" (lxxvii). Sally Sutherland

(Goldman) writes that "the Indian epic was not a 'text'[2] in the sense that the Western world understood" (86). "Vyasas's own words" come to the modern reader or audience through the complex interplay of multiple discourses and texts, including performative traditions, scholarly work, and translations in many languages. At best, therefore, we may surmise that Lal has adhered closely to the important Pune critical edition of the epic – published just ten years before Lal's volume – in Sanskrit.

In translating from Sanskrit, Lal has avoided a literalist approach, thereby making the work more readable. Lal himself describes the difficulty of translating the word "dharma" literally into English in the Introduction. Others, Lal comments, such as J.A.B. Van Buitenen in his three translated volumes published in the 1970s, have done an injustice to the lay reader by resorting to literal translation and archaisms (399). Lal has assiduously tried to avoid "a bland, urbane, scholarly pseudostyle" (54). This attempt, for the lay reader's sake at least, is commendable. For contrast, we can look at Lee Siegel's very literal translation of the *Gitagovinda*. In an attempt "to *show* in English what *is* in Sanskrit" (Siegel 238), Siegel goes so far as to present the alternate meanings of many Sanskrit words in parentheses above and below the word itself, thereby breaking the flow of the narrative. Barbara Stoler Miller's rendering of the same text, titled *Love Song of the Dark Lord*, as the title suggests, is far less academic, and more aesthetically inclined.

While the prose of Lal's transcreation itself is metrical and soothing to the ear, Lal often breaks rapturously into verse. For example, we can look at the following line from Lal's translation, in which Bhisma declares that the arrows piercing his armour must have been shot by Arjuna: "they are like a cold winter wind that cuts through a cow's skin. They cannot be Shikhandin's" (226). Note not only the alliteration between "c" and "w" but also the repetition of the "in" sound (wINter ... wINd ... skIN ... ShikhandIN). Particularly memorable are Lal's verse descriptions of the carnage of the war. In using nature-imagery to describe scenes of battle, his rendering is reminiscent of Homeric epics. Lal also claims to have used a deliberately colloquial style in order to preserve the oral character of the epic (54). He also preserves familiar Sanskrit words in the text where he feels a translation would not do justice. For instance, in order to preserve the *karuna-rasa* of Kunti's encounter with Karna before the war, Lal preserves the word "*Anjali*" to describe Karna's deeply respectful salutation of his mother.

A Modernist Doomsday Epic

It is arguable that Lal's rendering is not only a modernization of the epic, it is a moder*nist* rendering of it. Supriya Chaudhuri has suggested that Modernism made inroads into Indian cultural production as early as the first decades of the twentieth century, and that its popularity was partly on account of "the cultural work carried out by a highly educated bourgeoisie responsive to the latest international developments" (942). This educated colonial bourgeoisie – whose social reality has been studied by Tithi Bhattacharya, in her *Sentinels of Culture*[3] (2005) – was referred to in Bengal as *bhadraloks* or, pejoratively, as *babus*. Although Puroshottam Lal was born in Punjab, he settled in Kolkata at an early age, and was educated at the prestigious St. Xavier's College, Kolkata. His intellectual training and Westward-facing educational background, as well as his career as an academic based in Kolkata, can therefore help us locate him within the milieu of the elite colonial bourgeoisie classes, if not within the Bengali *babu* class itself.

Additionally, as a professor of English literature in St. Xavier's College, Calcutta, an elite missionary institution, Lal would have felt the enduring legacy of particularly the Renaissance, Romanticism, and High Modernism. As Rajeswari Sunder Rajan has pointed out, it was only after the "crisis in English studies in India" in the 1980s, following the turn to "theory" in the West, that English studies in India took a turn away from these thrust areas ("English Literary Studies" 67–69). In an essay on the English department in India,[4] Sanjukta Dasgupta points out that it was only in 1994 that Indian Writing in English, for instance, was introduced, and that it was only an optional course, while the core areas of study were "Greek and Latin classics, French and German classics, American literature, New Literatures in English" (229). Additionally, Lal, himself an Indian poet in English, would have, in the words of M.E. Gibson, defined himself "within, against, and across canonical understandings that included much of the British poetic canon, classical European and modern European poetry" (2).

One may argue then, that Lal, heavily influenced by Modernism, sees in the Hindu epic a specifically modernist iteration of a decaying moral order, the collapse of a golden age, a prophecy of dark days to come. The very quote with which Lal chooses to preface the narrative strikes the central chord of his reading – the loss of dharma in the world. In this, his voice quickly alternates between the passionate conviction of "I raise my arms and I shout" (Lal 1), and despondency, in "But no one listens!" He is also puzzled as to why, despite the certain promise of success and pleasure that comes from dharma, people fail to follow the path. His anguished cry, "Why is dharma not practised?" succinctly captures a sense of bewilderment (Lal 1).

G.H. Bantock, describing High Modernist literature, writes: "two basic themes of modern literature have been those of 'isolation' and of 'relationship' within what has been considered a *decaying moral order*" [emphasis mine] (Bantock 13). Modernist literature presents worlds where things fall apart, where morality is no longer a black-and-white matter. The same *weltanschauung* is repeatedly echoed in Lal's retelling. He writes: "Vyasa posits an intricate dharma, where right and wrong are bewilderingly mixed; he sits on one's back, relentlessly looking ahead to the end of a yuga" (3). The following quotation from the Introduction to Lal's retelling, alluding to W. B. Yeats' "The Second Coming," makes the comparison explicit:

> Vyasa portrays this massive moral collapse in terms that appear specially relevant to a century like ours that awaits the beast of a Second Coming slouching on slow hirsute thighs, and witnesses things falling apart, the centre refusing to hold, the best lacking all conviction and the worst full of passionate intensity.
>
> *(6)*

Here, as well as in descriptions of the battlefield during the Kurukshetra, Lal seems to be deeply influenced by Yeats's sense of doom and foreboding – "Jackals howled in the field; vultures circled in the sky" (260), Lal writes, in words that seem to echo the "indignant desert birds" of Yeats' poem (1196).

Lal infuses the last few chapters of his transcreation, particularly, with a characteristically Modernist sense of a world turned upside-down, one characterized by moral relativism, chaos, and destruction. While nothing in *The Mahabharata of Vyasa* is Lal's own invention, the space that the author gives in this short prose retelling, supposedly committed to a "hard core narrative," to poetically evoking this Modernist sense of civilizational crisis and disorder is telling:

> In the thirty-sixth year after the battle, many disturbing omens were seen by Yudhishtira. Dry, dusty storms blew into the city; birds wheeled backward; rivers flowed in reverse; a great fog always obscured the horizon ... fatal Time, bald-headed, bronze-skinned, stalked the streets; his fierce eyes peered inside every house ... Earthen pots cracked without cause; mynas chattered maddeningly day and night inside the houses; goats howled like jackals; asses were born to cows, elephants to mules, cats to bitches, and mice to mongooses.
>
> *(349)*

Depictions of ravaged landscapes occupy centre stage in the latter half of the retelling, in language that harks back to the poetry of World War I, particularly Wilfred Owen's anti-pastoral descriptions of the hellish experience of trench warfare. The similarity is made more evident by many of these passages being in verse. He writes, for instance, of the battlefield covered in "festering corpses," and stinking, "blood bespattered." Lal's descriptions of shattered bones, festering pus, "legless and armless corpses" with "guts strewn all over," a feast for crows and "iron-beaked vultures" (366) are eerily reminiscent of the mass technological slaughter of World War I, as described by English anti-war poets of the early twentieth century. Such passages are underpinned not only by a distinctly Indian Vibhatsya Rasa but also the aesthetics of Wilfred Owen, Siegfried Sassoon, and Isaac Rosenberg.

Lal also highlights what he sees as the individualism and moral relativism of many characters, in a manner that resonates with European Modernism. To begin with, he repeatedly stresses the unscrupulousness of the main characters. He depicts Krishna as a schemer, representing his killing of Shishupala as a vengeful act, denouncing his "theft" of Rukmini, and suggesting sexual tension between him and Draupadi.[5] Arjuna, to Lal, "suggests a restless twentieth-century hero." He asks whether "Arjuna's mental make-up is worrying and questing, *individualistic, even protestant*? [emphasis mine]" (32). He has also employed what he calls a "strong approach," choosing not to censor the text, but to highlight, for instance, that Draupadi was on her period during the game of dice. He has also stressed the strength and power of women in the text. In many ways, therefore, the text resonates with the literature of European Modernism.

Can the Mahabharata Be Read as a Modernist Epic?

Most notably, Lal's modernized epic is underpinned by what seems to be a distinctly Christian eschatology. It is arguable, though, that such teleological notions of time and history[6] are misapplied to the Mahabharata. Time, in the Judeo-Christian conception, is teleological – linear and progressive. Although there is a progression from *yuga* to *yuga* in the Hindu understanding of time, and a doomsday at the end of the Kali Yuga – this is not the ultimate end of time; the world is recreated after destruction, and this entire cycle is but an eyeblink in the lifecycle of Brahma, who himself is reborn after his destruction. It is widely accepted, therefore, that the notion of time in Hinduism is cyclical, and not linear (Basham 323–324; Eliade and Trask 112–118; Zaehner 5–6; Toynbee 28–29). Although, in the words of Basham, "each Yuga represents a progressive decline in piety, morality, strength, statute" (321), this decline is negated both by a cyclical return to a purer state, and by instances of divine intervention.

In Arvind Sharma's study, "The Notion of Cyclical Time in Hinduism," he notes that although in early Vedic Sruti literature, references to a cyclical notion are rare, Smriti literature, of which the Mahabharata is a part, is replete with references to a cyclical conception of time (30–32). He argues that the frequent divine interventions of Krishna in the Mahabharata, as epitomized in the Avatara verses of the Bhagavadgita, "clearly contradicts the inevitable character of the general decline of dharma from the apogee of the Kṛtayuga to the nadir of the Kaliyuga" (32). In the words of Sarvepalli Radhakrishnan, "The meaning of the birth of Krsna is the fact of redemption in the dark night. In the hour of calamity and enslavement the Saviour of the world is born" (35–36).

Platonic and Judeo-Christian thought tend to view the temporal world as a shadow realm, at a vast remove from the transcendent Reality. This two-world structure underlies Western thought from Plato through the Bible to Guy Debord's *Society of the Spectacle*. It is a loss of belief, or the problematization of belief in the transcendent world that led to the crisis of faith that marks Modernist literature. Hindu thought as embodied in the Mahabharata does not apprehend the universe in terms commensurate to the Modernist crisis of faith. The temporal is a manifestation of the atemporal, and therefore divine. The world we live in is not to be shunned – it too is Brahman, a product of divine play, or *lila*, the Supreme delighting in Himself.[7] How then could the same Modernist crisis of faith, brought on by the supposed rupture between the human and the divine, only possible in a two-world belief system, inform the Indian epics?

Temporal movement in Hindu thought is not as linear as in Western thought, which has since St. Augustine treated time as an arrow moving in one direction along a finite path. The temporal is in Hindu thought, blanketed or shrouded by the eternal. Radhakrishnan writes: "Time derives from eternity and finds fulfilment in it. In the Bhagavadgita, there is no antithesis between eternity and time" (38). Therefore, I argue that describing the Mahabharata in teleological terms as an epic of the end of time is, at least in part, a misreading.

It might be useful to note here that Lal is not alone in highlighting how the epic can be treated as chronicling the end of an epoch. Irawati Karve's important *Yuganta: The End of an Epoch*, first published in 1969, and a likely influence on Lal's understanding of the epic, is also invested in thinking through the sense of an ending in the Mahabharata. However, Karve takes a historical and anthropological view and, instead of highlighting a doomsday crisis of faith, carefully outlines how the Mahabharata marks a point of historical transition following which sweeping social changes occur, ushering in new class structures, rituals and conventions, eating habits, gender norms, political theories, literary modes, and attitudes towards devotion (183–217). She also takes pains to highlight lines of continuity, stating that "I do not mean to say that everything in it [the Mahabharata] came to an end or vanished" (183). She points out that much has persisted in India since the times of the epic, including the patriarchal household, relations between peasant society and forest-dwelling tribes, and the elasticity of religious thought (183–195). In comparing the epic's moral crisis to recent Western literature, Karve does initially suggest that "doubts regarding the nature of religion and human destiny" (195) bring the two into conversation and lend a certain topicality to the epic in the twentieth century. However, she goes on to carefully distinguish the "mood of questioning" (195) of modernist literature, which she sees as attendant on "loss of empires and their glories," with the mood of the epic. She argues that the figures of the Stranger and the Outsider that "one meets in modern literature" (196) are nowhere to be found in the epic, nor the existentialist belief "that human life is meaningless" (198). Instead, we find a "firm and hard" caste-specific morality, and an affirmation of existence based on "pity for the human condition" (198).

Conclusion

To sum up, Lal's retelling focusses on narrative, uses richly poetic language, and most importantly, presents the story of the epic from a distinctly Modernist lens. The Mahabharata is presented as a "doomsday epic," chronicling civilizational decay, moral relativism, and chaos. The moral order is collapsing in this ravaged world, while individualistic characters pursue their own ends, often unscrupulously. This is a world that seems to have been abandoned by god. I have argued that while Lal's modernizing of the epic in terms of style and language is commendable, in making the epic more readable, his reading of a distinctly Western Modernist crisis of faith into the Hindu epic is somewhat anachronistic, and a reflection of the transcreator's professional interest in modern English literature.

Notes

1 A vision explicitly detailed in his Introduction, in a section titled "The Message of the Mahabharata" (40–51).
2 On the other hand, several earlier commentators, invested in the methodology of textual criticism popular in the first half of the twentieth century, have argued *for* the existence of an ur-text. See, for instance, Fitzgerald, Dahlman, and Edgerton in Works Cited.
3 See also, in Batabyal; Ghosh.
4 For more on this topic, see Joshi; Paranjape, Rajendran and Sarwal; Sundar Rajan, *Lie of the Land*.
5 For a detailed scholarly discussion of the moral complexity of Krishna, as well as an attempt to historically locate and to an extent justify the same, see Matilal.
6 And Yeats is *not* the best example of such; his "The Second Coming," and other poems, underpinned by a cyclical notion of history as a product of interpenetrating "gyres"; a theory outlined in his *A Vision*. Arguably, though, the felt experience of "The Second Coming" is still one of "the breaking and fall of a culture" (Watson 32), of history as strongly directional and degenerative; the Olympian perspective of inevitable cyclical regeneration is not strongly felt in this particular poem, though it is in other poems such as "Under Ben Bulben."
7 As Klaus K. Klostermaier has pointed out, "Time is an instrument in the divine līlā (sport)" (873). Klostermaier's article on "Time" in *Encyclopedia of Hinduism* brings out the complexity of the discourse on time in the Hindu scriptures (872–874).

Works Cited

Bantock, G.H. "The Social and Intellectual Background". *The Pelican Guide to English Literature*, Vol 7. Ed. Boris Ford. Harmondsworth, England: Penguin Books Ltd., 1961.

Basham, A.L. *The Wonder That Was India*. London: Sedgwick and Jackson, 1956: 320–21.

Batabyal, Rakesh. "Who the 'Bhadralok' Was." *Economic and Political Weekly* 30.35 (2005): 3834–3836.

Bhattacharya, Tithi. *The Sentinels of Culture: Class, Education and the Colonial Intellectual in Bengal*. New Delhi: Oxford University Press, 2005. Print.

Chaudhuri, Supriya. "Modernisms in India". *The Oxford Handbook of Modernisms*. Eds. Osborne, Peter, et al. London: Oxford University Press, 2010: 942–60.

Dahlmann, Joseph. *Genesis Des Mahābhārata*. Berlin: F.L. Dames, 1899.

Dandekar, R.N. "The Mahabharata: Origin and Growth". *University of Ceylon Review* 12.2 (1954): 65–86.

_____, ed. *The Mahābhārata Revisited: Papers Presented at the International Seminar on the Mahābhārata Organized by the Sahitya Akademi at New Delhi on February 17–20, 1987*. New Delhi: Sahitya Akademi, 1990.

Dasgupta, Sanjukta. "To Be Or Not To Be Or How To Be: English Department in Indian Universities". *Indian Literature* 52.6 (2008): 223–238.

Edgerton, Franklin. "Sabhaparvan: Introduction". *Poona Critical Edition of the Mahabharata*. Vol. 2. Poona: Bhandarkar Oriental Research Institute, 1944.

Eliade, Mircea and Willard R. Trask. *The Myth of the Eternal Return*. New York: Pantheon Books, 1954.

Fitzgerald, James L. "India's Fifth Veda. The Mahabharata's Presentation of Itself". *Essays on the Mahabharata*. Ed. Arvind Sharma. Leiden: E.J. Brill, 1991: 150–170.

Ghosh, Parimal. "Where Have All the 'Bhadraloks' Gone?" *Economic and Political Weekly* 39.3 (2004): 247–251.

Gibson, Mary E. *Indian Angles: English Verse in Colonial India from Jones to Tagore*. Athens: Ohio University Press, 2011.

Goldman, Robert, and Sally Sutherland Goldman. "Introduction to Themes". Part of Volume 1 of an unpublished course reader, for a course titled "Epic in History, Epic as History: Reading the Ramayana and the Mahabharata as Documents of and Models for the Social and Political Life of the Indian Nation", taught at the Center for Historical Studies (CHS), Jawaharlal Nehru University, New Delhi, August–December 2010: 1–25. Available at the CHS library, New Delhi.

Joshi, Svati. *Rethinking English: Essays in Literature, Language, History*. New Delhi: Trianka, 1991.

Karve, Irawati. *Yuganta: The End of an Epoch*. Noida: Orient Blackswan, [1969] 2008.

Klostermaier, Klaus K. "Time (Kāla)". *Encyclopedia of Hinduism*. Eds. Denise Cush, Catherine Robinson, and Michael York. New York: Routledge, 2012: 872–4.

Lal, P. *The Mahabharata of Vyasa*. New Delhi: Vikas Publishing House, 1980.

Matilal, Bimal Krishna. "Krsna: In Defence of a Devious Divinity." *Essays on the Mahābhārata*. Ed. Arvind Sharma. Delhi: Motilal Banarsidass, 1991: 401.

Radhakrishnan, S., Ed. and Trans. *The Bhagavadgita*. Bombay: Blackie & Son, 1980.

Sharma, Arvind. "The Notion of Cyclical Time in Hinduism". *Contributions to Asian Studies: 5*. Ed. K. Ishwaran. Leiden: Brill, 1974: 26–35.

Sukthankar, V.S. "Prolegomena". *The Adiparvan, Being the First Book of the Mahabharata, The Great Epic of India.* Poona: Bhandarkar Oriental Research Institute, 1933.

Sunder Rajan, Rajeswari. "English Literary Studies, Women's Studies and Feminism in India". *Economic and Political Weekly* 43 (2008): 66–71.

Sutherland, Sally J. (Goldman). "The Text Which Is No Text: Critical Edition as Text". *Translation East and West: A Cross-Cultural Approach.* Ed. Cornelia N. Moore and Lucy Lower. Hawaii: East West Center, University of Hawaii at Manoa, 1992: 82–92.

Toynbee, Arnold. *A Study of History.* Vol. 4. London: Oxford University Press, 1939.

Watson, George. "Yeats's View of History: 'The Contemplation of Ruin'". *The Maynooth Review* 2.2 (1976): 27–46.

Yeats, William Butler. "The Second Coming". *The Norton Anthology of Poetry.* Eds. Margaret Ferguson, Mary Jo Salter, and Jon Stallworthy. New York: Norton and Company, 2005: 1196.

Zaehner, R. C. *Hinduism.* London: Oxford University Press, 1962.

8

IRREVERENT READERS, WORSHIPFUL VIEWERS

Post-emergency Epics and Diverging Indian Nationalisms

Sucheta Kanjilal

When the Pāṇḍavas won the Kurukṣetra war in the Mahabharata, their victory rang hollow because they found themselves ruling over a ruined land filled with orphans and widows. For the newly sovereign Indians, earning independence from the British after a challenging anti-colonial struggle brought about similarly contradictory feelings. Even though political autonomy had been achieved and celebrated, the young nation immediately began to stumble over widespread economic deprivation, social instability, and communal tensions. These frustrations rose to new heights during the declaration of a national Emergency between 1975–1977. At this time, the Sanskrit Mahabharata's impressive breadth, potential for tragedy, and philosophical complexities were revisited to contemplate new realities.

In what follows I investigate how the epic and the nation renewed the terms of their dialogue after the political crises brought on by the declaration of Emergency rule. First, I consider how Shashi Tharoor's English language text *The Great Indian Novel* (1989) rewrites an alternative, satirical version of Indian national history, beginning in the colonial period, working up to The Emergency and beyond. Tharoor employs the narrative framework of the Mahabharata to highlight the instability of the national project. In doing so, Tharoor exposes nationalism in India as a flawed and untidy mythology that demands quasi-religious devotion, which he asserts is ultimately detrimental to democracy.

Next, I examine a Hindi-language television adaptation of the Mahabharata, named *Mahabharat*, which appeared between 1988 and 1990 on the state-controlled, national television channel Doordarshan. I suggest that the televised epic, like Tharoor's novel, also arises because of anxieties about the state of the nation after the Emergency, which for many, signified

DOI: 10.4324/9781003516408-10

the failure of secular nationalism. However, where *The Great Indian Novel* uses the more recent past to underline that nationalism itself is an unstable mythology, the televised epics valorize and insist on a distant but stable mythological past. I demonstrate how *Mahabharat* positions itself as an authoritative retelling of the epic narrative that explicitly invites the audience's reverence. In doing so, the televised epic suggests that all could be well if a glorious, precolonial history and Hindu values could be reinstated. By comparison, Tharoor's novel is irreverent towards both Indian nationalism and its history. Although the novel remains comically pessimistic about the future, it does not abandon the project of nation-building. Instead, Tharoor suggests that self-critique will be essential in the quest to improve the nation.

Both texts also show how devotion has been infused into the Indian national imagination, for better and worse. The Sanskrit *Mahabharata* invites devotion. The first book explicitly mentions that reading the epic is as spiritually and intellectually important as reading the Vedas (*MBh* 1.2.235). As Arti Dhand, drawing on the work of Madeleine Biardeau, points out, in the *Mahabharata* "the symbolism of the Vedic sacrifice is retained, but recast in the devotional idiom of Bhakti. The epics are thus quintessentially works of Bhakti" (123–124). *Bhakti*, or deeply personal devotion, has a detailed and complex history in the Indian subcontinent. One of the key moments of *bhakti*'s articulation can be found in the mediaeval Bhakti movement, which arose as an anti-caste, individual-orientated alternative to mainstream Hinduism. The Bhakti movement is a broad rubric that includes the lives and works of a large group of poets from areas that correspond to contemporary Tamil Nadu, Karnataka, Maharashtra, and West Bengal.

Bhakti today still recalls a commonly shared devotion that emotionally and personally aligns the devotee with the higher power. However, unlike the mediaeval Bhakti movement's resistances to mainstream Hinduism, one of the ways in which *bhakti* is recalled in contemporary India doubles down on the superstructure of Hindu nationalism. In internet parlance, followers of Prime Minister Narendra Modi are often derided as "Modi-*bhakt*s," translating to Modi-devotees, or simply "*bhakt*s" by persons with more centrist or leftist views. The neologism's origins are uncertain, but many, including Congress Ex-General Secretary Digvijay Singh have used it (*The Economic Times;* Press Trust of India, "Digvijay Singh Takes a Dig"). These "*bhakt*s" are believed to be intolerant of any deviation from their own ideologies, which privileges the establishment of a Hindu nation. The term is a radical inflection of *des-bhakt*, a term in Hindi which aligns with the English word "patriotism" but literally translates to "devotees of the nation/country." Devotion continues to be a constitutive element of the very language that describes Indian national allegiance, especially that which privileges Hinduism.

The act of communally watching *Mahabharat* on colour television bolstered devotion for many viewers: in this case, seeing led to literally and religiously believing. This in turn gave the shows the power to support a hegemonic, Hindu nationalist worldview. As Sneha Roy Choudhury discusses in another Chapter of this volume, seeing the deities on this television show consolidated a particular kind of Hindu nationalist vision. Dipesh Chakrabarty has also written about the importance of "divine sight" in the Indian national imagination. Chakrabarty writes,

> There is a family of terms in north Indian languages for this activity of seeing beyond the real, of being in the presence of the deity. One of them is darshan (to see) and refers to the exchange of human sight with the divine that supposedly happens inside a temple or in the presence of an image in which the deity has become manifest (murati).
>
> *(173)*

Although in Benedict Anderson's account, the realist novel provides a worldview coexistent with the imagination of the nation, Chakrabarty shows that realism was, in fact, insufficient for realizing the whole spectrum of nationalist feelings in India. Although realism had its place, mainly in the realm of political critique, it could not stir up the feelings required to bring about patriotic loyalty and devotion. Instead, Chakrabarty argues that poetry and myth were more successful in consolidating patriotic feelings. He writes that the idea of seeing the divine and experiencing the uncanny is deeply entrenched in popular understandings of the nation. He provides examples of this phenomenon when he writes,

> [Tradition is] posed as a question of "divine sight," (divyadrishti, darshan) of a sight ... [L]ong before there were the newspaper and the novel, there was the age-old practice of darshan that came to constitute a critical element in the "performative" aspect of ... nationalism.
>
> *(Chakrabarty 175–177)*

One of the examples Chakrabarty discusses is a 1938 essay by nationalist writer Wajed Ali. Ali writes about how his faith in the continuity of tradition and community is affirmed by seeing two different persons reading the Ramayaṇa to groups of young children, twenty-five years apart. In the case of the televised epics in the 1980s, "darshan" found a similar platform to invite millions of viewers to perform Hinduism and nationalism on a weekly basis.

Further, the *Mahabharat* television show and Tharoor's novel proposed two distinct ways of coming to terms with nationalism and mythology, which become further polarized and entrenched in twenty-first-century Indian politics. Whereas the televised *Mahabharat* catalysed the Bharatiya Janata Party's (BJP) Hindu nationalist agenda, Tharoor's views represent an elite, western-educated, critical view of the nation that is shared by supporters of the Indian National Congress party. People associated with both texts also entered politics along specifically partisan lines: Tharoor is now a prominent Congress minister, while several actors who starred in the televised epic are working under the aegis of the BJP. This demonstrates the political power of texts, whether elite or popular, while showing how multiple media intersect and interact to shape religious and nationalist discourse.

Nationalism: A Cautionary Tale

Born in London to an elite Malayali family, Shashi Tharoor worked for the United Nations for nearly three decades until he left to join Indian politics. In March 2009, he contested and won the Indian general election as a candidate for the Congress in Thiruvananthapuram, Kerala. Since then, he has been Minister of State in the Government of India for External Affairs (2009–2010) and Human Resource Development (2012–2014). Currently, he is Chairman of the All-India Professionals Congress (since 2017) and Chairman of the Standing Committee on Information Technology (since 2019). *The Great Indian Novel* was published in 1989. In the novel, which was the first of his several works of fiction and non-fiction, Tharoor presents a vision of Indian nationalism and history that is self-critical but still invested in the tireless work of nation-building.

In *The Great Indian Novel,* Tharoor employs the framework of the *Mahabharata* to parodically retell the story of the modern Indian nation. It begins in the late colonial era and ends around the declaration of Emergency rule in 1975 while borrowing and repurposing many of the epic's devices and styles. Like the epic's eighteen volumes, *The Great Indian Novel* has eighteen chapters. The original epic's multiple narrators are adapted into an almost ridiculously unreliable and cynical single narrator named V.V.: a loose combination of Ved-Vyāsa, the compiler of the Sanskrit epic, and V.V. Giri, the fourth President of India. The book is consistently humorous, often supplementing its prose with doggerel and ditties to mock sombre epic or national events. In the novel, the altered narrative of the *Mahabharata* functions as a destabilizing force that challenges the grand narratives that help erect and support a homogenized nationalism.

Tharoor's *The Great Indian Novel* rewrites India's history with two pivotal moments: the anti-colonial struggle and the Emergency. The declaration of the Indian Emergency lasted twenty-one months between 1975 and 1977. It was orchestrated chiefly by Indira Gandhi, the then Prime Minister of India and the central figure of the Indian National Congress. Gandhi's popularity was on the decline following a number of social, economic, and political crises, including but not limited to a case of election malpractice filed against her and the rise of her son Sanjay as a dictatorial figure. To maintain power, she recommended to the President, Fakhruddin Ali Ahmad, that a State of Emergency be declared in the country, granting her rule of decree. During the Emergency, civil liberties were suspended, curfew was enforced, and leaders of the opposition were arrested. In his novel, Tharoor reimagines Gandhi as a feminine version of the epic hero Duryodhana. In comparison to the tragic ending of the *Mahabharata*, *The Great Indian Novel* ends comically, with India muddling through the twenty-first century with "computers and corruption, myths and politicians," after which the narrator returns to the beginning of his story (Tharoor 418). The beginning and end of the story are marked by the same words: "They tell me that India is an underdeveloped country" (Tharoor 17, 418). This repetition signifies that the story, much like the project of nationalism, is constructed – frequently rehearsed but still laughably unreliable.

Tharoor exposes and demythologizes the contents of national history for his own people by exposing its creators and characters as inherently flawed and comical. He draws together the imaginary of the Mahabharata with the standardized nationalist history taught in Indian schools to create a satirical counter-history. The novel is peppered with a host of caricatures of personages from Indian politics: Jawaharlal Nehru and Indira Priyadarshini Gandhi are re-imagined as the blind Fabian socialist King Dhritarashtra and shrewdly ambitious Priya Duryodhani.

Tharoor uses satire to make trenchant political critiques, especially of religious nationalism. Sneharika Roy contends that the novel is a move against the Hindu right's use of the Mahabharata to support fundamentalist ideologies as it "seeks to counter these ethnocentric forces by anglicizing, globalizing, and updating the Mahabharata" (59). However, while the novel does provide a counternarrative to Hindu fundamentalism's revisionist histories, the novel's intention is not necessarily to make the epic palatable for a global audience. Although the Mahabharata is recognized worldwide as a part of Indo-European mythology, the novel's specific references would be accessible or even palatable to just upper-class Indian English readers. Gayatri Chakravorty Spivak suggests that "[The novel is a] spoof that is inaccessible to the international readership of Commonwealth Literature. And...simply not a part of 'popular' culture on the subcontinent" (75). Furthermore, I would argue that the novel reads as an extended inside joke, mainly for elite Indian readers who are proficient in the Indian and British literary traditions.

As much as *The Great Indian Novel* challenges Indian history and its creators, its characters are a select group of native bilingual elite government officials, who are not altogether different from the intended elite readers or even the author himself. Kanishka Chowdhury critiques Tharoor for being a "westernized, middle-class Hindu [who] is unable to get beyond the habitual preoccupations of his class" (43). Frantz Fanon has also cautioned bilingual-elite writers of decolonized nation-states against employing older textual forms like the epic to erect an uncritical, monolithic vision of the past that glosses over the complexities of oppression and difference. However, Tharoor's satirical novel does not valorize the Mahabharata as the glorious past, but repurposes it to critique and unsettle the present. By doing this, he does what Fanon urged the decolonized intellectual to do, "[to write] for his people...to use the past with the intention of opening the future, as an invitation to action" (180). Fanon cautions thinkers against the fetishization of the mythic past in the construction of nationalism, urging them instead to mobilize the past to contemplate a more equitable future. Although Tharoor's novel gives no specific directives about the future, it uses the past to expose how national culture is constructed and must be re-examined constantly. In seeing this artifice, his readers would be compelled to consider dynamic ways in which the nation's present and future may be improved.

Democracy in Distress

A playful refashioning of Indian history, *The Great Indian Novel* exposes and critiques how nationalism in India invites religious fervour. This is further reinforced by narrativized mythologies of specific persons and institutions who have been elevated to godlike status in popular discourse. Through the novel Tharoor affirms that nationalism in India is not only affirmed through its connection with Hindu religious mythologies but is also performed like Hinduism. Like in Hindu mythology, Tharoor's epic too has its flawed but heroic demi-gods. For instance, the novel reimagines M.K. Gandhi as a figure called Gangaji, who has a large and devoted following. Shahid Amin argues that the tremendous following that Gandhi inspired was organized around a quasi-religious notion of "belief," with thousands gathering for his "darshan" or sighting with gestures, writings, songs, and poems that belied their reverence to him as a deity. The quasi-religious experience at the sighting of Gandhi has also been depicted in several media: for instance, it is a key moment in novels like R.K. Narayan's *Waiting for the Mahatma* (1995), Mulk Raj Anand's *Untouchable* (1935), and films like Deepa Mehta's *Water* (2005).

Unlike Narayan's optimistic nationalism, Tharoor shows how the nation malfunctions specifically because of its pantheon of figures like Gangaji who need to be appeased and celebrated in a manner that recalls distinctly Hindu modes of worship. The novel demonstrates how dominant ideology, here Hinduism, percolates through the education system and popular discourse so that conformist grand narratives and mythologies about the nation are repeated at the expense of truth, self-critique, and original thinking. In many ways, Tharoor's novel is an anti-textbook that challenges the homogenized, uncritical, heroic narrative of Indian nationalism by satirizing the state and exposing the ways in which it maintains dominance.

Tharoor also questions the stability of Indian nationalism by personifying democracy as Draupadi Mokrasi or Miss D. Mokrasi. Mokrasi's mother Georgina Drewpad is based on Edwina Mountbatten, the wife of Louis Mountbatten, the last Viceroy of India. Edwina's friendship with Jawaharlal Nehru has been fodder for gossip for decades. In Tharoor's novel, Georgina and her husband have an anglicized version of epic heroine Draupadī's father's name, Drupada, as their last name. Georgina's name is also a feminized version of the name of George VI, the last emperor of India. She comes to stand for Britain in the novel and even more during her intercourse, sexual and social, with Dhritarashtra/Nehru. Dhritarashtra is a blind king: where in the epic he is blind because of an error committed by his mother during his conception, in the novel, it is because of his political idealism.

When blind Dhritarashtra and flamboyant Georgina have an affair, it results in the birth of Draupadi Mokrasi. She is born prematurely on 26 January 1950, the date on which the Indian Constitution came into force to establish the nation as a republic. The novel playfully capitalizes on the fear that the colonizers were right because the whimsical and erroneous actions of the Indian politicians suggest that Indians were not ready to be democratic. Further, Miss D. Mokrasi's status as the bastard child of her Indian father Dhritarashtra and English mother Georgina also undermines the valorization of democracy. Democracy then is not the outcome of the sacrifices of the masses that participated in the freedom movement – a narrative that is frequently valorized by nationalists. Instead, Tharoor suggests that democracy was produced privately and almost exclusively for the pleasure of two specific and powerful parties, the bilingual-elite politician Dhritarashtra/Nehru and Britain, personified by Georgina.

Democracy/Miss D. Mokrasi, arguably one of the most controversial but celebrated outcomes of colonialism, is admired by the narrator and other characters in the novel. Just like in the epic, D. Mokrasi's beauty is celebrated for various political and aesthetic reasons, Tharoor's Miss D. Mokrasi is admired for her virtues and the political beliefs they represent:

[O]urs was an inevitably darker democracy, all the more to be cherished for the Indianness of her coloring … Draupadi's beauty attracted both men and women, both young and old. All sought to be a part of her beauty; no man presumed to attempt its submission … [She] was a flame in the brass lamp in a sacred temple of the people. Imagine, a flame nourished by a ceaseless stream of sanctified oil and the energy of a million voices raised in chanting adoration.

(Tharoor 309)

Here, Tharoor shows how democracy and Indian nationalism do not arise at the "dusk of religious modes of thought" as Anderson suggests is the case in Southeast Asia and other colonial nations (51). Instead, in India, the components of nationalism are reproduced as new religious modes of thought that flourish alongside majority religion, sometimes so closely that they appear indistinguishable. For this reason, in the novel, Miss D. Mokrasi is celebrated with acts and objects associated with Hindu prayer: chanting, sanctified oils, and brass lamps in temples.

When Miss D. Mokrasi is an adult, the five Pandava brothers marry her together. It is explained that Miss D. Mokrasi ends up with five husbands because she prayed to five different religious entities: Shiva, Jehovah, the Virgin Mother, Allah, and the Archbishop of Canterbury (Tharoor 316). Further, each husband stands for the institutions that protect democracy and the narrator spells this out transparently: Yudhishtira is a lawyer and a career politician, Bhim signifies the army, Arjuna is a journalist, Nakul represents the diplomatic corps, and Sahdev symbolizes civil servants (Tharoor 320). Even though Arjuna is the one who wins Draupadi's hand and consequently, heart first, he is compelled to share her with these others. In a sense, this is a self-conscious reflection on the role of the free press, including literature, in preserving democracy. Under ideal circumstances, they could have had a mutually pleasing and productive union, but other institutions always come in the way of their monogamous romance. D. Mokrasi's overzealous secularity becomes a threat to her well-being.

Although the institutions signified by the husbands routinely undermine Miss D. Mokrasi, it is eventually another woman who poses the greatest threat to her: Priya Duryodhani/Indira Gandhi. The two women are cleverly portrayed as half-sisters in the book, as they share Dhritarashtra/Nehru as a father. Miss D. Mokrasi is born and raised by an adoptive family, with Dhritarashtra only discreetly supporting her financially (Tharoor 261). D. Mokrasi grows up to have numerous qualities such as "a willingness to play with all the children in the neighbourhood, irrespective of caste, creed or culture" (Tharoor 262). In contrast, Dhritarashtra raises his legitimate child Priya Duryodhani with loving attention, even though he is initially disappointed that she was not the son he hoped for. In the novel, the narrator is enamoured of Draupadi while barely concealing his dislike of Duryodhani:

> [Duryodhani] was a slight frail girl … with a long thin tapering face like the kernel of a mango and dark eyebrows that nearly joined together over a high bridged nose, giving her the look of a desiccated schoolteacher when she was barely old enough to enroll in school.
>
> *(Tharoor 151)*

The narrator concedes shortly after that Duryodhani could have been physically unremarkable had it not been for her lustrous eyes, which show her dynamism and potential for leadership.

In the novel, appropriate feminine behaviour and its consequences are reinforced through a misogynistic comparison: Gandhi's ugliness, the lustre of her eyes notwithstanding, stands out in sharp contrast against Miss D. Mokrasi's beauty. But although Miss D. Mokrasi is beautiful, she has no will of her own. In keeping with the extended metaphor, she must be nurtured by her husbands or she deteriorates. As the nation's condition takes a turn for the worse, she slowly becomes less physically attractive. The narrator indicates that she gains weight and begins to age: "Draupadi Mokrasi, still beautiful, began to appear plump, her instinctive smile creasing the flesh of her face in the slightest hint of a double chin...sagging flesh [began] to mask her inner beauty" (Tharoor 342, 374). Here, the narrator indicates Miss Mokrasi's departure from beauty and femininity is as much of a catastrophe as the failure of democracy or, in Duryodhani's case, what motivates a female politician like Gandhi to become the chief threat to democracy.

However, Indira Gandhi's role in the traumatic Indian Emergency is far from fictitious. In *The Great Indian Novel,* the Emergency is called the Siege and occurs as a result of the Game of Dice, during which Draupadi is wagered by Yudhishthira. The Siege is described as a horrific time when millions suffer under Duryodhani's dictatorial rule:

[T]he Siege had become a licence for the police to do as they pleased, settling scores, locking up suspects, enemies, and sometimes creditors sometimes without due process and above all picking up young men ... to have their vasa cut off in fulfilment of arbitrary sterilisation quotas.

(Tharoor 384)

Although the narrator disapproves of The Siege, he emphasizes that Duryodhani has a change of heart shortly after. For reasons that are unclear – to her associates or the public – she ends The Siege and declares a general election in 1977, which she loses. However, she returns to power again in 1980 and remains the Prime Minister until her death in 1984. At this point, the narrator draws the story to a close:

I have portrayed the nation in struggle but omitted its struggles against itself and ignored the regionalists and the autonomists and the separatists and the secessionists who even today are trying to tear the country apart ... An India where a Priya Duryodhani can be re-elected because seven hundred million people cannot produce anyone better, and where her immortality can be guaranteed by her greatest failure.

(Tharoor 412)

The nation, despite its struggles, emerges damaged but alive. The narrator reflects on the irony that Duryodhani, despite her faults and role in The Siege, might have been a better politician than many others. In this way, Duryodhani is redeemed the way Duryodhana is in the epic, ultimately because both do their jobs as king or politician, even if their methods are suspect.

Tharoor demythologizes the very idea of a glorious national narrative because it is constantly punctured by the folly of individuals. Tharoor's principal project is retelling the story of the nation with comical irreverence. He is able to employ a grand narrative, the Mahabharata, to satirize the grand narrative of Indian nationalism, because they are similar in scale and import. Spivak contends that the novel is a critique of Indian politics, especially "the postcolonial politicians' fantasy to make the present identical with the hallowed past, and thus win votes for a politics of identity at degree zero of history" (75). The novel's view of history is antithetical to the televised *Mahabharat,* which does exactly what Tharoor and Spivak critique. The show turns the hallowed past into a highly accessible visual spectacle that helps Hindu-nationalist politicians establish and maintain power.

Seeing Is Believing

Around the time Tharoor published his novel, two Hindi-language, serialized adaptations of the Ramayana and the Mahabharata appeared on national television: Ramanand Sagar's *Ramayan* (1987–1988) and Baldev Raj Chopra and Ravi Chopra's *Mahabharat* (1988–1990) were originally telecast on Doordarshan. Even though these teleserials also retold the epics, they had a markedly different approach to both the epic texts and their new context. For Tharoor, the nation's history is the principal narrative while epic's style helps further his satirical intentions. In the television shows, the epics are a serious, central subject – the producers assiduously maintained that these shows did not deviate from the moral and political messages of the original epics. For this reason, the national audience was invited to view the shows with reverence, so that they could refamiliarize themselves with the allegedly true origins of their culture.

Even though the publication of Tharoor's text was contemporaneous with the shows, it could not compete with their reach. Where English language novels had, and indeed still have, a limited circulation, the shows had the potential to reach a larger audience since they were both in the widely understood official language of Hindi and on national television. Moreover, Doordarshan was virtually the only channel on television until that time, since private channels would not make an appearance until economic liberalization in 1991. Doordarshan's monopoly on the media market ensured the popularity of the mythological series. When the shows aired on Sundays, millions of Indian families tuned in together to experience their beloved mythological characters in living colour. B.R. Chopra and Ravi Chopra were long-time veterans of Bollywood and the Indian television industry. Together, they concocted a winning combination: they expertly melded Bollywood melodrama and ostentatious costumes with commonly known religious iconography and meditative practices. They strategically placed halos around the protagonists' heads and used chants in Sanskrit to begin each episode. Watching the show was meant to be a supplement to, or even a substitute for, family prayers.

The shows reappeared at an opportune time, when the citizens of the country were especially receptive to its messages. For many, the Emergency had recently and violently demonstrated the failure of secular nationalism. The televised mythological characters seemed to assure the public that all could be well again if there was a return to the values of a pre-secular past. The televised epics were so influential that they became new master texts that radically reorganized the way epic narratives are interpreted in popular and literary discourse in twenty-first-century India. Even today, many Indians continue to dogmatically refer to these televised adaptations as the dominant interpretation of both the epic narratives and in turn, Hinduism.

Both the shows were also an easily digestible supplement to oral retellings of the epic texts in countless homes because their visual and serial form lent itself well to ritualization. Purnima Mankekar writes of middle-class Indian families who bathed and purified themselves before the serial appeared on television, suggesting that the viewing of the serial itself was considered an act of worship. She notes that the relatively new visual medium of television recreated the Hindu ideal of "darshan," which she defines using Diana Eck's words "involves both seeing and being beheld by the deity" (qtd. in Mankekar 200). She writes,

> The viewers I worked with engaged the Ramayan with the same reverence they would have accorded a religious ritual: seeing Lord Rama on television became a form of darshan for them… For them, there was little difference between reading the Ramayana and watching it on TV.
>
> *(Mankekar 200)*

The show also made it possible for those who could not or did not read the epics in Sanskrit to engage with them more frequently. The shows were also in Hindi, a language which was, by then, the well-established lingua franca in the subcontinent. This made them popular and accessible even before they were dubbed into other Indian languages. The combination of a common language, national telecasting, and Bollywood-style *mise-en-scène* helped these elaborate and confident interpretations of the already-known narrative of the epics go even further than before. It helped that Sagar's and

Chopras' renditions of the epic stories were considered authoritative by their audiences. Mankekar found that few viewers doubted the "authenticity" of the epic's re-presentation in the television show (200, 223). The shows fortified the notion that epics were the dominant text through which to access a singular narrative of Hindu values, which in turn was conflated problematically with a monolithic Indian culture.

Mahabharat focused on the fractures and tensions in the epic text to relate it to the dire state of politics in the present day. The makers believed that each epic had different moral and political messages. B.R. Chopra claimed that "the Mahabharat was about the pervasiveness of politics in 'every aspect of life'" (qtd. in Mankekar 227). This was furthered by deliberately mining the tensions in the epic to yoke it to present times: the show rendered events of the war, assaults, and familial enmities in melodramatic detail. James Hegarty, for instance, has written about how the Chopra serial painstakingly spelt out the epic's links to nation and national culture. He argues that the show interpellated the audience as homogeneously Hindu and strongly suggested that its vision of the past was uncontestable (194–195). The *Mahabharata*, a text about numerous political conflicts that lead up to a tremendous and horrific war, provided many events that could be linked to topical concerns.

Many of the show's representations of epic events hit as close to home as the makers desired. For instance, Mankekar writes that the *Mahabharat*'s presentation of Draupadi's disrobing had a profound impact on a range of female viewers, including those who were not Hindus:

> Muslim and Sikh women, along with their Hindu counterparts, were extremely moved by Draupadi's disrobing: temporarily abstracting this episode from the rest of the televisual text, they saw it as yet another gripping tale of the injustices (zulm) perpetrated on women.
>
> *(Mankekar 228)*

Viewers, including myself, have vivid memories of first seeing this violent moment on television. The scene was particularly incongruous because it appeared in what had been otherwise deemed a family-friendly show. The depiction of sexual violence against women was a regular occurrence in Bollywood films but not in sanitized state-controlled programming. Mankekar notes that many female viewers discussed how violence depicted in the episode came uncomfortably close to their daily experiences of harassment or assault (245). Further, the Chopras' Draupadi, like the epic Draupadī, responds to her mistreatment visibly and vocally. The Chopra's *Mahabharat* provided compelling new visuals for already memorable epic events, including but certainly not limited to, Draupadī's disrobing.

The core narrative of the Mahabharata was confirmed by the Chopras as a historical mirror to the scourge of the present times. The Chopras rewrite the epic like Tharoor does but differed by doubling down on the text's solemnity and veracity. The television adaptations of the two epics worked together to present a powerful message: where Sagar's *Ramayan* was viewed as an epic about a common (Hindu) culture, Chopras' *Mahabharat* was an epic for the shared perilous present. They suggested to audiences that the failure to establish a *Ramayaṇa*-like ideal kingdom has led to Mahabharata-like chaos and corruption. Together, these two widely accessible televised adaptations ensured that the epics were more relevant by the last decade of the twentieth century than ever before.

Two Nationalisms and the Eternal Past

The impact of the epic serials on Indian politics has been powerful and enduring. Actors who starred in them became recognized all over the country as the mythological figures they played and were frequently treated as if they were divine in public. Actors such as Nitish Bhardwaj and Gajendra Chauhan played Kṛṣṇa and Yudhiṣṭhir in the *Mahabharat*, respectively, capitalized on the quasi-religious devotion they inspired by entering the political sphere as BJP candidates. Similarly, Tharoor remains widely recognized today not only because he is a member of the Indian National Congress but also as a writer and public intellectual. Tharoor currently has 8.4 million followers on the social media platform X, formerly Twitter, and is often in the news for his trenchant critiques of the BJP (*Sakshi Post*). Most recently, he has written books of nonfiction questioning the policies of the current Prime Minister Narendra Modi and arguing against Hindu nationalism called *The Paradoxical Prime Minister: Narendra Modi And His India* (2018) and *The Struggle for India's Soul: Nationalism and the Fate of Democracy* (2021), respectively.

The Great Indian Novel did not just anticipate Tharoor's political vision but also, the book's satirical tone and elite vocabulary forecasted Tharoor's current public persona. Tharoor's distinctively highbrow manner of public speaking and sesquipedalianism has itself been satirized, spawning internet memes and comic impersonations (Rizwan). Tharoor responds to such jokes about him with the good humour he demonstrates in his first novel (*MensXP*). He often appears on youth-orientated internet shows and even tried his hand at stand-up comedy (*The Quint; "One Mic Stand: Shashi Tharoor ft. Kunal Kamra"*). Many persons, including those who have not read *The Great Indian Novel,* recognize him from these internet appearances or follow his "word of the day" posts on Twitter (*The Economic Times*). These public engagements have earned Tharoor both visibility and goodwill among English-language-speaking Indians who share his views on nationalism: that self-critique and scepticism about history are necessary for improving the country.

Tharoor and the Chopras also demonstrate two distinctly different ways of reading both the *Mahabharata* and Indian nationalism: where Tharoor's vision is playful and self-critical without abandoning the project of nation-building, the Chopras suggest that *Mahabharat* is not even an adaptation but a solemn, historical truth that must be used to pivot the nation back towards Hinduism. *The Great Indian Novel* exhorts the reader to be irreverent towards mythologized history to better understand the country's problems, whereas the televised adaptations of the two epics functioned specifically to encourage reverence towards the epics, and by extension Hinduism, for the sake of the nation. In a sense, Tharoor's novel and the televised adaptations propose diametrically opposing ways to look at the same socio-political problem. After the Emergency, Tharoor suggests that it would be most productive to come to terms with the fact that the nation must be critiqued and re-worked rather than worshipped. On the other hand, the televised adaptations imply that even though the current state of the nation is undesirable, it can be redeemed and made worthy of worship again by reconnecting it with a specifically Hindu past.

The televised epics were essential in the recent revitalization of Hinduism. Dhand notes, "There's no denying … that the television epics have also had an immense impact on Hindu society and politics … the dramatisations have played a critical role in the revival and political self-assertion that has characterised Hinduism in recent years" (16–20). Further, the televised epics succeeded because they reproduced a powerful combination of vision and imagination. The practice of "darshan," which is now enhanced through the medium of television, is not just integral to Hindu worship, but also to the Indian national imagination.

By the end of the 1980s, India was moving towards becoming a key player in the global economy. In the decades following colonialism, the Indian government's economic policies had been protectionist, in promoting import substitution and building a large public sector. However, in 1991, the Indian government, headed by the BJP, initiated large-scale economic liberalization that would bring more foreign goods and ideas into the country than ever before. The televised epics became the unlikely mutual friend of both ethnocentric Hindu nationalism and globalizing economic liberalization. Arvind Rajagopal writes that in reimagining and consuming these epics, their primarily Hindu viewers "consume not only the product but the act of consumption itself, when they re-stage it in imagination, and perceive themselves as part of a grander design, proof of a larger intelligence at work than merely their own" (95) The powerful juxtaposition of the imagined past with a desirable future aided both the projects of Hindu nationalism and economic liberalization:

Audiences then experienced two events traveling in different directions, liberalization, as a portent of things to come, symbolized in the newly visible wealth of consumer goods, and the Ramayan serial, harkening back to a golden age. They were in a sense hinged together by television, as a device that brought past and future together while itself oscillating between time zones in a kind of eternal present.

(Rajagopal 74)

The new Indian consumer was thus empowered by these televised representations of what they conceived of as "our culture." Unfortunately, this new identity was also based on a largely reductive and problematic understanding of Indian culture as monolithically Hindu.

By the 1990s, the Congress' secular politics and power were increasingly being displaced by the rising right-wing opposition Janata Party. As many including Malik and Singh have suggested, Janata Party began as the Bharatiya Jana Sangh in 1955, primarily to provide an alternative to the secular politics of the Indian National Congress. At its inception, Janata Party was associated with the Hindu nationalist organization Rashtriya Swayamsevak Sangh (RSS). These groups were key agitators during the Emergency and protested to oppose Indira Gandhi's policies. The Janata Party won a majority in the elections for the first time in 1977, defeating Gandhi and the Congress. Although the party has varied its alignment with the Hindu nationalist cause over the years, it is noteworthy that the party was renamed the Bharatiya Janata Party (BJP) in 1980. "Bharat" is considered a Hindu space which is distinct from the secular, anglicized "India." In the classical epic, Bharata gestures to the text being a story of the descendants of a king named Bharata. In contemporary times, the use of the term *"bharat"* is significantly linked with conservative Hindu rhetoric, such as when RSS chief Mohan Bhagwat argued in 2012 that women are raped in India but not in *"bharat"* (*Press Trust of India*, *"Rapes Occur in 'India', Not in 'Bharat'"*). The fraught history of the word itself reveals that the epics, especially the *Mahabharata*, cannot be mentioned without recalling the always contested imaginings of India.

The constant resurfacing of the epic in literary productions shows that what is old, historical, or "traditional" does not simply vanish from the conceptions of the contemporary nation and its texts. Postcolonial texts in India and elsewhere often reveal that Independence and the official conferral of nationhood did not simply guarantee stability. Epic adaptations often emerge during moments of heightened national instability and show how thinkers attempt to grapple with new problems by both mobilizing and contesting premodern sociopolitical ideas. This demonstrates how Indian national culture is always in a state of renegotiation, constantly moving between interpretations of multiple pasts and presents.

Works Cited

Anderson, Benedict. *Imagined Communities: Reflections on the Origin and Spread of Nationalism*. 3rd ed. Verso, 2006.

Ali, S. Wajed. "Bharatbarsha" *Matriculation Bengali Selections*. Calcutta UP, 1938.

Amin, Shahid. "Gandhi as Mahatma." *Selected Subaltern Studies*, ed. by Gayatri Chakravorty Spivak and Ranajit Guha. Oxford UP, 1988, pp. 288–348.

Chakrabarty, Dipesh. *Provincializing Europe: Postcolonial Thought and Historical Difference*. Princeton University Press, 2008.

Chowdhury, Kanishka. "Revisioning History: Shashi Tharoor's Great Indian Novel." *World Literature Today*, vol. 69, no. 1, 1995, pp. 41–48. *JSTOR*, www.jstor.org/stable/40150855

Dhand, Arti. *Woman as Fire, Woman as Sage: Sexual Ideology in the Mahabharata*. State University of New York Press, 2008.

Eck, Diana L. *Darsan: Seeing the Divine Image in India*, Columbia UP, 1985.

Fanon, Frantz. *The Wretched of the Earth*. 1961. Penguin Books, 2001.

Hegarty, James. *Religion, Narrative, and Public Imagination in South Asia: Past and Place in the Sanskrit Mahabharata*. Routledge, 2011.

Malik, Yogendra K., and V. B. Singh. "Bharatiya Janata Party: An Alternative to the Congress (I)?" *Asian Survey*, vol. 32, no. 4, 1992, 318–336. *JSTOR*, https://doi.org/10.2307/2645149.

Mankekar, Purnima. *Screening Culture, Viewing Politics: An Ethnography of Television, Womanhood, and Nation in Postcolonial India*. Duke UP, 1999.

MensXP. "Shashi Tharoor's Reaction to a Comedian Mimicking Him Leaves People Looking for a Dictionary." *Mens XP*, 16 June 2020, https://www.mensxp.com/social-hits/news/77429-shashi-tharoors-reaction-to-a-comedian-mimicking-him-leaves-people-looking-for-a-dictionary.html.

Press Trust of India, "Digvijay Singh Takes a Dig at PM Narendra Modi's 'bhakts' after Spy-ring Bust." *The Economic Times*. 10 Feb. 2017, economictimes.indiatimes.com/news/politics-and-nation/digvijay-singh-takes-a-dig-at-pm-narendra-modis-bhakts-after-spy-ring-bust/articleshow/57085501.cms.

Press Trust of India, "Rapes Occur in 'India', Not in 'Bharat': RSS Chief." *Hindustan Times*, 4 Jan. 2013, www.hindustantimes.com/delhi/rapes-occur-in-india-not-in-bharat-rss-chief/story-KI7I22pPSgbqvrH5WRg3JL.html

The Economic Times. "Shashi Tharoor's 'Word of the Day' Is Algospeak, Twitter Comes up with Examples." *The Economic Times*, 20 July 2022, https://economictimes.indiatimes.com/news/new-updates/shashi-tharoors-latest-word-of-the-day-is-algospeak-twitter-comes-up-with-examples/articleshow/93004035.cms.

The Quint. "Shashi Tharoor Turns Quiz Master: Is Your Vocabulary up to Mark? | The Quint." *YouTube*, 15 Oct. 2019, https://www.youtube.com/watch?v=vNvNh9A4Lq4.

Rajagopal, Arvind. *Politics After Television: Religious Nationalism and the Reshaping of the Indian Public*. Cambridge University Press, 2001.

Rizwan, Sahil. "Shashi Tharoor's Extensive Vocabulary Became an Uproarious Meme Last Night Thanks to Arnab Goswami." *BuzzFeed*, 9 May 2017, https://www.buzzfeed.com/sahilrizwan/kya-bola-aapne.

Roy, Sneharika. "Postcolonial Epic Rewritings and The Poetics of Relation: A Glissantian Reading of Shashi Tharoor's *The Great Indian Novel* and Derek Walcott's *Omeros*." *Journal of Postcolonial Writing* vol. 51, 2015, pp. 59–71, https://doi.org/10.1080/17449855.2014.985030.

Sakshi Post. "Shashi Tharoor Uses New Word to Criticise BJP." *Sakshi Post*, 10 Jan. 2022, https://english.sakshi.com/news/national/shashi-tharoor-uses-new-word-criticise-bjp-149567.

"Shashi Tharoor ft. Kunal Kamra" *One Mic Stand*, directed by Kreeti Gogia and Angshuman Ghosh, dirs. Season 1, Episode, 5. Amazon Studios, 2019, https://www.amazon.com/One-Mic-Stand-Season-1/dp/B0875KHWDK.

Spivak, Gayatri Chakravorty. *An Aesthetic Education in the Era of Globalization.* Harvard University Press, 2012.

Tharoor, Shashi. *The Great Indian Novel.* Arcade, 1989.

9

ORALITY OF "THEN" AND "NOW"

Narrating the Mahabharata on Television

Sneha Roy Choudhury

> No Hindu ever reads the *Mahabharata* for the first time. And when he
> does get to read it, he doesn't usually read it in Sanskrit. A.K Ramanujan
> (Thapar, 2013: 58–59)

As the longer and the more complex of the two Indian epics, with 100,000
shlokas, it would be incorrect to categorize the Mahabharata as a work
widely read. Instead, the onus of its transference and preservation has fallen
upon oral, performative, and technologized narrations, true to the embedded narrative strategies locatable within the epic.

The text has also played a pivotal role in the formulation of a historical
consciousness, which, in turn, has been instrumental in shaping a tradition,
with its characteristic understanding of the past, transferred across changing social forms and to create a distinct social culture. This is emphasized
in the fact that the *Mahabharata* refers to itself as *itihasa*, a tale to be told
and retold, therefore propagated across generations (Majumdar, 1952: 38).
While traditional understanding has often equated *itihasa* with the Western
understanding of history, the term has incited more nuanced debates,[1] leading one to conjecture that the Indian understanding of history forms an
unbroken chain by which the past is indissolubly linked up with the present
(Chakrabarti & Bandyopadhyay, 2014: 38). These blurred lines in the understanding of history as *itihasa* are also indicative of the embedded "oral" in
the social culture. A second emphasis, on being repeated before posterity,
and on "telling" itself, as the narrative structure of the text envisages, coupled with the definite presence of bards, who chronicle the *itihasa*, forms
the locus of the argument of it having been part of an oral culture (*ibid*).
That the Mahabharata was said to have been an orally narrated text is well

DOI: 10.4324/9781003516408-11

known, although it taxes our modern mind and belief rather heavily, as the text consistently asserts that this gigantic composition was narrated orally (Ong, 2002: 23). Such stupendous feats of memory early Indians have been amply attested in other instances as well. The entire Vedic corpus was committed to memory and elaborate techniques were developed to help with memorization and correct recitation (Parry, 1971: 321). This is also foregrounded in the narrative structure of the text of the *Mahabharata*, particularly by including multiple levels of narration, which itself indicates the flow of the text down the ages, thereby contextualizing its journey for the present audience.

Understanding "Oral"

In order to situate the Mahabharata within orality, one needs to first overcome the chirographic and typographic bias which majority contemporary cultures have so deeply internalized that it has become the normative for thought and expression.[2] Having internalized a written culture, one tends to forget that there is no memory of words saved by the voice and the ear. We, who have lived our lives with books, have reached a point where the words on the printed page are more symbols for ideas than the record of speech; and it is our eyes which carry to our minds the author's thoughts rather than our ears. Yet if we would remember any sentence, even any phrase, we must say it to ourselves either aloud or beneath our breath, until the organs of our voice will repeat, at our bidding, the gesture of its utterance (Ong, 2002: 33–34).

Walter Ong, in *Orality and Literacy – The Technologizing of the Word*, attempts to critique this bias. He tries to understand the essential oral-aural consciousness that existed before the written word. Indeed, the written word is looked upon as an attempt to "pin down" (or pen down) thoughts as words, so as to make it easier to remember and to access. What, therefore, impedes an understanding of orality is the question about memory – how does one remember, record, and recollect in the absence of the written word? For Ong, besides the use of memorable stories, the key to this lies in the use of fixed formulaic structures, namely epithets, proverbs, or numerical sets, which are easiest to remember and retain. Therefore, primary oral culture[3] keeps its thinking processes close to the human life-world, personalizing things and issues, and storing knowledge in stories.[4]

If knowledge is thus stored in narratives, which are written down at a later date, after the advent of the written word, then, one may argue, on the lines of Milman Parry, that oral poetry is essentially an activity, accomplished by a group, rather than by individual effort. Since the poet in such a culture only has the spoken word at his disposal, the luxury of pondering over the next word, of rephrasing, or even looking back at his immediate composition is impossible. Even with a supposedly unusual memory, the oral poet cannot compose a poem of any length unless he uses word groups, made to fit his verse. He puts together phrases which he has himself heard or used before, grouping them in a fixed pattern of thought, which is but "natural" in the composition of the sentence and the verse. This also makes it easier for recollection because the poet is guided by the same play of words that he used before (Parry, 1971: 269–70).

The challenge of an oral culture is not just remembering but also recollecting the stories handed down through generations. The key to this is repetition: to preserve the essence of a culture, which is as transient as human memory, one must tell and retell. For the oral composer, "words" do not exist. What he uses in composing, instead, are expressions of ideas. Therefore, repetition, in the oral sensibility, does not imply word-by-word recollection, but a recollection of ideas which contrive a cultural whole. In this need to preserve an oral culture, its sensibility is targeted at holding things together, to make and retain agglomerates – the focus shifts from analysis, typical of a written culture, to retention and transfer of stories. The emphasis remains on the fact that if writing separates, orality accumulates (Parry, 1971: 270).

Even though the written text of the Mahabharata adequately foregrounds the fact that it is a narrative originating in orality as evident in its narrative technique and structures, once it passes into television, the chirographic/typographic bias builds up, and what is lost is the plurality of the text – a plurality arising from the innumerable times the text has been repeated orally, each repetition adding a new interpretation, thereby allowing the text to grow and develop into an *akhyana,* and then an *itihasa.*

One is, therefore, led to two conjectures. The first being that, while the oral is being erased, in favour of the written, a new and "objectified" body of knowledge is in turn created through manuscripts and later through the printed page. Objectification, here, implies the separation of the knower from the known. In an oral culture, the knower has no means of preserving knowledge (and therefore, culture) anywhere but in his own mind, recording it through an oral-aural interaction during the live narration itself. The knowledge, thus, is imbibed within the knower's self, rather than being objectified in the form of a written/printed text – an object, which one can hold and read.

The second conjecture is that the process reinstates the oral audience engaged in both learning and thereafter teaching, so as to transfer cultural knowledge. Their sensibility, then, has a delicate balance, allowing them to execute both social roles, of the learner and the teacher. In a written culture, however, the objectified text often takes over the role of teaching, and the reader, who is very much implied[5] in the text, is more engaged in the learning process. Even in handing cultural knowledge down the generations, what is actually handed over is the printed page, with its standardized content, and manipulated retention of an "oral" form. What is lost in the process, therefore, are the multiple retentions of the text among audiences – local versions of the story, which have been forgotten, as writing held the yardstick of authentication, thereby erasing the oral and the possibilities of plurality it invokes, in favour of a narrative of exclusion.

Situating the Mahabharata in Orality

The best way of knowing whether a style is oral and traditional is to hear it in use, or lacking that, to compare the recorded works of several poets who have made their verses out of the same formula (Hegarty, 2012: 50–53). However, in the absence of access to such sources, the written document, with its characteristic narrative structure, turns into an object of speculation. Scholars have discussed these techniques of narration and have therein linked them to the oral roots of the Mahabharata (Dayal, 2009: 193).

The layered narrative structure of the epic is best understood through the concept of "narrative frames," which is an obvious inheritance from its oral origins. James Hegarty understands this as placing stories within stories, wherein the content of each becomes the context of the others that follow. In this way, one may situate the layered narrative frame developed when Urgrasavas tells the story of Vaisampayana's recitation; or the added frame of Sanjaya's narration of the events of war to the blind monarch, Dhritarashtra (Thapar, 2009: 193).

The fact that intercultural exchanges took place in the form of storytelling is evident in the structure of frame narrations, which may be espoused through Naina Dayal's discussion of the many narrators within the epic is able to locate two categories of *Sutas*, namely, those attached to the court – they perform many roles, the charioteer, the bard, and the messenger (*Pratiloma Sutas* of mixed parentage); and the itinerant *Sutas* – they are the tellers of tales (*Pauranika Sutas* whose parentage is not mentioned) (Dayal, 2009: 193). Romila Thapar, however, suggests that as monarchy was consolidated, the bards' importance dwindled. The *Brahmanas* recognized the power involved in capturing and controlling the past and took over the oral records from the bards, converting them into more accessible written records[6] – the non-literate bard lost out to the literate *Brahmana* in maintaining the genealogies of those in power. The *Brahmanas*, on the other hand, used writing and Sanskrit; and when they appropriated and refashioned bardic lore, they also downgraded many of those from whom they had "purloined their material" (Eco, 1984: 3).

Multiple narrators imply multiple listeners, who are also purveyors of the tale (Hegarty, 2012: 7). The Mahabharata is indeed *A Forest of Stories*. Stories are used to propagate the complex philosophy of the text, and some, like the tales of Shakuntala and Dusyanta (*Adiparvan*) or of Nala-Damayanti (*Aranyakaparvan*), have become sagas in themselves, achieving an identity distinct from the master-text. The presence of narratives within the Narrative is indicative not only of the oral origins of the epic but also of the positioning of the listener within the text. On the lines of Umberto Eco, one may argue that the Mahabharata is a text, generated "cooperatively by the addressee" (*Ibid:* 13).

Indeed, the role of the listener is implied in more ways than this. In the *Svargarohanaparvan*, after having completed his tale, Sauti Ugrasravas addresses his audiences and narrates to them a *phalasruti* (*Svargarohanaparvan* 5. 24–52), listing the benefits of hearing the narration of this *kavya*. This not only emphasizes the centrality of the listener within the epic text but also reinforces James Hegarty's hypothesis regarding the role of the Mahabharatain shaping South Asian public imagination, where "narrative," itself was used as a means for instruction (Chakrabarti, 2014: 244). Thus

> the Mahabharata sought to constitute itself very self-consciously as *the* authoritative "reflective" or "theoretical resource for early South Asian religious and social life. In doing this, the text contributed to a major change in the form and content of public imagination in early South Asia. More specifically, the text presented a new orientation to both the significant past [time] and to significant place [space]. This new orientation was as much a matter of specific imaginative content as of establishment of the necessity of participation in story-telling and story-listening activities. The Mahabharata was a text that was intended *to be used* by an implied audience.
>
> *(Bandyopadhyay, 2016: 197)*

The presence of the listener within the narrative of the epic is also discernible from the fact that conversation is central to the dialectical moral thinking of the Mahabharata, echoing the pride of Classical Indian philosophy in ritual debate (Hegarty, 2012: 65–66). As it is, the narration is many-levelled; being so, different types of liaisons between *narrators* and *narrates* (meaning, the persons "inside" the text to whom the narrators are speaking) as well as actual recipients are intertwined in Vyasa's *itihasa*. This is closely aligned to the discourse of the "oral-formulaic," which Milman Parry and A.B. Lord have referred to. Therein, the characteristic oral poet is bound by tradition while writing as a technology, frees him of the bounds, invites individuality, but in turn destroys the participatory, composite culture of the oral.

Both the epic's conversational approach and the situation of its audiences within the narrative framework come together in the use of interjected vocatives – the terms of address such as "O brahmin" or "O king." These refer not to the characters who appear within a given story but to the person or persons who are hearing the narrative, reinstating the existence of a context of narration. They also refer back to that context even as a given "embedded" story progresses, so as to prepare the reader for a return to the place where the story is being told and heard (Deleuze, 2005: 280). Spatial linearity is, therefore, both challenged, yet curiously maintained.

Being an oral "text," the *Mahabharata,* in its employment of the techniques of narration, has challenged temporal linearity, in more ways than one – the chief among these being the employment of "flashback." Giles Deleuze, in his *Cinema 2: The Time-Image,* emphasizes the "archaic" air of the flashback. It is somewhat a closed circuit, which goes from the present to the past, then leads one back to the present, bearing the internal mark of the past from elsewhere. It belongs more rightfully to the realm of "descriptive actual-images" than to the realm of "subjective recollection-images," though it can also be employed for the purpose of shattering linearity and rebutting causality (Turim, 1989: 248–49). Flashback has also been understood as an instance of a time-reversal, during which the spectator-subject is transported back in time, radically contradicting the logic of positive time-entropy of the real world, implying a calculated omission of a time-span which is perceptible, but not quite measurable (Bandyopadhyay, 2016: 233). However, these temporal ruptures generated through flashbacks only apparently undermine the integrity of the narrative "whole" and themselves remain organic to the problems related to imagination, subjectivity, or multiplicity (Ramanujan, 2007: 427).

Sibaji Bandyopadhyay discusses the flashback with reference to the *Mahabharata* and with particular emphasis on its use in Sanjaya's warreportage, so as to cement his narration with the *dharma* espoused in the *Gita,* thereby emphasizing it as organic to the master narrative. He treats Sanjaya's *divya-chakshu* and the reportage that follows as an unarticulated commentary on the *Gita,* along with which the dual discourse on War and Peace is expostulated (Lord, 1960: 125). The flashback as a narrative technique used in orality, therefore, retains the capacity to broaden the narrative, spatially and temporally, without the evident standardizations it brings about in its usage as a written or visual device.

The oral narrator is free to formulate the flashback with absolute originality, both in terms of location and description. However, he remains tied down by the burden of propagation of an existing culture, as preserved in the narrations of his predecessors. The epic narrative houses ample such recollections, as *upakhyana*s, some of which have developed into independent narratives in their own right in later literature. These include the tales of Sakuntala, Nala-Damayanti, and even the *Gita* itself. These may also be allied to the technique of flashback, for instance, when Bhishma is about to take the vow of celibacy, the audience is reminded of Puru, who relinquished his youth to his father, Yayati, and is therefore blessed. The tale of Nala, too, is a reflection on Yudhisthira's own fate, whereby he gambles his kingdom and is out in egress. Ramanujan calls such *upakhyana*s "performative" in their capacity to project the past into the present and future, and in amassing repetitive networks and destiny to engender the heroes' lives, not as singular, but as tokens of a type (Ramanujan, 2007: 424). These take up various forms of narration – moral tales, discourses, or life accounts, but remain organic to the narrative, only broadening its spectrum and scope. Even in their appearance in the written text, where they take on a different bearing, they are evidently tinged with the obvious presence of the oral in them, thereby reinforcing the *Mahabharata* as an oral, plural epic.

Repetition is one of the aims of an oral narration – repetition, not of words, but of ideas, thereby producing a "composite text," which agglomerates ideas and expressions, so as to create and propagate a social culture (*Ibid:* 424). In the Mahabharata, repetition becomes one of the ways to guide the listener and ensure remembering. In the *Adiparvan,* there are three distinct abstracts of the main story, two in the very first chapter and one in the second. However, the "ethics" of repetition lend greater cultural significance to the abridged tales than simple word-to-word repetition, targeted at structuring memory. The first abstract (*Adiparvan 1.65–94*) is an objective, impersonal summary of events, relating to the reign of Pandu, leading to the Kurukshetra War. This is preceded by an invocation of the symbolic imagery of two trees, one of virtue and the other of wrath, signifying the clash of opposing values. This is followed by the second abstract, *Dhritarashtravilapa* (*Adiparvan* 1.95–159), which is a more subjective, personal, and heart-rending lament of a defeated king and a devastated father, recollecting his tragic destiny and inevitable doom. The third abstract is a more detailed summary of all the *parvans,* which are definitely targeted at inscribing the story in the minds of the listeners (Bhattacharya, 2014: 41–42). Thus, repetition becomes more than a device to aid word-to-word remembering – it is but a narrative trope itself targeted at a philosophical progression of the text, and its retention as a cultural memory.

A.K. Ramanujan extends the idea of repetition, beyond mere episodic repetitions to the recurrence of symbols and motifs within the Mahabharata, which foreshadow later events and recapture earlier ones (Chakrabarti, 2014: 244–283). For instance, the motif of fire occurs over and over again. Duryodhana conspires to burn the Pandavas in the house of lacquer, but in their stead a hunter woman (*Nisada*) and her five sons die – as later in Ashwatthama's rampage, the Pandavas' own five sons die as surrogates for the Pandavas (Mankekar, 1999: 224). The motif recurs in other episodes including the birth of Draupadi and Dhristadyumna, as well as the burning of Khandavprastha.

The typical techniques, namely multiple narrators, flashbacks, disruption of linearity and spatio-temporal chronology, and evolution as a conversational text,[7] are themselves, therefore, standards for recreating orality in a literate culture. The text in its "oral" form, therefore, can only exist among its audiences through their involvement – how they retain and recollect the text is what determines the survival of a culture. It may thus be argued that the process of standardization necessitates the retention of the form, but with a manipulation of the content. The "oral" emphasizes a plural form and content, while the written relies on structuring and singularizing both. This becomes more interesting with the introduction of the third paradigm, that of the visual, wherein the *Mahabharata* is narrated in performance and television.

Visualizing the *Mahabharata*

The *Mahabharata* is an ancient tale re-told by Indian television. Like all tales, its meanings acquire new valence with every telling. Serialized on Doordarshan from September 1988 to July 1990, it was watched by more than 200 million viewers throughout India (Hegarty, 2012: 192). One of the reasons the serial held the attention of viewers from different communities and drew "ratings" unsurpassed in Doordarshan's history was its deployment of a combination of techniques drawn from various sources, the modes of address and performative traditions of Hindi film melodrama, the use of background music and song, the narrative rhythms of soap operas, and the iconography of religious calendar art (Gonda, 1969: 9).

The role which television has played in integration of Indian audiences into a "national" whole has hardly been overstated. Media scholarship has focused on the history of Doordarshan, with particular emphasis on policy-making, to understand how television in India had been introduced and popularized as an important part of the project of national integration, bringing the diverse cultures within the nation into a mediated interaction with the equally diverse and ever-expanding audiences, thereby blurring the lines between the established categories of the local and the national, into the inclusive, transnational (Babb, 1981).

Moreover, the centrality of the visual in Hinduism has also contributed to the popularity of the mythological on television. The *Brihadaranyaka Upanishad* pronounces: I have seen, that is the truth (Mankekar, 1999: 230).

In scriptural Hinduism, as well as in religious practice, a sensuous approach to perception of the divine is adopted, within which the primacy of "seeing" is stark. The emphasis, here, is on *Darshana*. It implies "seeing," more specifically religious seeing or visual perception of the divine, as also on "being seen" through the "auspicious sight" of the divine. Beholding the image is an act of worship, and through the eyes one gains the blessings of the divine (Eck, 3). As Lawrence A. Babb notes: "It depends on the idea that seeing itself is extrusive, a medium through which seer and seen come into contact, and, in a sense, blend and mix" (Chakrabarti, 2014: 244–283). The experience of watching the Mahabharata on television, thus, for many could also become an act of worship, a televisual *darshana,* which can barely be understood in isolation from its religiosity.[8]

The essence of a civilizational epic, such as the Mahabharata, essentially lies in its oral origins – orality endows the epic with its characteristic inclusive space, wherein the narrator and the narratee are both participating in the narration, which itself is less didactic, and more conversational in its approach.[9] On the contrary, in the process of being written down, the epic narrative is standardized, whereby one narrative is attempted to be emphasized as the only possible direction in the multiplicity of stories. On television, too, the same story is repeated, pushing others into oblivion, in the attempt to present a unified "national" narrative before an otherwise diverse audience, as part of the state agenda of national integration.

Arguably, in standardizing the epic into a didactic text on television, what is significantly evident is its *Gita*-centrism. The opening sequence commences with a verse from chapter 2[10] and ends with one from chapter 4[11] of the *Gita*. Significantly, the sequence is accompanied by a slideshow of images, which depict Krishna and Arjuna on the chariot, either at war or during the prophetic *Gita* episode, and Krishna in his *Vishvaroop* (Bandyopadhyay, 2016: 18–27). The lyrics of the opening sequence, too, emphasize Krishna as the *sarathi,* harping back upon the *Gita* episode. This evident *Gita*-centrism contradicts the agenda of "national" integration which Doordarshan set forth in serializing the epic. This also reiterates the fact that the serial is based on the written text, V.S. Sukhthankar's *Critical Edition* is acknowledged, thereby caring little for the local epics that are lost in the process of constituting the standardized written one. In the episodes where the *Gitavachana* is depicted, Hindi dialogues are interspersed with Sanskrit *shlokas,* thereby making the standardization more obvious (*Ibid:* 31–32).

Scholars of the *Mahabharata* have examined this process of bringing Gita to the centre of discourse and have called this *Gita*-centrism. It seems that the process began with the pre-modern commentaries on the various verses of the *Gita,* particularly 2.47. However, in modern times the first clear evidence of making Gita the central text of the Indian non-Christian and non-Muslim population comes with Warren Hastings' commentary on Charles Wilkins' translation (Sharma, 1978: 263).

This *Gita*-centrism has indeed negated the orality of origin and spirit of the epic narrative – in being transferred from the oral, to the written, to the televised, the epic has, therefore, been standardized and structured across the process of its transference. One religious *Gita* is therefore created from the many *Gitas,* which appear in various forms in Puranic literature.

For example, the *Ishvara Gita* portrays Shiva as the supreme divinity, while the *Kapila Gita* is heavy in its reliance upon the epistemic authority of a god, despite the text being structured as a conversation between two human beings, sage Kapila and his wife; and the *Astavakra Gita,* again a conversation between two human beings, asserts the nature and glory of a supreme reality (*Ibid:* 264–65). *Anugita* too should be mentioned in this context. Besides, an extract of it appears in the *Ashvamedhikaparvan* of the *Mahabharata,* wherein Arjuna requests Krishna to repeat to him what he had heard before the Kurukshetra War. Krishna narrates the same, however, this time in the form of stories. Arvind Sharma has argued that "the *Bhagvadgita* recollected in tranquillity" (*Ibid*), instead of recapitulating the former, elaborates on the trichotomy of *karana, karta,* and *karma,* and introduces a new theme on the relation of thought and speech (Thapar, 2013: 202).

Along with the many *Gitas,* therefore, the catholic spirit of the *Mahabharata,* too, is neglected, across media performances of it. There has always been a tendency, in performance and media narrations of the epic, towards reinforcing unity in the *Mahabharata,* of creating a "one" from the spirit of the "many" which the epic exuberates. This, as argued within the scope of this research, has been a result of its transference from an oral culture to that of a written. The opening sequence of B.R. Chopra's *Mahabharat* is followed by an introduction of the narrator, *Kaal,* Time itself.[12] The visual images used for the representation of time are significant here – a *chakra* and the image of a sage, in the backdrop of a star-studded galaxy – these together represent Time, as cyclic and cosmological.[13] The narrator claims himself to be omnipresent and all-seeing and is therefore the only possible narrator of the epic saga – the one who has witnessed all the events in history unfold and pass before him.

If the image of the *chakra* represents cyclic time, the sage presumably represents Vyasa, the witness and the first narrator of the *Mahabharata.* Significantly, the other narrators, namely the *sutas,* are denied narratorial authority here, evidently distancing the narration from its earthly, oral roots and at the same time denying the conversational ethics of the epic saga, by severing possibilities of weaving new interpretive meanings into the story through wider participation, particularly from later audiences (Bandyopadhyay, 2016: 229).

In an oral narrative, one of the techniques of narration is the use of flashback. In orally narrating a tale, however, flashback, as a technique, has different forms and implications, distinct from its usage in written or televised narrations. In a many-layered, oral narrative, the flashback is important, and is often considered as a disruption to linear narration, taxing the listener's memory, though it serves to contextualize stories and characters within the larger narrative framework. The same technique, however, when applied in writing has different implications. Here, one needs to compare it with the same technique used in the cinematic mode. Giles Deleuze's observation about flashback in cinema reiterates it as a closed circuit which goes from the present to the past, then leads one back to the present (Bandyopadhyay, 2016: 233). The *kala*-narrator, in B.R. Chopra's *Mahabharat*, relates spatio-temporal shifts to his dialogues, and therein connects the tales narrated in flashback to the larger narrative. The tale of Krishna's childhood in Dwarka culminating in his killing of his demon-uncle, Kamsa, is narrated in this manner. Significantly, Indra serves as the narrative link between this narrative and that of the Mahabharata, when he requests Krishna to protect his son, Arjuna, after his *Vajra* and the torrential rainfall it brings to Gokul is neutralized when Krishna protects his people by lifting Giri Govardhana mountain on his little finger.

Another important flashback episode from the epic is that of Sanjaya's war-reportage to Dhritarashtra. Sibaji Bandyopadhyay finds Sanjaya's war reportage many layered. "At one level," Bandyopadhyay notes, "it is an after-account" (Bandyopadhyay, 2016: 229). "Being so," he continues, "the verbal form of Sanjaya's reportage is in the past tense. But given the flashback's working, the verbal form simultaneously indicates another order of narratorial tense. Sanjaya speaks in the *past-in-present* tense" (Hegarty, 2012: 196).

B.R. Chopra's narration hardly explores the narrative possibilities of Sanjaya's *divyacacshu*, but the 2013 Star Plus narration does better in this case. The war scene opens through the eye-divine, and progresses without going back and forth to Hastinapur. If Krishna's narration of the *Gita*, wherein he awakens in the dispirited Arjuna the will to battle, and Sanjaya's deferment of the descriptions of horrific incidents in the battlefield are connected to the point of being interactive, then the narrative style of the later serial seems more meaningful, presenting a better narration of the dual discourse on war and peace, as postulated by the two (Ramanujan, 2007: 435).

In analysing the televisual *Mahabharat*, James Hegarty points out how it exhibits a standardization beyond even the written: "The Sanskrit *Mahabharata*'s descriptions of almost all its major characters as incarnations of various divine and demonic beings in order to unburden the earth of a factitious warrior caste is replaced with a unified, Krsna-focussed doctrine" (*Ibid*: 435–36).

Indeed, standardization does not limit itself merely to *Gita*-centrism, but is evident in characterization and construction of the plot. Many minor characters are allotted no space in the television text, and many significant digressions and stories are omitted. In fact, the narrative ends with the death of Bhishma, and therefore, does not even cover all the *parvans* of the text. Thus, the attempt here is definitely to construct certain meanings from the text to interpolate a large audience with a religious message, rather than highlighting the plurality of the epic. Heroes are made out of characters, and their shady, rounded construct is ignored in contrast to the fact that the epic is a study of human frailties and the tragedy that it brings about.

In analysing the *Mahabharata*, A.K. Ramanujan points out that ambiguity is not merely notable in the narrative structure and the philosophy of the epic but is intensified by the

> ineradicable mixture of good and evil in each of the main characters. The Pandavas, with Krishna, who are "the good guys", manage to kill every Kaurava hero, Bhishma, Drona, Karna and Duryodhana, by foul means. And the Kauravas, especially Duryodhana and Karna, are not just villains but heroic and honest warriors despite everything.
>
> *(Mankekar, 1999: 225)*

Moreover, folklore and later retellings, like the Tamil Bharata of Villipputturar, the Kannada one, and a Tamil chapbook reinvent an episode in the *Vanaparva* to question Draupadi's chastity (*Ibid*: 229). The television *Mahabharat,* however, is unable to either uphold this inherent ambiguity or to attempt any oppositional readings of characters. Instead, in the presentation of characters and their attitudes, their righteousness or turpitude becomes evident. Part of it is also suggested through the costumes and the background music, thereby leading the audiences to a certain defined understanding of characters and situations. Purnima Mankekar, commenting on the semiosis of the interpretive processes, notes "texts are hardly open-ended and that viewers/readers are rarely, if ever, in a position to 'choose' the meanings they want to 'produce'" (Hegarty, 2012: 197).

Bhishma and the Pandavas are dressed in white, while Shakuni in black.[14] Thus, despite the characteristic resoluteness which marks both, they are placed as counterpoints to one another in the court scenes, particularly. Shakuni is hardly contextualized in B.R. Chopra's rendition. The 2013 production has attempted to bring out the nuances of his character by projecting him, both, as a caring brother and uncle, and resolute politician and manipulator. By so contextualizing characters, the later adaptation looks at them as more human and rounded entities, but in B.R. Chopra's adaptation, deification is starkly evident, thereby formulating flat characters, devoid of the essential "greyness" which, I have argued, is but one of the major concerns of the epic narrative in keeping with its larger open-ended enquiry into *dharma*.

Conclusion

This journey of the Mahabharata, as a civilizational epic, from "then" to "now," has been situated within the scope of this chapter, as a journey across multifarious cultures of narration, oral, written, and visual. It becomes imperative, in conclusion, therefore, to situate the socio-cultural implications of such a reading. The televisual *Mahabharata* presents the past in such a way that it is closed off from debate and subordinated to the delineation of a national ideal. It also articulates a view of India that suggests that it is "aboriginally" democratic; it is Hindu and indeed Vaishnavite; that it is culturally Gangetic and Hindi speaking, and is characterized by the triumphal aspect of the epic, in denial of the interrogative.[15] It is this religiosity wherewith at crucial historical junctures the televised epics have been telecast on television. While the first telecast is linked to the consolidation and mobilization of a Hindu nationalist agenda, the second telecast of 2020,[16] amongst an audience, locked down in their houses due to the COVID-19 pandemic, may also be read as part of a similar agenda in the wake of sporadic riotous outbreaks in the national capital surrounding the NRC-CAA protests.[17] The argument, then, emphasizes a return to the open-ended universalistic spirit of the Mahabharata as narrated socially by the *Sutas* to their implied audiences, and domestically by grandparents to children – a narrative essentially locally conceived and contextualized.

Notes

1 Though Vyasa had "seen" the war, the present narration is received, not from the "seer," but from its "hearers," since both Vaisampayana and Ugrasravas had "heard" the epic being narrated at different points in time. This emphasis on hearing, as will be argued here, is indicative of the oral inception and propagation of the text, and at the same time of the importance of listeners, themselves narrators of this oral history.

2 Primary orality is the orality of cultures where writing is unknown while secondary orality refers to the electronic orality of radio and television. Ong, Walter. *Orality and Literacy* (1982), Routledge, London, 2002, pp. 34–35.

3 Separation is manyfold – detaching the knower from the known (by creating new knowledge, technologized in print or electronics, for a knower to locate and interpret), separating interpretation from data, estranging word from sound, distancing the source of communication from the recipient (by creating spatial and temporal distance between the writer/narrator and the reader/audience), rifting the past from the present (instead of using the past to explain the present, writing creates a distanced past, hardly relatable), creating abstraction, and parting the being from time – these are a few ways it accomplishes separation (Ong, 1986).

4 See Eco, Umberto. *The Role of the Reader: Explorations in the Semiotics of Texts,* Indiana University Press, Bloomington, 1984.

5 See Bandyopadhyay, Sibaji. *Three Essays on the Mahābhārata: Exercises in Literary Hermeneutics,* Orient Blackswan, New Delhi, 2016 and Dayal, Naina. *Tellers of Tales: Pauranikas, Sutas, Kusilava Vyasa* and Valmiki, http://hdl.handle.net/10603/17668, Centre for Historical Studies, JNU, 2009.

6 Ashok Banker's title for his retelling of the Mahabharata, which the author claims is a paraphrase of the entire text, verse for verse, from the Sanskrit "original" – the chirographic influence is aptly stated.

7 Arvind Rajagopal equates melodrama with the mythological, as represented on television. See Rajagopal, Arvind. 2001, pp. 96–97.

8 Your right is only in the action and not the fruit of it.
  Let not the results of action be your motive, nor let yourself be attached to inaction (Translation mine)
  Bhagvad Gita, Chapter 2, Verse 47
9 Whenever righteousness wanes, O Bharata; and the nefarious is rampant, I evince myself.
  I manifest from Age to Age, to save the devout and destroy the unholy. (Translation mine)
  Bhagvad Gita, Chapter 4, Verse 7–8
10 Carl Becker notes:
  Essentially, the Vishwarupa is the story of evolution... It is the greatest story that can ever be told because it includes all stories.
  (Becker, Carl J. *A Modern Theory of Evolution,* iUniverse Inc, New York & Bloomington, 2010, p. 330)
11 Krishna, while delivering the message of the *Gita* in Hindi, quotes from several verses of it and the scene continues through his commentaries on the *shlokas* in Hindi.
12 Conversation, including requests for narration it has been argued on various platforms, has been central to Indian philosophy.
  See Hegarty, James. 2012, p. 64.
  See also Chakrabarti, Arindam. 2014, p. 244.
13 Deleuze, quoted in Bandyopadhyay, Sibaji, 2016, pp. 227.
14 See Verma, Rahul. "The Ramayan: Why Indians are Turning to Nostalgic TV," *BBC,* May 2020. Accessed 15 August 2020 https://www.bbc.com/culture/article /20200504-the-ramayan-why-indians-are-turning-to-nostalgic-tv
15 See See Pokharel, Krishna. "India Citizenship Protests Spread to Muslim Area of Capital," *Wall Street Journal,* 17 December 2019 Accessed 15 August 2020 https://www.wsj.com/articles/india-protests-against-new-law-spread-to-muslim -area-of-capital-11576596978
16 For a brief account of the translators, see (Modi 96–99).
17 For a complete translation, see Husain 275–80; Ernst 180–82.

Works Cited

Babb, Lawrence A. "Glancing: Visual Interaction in Hinduism." *Journal of Anthropological Research,* vol. 37, no. 4: 1981, pp. 387–401.

Bandyopadhyay, Sibaji. *Three Essays on the Mahābhārata: Exercises in Literary Hermeneutics,* Orient Blackswan, New Delhi, 2016.

Basu, Rajshekhar. *Krishnadvaipayan Vyas Krita Mahabharat,* M.C Sarkar & Sons Private Limited, Calcutta, 1949.

Buitenen, J.A.B. van trans. ed. *The Mahabharata, Book 1: The Book of the Beginning,* The University of Chicago Press, Chicago & London, 1973.

Chakrabarti, Arindam & Bandyopadhyay, Sibaji ed. *Mahābhārata Now: Narrative, Aesthetics, Ethics,* Routledge, New Delhi, 2014.

Chopra, Ravi. *Mahabharat,* B.R. Films, 1988.

Dandekar, Ramchandra Narayan ed. 'The Anusasanaparvan', *The Mahabharata* (Vol. 1, Part I), Bhandarkar Oriental Research Institute, Poona, 1997.

Dayal, Naina. *Tellers of Tales: Pauranikas, Sutas, Kusilava Vyasa and Valmiki,* Centre for Historical Studies, JNU, 2009. http://hdl.handle.net/10603/17668.

Eck, Diana L. *Darsan: Seeing the Divine Image in India.* Columbia University Press, New York, 1984.

Eco, Umberto. *The Role of the Reader: Explorations in the Semiotics of Texts,* Indiana University Press, Bloomington, 1984.

Hegarty, James. *Mahābhārata in Religion, Narrative and Public Imagination in South Asia,* Routledge, London, 2012.

Hiltebeitel, Alf. *Rethinking The Mahabharata,* University of Chicago Press, Chicago & London, 2001.

_____. *The Ritual of Battle: Krishna in the Mahabharata,* State of New York Press, Albany, 1990.

Karve, Irawati. *Yuganta,* Orient Longman, New Delhi, 1991.

Lord, A.B. *The Singer of Tales,* Harvard University Press, London, 1960.

Majumdar, Subodhchandra ed. *Kashidashi Mahabharat,* Deb Sahitya Kutir Private Limited, Kolkata, 2006.

Mankekar, Purnima, *Screening Culture, Viewing Politics: An Ethnography of Television, Womanhood & Nation in Postcolonial India,* Duke University Press, London, 1999.

McLuhan, Marshall. "Electronics and the Changing Role of Print." *Audio Visual Communication Review,* vol. 8, no. 5, 1960, pp. 74–83.

Mitra, Ananda. *Television and Popular Culture in India: A Study of the Television Mahabharat,* Sage Publications, New Delhi, 1993.

Ong, Walter. *Orality & Literacy,* Routledge, London, 2002.

Parry, Adam ed. *The Making of Homeric Verse: The Collected Papers of Milman Parry,* Clarendon Press, London, 1971.

Rajagopal, Arvind. *Politics After Television: Religious Nationalism & the Reshaping of the Indian Public,* Cambridge University Press, London, 2001.

Ramanujan, A.K. "Where Mirrors Are Windows: Toward an Anthology of Reflections." *History of Religions,* vol. 28, no. 3, 1989, pp. 187–216.

Sharma, Arvind. "The Role of the Anugītā in the Understanding of the Bhagavadgītā." *Religious Studies,* vol. 14, no. 2, 1978, pp. 261–267.

Sukhthankar, Vishnu S. ed. 'The Adiparvan', *The Mahabharata* (Vol. 1, Part I), Bhandarkar Oriental Research Institute, Pune, 1933.

Thapar, Romila. *The Past Before Us: Historical Traditions of Early North India,* Harvard University Press, London, 2013.

Turim, Maureen. *Flashbacks in Film: Memory and History,* Routledge, London, 1989.

10

PSYCHOBIOGRAPHY AND AUTHORIAL SUBJECTIVITY IN THE (RE) PRESENTATION OF DRAUPADI

Towards a Feminist Mythopoeia in Select Retellings of the Mahabharata[1]

Komal Agarwal

> *We'd had to cobble it together from rumors and lies, dark hints Dhai Ma let fall, and our own agitated imaginings. Perhaps that was why it changed with each telling. Or is that the nature of all stories, the reason for their power?*
>
> – Panchaali in *The Palace of Illusions*
> (Divakaruni15, italics in original)[2]

Anecdotes, stories, narratives, and myths are treasures humans inherit from their predecessors, and for as long as they survive, this treasure trove will perpetually be circulated – albeit in myriad ways – through innovations, re-narrativizations, and retellings of familiar myths, tales, narratives, and chronicles. However, one is inclined to interrogate what necessitates contemporary renditions of traditional material and at what point in the history of cultural phenomena does a retelling become necessary? Is it owing to some inadequacy, some gap/fissure in the original, the desire for further aestheticization of available material, or merely the spirit of experimentation and inquiry that fuels such retellings? Other questions such as what is the mechanism employed and who are the readers/consumers of the retellings also merit attention. Of course, such questions assume greater significance when the retellings being discussed are those of the monumental epic, the Mahabharata.[3]

This chapter investigates the politics of narration in the (re)presentation of the character Draupadi in select retellings of the Mahabharata namely in Pratibha Ray's *Yajnaseni* and Chitra Banerjee Divakaruni's *The Palace of Illusions*, employing a feminist myth critical lens. The chapter primarily investigates the following conundrums: who re-narrates Draupadi's story,

DOI: 10.4324/9781003516408-12

why and how does she revisit a mythical paradigm to (re)tell a familiar story, and what role does authorial subjectivity play in the process vis-à-vis the psyche of the central hero(ine)? Can one postulate that the authors retelling Draupadi's story attempt to recreate a psychobiography of a character who remains a perennial favourite with people in the Indian subcontinent? Can one posit that such retellings are a blend of psychobiography of the central character and the author's own subjectivity, and that this admixture of the two psychoanalytic approaches constitutes the author's feminist myth critical approach to the epic?

In addition to interrogating the questions outlined above, the chapter argues that with each retelling, the narrative of Draupadi becomes more and more poignant, pointing to a sense of inherent continuity in the apparent discontinuities of time, place and milieu. This chapter further establishes that the numerous retellings of the epic from the vantage point of Draupadi constitute a watershed contemporaneous moment in the continuum of epic and narrative literature on the Mahabharata, ensuring not only a sustained perpetuation and progression of Draupadi's life story, but also informing the epical "time-loop" by throwing into sharp relief the oldest version of the Draupadi story ever told! At the same time, all such revisionist recreations/retellings, taken together, form a meta-character/meta-narrative of Draupadi. Thus, Draupadi – in the present discussion, as also any other epical character – and the epic Mahabharata will forever remain contemporaneous, germane, and appurtenant.

Scholars of the Mahabharata propose that the epic should not be read as a singular, unitary text, but as a text that is simultaneously constituted by and constitutes all its literary, creative, performative, critical, and ritualistic renditions.[4] Alf Hiltebeitel observes that

> one must ... interpret the Mahabharata not only retrospectively but, in a sense, prospectively. Possibly the epic simply anticipates later forms ... . It is ... impossible to study the epic as a story frozen in its Sanskrit textual forms.
>
> (When the Goddess 57–58)

In the literary sphere apropos of the epic, one comes across an almost insatiable, endless number of retellings in various Indian languages as well as in English.[5]

Malinowski is of the opinion that

> [q]uestions about myths may need to go beyond the literary level of a myth, beyond the text, to the situation and *intentions* of their collective

or individual creation ... myths are not mere "texts"; they are at least texts in contexts.

(qtd. in Strenski xxi)

What Malinowski notes about myths is equally true of the retellings or adaptations of myths. It is interesting to analyse how the writers who retell/ adapt the epic reinterpret the characters and incidents in the epic, how they (re)present the mythical past and the long epical tradition, and especially, the ways in which they employ myths to their creative ends. Writers of retellings step into the gaps and fissures of the "epic original" or the "original myth" and creatively play with or tie up the loose ends. In so doing, the writers of retellings breath fresh air into old tales, place their protagonist centre stage, replenish the mundane details with vibrant descriptions or maybe even a few imaginary incidents, and weave an altogether new world in their retellings.

Perhaps no other woman in Vyasa's epic plays such a pivotal role as Draupadi. The narrator of the battle books in the innermost frame of the epic, Sanjaya, refers to her as *"rajaputri satyavrati varapatni saputri manasvini'*a princess, virtuous, wife of warriors, mother of sons, esteemed" (McGrath 116). However, one often tends to forget that Draupadi was also "quite human with human emotions and feelings like anger, love, hate, happiness and grief," she was both "flawed and paradoxically human" (Bhawalkar 141; Mukhoty 22).

Writers, playwrights, and artists alike have been fascinated by the character of Draupadi since times immemorial. Bhattacharya notes how she became "the central figure in a number of bardic epics between the twelfth and fifteenth centuries" (102). In recent times, there has been an astounding resurgence in engagement with the character of Draupadi by creative writers.[6] While retellings from the vantage point of other significant women of the epic, namely Kunti and Gandhari, as well as other female characters both from the main narrative as well as the sub-narratives of the epic – like Karna's wife, Satyavati, and Shakuntala – have been flooding the market in the last two decades, the re-narrativizations from the vantage point of Draupadi undoubtedly rule the roost.[7]

Interestingly, most of the critically acclaimed retellings of Draupadi's story are by women writers. Maggie Humm's elucidation of why women writers are drawn to myths comes in handy:

Literature, especially the novel, offers a writer the space and complexity necessary to represent *probable* truths as well as "truthful" reality ... many women writers turn to myths as familiar frames which can be reshaped ... to give a truer picture of women's experience.

(Practicing 24)

Elsewhere, Humm also suggests that myths appeal to women because they often portray "the informal and the private experience of women's lives.... What had previously been dismissed as trivial, ordinary or gossip has been collected by feminist myth-critics and recreated as wives' new tales" (*Reader's Guide* 60). In trying to salvage the women characters from the hubris of a largely male-dominated literary discourse, the writers of the retellings paint an empathetic, often empowering, and possibly also a "private" and "truthful" picture of the women in the epic.

Ray and Divakaruni investigate, in their respective novels, how Draupadi's life is determined by the choices that are thrust upon her by the patriarchal society while also exploring the subversive possibilities latent therein, also probing if Draupadi has been successful in employing them and challenging the gendered dimensions of the society. In so doing, Ray and Divakaruni use Draupadi as their mouthpiece and employ the method adopted by Susie Tharu and K. Lalitha for their project of identifying women's writing in India starting 600 BC. In outlining the major principle behind their choice of texts for their anthology of women's writings which runs into two volumes, Tharu and Lalitha explain that they were interested in "[w]hat modes of resistance did ... [women] fashion? How did they avoid, question, play-off, rewrite, transform, or even undermine the projects set out for them?" (40)[8]

Pratibha Ray's *Yajnaseni* is an epistolary novel. Writing a long letter towards the very end of her life to Krishna, her friend and spiritual companion in the novel, Yajnaseni affirms that she is writing a "blood-drenched autobiography"; the dying Draupadi pleads to Krishna: "Only let me tell my story – standing at death's door" (Ray 3–5). When she falls during her last journey to heaven at Himavant, she wishes to recollect all that transpired in her life, laying bare "each hair-raising incident" of her life so that "the people of Kaliyuga will be able to decide whether the insults Draupadi suffered have ever been borne by any woman of anytime" (Ray 4). Divakaruni structures *The Place of Illusions* like a bildungsroman, where she traces the trajectory of the life of Draupadi right from her birth, to her childhood, adolescence, and her coming of age mainly though her own efforts at self-education and assisted by "lowly" or othered women like her Dhai Ma (her nurse and mother-figure), her sister Shikhandi, and a sorceress who miraculously enters her life for a brief period to give her crucial lessons in life, love, and survival strategies. Divakaruni's mythical tale unfurls through the eyes of Panchaali, who "resonates the aspirations and anguish; the agony and ecstasy of every female in a timeless world" (Multani 221).[9]

Explaining the significance of myths with respect to women's subjective experiences and social formations, Maggie Humm opines:

> Myths can depict in imaginary and symbolic form some of the social processes affecting women.... [Hence,] many women writers turn to myths

as familiar frames which can be reshaped and remade to give a truer picture of women's experience.

(Practicing 24)[10]

Ray's Yajnaseni is on a spiritual quest, and is patient, mature, and wise. Divakaruni's Panchaali is young and spirited, impatient and resolute. Placing a woman at the centre of an epic or choosing a female narrator is indeed a significant departure from the established conventions of epic narrative. Explaining the feminist politics behind her aesthetic choice, Divakaruni asserts:

[P]lacing a woman in the center of your work is radical enough, giving her the humanity, allowing her to tell her story. It makes her into a hero because she is interpreting the world for us through her eyes .... [My] Panchaali ... is the teller of everything, and everything in the book is what she has seen, heard, and interpreted, sometimes on a literal level, but sometimes through dream visions, which is also a part of the mythic tradition.

("Power of Storytelling" 92)[11]

Pratibha Ray also outlines her motivations behind writing Yajnaseni: "It has been my lot to speak for such persons in society who are grossly misunderstood and ... seem to be mute, inarticulate or voiceless ... they challenged me to portray their true faces" ("Sky is Not" 83).

At several places in her novel, Divakaruni highlights the act of telling a story or re-telling a mythical story/epic poem by employing fascinating revisionist strategies. Divakaruni's Panchaali expresses wonder at her discovery that "a story gains power with retelling" (Divakaruni 20).[12] Later in the text, Panchaali exclaims: "Stories were important. Even when I was a child, I'd realized that they had to be understood and preserved for the future, so that we didn't make the same mistakes over and over" (Divakaruni 270).

Elaborating upon the potential that myths hold with respect to a recreation of women's subjective experiences and history, Maggie Humm writes, "Mythology can help to reformulate traditional historical accounts of women's lives with female centred stories" (Practicing 17). Lakshmi Bandlamudi poses a very significant question regarding the social or political relevance of such an exercise, of using a mythic-epic story to understand social and gender relations in contemporary times. She begins by asking, "Is Draupadi a necessity for the present day in order to wage the current gender battle?" and answers it in the same breath: "[O]ne needs to 'reclaim' her and 'reconstitute' her to suit the individual and cultural needs. In such a reconstitution," she is careful to point out, "she simultaneously becomes both a victim and a victor" (141).

A significant strategy to rewrite women's history is to deconstruct and defamiliarize existing myths, especially with respect to the female characters: their portrayal, absences, silences, and voices have to be punctured, and their deification and divinization undone. Another allied measure adopted by writers of retellings is to humanize their characters, empathizing with her "impossible longings," "small betrayals," and "need for justice above everything else" (Mukhoty 22).[13] Vyasa's *Mahabharata*, the length of which exceeds one lakh verses, does not even spare a verse or two for delving into the heart of Draupadi, or describing her reactions to the purpose of her birth, the incidents of her girlhood, she being unwittingly pushed into perilous situations throughout the course of her life, especially at the time of her *svayamvara* and her lack of choice in a ceremony of choice, the event of polyandry thrust upon her by her mother-in-law and its ramifications, the unforgettable humiliation and violence she experiences during the fateful game of dice, or even her fall during the final journey which she undertakes along with her husbands. A significant intervention on the part of Ray and Divakaruni is their exploration of the interiority and the subjectivity of their central characters. Both of them provide a considerable narrative depth to the individual psychological tendencies and conflicts in the mind of Draupadi.

Any avid listener/reader of the epic would be disappointed in the fact that Draupadi is born as a full-grown woman from a sacrificial altar, and one is deprived of the anecdotes of her childhood and adolescence. It is interesting to note that in both the novels, Draupadi grows up in the absence of the loving care and upbringing of a mother. This is supplanted by Ray and Divakaruni, who bring to their readers the tales of Draupadi's "formative" years; the novelists explore at length the trials and tribulations of Draupadi as a young girl. They take the readers through an exploration of Draupadi's psyche and her heart as she jostles her way through life.

Prema Jagannathan maintains that Draupadi emerges as "the archetypal victim, a much wronged woman" (92). One can take, for instance, the story of how Draupadi was married to five brothers at the command of her mother-in-law Kunti.[14] There is a significant silence in Vyasa's epic about the reaction of Draupadi to such a proposal: "[N]obody asked Draupadi what *her* thoughts and feelings were on this subject" (Badrinath 182). What makes matters worse is that except Draupadi's father, the command of Kunti is attested to by several men in positions of authority, both in the epic as well as the two novels.[15] Both Yudhishthira and Vyasa provide by way of examples precedents of polyandrous marriages in the scriptures.[16] Whatever the reasons provided by the men and Kunti, one cannot dismiss the fact that the Pandavas seek to remain united and establish dharma by partaking of the common female body; a woman and her sexuality are reduced to the status of playthings in the hands of male sexual desire.[17]

Draupadi's life arouses curiosity as well as invites barbed comments, especially because of her multiple marriages, all of which boils down to an understanding of her "hyper-sexuality.'[18] Many scholars have attempted to understand Draupadi's polyandry not as a reality, but in symbolic terms.[19] Gurcharan Das maintains that though polyandry was not widely practised, but suggests that Draupadi's polyandrous marriages can be read as "the epic throwing a challenge to the audience's paradigm of patriarchy" (44). Moreover, Draupadi's epical silence on such a momentous – and arguably also tragic moment in her life – ensures that Ray and Divakaruni step in with their feminist lens, de-divinize Draupadi and humanize her reaction to the situation. As Hiltebeitel explains:

> The *Mahabharata* keeps Draupadi quiet on the *dharma* of her polyandry, but folklores and modern fictions give her plenty of complaints ... [the audience/readers can see how] the questionable *dharma* of her marriage implies her complicity in its outcome no less than her mother-in-law's, her husbands', the author's, and Kaurava's ... One can only imagine what she was thinking.
>
> *(Dharma 495)*

Ray's and Divakaruni's retellings of the episode take us through the mental agony that Draupadi suffered, the tumult in her heart, the muted protest that her mind raged with, while also recreating the situation in which her silence might have been justified, or her objections might have gone unheeded. Ray's Yajnaseni flares up at the suggestion and is deeply disturbed about her very name becoming tainted for all of posterity. The predicament of having to marry five men baffles her: "My mind rebelled. Did I have no say? Then what was the meaning of *svayamvar*? ... Why should I accept the other brothers as husbands? ... Why should I silently bear such an insult?" (Ray 56)[20] It was a "desperate dilemma" for Yajnaseni which she holds to be far worse than the predicament of Sita in the *Rāmāyaṇa* (Ray 62). Divakaruni's Panchaali is flabbergasted, as if turned into a stone: "I stared at her... Was she joking when she said they must all marry me? ... I wanted to shout, Five husbands? Are you mad? I wanted to say, I'm already married to Arjun!" (Divakaruni 108). Panchaali feels cheated and humiliated at the hands of Kunti.

At the same time, one must point out that Divakaruni juxtaposes history, myth, and magic with elements of the modern and contemporary in her novel. Zupančič, making an interesting observation about Divakaruni's narrative stylistics, observes how she combines "the human and the divine" in a mode of "spiritual writing" ("Storytelling" 89). Elsewhere, Zupančič lauds Divakaruni for ensuring that she "did not make Draupadi into a goddess, while taking the freedom to render this character's psyche and her quest much closer to the modern perception of self-affirmation" ("Feminine

Myths" 19). In yet another move to subvert the male stereotypes of epic conventions, Divakaruni invests Panchaali with extraordinary powers of dreams and visions, which enable her to witness the war scenes of the epic story which were traditionally not revealed/accessible to women.[21] In her feminist revisionist representation of Draupadi, the author re-examines to borrow an apt description from Vaishali, "the most ancient and universal of myths re-articulated by Simone de Beauvoir in *The Second Sex*: women as sorceress, an enchantress, casting a spell over men and women as a formidable enigmatic 'other'" (212).[22]

However, Divakaruni's Panchaali becomes etched in the memory of her readers because she is as much a dreamer as a fierce realist; she is unique but also quite human and hence relatable for her readers. Ray's Yajnaseni is philosophical and wise, but also feels the basic human instincts and pains of love, separation, jealousy, and motherhood as passionately as any woman in her position would, while also holding close her spiritual friendship with Krishna, her guide, and ultimate refuge.[23]

"Myths are particularly important sources of alternative history for groups denied a place in mainstream culture," writes Humm (*Practising* 25). Writers of retellings bring fresh perspectives to a mythological retelling, thereby also creating an alternative historical account, by usually bringing one character centre stage. Both Divakaruni and Ray make their novels about the quest of their heroine, Draupadi: the novels are about the exploration of her identity, her coming home to love, and ultimately, the dawning of and fulfilment of her purpose in life. This is indeed a remarkable feminist departure from the preoccupation of myths with the journey of a male hero. The novelists delineate the heroism of their central female characters: they trace the trajectories of the many fights they wage against patriarchy and societal norms, and their resilience in the face of pain and suffering. In a nutshell, the novelists flesh out the biographical details of an unforgettable and immortal fictional character, Draupadi.

While Pratibha Ray identifies the preservation of dharma on earth to be the purpose behind Yajnaseni's birth, Divakaruni indicates right at the beginning of her work that Panchaali is born to change history:

At my birth there was a prophesy: "This woman has taken birth to avenge your insult. She has appeared to fulfil a vow. By her, dharma will be preserved on this earth, kshatriyas will be destroyed. She will be the destroyer of the Kauravs."

(Ray 8)

And then the voices came again. They said, *Behold, we give you this girl, a gift ... Take good care of her, for she will change the course of history.*
(Divakaruni 4–5, italics in original)

The novelists also spend considerable time discussing the life of Draupadi from the dicing match and its consequences, the cataclysmic war and its aftermath, and the depiction of the final journey to heaven.[24] "Panchaali is continuously forced to recreate her own universe and to learn from her mistakes, her hubris, and mainly from her deep yearning," writes Zupančič ("Wisdom and Compassion" 111).

The novelists also discuss love and sexuality in relation to Draupadi: she does not have reservations against expressing her love, hinting at her thwarted love, and according significance to material relationships. Both Ray and Divakaruni provide her with the opportunity to imagine the exploration of love elsewhere: Draupadi harbours spiritual love for Krishna in *Yajnaseni*, and longs for Karna in *The Palace of Illusions*. Though their desires do not find fulfilment, the novelists do give their central characters the freedom to explore love other than marital love. Iravati Karve reiterates: "The Draupadi of the Mahabharata stormed and raged, but to the last moment she remained a faithful wife" (95). Needless to say, Karve's observation holds true for the epic Draupadi as well as the one in the two novels.[25]

In Draupadi's life quest in the two novels, war and massacre, which have traditionally been male prerogatives, are viewed as absolute unnecessities. Both Panchaali and Yajnaseni seem to be asking a poignant question with respect to wars: why cannot there be a world of love and harmony, rather than war and bloodshed? In Divakarni's novel, a night before the war, Krishna imparts the same lessons to Panchaali in her dream as he would to Arjun at the start of the war. This is a significant feminist intervention by the author: the teachings of the *Gita* are imparted to her before they are to Arjun. It is also a significant rupture in the convention of men being the recipients of spiritual experiences. Also, Divakaruni's Panchaali virtually participates in the war in viewing the gory scenes of the war through the gift of the divine vision – the violence and the bloodshed, thousands of innocents being razed to dust, the killing and mutilation of her own kith and kin – unlike the epic where the proceedings of the day are just reported to women in their camps every evening. One can only imagine the horror that Panchaali takes upon herself as a result! However, in the process, the reality of the world of men and wars is also laid bare before the eyes of a woman: "I realized then that the sight allowed me to penetrate the masks of men and look into their core, and I was at once elated and terrified" (Divakaruni 261). Ray evades a detailed description of the war, and her narrative fast forwards to only some significant episodes of the war. Of course, her silence on the war speaks a million words! After the war, Divakaruni's Panchaali resolves to form a separate court for women, presided over by women, namely Kunti, Gandhari, Subhadra, Uttara and herself "a place where women could speak their sorrows to other women" (Divakaruni 323). As Divakaruni would elaborate with numerous instances, the women prove to be astute administrators too.

Both the novelistic narratives close with an analysis of the *mahaprasthanam* (the final journey) that Draupadi undertakes with her husbands, and give alternative accounts of her fall. Draupadi is not too keen on proceeding on the final journey but is nevertheless coerced into following Yudhisthira to heaven. Shattered by the indifference of Yudhishthira – when he does not turn back to rescue Draupadi when she falls, nor does he allow any of her other Pandava husbands to reach out to her – Yajnaseni regrets why she had to "bear the burden of the whole world's mockery, sneers, innuendos, abuse, scorn, and slander for the sake of preserving Yudhishthir's dharma" (Ray 3). Panchaali muses:

> It was clear that we wouldn't last long enough to reach any peak, sacred or otherwise... . But what I resented was this: when we fell, our failure would be ascribed not to a physical limitation but a moral one
>
> *(Divakaruni 245)*[26]

In Ray's novel, Yajnaseni rejects *moksa* (liberation from the cycle of births and deaths), which has remained a largely male desire in the Indian philosophical discourse in favour of rebirth. In Divakaruni's novel, Panchaali proceeds to inhabit a formless, genderless world. Draupadi's grit and determination in the face of violence, hardships, and pain result in her final triumph at the hands of the novelists, when she is redeemed from her husbands – hopefully, forever. Daschaudhuri writes, "The two narratives may differ in their vision and style, yet, both these narratives succeed, in their unique way, to deconstruct the image of a deified ideal wife" (177). By the end of the two novels, the readers get a fuller picture of Draupadi, who unquestionably emerges as the real hero who continues to the finishing line and wins over all odds.

Hiltebeitel makes a considerable observation about the new, "reconstituted" narratives of Draupadi:

> Each heroine ... is "the subject of a fragmented countertext ... that the poets leave readers to piece together from segments where she is part of the main story and patches where she is the subject of selected memories—not only others' memories but her own." The two epics tell us enough about ... their chief heroines to allow a scholar, novelist, a filmmaker to reconstruct their biographies.
>
> *(Dharma 484)*

The reconstruction of the heroine is thus a two-fold exercise: going back to the original "fragmented countertext," and rummaging through one's memory as well as that of the subject of recreation, and this holds true both for the creative writer and the readers. "Myths are created by writers, and existing myths drawn upon by writers, to make imaginative interpretations of the psychological states of characters," writes Humm (*Practicing* 23–24). Furthermore, "Malinowski believed that myths provided access to the desires and beliefs of the mythmakers," writes Strenski (xxiv). Malinowski's argument can also be extended to an understanding of modern mythmakers, or writers of mythological retellings. From the foregoing discussion, one can surmise that the author's own subjectivity (female subjectivity in this case) comes in handy for sketching out the character's psychobiography. One can suggest that creative writers of mythological retellings almost treat their characters living beings/entities, place themselves into the shoes of their characters, and attempt to think and feel like their characters to add the shades of realism and humanness to their fictional characters. This ensures that the readers simultaneously hear two voices in the narrative: the voice of the character (here, Draupadi) and the voice of the storyteller/authorial voice (Ray and Divakaruni in this context).

Both Ray and Divakaruni place Draupadi's plight at the heart of their novels. In trying to salvage the women characters from the hubris of a largely male discourse on dharma and propriety, both the writers paint an empathetic picture of Draupadi. The words, rage, and venom that Draupadi spews during her humiliation and disrobing in the assembly hall of Hastinapura could only have come from the pens of female authors who feel the unfathomable pain and uncontrollable anger of Draupadi.[27] Ray's Yajnaseni cries out: "Such a gross outrage on womanhood will never be wiped out in history.... For this insult there is no forgiveness, for this sin there is no expiation" (Ray 241–42). Moreover, she makes a piercing feminist proclamation: she refuses to own her own body, so that the shame does not befall her. One must reiterate that a woman's body, which has been seen as a source of deep trouble and the root of numerous problems, is disowned by Ray's Yajnaseni. Divakaruni's Panchaali reassures herself, "*No one can shame you, ... if you don't allow it ...*). Let them stare at my nakedness, I thought. Why should I care? They and not I should be ashamed for shattering the bounds of decency" (193, italics in original). The outrage in the heroine's voice, her ominous words, and her feminist position of disowning her body and hence also the shame clearly demonstrate the psychological states of the writers who narrate her story, and in so doing, feel her pain closely and deeply.

In order to delve into the minds of their characters and apply their subjective takes to their creative works, the writers take recourse to dialogical discourses, which provide enough room for creative departures and critique. The genre employed – the novelistic genre, which comes with the Bakhtinian possibilities of polyphonic voices and heteroglossia, is often the genre that writers of retellings often take recourse to. Moreover, they usually employ diegesis or dialogism, or both, to provide an internal view of the world of the central character of their respective novels, fleshing out their characters through plentiful dialogues. Thus, the novelistic mode, the technique of diegesis, and sometimes also dramatic/reflective monologues, aid the writers of retellings in penning down the psychobiography of their pivotal character.

Storytelling is "very powerful. It transforms … the teller as well as the listener" (Zupančič, "Storytelling" 90). Mythological stories, narratives, adaptations, and retellings are ceaselessly circulated generation after generation primarily because their listeners and audience have an inexhaustible desire to hear more.

Malinowski believed "that a deeper, perhaps more potent, level of meaning existed" in myths, which "come not from the mythmaker, but from how … the myth affects its audience – how it *functions*" (Strenski xxii). Writing about the interconnectedness of writers who draw on myths and mythical symbols, the subjectivity/psychological states of the creative writers and the effect that the mythical symbols have on readers, Humm explains:

> Myth critics argue that literary symbols often make provocative disclosures of writers' psychological conditions. And in turn that these psychological conditions take certain regular and archetypically symbolic forms which may help the reader to understand her own archaic images and pulsations.
>
> *(Reader's Guide 60)*

Draupadi as a character has remained one of the most fascinating heroines from Indian mythology. Readers are introduced to the many nuances of her personality when her story is read and reread, either as an epic heroine or as a woman in flesh and blood in the novelistic/literary/dramatic retellings of her life-story mired in the entanglements of life and the conflicts of dharma. The body of revisionist literature that the retellings comprise is indeed topical, born out of the author's own spacio-temporal context and subjective reflections. And yet, in the retellings by Ray and Divakaruni, Draupadi simultaneously cuts a picture of a fierce feminist as well as a fellow human, who is not afraid of voicing out her innermost travails and conflicts, a voice that is largely amiss and replaced by a conspicuous silence in the epic on critical, even momentous occasions.

Draupadi is made and remade every time a writer tells the story of her life, afresh. The writers of retellings employ feminist revisionist strategies and make narrative innovations to project the character of Draupadi not as divine, inaccessible, and intangible, but as a woman with her fair share of foibles and follies who commands respect because she stands her ground in spite of all adversities. This quintessential mix makes her a fairly relatable and unforgettable character, a result of the carefully measured deviations that the creative writers retelling her life make by rupturing the silences and fissures in the epical story, first as readers of the mythological story, and then as writers of a fresh tale of Draupadi. The readers also never tire of listening to the gripping narrative of her life. Moreover, considering the sheer number of times and the myriad ways in which Draupadi's story has been retold and performed, one feels that Draupadi is still a puzzle writers and artists are trying to piece together, a character whose life narrative is still in progress. Draupadi is undoubtedly and truly contemporary, and will remain so for as long as the human civilization exists, and with her, also the Mahabharata.

Notes

1 Many arguments in this chapter derive from the original and as yet unpublished doctoral thesis of the scholar, entitled *The Shifting Paradigm of Dharma: A Study of Select Modern Retellings of the Mahābhārata*, submitted to Jawaharlal Nehru University (2019).

2 Divakaruni's protagonist Panchaali muses over how stories are constructed. Devoid of the real story behind their births, Panchaali and her brother Dhri try to recreate the same and also that of their father's past by any means possible, employing sources which are mostly inauthentic, imagined, and fictional. Moreover, one can discern that Divakaruni engages in a self-reflexive act: her thoughts about the birth of narratives and their nature and functions are partly directed towards herself; she is theorizing her own act of not only telling a story and creating a work of fiction but also of retelling one of the most popular and voluminous epics of all time. One is reminded of A.K. Ramanujan's observation in "Where Mirrors are Windows: Toward an Anthology of Reflections": "[W]orks of Indian literature are inherently self-reflexive in that they offer reflections on themselves as stories" (qtd. in Hudson 50).

3 The Mahabharata is undoubtedly the shining glory of the collective memory of India. V.S. Sukthankar remarks that the epic, a "dateless and deathless poem … which forms the strongest link between India old and new," is "still living and throbbing in the lives of the Indian people" (32, 29). The epic makes a resounding proclamation about itself: *yannehsti na tadkvacit* "what is not here is not found anywhere else." The epic is indeed "an encyclopedic repository of ancient Indian myths, legends, ideals and concepts" (Miller 123).

4 Perhaps more than any other ancient text in India as well as the world, the Mahabharata's versions "recur throughout India in a wide variety of literary, performative, ritual, and political contexts" (Brodbeck and Black 1).

5 The *Mahābhārata* has always given creative impetus to the authors over the ages, and numerous versions and interpretations of the same abound. The retellings of the characters and incidents of the *Mahābhārata* date as far back as the Sanskrit playwrights Bhāsa (third century), Kālidāsa (fourth–fifth century), Bhāravi (sixth century), and Bhaṭ ṭa Nārāyaṇa (eighth century). However, in the last century, there was a sudden spate in the retellings of the *Mahābhārata* in the latter half of the twentieth century, in numerous languages such as Marathi, Tamil, Bengali, Kannada, Oriya, Telugu, Hindi, and English, to name a few. Most of them were either retellings of the entire story of the epic or retellings from the vantage point of a specific character. While Krishna, Bhisma, Karna, Arjuna, and Kunti continued to remain some of the favourite characters from whose point of view the retellings were usually narrated, it can be said without an iota of doubt that Draupadi was and still remains the most favoured character of all when it comes to character-based retellings of the epic: Iravati Karve's heart-touching and oft-quoted study of Draupadi in *Yuganta: The End*

of an Epoch (in Marathi), or Pratibha Ray's *Yajnaseni* (in Oriya), Mahasweta Devi's story "Draupadi" (Bengali), and Divakaruni's English novel *The Palace of Illusions* are the more popular ones among the long list of creative works retold from Draupadi's perspective, and many more perpetually continue to be released every year.

6 Mukhoty notes that the renewed interest in Draupadi has largely to do with the allure held by her "polyandrous marriage or her imagined love interest," which, for her, amounts to a reduction, a "grave injustice" towards her character (21–22; 22). But one is of the opinion that there is a lot more to the character of Draupadi than her polyandry.

7 In addition to the literary retellings of the hardships of Draupadi mentioned above, some others published in the recent past are Subramania Bharati's *Panchali's Pledge*, Yarlagadda Lakshmi Prasad's *Draupadi*, Pavan K. Verma's *Yudhisthir and Draupadi*, and M Veerappa's Moily's *Draupadi*. These are just a few examples (in English or translated into English) that far outnumber the narratives from the perspectives of other women of the epic.

8 Tharu and Laitha also argue in favour of reading the texts chosen by them for "the gestures of defiance and subversion implicit in them" (39).

9 Yajnaseni and Panchaali are two of the many names by which Draupadi is known.

10 Elsewhere, Humm notes, "It is crucial that feminist critics address myth since ... the process of reclaiming and recreating myths is a central activity in the work of many feminist poets" (*Reader's Guide* 68).

11 In the *Author's Note* to the novel, Divakaruni explains that she felt unsatisfied when growing up, she listened to the stories from the epic. She could notice that something was wanting in those narratives, especially regarding the female characters: "It wasn't as though the epic didn't have powerful, complex women characters ... But in some way, they remained shadowy figures, their thoughts and motives mysterious, their emotions portrayed only when they affected the lives of the male heroes, their roles ultimately subservient to those of their fathers or husbands, brothers or sons" (*Illusions* xiv). She was determined to remedy this lack herself: "If I ever wrote a book ... I would place the women in the forefront of the action... [and] uncover the story that lay invisible between the lines of the men's exploits .... I would have one of them tell it herself, with all her joys and doubts, her struggles and her triumphs, her heartbreaks, her achievements, the unique female way in which she sees her world and her place in it. And who could be better suited for this than Panchaali? (*Illusions* xiv–xv).

12 All references to Divakaruni, unless otherwise indicated, are from her novel, *The Palace of Illusions*.

13 An anthropological or sociological investigation of the rendering of Draupadi in folklore and rituals brings to light the deification of Draupadi from a mythological heroine to a folk goddess or local deity. For further details, see Hiltebeitel (1988, 1999, and 2011) and Gupta and Ramachandran (1976).

14 Bhattacharya observes: "If Draupadi [in the epic] had hoped to find her missing mother in her mother-in-law, she is tragically deceived as Kunti thrusts her into a polyandrous marriage that exposes her to salacious gossip which reaches a horrendous climax in Karna calling her a public woman" (94).

15 Drupada in the epic and the novels under discussion, as well as scholars such as Mukherjee (23), Matilal (xi), and Kavita Sharma ("Eyes of Women" 110–111) summarily condemn Yudhishthira for his support to Kunti's command as the dharmic way for all.

16 Vyasa in Divakaruni's novel does not come himself, but sends a prompt verdict when the matter is brought to his notice.

17 In Divakaruni's novel, Panchaali, who is present when the men are debating the matter, is completely taken aback. Even though she does not intervene to apprise them of her sentiments and reaction, she is evidently traumatized by her treatment as a mere commodity, and the selfishness she can smell in the motives of all the men deciding her fate.

18 The society, according to Kavita Sharma, operates on the formula of a duality: it sees "women's sexuality ... as a potentially ... destructive force in front of which the mightiest of men are rendered helpless," while simultaneously believing in the fact that "it can be put to great use once it is subordinated and regulated by men" (*Dicing* xxxii). Feminists today negotiate the conundrum by foregrounding the woman's point of view, more specifically by retelling ancient stories from a woman's perspective. Also see, Kavita Sharma (*Dicing*), Bhattacharya, Mukhoty and Doniger for detailed discussions of Draupadi's polyandry.

19 See, Sukthankar (21) and Miller's "India's Great Epic" (126–27).

20 All references to Ray, unless otherwise indicated, are from her novel, *Yajnaseni*.

21 Divakaruni's Panchaali gets the gift of divine eyes from Vyasa for witnessing the war and bearing testimony to it. She is indeed fierce, for she takes on the fathomless pain and agony of seeing the men fight and die, and yet be in the battlefield – though virtually. One must be reminded of the fact that traditionally, wars or any associations with wars have been male prerogatives.

22 Vaishali uses these lines in her study of the works of Namjoshi and Atwood, writers who have been credited with being feminist revisionist mythmakers.

23 Humm suggests that "[m]otherhood ... is the one place from which criticism could begin to reformulate the representation of women in myth" (*Reader's Guide* 61). Pratibha Ray lays considerable emphasis on the maternal instincts of Yajnaseni, who even feeds a tribal child when in exile.

24 While the treatment of each of these topics by the two novelists merits a special discussion, especially the humiliation of Draupadi during the dicing match, one has to refrain from attempting the same in this paper. They have been discussed in detail with respect to the epic and in Divakaruni's novel elsewhere by the author. See Agarwal (2017) and Agarwal (2016).

25 Karve unabashedly takes Draupadi's side in asking, "If she had loved Arjuna most, was there anything astonishing about that?" (103). Bhattacharya also echoes the same concern: "Draupadi never enjoys possession of her first love" (80). Draupadi's jealousy of her co-wives, which is, of course, born out of love for thwarted love for Arjuna, is reproduced both by Ray and Divakaruni.
Several retellings of the *Mahabharata* also project Draupadi realizing very late in her life that Bhima had loved her more than any of the other brothers. Bhatta Narayana develops this theme in his play *Venisamhara*, Iravati Karve makes this imaginative departure in her study, and M. T. Vasudevan Nair also renders this understanding in his *Randamoozam* (*The Second Turn*).

26 Iravati Karve in *Yuganta* uses this part of the story to recreate a narrative of Draupadi's life where she realizes only after her "fall" on the final journey that it was Bhima, the second Pandava, who loved her the most!

27 Draupadi in the epic is not subjected to violence only in the *sabha* at Hastinapura. She is abducted twice after that nightmarish day in the Kuru court: first by Jayadratha, her brother-in-law (husband of the only sister of the Kauravas, Dushala) in the forest during their exile, and then by Keechaka, a general in the army of King Virata, in whose kingdom the disguised Pandavas and Draupadi spend their last year of exile as part of the terms of Duryodhana.

Works Cited

Agarwal, Komal. "Draupadi Jeopardizing Jurisprudence: A Critical Analysis of Dharma as Law in the Light of Draupadi's Question(s) in the Sabha." *The Rupkatha Journal on Interdisciplinary Studies in Humanities* IX.1 (May 2017): 133–39. Web. 20 Oct. 2020.

———. "The Story of a Feminist Woman-Goddess: Re-reading, Re-telling and Ritualizing Draupadi in India Today." *Re-reading Myths at the Beginning of the Twenty-first Century*, special issue of *HyperCultura* 5.2 (2016): 2–9. Web. 20 Oct. 2020.

Badrinath, Chaturvedi. *The Women of the* Mahabharata: *The Question of Truth.* New Delhi: Orient Longman, 2008.

Bandlamudi, Lakshmi. *Dialogics of Self, the* Mahabharata *and Culture: The History of Understanding and Understanding of History.* London: Anthem, 2011.

Bhattacharya, Pradip. *Panch-Kanya The Five Virgins of Indian Epics: A Quest in Search of Meaning.* Kolkata: Writers Workshop, 2005.

Bhawalkar, V. *Eminent Women in the Mahabharata.* Vol. I. Delhi: Sharada, 2002.

Brodbeck, Simon, and Brian Black. Introduction. *Gender and Narrative in the Mahabharata.* Eds. Brodbeck and Black. Oxon and New York: Routledge, 2007. 1–34.

Das, Gurcharan. *The Difficulty of Being Good: On the Subtle Art of Dharma.* New Delhi: Penguin, 2009.

Daschaudhuri, Mohar. "Re-Writing the Myth of Draupadi in Pratibha Ray's Yajnaseni and Chitra Bannerjee Divakaruni's The Palace of Illusions." *Athens Journal of Philology* 7.3 (Sep. 2020): 177–88. Web. 10 Sep. 2020.

Divakaruni, Chitra Banerjee. *The Palace of Illusions.* New Delhi: Picador, 2008.

———. Interview by Metka Zupančič. "The Power of Storytelling: An Interview with Chitra Banerjee Divakaruni." *Contemporary Women's Writing* 6.2 (2011): 85–101. Web. 27 June 2017.

Doniger, Wendy. *Hinduism.* Gen. Ed. Jack Miles. New York: Norton, 2015. The Norton Anthology of World Religions.

Gupta, S. P. and K. S. Ramachandran, eds. Mahabharata, *Myth and Reality: Differing Views.* Delhi: Agam Prakashan, 1976.

Hiltebeitel, Alf. *Rethinking India's Oral and Classical Epics: Draupadi among Rajputs, Muslims and Dalits.* Chicago: The U of Chicago P, 1999.

———. *The Cult of Draupadi: Mythologies: From Gingee to Kurukshetra.* Chicago: The U of C Press, 1988.

———. *When the Goddess was a Woman: Mahabharata Ethnographies—Essays by Alf Hiltebeitel, Volume 2.* Eds. Vishwa Adluri and Joydeep Bagchee. London: Brill, 2011.

Hudson, Emily T. *Disorienting Dharma: Ethics and the Aesthetics of Suffering in the* Mahabharata. New York: OUP, 2013.

Humm, Maggie. *A Reader's Guide to Contemporary Feminist Literary Criticism.* London: Routledge-Taylor & Francis, 2015.

———. *Practicing Feminist Criticism: An Introduction.* London: Prentice Hall-Harvester Wheatsheaf, 1995.

Jagannathan, Prema. *The* Mahabharata *and Contemporary Indian Novel.* New Delhi: Prestige, 2010.

Karve, Iravati. *Yuganta: The End of an Epoch.* Hyderabad: Disha-Orient Longman, 1991.

Matilal, Bimal Krishna. "Introduction." *Moral Dilemmas in the* Mahabharata. By Matilal. Simla: Indian Inst. of Advanced Study; Delhi: Motilal Banarsidass, 1989. ix–xiv.

McGrath, Kevin. *Stra: Women in Epic Mahabharata*. Boston, Massachusetts: Ilex Foundation; Washington, DC: Center for Hellenic Studies, Trustees for Harvard University, 2009. Ilex Foundation Ser.

Miller, Barbara Stoller. "The Mahabharata, including the *Bhagavad Gita*: India's Great Epic." *Masterworks of Asian Literature in Comparative Perspective: A Guide for Teaching*. Ed. Miller. New York: East Gate-M.E. Sharpe, 1994. 123–32. Columbia Project on Asia in the Core Curriculum.

Mukherjee, Prabhati. *Hindu Women: Normative Models*. New Delhi: Orient Longman, 1978.

Mukhoty, Ira. *Heroines: Powerful Indian Women of Myth & History*. New Delhi: Aleph, 2017.

Multani, Geetanjali. "Tradition of Myth in Chitra Banerjee's *The Mistress of Spices* and *The Palace of Illusions*." Ed. Vandana Sharma. *Studies in Myth, Orality and Folklore in World Literature*. New Delhi: Atlantic, 2013. 214–25.

Ray, Pratibha. "Sky is Not the Limit." *Growing Up As A Woman Writer*. Ed. Jasbir Jain. New Delhi: Sahitya Akademi, 2007. 77–84.

——. *Yajnaseni: The Story of Draupadi*. Trans. Pradip Bhattacharya. New Delhi: Rupa, 1995.

Sharma, Kavita A. Introduction. *The Dicing and the Sequel to Dicing*. Trans. and Ed. J. A. B. van Buitenen. New Delhi: Doaba, n.d. vii–lxiii.

——. "Mahabharata through the Eyes of Women." *Women in Dharmasastras: A Phenomenological and Critical Analysis*. Ed. Chandrakala Padia. Jaipur: Rawat, 2009. 107–30.

Strenski, Ivan. *Malinowski and the Work of Myth*. Princeton, New Jersey: Princeton U P, 1992.

Sukthankar, V. S. *On the Meaning of the* Mahabharata. Bombay: The Asiatic Soc., 1957.

Tharu, Susie and K. Lalita, eds. *Women Writing in India: 600 B.C. to the Present*. Vols. 1 and 2. New York: The Feminist Press, 1991.

Zupančič, Metka. "Ethics of Wisdom and Compassion in the Novels by Chitra Banerjee Divakaruni." *Asian Studies I* XVII.1 (2013): 105–17. Web. 25 Aug. 2020.

——. "New Feminine Myths as Builders of New Transcultural Horizons." *Transcultural Negotiations of Gender: Studies in (Be)longing*. Eds. Saugata Bhaduri and Indrani Mukherjee. New Delhi: Springer, 2016. 15–24.

——. "The Power of Storytelling: An Interview with Chitra Banerjee Divakaruni." *Contemporary Women's Writing* 6.2 (2011): 85–101. Web. 27 June 2017.

11

A WORLD OF IMAGES

The Visual Identity of the Mahabharata

Sankha Banerjee

In the twenty-first century, visual culture is celebrated almost everywhere. We live in a world that's overloaded with visuals. A camera, no larger than a bee, can capture 4K videos and is available as an accessory gadget in mobile phones. We upload millions of gigabytes of data on social media every day. When any incident or news comes to our notice, we instinctively look for its visual representation. People encounter photos and videos by the thousands every day. Words like "surveillance," "gaze," "gallery," "image," and "selfie" have connotations which open up altogether new dimensions of possibility. The power of the visual is so profound that even the shape of ossified, traditional rituals in India is gradually changing – visual memories deposited in movies or photographs are helping to recycle those same rituals at a much faster tempo than before. Even two decades ago, we could not have imagined that a marriage ritual would be paused by the photographer or videographer to capture the "right moment" of some specific. We love to construct our memories based on visuals, or better to say, "captured" visuals.

With the help of high-end lenses and imagination crafted with 3D software, we have managed to construct the fight between two microscopic creatures: paramecium and its enemy dileptus inside a dewdrop. Thanks to technology, we can now watch and reconstruct the Tardigrade (Miller 2017), the animal smaller than a ballpoint dot, which has inhabited this planet for more than 500 million years! We capture photographs of galaxies, supernovas, and distant celestial objects using ultra-powerful lenses. We anticipate being able to visualize almost any concept within our perceived reality. Whether it is nature, from the largest animal to the tiniest creature, distant giant nebulas, events in an ongoing riot, war, or the evolving visuals of a marriage, or even the kitchens of an Afghan tribe in a remote hamlet

DOI: 10.4324/9781003516408-13

– everything that exists can be perceived as a visual memory, and that in turn ignites in us the desire to see it all. We are also continually developing more powerful ways to bring our imaginations to life.

Now, can we create a visual representation of an age-old poem? A poem that has been composed for nearly eight hundred years by countless poets (Buitenen 1983) – can we visualize it? Can we visually reconstruct the imagery from the ancient poets? Can we see their characters, the cities, the lands, or the wars described in the poem? Can we see the Mahabharata?

1.

Contemplating problem, I thought of constructing an amalgam of words and images; in other words, a graphic novel, a narrative built on the logic of sequential art form. While there was the temptation to make a movie on the Mahabharata, when I considered the project, I found myself more comfortable working with mediums that involve physical contact, such as drawing and painting. Additionally, filmmaking comes with additional challenges related to budget and management, which, at that time, I was not prepared to handle. Furthermore, I had the strong desire to work with ink, colour, texture, and the juxtaposition of images.

I had previously created a few graphic novels before *Vyasa: The Beginning*, most of which were commissioned works, with some of them revolving around the stories of Greek mythology and one on Nelson Mandela. When I made the decision to create a graphic novel based on the Mahabharata, I had not yet met Sibaji Bandyopadhyay. I reached out to him with the intention of learning more about the Mahabharata, and we eventually ended up collaborating on the same subject. It was certainly a remarkable journey from my perspective.

2.

We have visual representations of and references to the *Mahabharata* in almost every medium of visual art. We have seen sculptural representations of the Mahabharata war in Ellora, in the Kailashnath temple (c. 756 CE), Arjuna's penance in Mahabalipuram (c. seventh century CE), the Pandavas and Draupadi (c. sixth century CE), and an intriguing depiction of the Chakravyuha in Hoysalewara temple, Halebidu (c. 1160 CE). Unfortunately, the names of the artists and artisans from this period remain unknown.

During the Mughal period, we can marvel at the amazing paintings in the *Razamnama* (c. 1616–1700), commissioned by Mughal Emperor Akbar (1542–1605), edited by Abul Fazal (1551–1602), and Abdul Qadir Badayuni (1540–1605), and executed by artists like Mushfiq, Basawan (who flourished 1580–1600), Daswanth (d. 1584), and Lal. We read the analysis of its development in detail in another chapter of this volume. Their collaborative work exhibits a connection with the narrative style of a graphic novel, particularly when it comes to the juxtaposition of images. This connection is seen not only in Mahabalipuram's Arjuna's penance but also in the artistry of the *Razamnama*.

There is a continuous flow of images and stories related to the Mahabharata across various artistic mediums and historical periods. Rajput miniatures and *patachitra* stories from Bengal and Odisha have contributed to a rich tradition of visual storytelling.

In the modern era, we have witnessed the artistic works of Raja Ravi Varma, the comics of "Amar Chitra Katha," and representations in audiovisual media, such as B.R. Chopra's TV-*Mahabharata* as well as the innumerable movies based on the epic. In the realm of performing arts, we have seen the *mahakavya* depicted through forms like Kathakali and Kudiattam in Kerala. We have also enjoyed the lively performances of Tijan Bi (born 1956), a practitioner who sprang from the oral tradition and continues to work within it.

Many Bengali readers still cherish the comic adaptation by Purna Chakraborty meant for children. Peter Brook's *Mahabharata*, a unique audiovisual performance of the epic, stands as a thought-provoking and aesthetically enchanting masterpiece.

3.

Scholars say, the composing of the Mahabharata was completed by 450 CE. In the stories of the *mahakavya,* we find Greeks, Shaka, Bactrian, Chinese, and many such people (Sukthankar 1997). Who knows, if poets had continued to add episodes beyond 450 CE, we might have come across the Mughals in the Mahabharata! But here is the interesting aspect. Visuals can create their own text. In the artwork of *Razamnama*, the Persian adaptation of the Mahabharata, the characters wear contemporary Indian dresses and attire. Visually speaking, Arjuna and Krishna, the Pandavas and the Kauravas, all belong to the Mughal period. For instance, in the painting called "The Burning of the Khandava (Forest)" (Folio 46r., Inscribed: Tarah Lal, Amal Bhagwan), we can see Agni, disguised as a huge golden-hued brahmana wearing a Mughal court-turban (Das 2005). In "The battle of Kurukshetra war-scenes: Bhima kills the King of Kalinga" (Folio 234v, Inscribed: Tarah Tulsi, Amal Farrukh) – this battle-painting immediately reminds us of Rajput war paintings; Bhima beheads the king of Kalinga with a Mughal sword wearing a Mughal dress (Das 2005). In brief: at the least, in terms of the visual lexicon, the narration of the Mahabharata need not be frozen in some (imagined) ancient time even if its words, collected and collated from various manuscripts, are more or less fixed. Therefore, anyone who decides to visually *re-present* the Mahabharata is not obliged to producing replicas of some fossilized entity.

4.

The ancient bards, like the Suta and the Magdhi people, used to recite the stories of the Mahabharata. In all probability, they used to sing, perform the stories, and even compose new verses. The stories continually underwent textual shifts. Scholars have identified three different stages of the Mahabharata, namely "Jaya," "Bharata," and "Mahabharata" (Bhattacharya 2015); but it is next to impossible to pinpoint the precise time period of these stages – there could be a gap of a hundred or even five hundred years between these sections. Hence, we do not have any exact visual idea of the stages either. At the end of it all, the vast poem has amassed a huge range of, often contradictory, words, thoughts, and images from different historical eras and various people.

The multiple historical layers the Mahabharata contains are the primary reason behind ceaseless disputes over its characters, discussions about the breaks which disrupt the "continuity of action." The poem has collected layers like a snowball, and a single story may have travelled for years, gathering flesh in its body. The visuals from the post-Iron Age period or the Kushan period could thus have gotten fused with those of the post-Mauryan or Gupta period. Additionally, in the ancient age when the composition of the Mahabharata was underway, there were no available visual representations of the stories. So, when we read the Mahabharata, we either refrain from visualizing the poem, or if we choose to imagine, we create a room of visuals based on our visual memory and ideas, and we blend the two streams together. In the *Razamnama*, the characters were depicted as Mughals because the patrons were Mughals; in B.R. Chopra's TV-*Mahabharata*, the characters wore dresses that conveyed a glossy and extravagant idea of the period. Therefore, we often encounter people who may agree with the words but do not agree with the visual representation of the poem. A significant debate emerged when Peter Brook mixed the actors of his Mahabharata with a variety of ethnicities like Indian, African, French, Japanese, etc. Visually, the people looked strikingly different from each other. Brook's imaginative portrayal of diversity did not align with the visual memory or imagination of many people.

5.

We decided to narrate the Mahabharata in the genre of a graphic novel. The term "graphic novel" was coined by Richard Kyle in an essay in the November 1964 issue of the comics fanzine "Capa-Alpha" in the USA (Schelly 2010 117). In Europe, people mostly refer to it simply as "comics." Comics are closely connected with fine arts; in fact, any form of sequential art can be read as comics. Comics technically are also juxtaposed images. Any two images side by side, communicating information can be called comics (Gavaler 2021). This format is open to interpretation. If the artist creates pictures with borders, usually they are called panels; the space between two panels is called gutter space (McCloud 1994), and the full-page artwork is called a splash page. These are terms usually used to describe the comic medium, but we also need to understand that like every medium, these elements are not an essential part of comic form. Comics form is open. When we read comics, we can see two pages at a time. The reader may also choose to read the images right to left or left to right or clockwise or anticlockwise – comics are very amenable to such flexibility.

The long and the short matter is, whether it's a Yama-pata of West Bengal, India, telling the story of human life through pictures accompanied by singing, or the 35,000-year-old drawings on the walls of Chauvet cave in France, where we can see a pride of lions chasing a group of rhinos and buffaloes, or the Greek vase of black-figure style depicting the story of bowel movement after overeating, all of them can be interpreted as comics.

The longer format, often referred to as the "graphic novel," can sometimes be more serious and targeted towards mature readers. Works like David Mazzucchelli's *Asteroid Polyp*, Art Spiegelman's *Maus*, and Marjane Satrapi's *Persepolis* are widely recognized as such.

6.

So, after we decided to tell the story in the graphic novel format, Sibaji Bandyopadhyay created the scripts for both *Vyasa* and *Panchali*. From the start to finish, the basis of his scripts was the Critical edition of the Mahabharata brought out by Pune's Bhandarkar Oriental Research Institute. Therefore, this is probably the first-ever graphic-novel adaptation of the Mahabharata based on the critical edition. Bandyopadhyay undertook the enormous task of constructing the canyon of the two books, *Vyasa: The Beginning* and *Panchali: The Game of Dice*, both published by Penguin Books. In both cases, he wrote the stories. While *Vyasa* follows the zigzag pattern intrinsic to the epic, *Panchali* develops linearly by more or less sticking to the Kaurava-Pandava animosity. Graphic novels can have their own narration with images: as I illustrated Bandyopadhyay's story, I also simultaneously tried to do parallel narrations with artworks. Adhering strictly to the Critical edition as Bandyopadhyay did, there is no mention of Ganesh the scribe in his rendition.

According to the poem, Vyasa composed the poem; Vaisampayana was the first receiver and reciter. Then, Sauti listened to the poem from Vaisampayana at the Snake Sacrifice ceremony of King Janamejay and became the second reciter (Buitenen 1983). Throughout the poem, Sauti recites the poem, saying, "thus Vaisampayana spoke." Bandyopadhyay's Sauti is not just a humble narrator; he also, at points, raises critically important ethical issues during his recital. The four listeners of the poem in *Vyasa* represent four philosophical schools of ancient India. The young listener with a shaved head represents a Sramana school opposed to Brahminism and the old Brahmin is a staunch conservative. These characters frequently make comments on the stories, as do the commoners.

Bandyopadhyay had told me that the narrator Sauti was a story-peddler. So, I imagined him as being very colourful character. He is an entertainer, a person who keeps travelling with stories, and the stories grow. His surroundings and backgrounds often depict small, mundane stories of daily life. For instance, in *Vyasa*, we can see honey collectors with masks and wearing leaf protection (page 19), woodcutters (page 50), cooks and food (page 84), labourers carrying vegetables (page 85), travellers in the Himalayas (page 97), etc. Sauti of the two graphic novels is completely free of the toxic masculinity which scars many a character of the epic. He loves makeup and decorates himself before his performances. I took inspiration from various traditional performing arts in India, like Kathakali and Theyyam. In *Panchali: The Game of Dice*, Sauti tells stories with the traditional tribal dolls of Chadar-Badar performance art.

7.

Vyasa explores the genealogy of the principal players of the Mahabharata. Bandyopadhyay began with Pururava, the first ancestor of the Kuru dynasty who often goes unmentioned. Pururava, who was against any kind of animal sacrifice in rituals and was a prominent voice against animal cruelty. Brahama's son Sanat Kumar kills the anarchist Pururava, "anarchist" from the point of view of the proponents of Brahminism. Pururava raised questions like "If bad things can affect the bad and good equally, what can be the reason for being good?" or "Can it be proved that it's wrong to do what's wrong?" Any artist would be tempted to draw a character like this who moves with a lot of animals. And here comes the most important part, the flesh and skin of graphic novels, the word and image pairing.

8.

In graphic novels, the pairing of words and images, and the relationships between them, make the reading experience enjoyable. This relationship can sometimes be straightforward or quite intricate. According to Chris Gavaler, a comics scholar, there are primarily four kinds of relationships.

What Sibaji Bandyopadhyay narrates through words and what I convey through images can sometimes duplicate each other. This form of storytelling offers a low-resistance experience for the readers. In *Vyasa*, when Sanat Kumar burns Pururava (page 61), it reads, "A fire engulfs Pururava, and within a twinkle, he is turned into ashes." The image also depicts a burning skeleton. Both convey the same information. However, in these cases, the background image tells additional stories. Throughout the scene, we see Pururava surrounded by various kinds of beasts. When he is burning, one of the beast's heads falls, resembling a human mask.

When words and images complement each other, it forms another kind of relationship. In *Vyasa*, in the Ekalavya story (page 191), we see Ekalavya saying, "Here is Nishada's *gurudakshina*." The image shows a freshly chopped-off thumb placed on a Sal leaf. The words do not explicitly state what the *gurudakshina* is, and the image doesn't convey its identity. However, when readers see the image along with the words, they get a complete idea of the incident.

The third type is contrast-pairing. In *Vyasa*, on page 129, Vyasa appears to impregnate Ambalika. In the fifth panel, he says to Ambalika, "It's me, Vyasa, your brother-in-law." This seemingly humble introduction is not humble at all. The image shows Ambalika looking scared, and those apparently humble words take on a chilling undertone when we notice the relationship between them.

The fourth kind is when words and images diverge from each other. This relationship creates a stronger resistance for the reader. Both books use this relationship numerous times to add depth to the narration. In *Panchali: The Game of Dice*, when Yudhisthir is gambling and using his wife Panchali as a bet, he describes Panchali (Draupadi). He says (page 187), "hair, long, eyes, copper-colored; face, lotus-like; waist, slender as a sacrificial altar." The images do not directly mirror the words. Instead, we see in the previous panel that Yudhisthir is riding on a giant locust on the board and from the dots of the dice crops are coming out: and the locust is approaching them. The background is dark, resembling a theatre-stage. If we recall, when Draupadi had come to Hastinapur on page 99, a locust had landed on her hair, which Yudhisthir had taken away. During the dice game, as Yudhisthir recites the beauty of Draupadi, we see four phallus-like shapes emerging from his wide-open skull. A distorted branch of a tree with dry leaves is shown in the background. This entire page showcases the power of comics and graphic novel narration, where the reader can interpret the word-image pairing in multiple ways. The information is open-ended, and the human mind naturally seeks to explore the meaning, creating an engaging experience. In *Panchali*, in the same episode, on page 185, we observe Yudhisthir, now neurotic, saying, "The last bell is yet to toll, Sakuni. My seventeenth bet is on Arjuna. The invincible world-hero." The image shows a bird-like beast eating his brain. Yudhisthir is seated on a cloud-shaped brain with two menacing eyes looking at the readers. This cloud is being devoured by a crow, taking the form of Sakuni himself. The crow exclaims "Krita-Krita" (success), and Sakuni simply says, "Won" in a dark speech bubble.

9.

Graphic narration of the Mahabharata delves into various aspects, where ink, scratches, and lines create narratives in both books. Words also create images. In *Panchali* (27), Purochana, a minister and co-conspirator of Duryodhana, shows the house of Lac to the Pandavas. He tells Sahadeva, "It won't be an exaggeration to say that, besides being snugly secure, this tower of a building trumps every other building." While the employment of the word "trump" is innocuous enough, it does here obliquely refer to the Tower in New York named after the modern-day villain of epic dimensions, Donald J. Trump of the United States. Contemporaneity of the Mahabharata is thus never propounded or illustrated loudly – put in philosophical terms, it is never *said* but *shown*.

In the dice-game section, Bandyopadhyay has surreptitiously slipped in a poem on the game straight from the *Rigveda* – and, the poem is unquestionably remarkable. Over and above that, he has spelt out the rules of the game. Moreover, he has connected the number of faces of the ancient dice, which was four, to lay out a number theory focussed on four. Number four plays an intriguing part in ancient Indian narrations and philosophies. In the "Sign of Four" sub-section of Episode 6, Bandyopadhyay lets us know via Sauti:

> A player grasps a bundle of dice and throws the lot on the game-board. If the total count is divisible by four, he obtains Krita or winnings. If after dividing the count by four the remainder is three he obtains *treta* or *treya*. By the same arithmetic if the remainder is two he gets Dvapara or deuce. Alas! If the remainder happens to be one, he earns Kali or losing.
>
> *(161)*

This is the part in the graphic novel which is represented in terms of informative visuals. So, in the pictures we see, against a flat background, the dice and a series of mathematical equations – it appears as though the page has floated in from a science textbook. And, indeed, there is a modern theory of Physics in play at the core of the unfolding of the dice game in the graphic novel. Bandyopadhyay has introduced aspects of Chaos Theory which speaks of what is known as the "butterfly effect." He writes "If the balance gets upset, the tiniest addition might bring the orderly arrangement to the brink of chaos" (177). To bring this point to the fore, the illustrations here are divided into almost identical panels but without any boarder. In contrast to others, these three panels render visibility to slow motion.

10.

Panels too tell stories. On pages 172–173 of *Panchali*, panels are connected with geometrical shapes with the express intent of depicting the psychological turmoil of Yudhishthira during the dice game. On page 173, he is shown holding the gutter space (the empty space between panels) like a prisoner holds the bars in a cage. Yudhisthira is breaking the fourth wall on this page. On page 178, the panels are arranged like zigzag folds and Yudhisthira is sitting in the middle. Simultaneously, Shakuni is endowed with multiple impressions and multiple voices. The shape of the panels has broken with conventional patterns.

In *Vyasa*, the gutter space and the white space play a major role in narration. Fragmented panels, fragmented visuals, scattered visuals without any definite borders, interchanging images are all over *Vyasa,* calculated to give expression to many short but multi-dimensional stories. On page 40 of *Vyasa*, young Devabrata is dealing with his father's depression – shortly, in order to assuage his father that he would pose no obstacle to his desire to marry Satyavati, the young man would decide to sacrifice his libido for the rest of his life. Devabrata says "I've been informed by your well-wishers. And believe me, father, the remedy is at hand. Be patient." In the visuals, we see in the background a red tree gradually becoming the throat tendons, veins, and muscles of Devabrata. The two panels there are so connected that they together tell a fantastic tale.

The body plays a crucial role in the stories of the Mahabharata. Take for instance these events: the father-son Yayati-Puru age exchange, the public humiliation of Draupadi, Bhisma's bed of arrows, Bhima's drinking of his cousin Duswasana's blood.

We come across a number of melancholic scenes in the post-war moment at which mothers, wives, and sisters, lamenting the loss of their loved ones, search for their scattered body parts. One of the foremost examples in this procession is the wife of Karna who has her husband's head in her hands. One can never forget that during the Bharat-Yuddha, which indeed is the epicentre of the Mahabharata, the majority of the valiant heroes of the epic were busy from dawn to dusk in destroying human bodies.

For the artist of any graphic novel, the imagining of the human anatomy, of body parts, and of costumes are of critical importance – it is through these that he attempts to make the characters convincing. From the first, I thought of the characters in terms of theatrical performance. For me, the Mahabharata is raw, its texture is rough, not glossy. Whenever I try to imagine its characters, they come with such complicated emotions that they, on their own, set a mood as rough as the tree skin. The Vyasa who sings the Mahabharata in the graphic novel is thus raw as mud, real, palpable as the smell of newly harvested crops.

The designing of illustrations with movements of figures, hand gestures, expressive faces, bending, and stretching of bodies, was absolutely central for me. In *Panchali*, Duryodhan often talks with a lot of hand movement; theatrically speaking, he often carries "spaces" around him. Conversely,

Yudhishthira is calm, his eyes are wide; we hardly can see him with body movement except when he plays the dice game and loses his mind.

For most part, the dresses are conceived in accordance with social rank. A king or a prince wears multi-pleated dresses, and the stitches are fine. Using folds without stitches is taken to be fashionable in the books. Often the waves of the clothes give dynamism to the characters. Hand-woven thick clothing is given to characters possessing a strong personality, such as Vyasa, or to persons of intense personality, such as the one-eyed dice-game player in *Panchali*.

Forests and trees are characters in the narration. The trees cry during the burning of the Khandava forest; they laugh when sage Kindama makes love before being killed by Pandu; they get angry, pose seductively, display eerie forms, etc. either in the background or in the foreground. It is as though the trees have their own take on the various *Mahabharata* episodes, something that is never revealed to humans.

11.

The Mahabharata is the poem of the people. We see countless unknown people of different races, ethnicities, colours, and professions throughout the epic. In *Vyasa* we see silent toilers working in the background in all the chapters; most of the time we can't see their eyes as if they don't have any identity.

Bandyopadhyay writes in *Panchali*, "Many a bard has recycled the poem in many a tongue, in many a style" (14). In *Panchali*, we see suddenly one of these toilers, during the making of the city, Indraprastha, pops up in a splash page with wide eyes and strong face. Also, during the insult of Draupadi in the royal court, we see Draupadi's eyes in a close-up and then in a big close-up. The face of the toiler, straight looking at the reader or Draupadi's eyes, has a larger-than-life function in the book – the canvas size of the graphic novel appears to be far too meagre to capture the pain or struggle of the oppressed. Such challenges need to be encountered and solved at every turn of turning the narrative into a contemporary graphic narrative.

Works Cited

Bhattacharya, Sukumari. 2015. *Prachin Bharat: Samaj O Sahitya*, Ananda Publishers Pvt LTD.

Buitenen, J. A. B. 1983. *The Mahabharata – 1*; The Book of the Beginning, "Introduction". The University of Chicago.

Das, Asok Kumar. 2005. *Paintings of Razamnama*, Mapin Publishing, India.

Gavaler, Chris. 2021. *How to Make Comics: What Are Comics?*, Museum of Modern Art, New York.

McCloud, Scott. 1994. *Understanding Comics: The Invisible Art*. William Morrow, New York.

Miller, William. 2017-02–06. Retrieved 2018-04–13. 'Tardigrades', *American Scientist*.

Schelly, Bill. 2010. *Founders of Comic Fandom: Profiles of 90 Publishers, Dealers, Collectors, Writers, Artists and Other Luminaries of the 1950s and 1960s.* McFarland & Co., USA.

Sukthankar Vishnu S. (ed.). 1997, *Mahabharata* Vol II., Bhandarkar Oriental Research Institute, Poona. 4.19.

PART II

12

THE "AVENGERS" IN AN *ITIHASA*

Reading Revenge in the Mahabharata

Kanad Sinha

The Vengeful Hero and the Mahabharata

Revenge is a frequently used theme in the popular narratives about heroism. In heroic literature, especially in Indo-European mythology, successfully avenging insult and death is often the yardstick of heroism. Thus, in Homer's *Iliad*, numerous Hellenic heroes undertake a risky journey to distant Troy to avenge the abduction of Helen. The epic narrative culminates with Achilles, the supreme hero, avenging the death of his beloved Patroclus, by killing Hector in a duel. In the Odyssey, an epic sequel to the Iliad, Agamemnon, king of Mycenae, returns from Troy after the Hellenic victory, only to be killed by Aegisthus, the lover of his wife Clytemnestra. Orestes, the son of Agamemnon, avenges his father's death, by killing both Aegisthus and Clytemnestra, despite the risk of inviting the wrath of the deities for committing the sin of matricide. If we look at the ancient Indian epic Ramayana, Ravana avenges the humiliation of his sister Surpanakha at the hands of Rama and Laksmana by abducting Sita, the wife of Rama, while Rama avenges this by killing Ravana. Even in modern popular culture, the idea of revenge is so much entrenched with the idea of heroism that the heroes who represent justice are still shown as righteous avengers of insults and deaths. For instance, the sleuth Sherlock Holmes, usually a strong adherent of the Victorian ideals of justice, occasionally endorses revenge when a guilty cannot be brought to justice by legal mechanism. In *A Study in Scarlet*, the novel where Holmes makes his appearance, Arthur Conan Doyle paints the character of Jefferson Hope who murders the ones responsible for the death of his murderer with romantic empathy, a feeling possibly shared by the narrator Watson if not by Holmes himself, and spares him a legal trial by

DOI: 10.4324/9781003516408-15

his death before the court could punish him. In several adventures, including *The Adventure of Black Peter*, *Adventure of the Illustrious Client*, and *Adventure of Charles Augustus Milverton*, Holmes appears in full sympathy with the ones committing crimes to avenge wrongs, and often lets the criminal go. In certain cases, Holmes is shown to have considered revenge and justice complementary to each other. For instance, in the case of *The Resident Patient*, when he failed to protect Sutton, a former bank robber eventually found and murdered by his gang, he declares:

> However, wretch as he was, he was still living under the shield of British law, and I have no doubt, Inspector, that you will see that, though that shield may fail to guard, the sword of justice is still there to avenge.
>
> *(1. 155)*

The two sets of superheroes, originating in comic books published by DC and Marvel and extremely popularized by a series of Hollywood movies of the last few decades, highlight the spirit of revenge as a key factor in the making of heroes. The most popular superhero of DC Comics emerges when Bruce Wayne resolves to avenge the murder of his parents and transforms into the Batman. The team of superheroes popularized by the Marvel Comics and the Marvel Cinematic Universe call themselves "The Avengers."

The Mahabharata is often considered one of the Indo-European heroic epics, and revenge is considered a key theme in the text. Popular culture associates the Mahabharata heroes with the ideal of revenge. For instance, allusions to the Mahabharata are frequent in the revenge-themed Bollywood film *Badla*, directed by Sujoy Ghosh. There, the protagonist, played by Amitabh Bachchan, repeatedly hints that the Mahabharata is to be understood as the revenge story of Draupadi. Indeed, in popular understanding, the Mahabharata is the story of a war where the Pandavas avenged the atrocities of the Kauravas, especially the humiliation of Draupadi, by fulfilling various vows of revenge. Arjuna killed Karna who had called Draupadi a harlot and ordered her disrobing. Sahadeva killed Sakuni whose cunning at the game of dice led to the Pandavas losing their kingdom and Draupadi being staked and lost. Bhima shattered the thigh of Duryodhana who had made an obscene gesture to Draupadi, and drank the blood of Duhsasana who pulled Draupadi's hair and tried to strip her. Woven into these vivid scenes of heroic revenge are sub-stories also culminating in the war. Amba, who had committed suicide with a vow to avenge her abduction from her svayamvara by Bhisma, was reborn as Sikhandi who caused Bhisma's death (Hymns of the Atharvaveda, 8.10.22). When Drupada, the king of Panncala, humiliated the poor brahmana Drona, his boyhood friend, and denied the promises made earlier on the ground that friendship was possible only between equals, Drona avenged his insult by getting Drupada captured by the Kuru princes, as a payment for teaching them martial skills, and forcing him to share his kingdom with him and to acknowledge his friendship. Drupada's sacrifice to avenge this insult gave birth to Dhristadyumna who eventually killed the unarmed Drona in the war (*Hymns of the Atharvaveda*, 8.10.29, 8.14.14, 4.6, 5.13, 6.12). Reading the Mahabharata as a story of heroic revenges is, therefore, very much plausible.

However, this chapter argues that the Mahabharata differs from the epics discussed above in its approach to heroism. It is one of the earliest texts to have questioned the valorization of violence and martial heroism in a "heroic society." Though revenge, and the fulfilment of vows of revenge, was highly valorized in the society the text reflects, particularly among the martial class – the kshatriyas, the Mahabharata – at least in its older sections – questions rather than espouses the stereotypes of *kshatradharma* including the glorification of revenge. This chapter shall show that revenge had gradually become a dominant theme of the text with its reworking by the Bhargava brahmanas, but the message of the older sections was possibly quite contrary. In the older sections, the poet/s of the Mahabharata actually posed the question whether revenge could fulfil the cause of justice or started an endless chain of violence. Looking back at these debates is essential at an age when aggressive militant nationalism is glorifying a dangerous politics where narratives of populist violent revenge are being glorified and policies of peaceful diplomatic deliberation are being portrayed as "weak," despite the lesson learnt from two World Wars. Is heroism entailed in vengefulness or in a peaceful quest for justice? Thankfully, the contemporary popular culture mentioned above, despite using the trope of vengefulness as a marker of heroism, shows the responsibility to point out the difference between "revenge" and "justice." The "Avengers" hardly "avenge" in the Marvel Cinematic Universe. When they try to avenge earlier deaths, it only leads to a civil war, whereas they succeed when they unite for the cause of justice. In Christopher Nolan's *Batman Trilogy*, Bruce Wayne is taught by his love interest Rachel Dawes the difference between "revenge" and "justice." It is the commitment to the latter that characterizes the Batman and distinguishes him from many of the villains he fights. Populist politics, however, often does not show the responsibility that popular culture does. The epics are often invoked to justify the rhetoric of populist politics. Therefore, it is essential to read the debates around the idea of heroic revenge in the Mahabharata and understand how the text's position changed through its millennium-long composition.

It is not only that the Mahabharata's central narrative appears to be a story of heroic vengeance, it is framed in a context of revenge. The central narrative around the Bharata War, whose composition is attributed to Krishna Dvaipayana Vyasa, is presented as retold by Vaisampayana, one of the disciples of Vyasa, to the Kuru king Janamejaya. The context of

Vaisampayana's performance is Janamejaya's sacrifice intending to kill all the Nagas, especially the Naga Taksaka who had killed Janamejaya's father, Parikshit. Thus, genocidal vengeance provides the context for the first public performance of the Mahabharata. The Nagas, whose slaughter Janamejaya desired, appear in the Mahabharata at times as snakes, at times as humans, and at times as both. They could have been easily dismissed as fantastic mythological creatures, had they not been present in various historical sources throughout early Indian history. They were a powerful group, who were sometimes allies or antagonists of the ksatriya rulers. Some of the major Naga figures, such as Dhritarashtra Airavata, Taksaka (Minkowski 2011), and Arbuda Kadraveya, are well-known characters in Vedic literature. One of them, Arbuda Kadraveya, is also considered the poet of Rg Veda X.94, while Taksaka seems to be a Later Vedic figure, well-known to the *Atharva Veda*. Christopher Minkowski has shown that the sarpasatra itself has Vedic precedents, and Janamejaya is a well-known Later Vedic figure. However, rather than being a rite to exterminate all Nagas, it seems to be a Vedic rite practised by many communities including the Nagas. The rite is known to various Vedic texts. Interestingly, some of them mention among the previous performers of the rite Janamejaya as well as his principal adversary Taksaka (Raychaudhuri 2006 489). The Nagas were powerful at least till the Gupta Period (fourth–fifth centuries CE) when they were the main antagonists of Samudra Gupta (1. 206), whereas Chandragupta II married a Naga princess (Kosambi 1964 39). Similarly, in the Mahabharata, marital alliance between the Kurus and the Nagas is mentioned. Arjuna marries the Naga widow Ulupi who keeps her son with her, possibly following their own matrilineal custom. D.D. Kosambi notes the importance of the Naga cycle in the epic, reflected in the Naga aid to Bhima, Nahusa's conversion into a Naga, Balarama's transformation into a Naga, and Dhrtarastra's assumed Naga characteristic (Sinha 2014). But, the Nagas were also antagonistic to the Kuru heroes and their associates. Legends hold that Krishna subdued Kaliya Naga on the banks of the Yamuna (Minkowski 390). The sarpasatra in the Mahabharata is not a stray incident but is located within a chain of events depicting the clashes between the Kurus and the Nagas, possibly starting with the violent destruction of the Khandava Forest, where the Taksaka family lived, by the Kuru prince Arjuna and his friend Krishna, for the extension of habitable and cultivable land in the settlement of Indraprastha (17.5.29).

Interestingly, the *Baudhayana Srauta Sastra* locates the original sarpasatra at Khandavaprastha, not only a part of the Kuru kingdom but also the original abode of Taksaka in the Mahabharata (Fergusson 1868 44–47). Even more interestingly, the sarpasatra of Janamejaya took place at Taksasila (1.118.1–11), the place where the Khandava Nagas might have shifted their base after they were driven away from the Khandava Forest. This assumption is strengthened by the experience of Onesikritas, a companion of Alexander to India in the fourth century BCE, who encountered a community of huge number of snakes and snake-worshippers at Taxila (8.66.1–24).

In the Mahabharata, the Nagas had an overall troubled relationship with the Kurus, despite Arjuna's marriage with Ulupi. The animosity started with the eviction of Taksaka's family from the Khandava Forest by Arjuna and Krishna, including the killing of Taksaka's wife by Arjuna (1.45.6). Asvasena, Taksaka's son, wanted to avenge the death of his mother by aiding Karna in killing Arjuna during the Bharata War, but Karna refused the aid (1.51.16–1.53.14). Taksaka, however, killed Arjuna's grandson, Parikshit. Janamejaya's vow was to kill Taksaka and exterminate all the Nagas. Thus, it became a series of seemingly endless violence that culminated in the sarpasatra of Janamejaya. However, the satra was halted midway by Astika, a half-brahmana half-Naga. This became the occasion for Vaisampayana's narration of the Mahabharata.

Therefore, the Mahabharata was to be recited amidst an ongoing feud of violent vengeance which was temporarily halted by a seemingly neutral person. Thus, in a way, the Mahabharata itself was addressing a crucial question: is vengeance the right solution? Before we find out what answer the text provides, it is, therefore, important to consider who asked this question and at what context. The tale of the Bharata War was told by Vyasa, and Vaisampayana narrated Vyasa's tale to Janamejaya. But who was telling the tale of Vaisampayana and Janamejaya? Who were the authors of the frame story of the Mahabharata?

Incidentally, the Mahabharata itself says a little about its textual history. Thus, it itself provides us with two frame stories. Vaisampayana's narration to Janamejaya, thus, is usually called the "inner frame" which itself is contained within the "outer frame" where the bard Ugrasravas addresses an assemblage of sages at the Naimisa Forest, led by the Bhargava kulapati Saunaka, gathered for a twelve-year long sacrifice. Vaisampayana and Janamejaya are figures known to Later Vedic texts. This Saunaka and the bard Ugrasravas (and his father Romaharsana) were probably mythological characters. However, even if the characters and context mentioned in the two frame stories are not exactly factual, they possibly say a lot about the Mahabharata's textual journey. Both seem to be bardic performances at grand sacrifices, but patronized by the Kuru court interested in their own past and the Bhargava-led brahmanas interested in an interesting narrative, respectively. It is highly possible that the Mahabharata emerged as an itihasa (bardic historical tradition) of the Later Vedic Kurus, but was gradually controlled by the brahmanas, especially the Bhargavas who canonized it. Ugrasavas's narration indeed contains a mini-epic on Bhargava mythology. V.S. Sukthankar had first addressed the possibility of Bhargavization of the text, a theory also supported by the findings of later scholars, such as Robert P. Goldman (Sullivan 9). Kevin McGrath showed how Bhargavization created a new theology by associating Krishna with an old divinity named Narayana, possibly of pre-Aryan origin, and identifying Arjuna with Nara, the companion of Narayana, and how often the Bhargavized sections justify their claims by drawing on traditions and stories referring to ancient times, mainly through the authoritative figure of Narada who is depicted as the repository of divine and all-pervading knowledge and is the representative of oral traditions within the text. Bruce M. Sullivan also notes how the portions contained within Ugrasravas's narration within the text are self-consciously later than others (Buitenen 1973 xxiv). On the other hand, though the composition of the text has usually been dated between 500 BCE and 500 CE, historians like Romila Thapar and R.S. Sharma – who have pointed out the difference between the narrative and didactic sections of the text – note that the older narrative sections represent the context of the period of the Later Vedas (c.1000–600 BCE). A similar view has been expressed by J.A.B. van Buitenen, on the basis of the seemingly Later Vedic context of the Mahabharata narrative and the Vedic location of some of the Mahabharata characters, that: "It seems more likely than not that the origins of The Mahabharata fall somewhere in the eighth or ninth century" (6.32.15, 6.32.37).

Therefore, it can be argued that the central narrative of the Mahabharata addresses the concern of the Later Vedic clan societies of the Kuru-Pancala region. But, the text had been thoroughly reworked by the brahmanas between 500 BCE and 500 CE, with the Bhargavas playing a prominent role in its refashioning, and the outer frame had been added to the text within this process. Therefore, the authors of the outer frame, possibly Bhargavas, devised the context of the inner frame as the sarpasatra of Janamejya, who wanted to look at the Mahabharata with an emphasis on heroic vengeance. Perhaps, heroic vengeance was a theme that coloured the Bhargava imagination, as can be seen not only from their framing of the Mahabharata narrative but also from the recurrent appearance of revenge-themed myths in the later accretions to the story, mostly evolving Bhargava heroes like Ruru and Aurva, and culminating in the legends of the vengeful Bhargava superhero, Parasurama.

Parasurama and Bhargava Vengeance

The Bhargavas – particularly the Grtsamada-Saunaka branch – have played a very interesting role in the history of Sanskrit text creation. They might have been very prominent in pre-Vedic time, but in the Rgvedic history they were subdued by the Angirasas at first and the upstart Vasistha later. The Grtsamada Saunakas, the family to whom the Book II of the *Rg Veda* is attributed, were Bhargavas by adoption. The main line of the Bhrigus has no family book of their own in the *Rg Veda*. The most prominent Bhargava poet of the text is Jamadagni (3.62.16–18, 8.101, 9.62, 10.65, 9.67, 9.107, 10.110). There are several references to the clan. But Bhrigu himself is a shady and mythical figure in the text. Only IX.65, which seems to be Jamadagni's composition, has sometimes been attributed to Bhrigu. Bhrigu's son Kavi is the poet of IX.47–49 and IX.75–79. Usanas (VIII.84, IX.87–89), son of Kavi, seems to be the most famous poet of his time. Even Vasistha and Vamadeva, by no means affiliated to the Bhrigus, remember him as a great poet (Sinha 2014). Even in the much later text of the *Bhagavad Gita*, Krishna describes himself as Bhrgu among the sages and Usanas among the poets (*RV* 7.18). Despite the influence of the Bhargavas on the contemporary intelligentsia, and the fame of Usanas, it is strange that the Bhrigus have so little composition in the text. Possibly, they were not very enthusiastic about the form of religion practised in the Panjab. This made them an unorthodox group of brahmanas often associated with magic and sorcery (probably remnants of pre-Vedic shamanism). The association of the Bhargavas with the Asuras (possibly representative of the Indo-Iranians of pre-Vedic days) who are said to have possessed magical power (maya) is probably a result of that. The famous Bhargava figure Usanas Sukracarya is thus also renowned as the teacher of the Asuras, whereas the Angirasa Brhaspati is known to be the teacher of the Devas. It is possible that the separation between the Indo-Iranians and Indo-Aryans in the pre-Vedic period had something to do with cultic confrontation. The Deva-worshipping Indo-Aryans migrated to the Indian subcontinent, their religion being predominated by the Angirasa priests, while the Asura-worshipping Indo-Iranians – with a predominant presence of the Bhargavas who believed in sorcery and shamanism – remained in Iran. This hypothesis is supported by the fact that Ahura (Asura) is the epithet of the Iranian Supreme Deity Mazda, and the Avesta is very much aware of the "Atharvan" (Bhargava) priests.

Thus, the famous Bhargava poets of earlier days are remembered in the *Rg Veda*, while the Bhargavas have little presence in the text. In the most famous political event of the Rgvedic period, the Battle of Ten Kings, the Bharata chief Sudas, aided by his upstart priest Vasistha, defeated a confederacy of ten clans brought together by Visvamitra and his Bhargava friends (Sukthankar 1936–7 335). This victory established Vasistha as the most important religious ideologue of the time and marginalized the Bhargavas further. Later, the Bhargava Saunakas compiled the most popular recension of the *Atharva Veda*, the Saunaka Samhita, which deals with mainly magic and sorcery, and which was grudgingly accepted as the fourth Veda. When the Bhargavas started taking serious interest in the literary field, they also provided their interpretation of the *Rg Veda* in the Brhaddevata, attributed to a Saunaka. The Bhargava myths indicate a close link between the Bhargavas and the kshatriyas who might have benefited from the Bhargava tradition of sorcery and text-creation (since both could be sources of royal legitimacy).

So, when the Brahmanical authority was questioned by the rise of heterodox religions, many of which received considerable royal patronage, it was the Bhargavas who might have suffered substantially by losing a good share of their monopolized patronage. This is probably the context of the Bhargavas emerging as the main mouthpiece for a varna-ordered society protected by a dharmika king defending the caturvarnya and patronizing the brahmanas. The Bhargavas seem to be instrumental in articulating this vision of kingship in the post-Maurya period (c. BCE 200–300 CE). The strongest propagation of this theory was presented in the archetypal lawbook *Manu Smriti* also known as the *Bhrigu Samhita*. However, this was the period which had witnessed major modification of both the Ramayana and the Mahabharata as well. The principal additions to the Ramayana were the "Uttarakanda" (the last book) and parts of the "Balakanda," which turned the erstwhile heroic romance in the story of an ideal dharmika king who ruled according to caturvarnya, and deified the hero Rama into a Vaisnava incarnation. The Bhargavas seem to have some role in the process, at least in claiming a Bhargava identity for the poet Valmiki if not in anything else (3.115–117). The Mahabharata witnessed a similar process of Brahmanization and Vaisnavization, and with a much more pronounced body of Bhargava myths. In fact, there seems to be a close relationship between the composition of the Manu Smrti and the Bhargavization of the Mahabharata. Sukthankar has pointed out that about 260 stanzas of the Manu Smrti (about 10% of the total) are found verbatim or with slight variations in the Bhargava sections of the "Aranyakaparvan" and the later Bhargava books "Santiparvan" and "Anusasanaparvan"(1.2.3–9). Thus, the Bhargavized sections of the Mahabharata propound the theory of a varna-based polity with a symbiotic relationship between the brahmana and the kshatriya. An ideal king was to be an upholder of the brahmana's social supremacy. A failure from this ideal might lead to a violent purge of the demonic unlawful kshatriyas as witnessed in the Bharata War that took place at the same spot (Kurukshetra) where Rama Jamadagnya (or Parasurama), the Bhargava superhero, had celebrated his ruthless massacre of all kshatriyas to avenge his father Jamadagni's murder.

Jamadagni was a Rgvedic figure. But this son of Jamadagni is unknown to the Rg Veda. The word "Parasurama" is a very late Puranic epithet, and in earlier references, the figure is known as Rama Jamadagnya, Bhargava Rama, or simply Rama. Who was this Rama Jamadagnya? His legend has been narrated in the Mahabharata by his follower Akrtavarna to Yudhisthira. It started with Rcika, the father of Jamadagni, who married Satyavati, the daughter of king Gadhin. Satyavati and her mother confused the separate childbearing potions prepared for them by Rcika. Thus, the queen bore a son of brahmana sensitivities, the future Visvamitra. Satyavati was to bear a son of ksatriya spirit. But, Rcika could defer it for a generation. Thus,

Jamadagni was born with brahmana sensibility, but with ksatriya inclinations subdued in his gene. Like his father, Jamadagni married a princess, Renuka. They had five sons. One day, Renuka was aroused by witnessing the watersports of King Citraratha and his wives. Angrily, Jamadagni asked his sons to kill her. Though the first four refused to do so, and were cursed by Jamadagni, Rama followed his father's command.

Much attached to his father, Rama was furious when Jamadagni's hermitage was ransacked by the proud Haihaya king Kartavirya Arjuna. With his kshatriya spirit aroused, Rama went to fight Kartavirya whose men (or sons) used Rama's absence to kill Jamadagni. It caused the world-shattering wrath of Rama who brutally massacred all kshatriyas. He repeated this feat twenty times more, conquering the entire world. His violent career at last ended when he gifted the earth to the great sage Kasyapa who banished him at once from his domain (1.98.5).

The account of Akrtavarna is the most extensive description of Rama Jamadagnya's life in the Mahabharata, but it is not the only one. Sukthankar notes that the birth story of Parasurama had been narrated at least four times in the Mahabharata, and his destruction of the kshatriyas referred to at least ten times. In fact, the Bhargava reading of the Mahabharata has to begin with a connection made between Parasurama's destruction of all the kshatriyas and the death of many kshatriyas in the Bharata War, both culminating at the same venue, Samantapancaka or Kurukshetra (7.70). Moreover, the new kshatriyas are described as nothing but creation of the brahmanas who cohabited with the widows of the kshatriyas killed by Parasurama (7.34). In the "Dronaparvan," the exploits of Parasurama are described in vivid detail as a part of the Saga of the Sixteen Kings (9.52–56). The "Karnaparvan" extends Parasurama's exploits to a victory over the Daityas as well (9.48–49). The story of Parasurama is narrated in full in the "Anusasanaparvan" too, and there the reversal of the caste roles of Visvamitra and Parasurama is further explained as a result of the Bhargava Cyavana's prophetic blessing to Kusika who served him like a slave (Goldman 161–173).

However, the Bhargava accounts in the "Santiparvan" have a milder tone than the ones in the "Adiparvan," "Aranyakaparvan," "Dronaparvan," "Karnaparvan," and "Anusasanaparvan." Therefore, in the "Santiparvan," the new ksartiyas are genuine kshatriyas, since nature protected some of their ancestors from Parasurama's campaign. This "Santiparvan" account of Parasurama's career, placed in the mouth of Krishna, also differs from Akrtavarna's account in the characterization of Kartavirya Arjuna. The cruel, proud, and oppressive king of Akrtavarna's account is a perfectly noble one in Krishna's narrative. His sons created the trouble in the latter account (1.169.10–25). Again, the Saga of the Sixteen Kings, in the "Santiparvan," does not include Rama Jamadagnya, but an actual king, Sagara, as the sixteenth one.

Goldman thinks that Krishna's version of the Parasurama legend ended up as an apologia for the warrior race and their right of sovereignty, and perhaps developed later than the Akrtavarna version. He points out that the Akrtavarna version – which contains a long lamentation by Parasurama after Jamadagni's death, shows Kartavirya as arrogant and brutal, and makes his destruction of the kshatriyas final – is sympathetic to the hero and shows him as a grief-stricken son avenging his father's death. On the other hand, Krishna's version shows Kartavirya as a pious, dutiful, and generous ruler, contains no lamentation, makes Parasurama's successive destruction of the kshatriyas a result of a taunt by Paravasu who mocked him for a false pledge, makes some kshatriyas survive the slaughter, is pro-ksatriya, and shows Parasurama in a negative light as a ruthless murderer who goes on killing people to boost his own ego and whim (Choudhary 47–8).

However, a closer scrutiny of the two versions indicates that the distinction may not be so clear. After all, in both the versions, Parasurama reacted to the killing of his father by the kshatriyas. The presence or absence of a vilapa does not alter this scenario, and Parasurama remains a grief-stricken son in both. The massive slaughter no doubt hurts our sensibilities, but in the epic context it is probably the fulfilment of the vow that matters most. Therefore, the representation in Krishna's version may not be so negative for Parasurama as Goldman thinks, and – in any case – the slaughter is equally gruesome in both the accounts. The survival of the kshatriyas, in fact, points to Krishna's version's priority in date. If some kshatriyas were not shown as surviving in each round of slaughter, the very myth of twenty-one slaughters could not even be generated. It seems that in later times, when Parasurama had attained the status of a superhero, his followers – which Akrtavarna reportedly was – made his slaughters even more complete, turning the later kshatriyas in creations of the brahmanas. Moreover, the way the "Santiparvan" version of the *sodasarajopakhyana* (*Tale of Sixteen Kings*) has been Bhargavized in the "Dronaparvan" would point towards the priority of the former one.

The highly violent Brahmanical and patriarchal overtone of the Parasurama legend is quite apparent. The legend shows a point of rupture when even reconciliation between the brahmanas and the kshatriyas seemed improbable, and when the brahmana aspiration was to purge the earth of all the kshatriyas. What antagonized the Bhrgus this much? What necessitated the conception of Jamadagnya Rama?

The answer possibly lies in another legend in the Mahabharata. It says that the noble Haihaya king Krtavirya had distributed a huge amount of wealth among the brahmanas. However, his descendants – when in distress – wanted the wealth back. Many Bhrgus returned the wealth, while many others did not. The angry Haihayas killed all the Bhrgus, down to the children in the womb. Of course, the Bhrgus did not let the story end in this fashion. They brought in the infant Aurva who blindfolded the Haihaya persecutors and prepared to destroy the evil world. He only stopped when his ancestors appeared to reveal to him the secret that the puny kshatriyas were no match for the Bhargavas and would never be able to kill them. Actually, the Bhargavas, who were tired of their lives but were virtually immortal (as death feared to approach them), had to create a pretext for dying. Otherwise, they never desired any wealth except the heaven (Sukthankar 327). However, despite this Bhargavized defence, a large-scale persecution of the Bhargavas, who hoarded undue wealth, is indicated.

The legend of Aurva indeed had the potential of what the Parasurama legend became. But, Aurva stopped twice on the verge of becoming a great annihilator. Pradeep Kant Choudhary assumes several reasons behind this, including the followers of Aurva losing importance, some actual memory of a historical Parasurama, and the appeal of a warrior hero than a hero using sacrificial means to accomplish his task (AV 5.18.10, 5.19.1). However, it seems that the Aurva legend is a bit older than the Parasurama legend, representing an immediate response to the persecution they were facing. An immediate justification of their fate was conceived as a design made by the Bhargavas themselves. However, when the wave of persecution was over, the Bhargava vengeance was crystallized in conceiving their ideal hero, one capable of combating the kshatriyas on the battlefield.

This possibly explains the violent anti-kshatriya stance of the Bhrigus whose relationship with the rulers had a complicated history. Sukthankar rightly shows that the Bhrgu legends show their close relationship with the rulers, including several marital ties (Choudhary 43–44). Neglected in the days of Kuru-Pancala dominance, they possibly sought patronage under some lesser Vedic tribes, maybe the Haihayas. No doubt, the Bhargavas composed and controlled a good number of texts. But, they probably never succeeded in regaining the social prominence they desired. They were engaged in long struggles against the kshatriyas. Their own text, the *Atharva Veda*, speaks of how the Vaitahavyas perished because of slaughtering the cows of the Bhrigus (Fitzgerald 52–74). Choudhary suggests that the Vaitahavyas joined the Haihaya tribe, which is not improbable (1.9.10). The final blow was probably a violent persecution at the hands of the Haihayas. In fact, they could not do much against the existing political power. But, in their texts, they could dream of a role reversal led by a Bhrigu hero. That could have given birth to Aurva, and ultimately to Jamadagnya Rama. The Bhargava individual, in this case, was a superhuman figure who could extend this conflict to all the kshatriyas.

Thus, following scholars like Sukthankar, we can assume that the creation of Parasurama was a psychological overcompensation of the Bhargava brahmanas against their subjugated real-life status and to propagate their own social superiority. James L. Fitzgerald is probably right in thinking that the

Mahabharata, as we find it now, is primarily a religious epic, a response of the "Brahmanical Renaissance" to the empires of Pataliputra, which patronized the heterodox religions. The principal agenda of the text is to espouse an ideal polity under a king who subjects himself under the brahmanas whom he supports materially and preserves from all harm. The ideal society is conceived as one where all the varnas perform their specified duties. The Brahmanical rage against the contemporary ruling class is presented within an overall narrative of demonic, unlawful kshatriyas being purged by the divine kshatriyas allied with the brahmanas. The narration unfolds in genocidal hatred of a sacrifice to kill all the Nagas, with Rama Jamadagnya's genocidal rampage against all the kshatriyas at the backdrop, gradually moving towards the violent purge of the kshatriyas in the Bharata War (*RV* 10.98). Thus, heroic vengeance was a key question in the Bhargava reworking of the Mahabharata, and the redactors provided the central narrative with a frame story that would prioritize this question. The concept of the inner frame, a massive initiative to destroy all the Nagas to avenge the death of a loved one, was possibly derived from another Bhargava myth in which the Bhargava sage Ruru endeavoured to kill all snakes after the death of his betrothed Pramadvara off snake-bite (*AV* 20.127.7–10). Interestingly, the chief priest in Janamejaya's snake sacrifice was also named Candabhargava (angry Bhargava). However, though the narration of the Mahabharata took place within a context of heroic vengeance, the intervention of Astika had halted the process. Janamejaya was to listen to the account of his ancestors and consider if vengeance was the solution. What answer did the Mahabharata narrative provide?

Revenge or Justice: Yudhisthira's Solution

As indicated earlier, the narrative section of the Mahabharata possibly addresses the context of the clan societies of the Later Vedic period. The Kurus and the Pancalas were the most important clans in the early part of the Later Vedic period. The legends of the Kuru chief Santanu appear in the Tenth Book, the latest part, of the *Rg Veda*. The Kuru chief Parikshit is celebrated as a contemporary ruler in the *Atharva Veda*. Parikshit's son Janamejaya was a well-known Later Vedic figure (Witzel 27–52). By the time of the composition of the *Brihadaranyaka Upanishad*, one of the earliest Upanisads, the descendants of Parikshit were no longer there. The Mahabharata narrative, concerning the generations between Samtanu and Parikshit, definitely addresses the early centuries of the first millennium, when the Later Vedic janapadas settled down and the Vedic varna orthodoxy and orthopraxy were crystallizing, as Michael Witzel argues, in the Kuru realm (Panini 4.3.98). Vaisampayana was associated with the teaching of Mahabharata in the Asvalayana Grhya Sutra, and the worship of Krishna Vasudeva and Arjuna was prevalent during Panini's time (2.25–42).

Therefore, the hereditary ruling authority of the ksatriya dynasties was consolidating in the period which concerns the Mahabharata narrative, and the ksatriya code of martial valour (*kshatradharma*) was valued much by the ruling clans. This explains why violent heroic vengeance is integral to the various personal battles within the Bharata War, including Bhisma's killing involving Sikhandin, Drona's death at the hands of Dhrstadyumna, Bhima's fulfilment of violent vows to kill Duryodhana and Duhsasana, Arjuna's killing of Karna, and Sahadeva's killing of Sakuni. Thus, it may seem that revenge is a celebrated martial value in the Mahabharata narrative. Yet, Krishna, just before the commencement of the Bharata War, delivers the *Bhagavad Gita* to encourage Arjuna to fight, without uttering the issue of revenge once. Rather, Krishna's espousal of niskama karma (desireless action) would hardly consider goal-orientated vengeance advisable. The *Gita* is a didactic section, and its date has been debated a lot, but Krishna's own actions throughout the narrative present an alternative to the idea of revenge, the ideal of forgiveness till violence is the only option left to assure justice. Thus, Jarasamdha attacked Mathura to avenge the killing of his son-in-law Kamsa by Krishna. Krishna left Mathura and fled to Dvaraka. He did not seek revenge on Jarasamdha till the latter was about to organize a human sacrifice of a hundred kings. Then, Krishna got him killed by Bhima (7.53.2–3). Similarly, Krishna forgave a hundred offences by Sisupala before he had to kill him when he was about to jeopardize Yudhusthira's rajasuya (1.155). Therefore, during the Bharata War, when Arjuna vowed to kill Jayadratha before the next sunset to avenge the death of his son Abhimanyu, Krishna criticized the rashness of the vow, even though Abhimanyu was his own nephew and disciple (McGrath 2011 54).

However, even if Krishna was not a champion of heroic vengeance, it can be denied that the idea was very much behind the Bharata War. The war was, at least to Draupadi, a way to avenge her humiliation. However, the strongest criticism of this ideal came from the victor of the Bharata War, Yudhisthira. If Draupadi's humiliation was to be avenged at the Bharata War, Yudhisthira was expected to be the keenest person to seek revenge. After all, it was Yudhisthira, the eldest of Draupadi's five husbands, who had staked and lost Draupadi in the fateful dicegame where Duhsasana tried to strip her and Duryodhana made obscene gestures at her. Draupadi was not to let it go unavenged. She was, after all, supposed to be born out of the fire of Drupada's sacrifice to avenge his insult at the hands of Drona and the Kurus. Naturally, Draupadi herself took a pledge not to tie up her hair as long as it was not washed in Duhsasana's blood, inspiring Bhima to eventually accomplish this terrible deed. McGrath rightly notes that "women in epic Mahabharata, more than male heroes, speak what is considered to be social truth: what is right for kshatriyas and what constitutes good behaviour" (12.14.4). Draupadi, being the highest epitome of such ideal kshatriya woman, repeatedly tried to inspire Yudhisthira to the martial heroism extolled within his caste.

However, Yudhisthira remained steadfast in his own virtue of *anrsamsya* (non-cruelty) and *anukrosa* (considerate empathy) (4.17.1), which cared little for inherited varna identity. Thus, the poet describes the character of Draupadi as one who is perpetually offended particularly with Yudhisthira (*abhimanavati nityam visesena yudhisthire*) (3.28), which is testified by Draupadi's comment, "*asocyam nu kutas tasya yasya bharta yudhisthirah*" (What pity doesn't a woman deserve who has Yudhisthira for her husband?) (3.29). Repeatedly complaining about Yudhisthira's lack of anger (3.31.4), she forcefully argued why neither extreme vengeance nor extreme forgiveness was desirable, and one had to maintain a balance of both in his dealings (3.13.58–59). She went to the extent of arguing that gentleness, patience, uprightness, and tenderness – the cornerstones of Yudhisthira's cherished dharma – were futile (3.13.112–113). She had also lamented to Krishna:

garhaye pandavams tv eva yudhi sresthan mahabalan/
ye klisyamanam preksante dharmapatnim yasasvinim//
dhig balam bhimasenasya dhik parthasya dhanusmatam/
yau mam viprakrtam ksudrair marsayetam janardana//
(I detest the Pandavas, those grand strongmen in war, who looked on while their glorious consort in Law was molested! A plague on the strength of Bhimasena! A plague on the bowmanship of the Partha! Both stood by, Janardana, when churls manhandled me.) (3.255–45)

She also complained:

naiva me patayah santi na putra madhusudana/
na bhrataro na ca pita naiva tvam na ca bandhavah//
ye mam viprakrtam ksudrair upeksadhvam visokavat//
(I have got no husbands, no sons, Madhusudana, not a brother nor a father, nor you, nor friends, if you mercilessly ignored me when I was plagued by the vulgar.) (4.15.20–36)

When Jayadratha tried to assault Draupadi, she physically resisted him, and then wanted to avenge her insult by killing him. Infuriated by Yudhisthira's passivity, she urged Bhima and Arjuna:

kartavyam cet priyam mahyam vadhyah sa purusadhamah/
saindhavapasadah papo durmatih kulapamsanah//
(If you want to do me a kindness, kill off that wretched abortion of the Saindhavas, the evil, ill-minded defiler of his race.) (5.80.31–41)

Similarly, when in disguise in the Matsya realm, she was sexually assaulted by Kicaka, the king's brother-in-law, in front of the passive Yudhisthira, she became vocal in rage against her husbands and even admonished the king Virata and his court, despite being in the disguise of a mere maidservant:

> Where on Earth are the great warriors roaming in disguise, they who were the refuge of those who sought shelter? How can those powerful, boundlessly august men like castrates suffer that their beloved and faithful wife is kicked by a suta's son? Where has their intransigence gone, where their virility and splendor, if they choose not to defend their wife who is being kicked by a blackguard? What am I to do with Virata here who sees the Law violated, an innocent woman kicked, and allows it? King, you do not act like a king at all in the matter of Kicaka, for your Law is the Law of Dasyus and does not shine in the assembly! Neither Kicaka nor the Matsya abide in any way by their own Law. I don't blame you, King Virata, in the assembly of the people, but it is not right that I am struck in your presence, Matsya! Let the courtiers bear witness to the crime of Kicaka.
>
> *(5.79.1–4)*

Thus, Draupadi was insistent on a war to avenge her humiliation:

> A curse on Bhimasena's strength, a curse on the Partha's bowmanship, if Duryodhana stays alive for another hour, Krishna! If you find favour in me, if you have pity on me, direct your entire fury at the Dhartarastras, Krishna.

This hair was pulled by Duhsasana's hands, lotus-eyed Lord; remember it at all times when you seek peace with the enemies! If Bhima and Arjuna pitifully hanker after peace, my ancient father will fight, and his warrior sons, Krishna! My five valiant sons will, led by Abhimanyu, fight with the Kurus, Madhusudana! What peace will my heart know unless I see Duhsasana's swarthy arm cut off and covered with dust! Thirteen years have gone by while I waited, hiding my rage in my heart like a blazing fire. Pierced by the thorn of Bhima's words, my heart is rent asunder, for now that strong-armed man has eyes for the Law only (5.135.16–17).

She had full-throated support from many voices including that of her mother-in-law, Kunti:

> Not the rape of the kingdom, not the defeat at dice, not the banishment of my sons to the forest grieves me, as it grieves me that that great dark woman, weeping in the hall, had to listen to insults.
>
> *(5.158.9)*

The idea these women believed in had its supporters among the Pandavas. Thus, Bhima earnestly fulfilled Draupadi's wish. Sahadeva clearly stated in the deliberations before the war:

> What the king has said is the sempiternal Law, but see to it that there be war, enemy-tamer! Even if the Kurus should want peace with the Pandavas, you should still provoke war with them, Dasarha! How could my rage with Suyodhana subside after seeing the Princess of Pancala man-handled in the hall? If Bhima, Arjuna and King Dharma stick with the Law, I want to fight him in battle, and begone with the law *(yadi bhima-rjunau Krishna dharmarajas ca dharmikah/ dharmam utsrjya tenaham yoddhum icchami samyuge).*
>
> *(5.70.46–49)*

In fact, it was Yudhisthira's reluctance to follow the ksatriya code of violent, martial vengeance that seemed unrighteous to his cousin and arch-enemy Duryodhana. Therefore, on the verge of the war, after all attempts at peace failed, Duryodhana's message to the Pandavas would be:

amarsam rajyaharanam vanavasam ca pandava/
draupadyas ca pariklesam samsmaran puruso bhava//
(Be a man, remember your banishment from the kingdom, your hardships, your forest exile, the molestation of Draupadi, Pandava!) (5.70.53–59)

However, Yudhisthira was equally steadfast in his allegiance to dharma. He clearly stated his disapproval of the idea that a person had to be violent and unforgiving just because he belonged to a certain caste by birth. War to him was evil by all means and so was the ksatradharma that endorsed it:

> What is pretty in war? It is the evil Law of the kshatriyas...ksatriya kills ksatriya, fish lives on fish, dog kills dog.
>
> *(10.10–16)*

Yudhisthira provided us with one of the earliest and strongest statements against war and violence, standing in an era when heroism was the most respected manly virtue:

> War is evil in any form. What killer is not killed in return? To the killed victory and defeat are the same, Hrishikesa *(sarvatha vrjinam yuddham ko ghnana na pratihanyate/ hatasya ca hrisikesa samau jayaparajayau).*
>
> The victor too is surely diminished: In the end some others will kill a loved one of his; and behold, when he has lost his strength and no longer

sees his sons and brothers a loathing for life will engulf him completely, Krishna...There is always remorse after the killing of others, Janardana.

Victory breeds feuds, for the defeated rest uneasy. But easy sleeps the man who serenely has given up both victory and defeat (*jayo vairam prasrjati duhkham aste parajayam/ sukham prasantah svapiti hitva jayaparajayau*).

Thus, Yudhisthira viewed heroism as a "powerful disease that eats up the heart."

The issue of heroic vengeance, thus, was debated heatedly in the Mahabharata narrative. The ideal was too powerful to be ignored. When all attempts at peace failed, Yudhisthira himself had to agree to fight the war which, as discussed earlier, became a platform for exacting several personal revenges. However, the worst sufferer of this battle was Draupadi, the most vocal advocate for the battle. She lost her father in the battle, and the night attack by Asvatthaman on the Pandava camp took away the lives of her brothers and all her five sons. Interestingly, Asvatthaman commit-ted this heinous deed also to exact revenge for the deceitful killings of his father Drona and his friend Duryodhana. This was the pivotal moment that showed the vagary of violence, since a war to avenge the humilia-tion of Draupadi produced the worst consequences for Draupadi herself. Given her natural inclination, she initially wanted a violent revenge, the death of Asvatthaman. However, eventually she settled for the gemstone on Asvatthaman's head and placed it on Yudhisthira's head. Thus, the cycle of cruelty and violence ended when the crown gem of the nrsamsa Asvatthaman was passed on to the anrsamsa Yudhisthira. This transfer was prompted by Draupadi herself, indicating the eventual futility of an endless chain of revenge to ensure justice. The Bhargavas might have situ-ated the Mahabharata amidst a vengeful sacrifice, with several revenge sto-ries as the backdrop. Yet, they possibly understood the central message of the Mahabharata narrative was not in accomplishing the vengeful deeds, but in understanding the difference between revenge and justice, recogniz-ing the futility of violence, and appreciating the value of dialogue and for-giveness. After the war was over, the forgiving Yudhisthira took utmost care of Dhrtarastra and Gandhari, the parents of his life-long rival and tor-mentor. After Vaisampayana's narration was over, the sarpastra remained unfinished, as Janamejaya decided to let the Nagas live. The Bhargavas responded to the need of their time. But they could not eradicate the time-less message of the Mahabharata that violent revenge is an endless cycle that cannot ensure justice. The real heroism was in the ability to forgive, the principle of non-cruelty and empathy, the recognition of the necessity to live and let live.

Note

All references to Vyasa's Mahabharata are from the multi-volume Critical Edition prepared under the general editorship of V.S.Sukthankar, published from the Bhandarkar Oriental Research Institute, Poona. The translations which have been followed are: Vyāsa, *The Mahābhārata* (Vol.I), translated by J.A.B. van Buitenen, University of Chicago Press, Chicago, 1973 (for the 'Adiparvan'), Vyāsa, *The Mahābhārata* (Vol.II), translated by J.A.B. van Buitenen, University of Chicago Press, Chicago, 1975 (for the 'Sabhaparvan' and the 'Aranyakaparvan'), Vyāsa, *The Mahābhārata* (Vol.III), translated by J.A.B. van Buitenen, University of Chicago Press, Chicago, 1978 (for the 'Virataparvan' and 'Udyogaparvan'), Vyāsa, *Mahābhārata* (Book Six): Bhishma (Vols. 1 and 2), translated by Alex Cherniak, New York University Press, New York, 2008 (for the 'Bhismparvan'), Vyāsa, *Mahābhārata* (Book Nine): Shalya (Vols.1 and 2), translated by Justin Meiland, New York University Press, New York, 2007 (for the 'Salyaparvan'), and Vyasa, *The Mahābhārata* (Vol. VII), translated by James Fitzgerald, University of Chicago Press, Chicago, 2004 (for the 'Striparvan' and 'Santiparvan' 1–167). For the rest of the text, the translations are mine unless otherwise specified.

Works Cited

Choudhary, Pradeep Kant. *Rāma with an Axe*, Aakar, New Delhi, 2010.

Fergusson, J. *Tree and Serpent Worshippers*, India Museum, London, 1868, pp. 44–7.

Fitzgerald, James L. 'Mahābhārata' in Sushil Mittal and Gene Thursby (eds.), *The Hindu World*, Routledge, New York, 2004, pp. 52–74.

Goldman, R.P. 'Akṛtavarṇa vs Srīkṛṣṇa as Narrator of the Legend of the Bhārgava Rāma: Apropos Some Observations of Dr. V.S. Sukthankar' in *Annals of the Bhandarkar Oriental Research Institute*, Vol.53, 1972, pp.161–173.

————. *Gods, Priests and Warriors*, Columbia University Press, New York, 1977.

Hymns of the Atharvaveda (Vols. I and II), translated by Ralph T.H. Griffith, Munshiram Manoharlal, New Delhi, 2002.

Jaiminīya Brāhmaṇa, edited by Raghu Vira, Sarasvati Vihara, Nagpur, 1934.

Jaiminīya Upaniṣad Brāhmaṇa, translated by H. Oertel in *Journal of the American Oriental Society*, Vol.16, 1896, pp.79–260.

Kosambi, D.D. 'The Autochthonous Element in *Mahābhārata*' in *Journal of the American Oriental Society*, Vol.84, No. 1, January-March 1964.

McGrath, Kevin. *Strī: Feminine Power in the Mahābhārata*, Orient Blackswan, Hyderabad, 2011.

————. *Arjuna Pāṇḍava: The Double Hero in Epic Mahābhārata*, Orient Blackswan, Hyderabad, 2016, pp. 119–167.

Minkowski, Christopher. "Snakes, Sattras and the *Mahābhārata*' in Arvind Sharma (ed.), *Essays on the Mahābhārata*, Motilal Banarsidass, Delhi, 2011, pp. 384–400.

Pāṇini, *The Ashtadhyayi*, edited by Srisa Chandra Basu, Motilal Banarsidass, New Delhi, 2003.

Raychaudhuri, H.C. *Political History of Ancient India*, new edition with a commentary by B.N. Mukherjee, Oxford University Press, New Delhi, 2006.

Sinha, Kanad. 'A Tale of Three Couples and their Poet: *Rāmakathā*, Love and Vālmīki in South Asian Tradition' in *Studies in Humanities in Social Sciences*, Vol. XVIII, Nos. 1–2, 2011, pp. 43–80.

————. 'The Devas, the Asuras and Gilgamesh: Exploring the Cross-Cultural Journey of Myths' in *Vedic Studies*, Vol.VI, 2014, pp.360–401.

_____. "Mahabharata's Spatial Politics and the Khandavadahana" in *Coldnoon: Travel Poetics*, Vol. 3, No. 2, 2014, pp. 79–105.

_____. Redefining *Dharma* in a Time of Transition: *Ānṛśaṃsya* in the *Mahābhārata* as an Alternative End of Human Life, *Studies in History*, Vol. 35, No. 2, 2019, pp. 147–161.

Sukthankar, V.S. 'The Bhṛgus and the Bhārata: A Text Historical Study' in *Annals of the Bhandarkar Oriental Research Institute*, 18, 1936–7.

Sullivan, B.M. *Kṛṣṇa Dvaipāyana Vyāsa and the Mahābhārata: A New Interpretation*, E.J. Brill, Leiden, 1990), p. 9.

Thapar, Romila. 'The Historian and the Epic' in *Cultural Pasts* (Oxford University Press, New Delhi, 2008), pp. 613–629.

Vyāsa, *The Mahābhārata* (Vol.I), translated by J.A.B. Van Buitenen, University of Chicago Press, Chicago, 1973.

Witzel, Michel. 'Early Sanskritization. Origin and Development of the Kuru State' in B. Kolver (ed.), *The State, Law and Administration in Classical India*, R. Oldenbourg, Munich, 1997, pp. 27–52.

13

OTHERWISE THAN BEING

The Mahabharata, the Animal, and the Eruption of the Ethical

Anirban Bhattacharjee

> *The mortals are human beings. They are called mortals because they can die. To die means to be capable of death as death. Only man dies. The animal perishes.*

(Heidegger 2001 176)

While animals "die," they do not live with the possibility of death as a "certainty" ahead of them, nor need they cover up their impending demise. Heidegger holds on to the idea that the animal, in contrast to man, has no explicit relation to death. He further links this possibility of death "as such" to the possibility of speech; and in a certain circuitous logic, the animal, the living thing "as such," is, therefore, not properly mortal.

Death preserves the infinity of the infinite that indicates a way of concerning the being without entering into conjunction with it. The understanding of death as a disruption of the everyday – the ultimate exterior and yet the most intimate – opens up the space for ethics, for thinking singularity as such. The trace left by the "event" is not the residue of a presence; rather it demands a new sort of responsibility when one is obliged without the obligation having begun in oneself. The notion of death and the animal as ungraspable, with all the ontological conundrums, gears toward a solitary and silent friendship with ethics and finitude.

We here begin with a question – the question that is most fundamental, primary, and elemental. Interestingly, we all know the answer. But the most curious and contradictory thing is that we never think seriously of it. It is, as if, we know the answer but we are incapable of thinking it.

DOI: 10.4324/9781003516408-16

Ka ca barta kimascaryam kah panthah kah ca modate?

To know the "exact" answer, one must take recourse to the *Mahabharata*. During their exile in the forest in the *Aranyak Parva*, the Pandava brothers, once exhausted and full of fret, went in search of water. On the bank of the Lake of Death, the younger four met a Yaksha living in the form of a crane. Each of them heard a strong and clear voice of warning: "Do not dare to touch that water. You must first answer my questions!" Due to sheer fatigue, each of the Pandava brothers ignored the warning, drank the water and immediately fell dead. Now it was left to the eldest, Yudshishthira, to recognize the power of the Yaksha, to answer the questions he put to him, and to thus revive his dead brothers with the blessings of the Yaksha. One component of the final question was: *kimascaryam?* "What is it that causes the greatest wonder in the world?" Yudhshthira answered: "Day after day countless people are going to the abode of Yama, yet those that remain behind count themselves as immortal, what can cause greater wonder than this?"

The question brings forward the most singular aspect of human form of life. The propensity to deny at every moment one's mortality – our forgetfulness towards the fact that we all are born in *debt to death* is that which distinguishes humans from animals. It dissimulates all questions of ontological intelligibility (Bhattacharjee). But it forces us to think of a sphere, a state which is not that of being while not being non-being – but which is *otherwise than being* (Levinas). It signals a profound issue: our incapacity to imagine our own death – to have a genuinely embodied sense of being extinguished. The state of non-being necessitates the thinking of the animal. Thinking the animal is thinking death. This is an ontological statement that implicates the privation and interiority of the "as such" of death. We would try to understand and explore if our *conscious amnesia* towards the "proper possibility" of death has any linkage to the sacrificial logic of "killing" animals as elaborated in the Vedic hermeneutics.

Man-animal relationship underlies a crossing of borders. Nietzsche has put in *Beyond Good and Evil* (2002) that man is the as-yet undetermined animal – an animal lacking in itself. The ends of man "I" come to the animal – the animal in me (Nietzsche 1996). I feel an intolerable proximity with the animal. My "self" is constitutive of the animal other – the animality which is born out of muteness and of unspeakability (Derrida 2002). This fundamental muteness is the singular property of the animal that resists human accessibility. It is not simply linguistic, rather it derives the properly phenomenological impossibility of speaking the phenomenon whose phenomenality "as such" does not appear to the animal or, as Derrida says, does not unveil "the being of the being" (Derrida 1989). Hence, to grasp animality is to grasp it as a mode of being from which human beings are fenced out, that they can grasp only as "beyond" them. Thinking the animal is, therefore, thinking beyond. Logically put, the ungraspable weirdness of the animal world is experienced as somewhat similar to our strange relation between death and actuality [*Wirklichkeit*]. It implies that death is what is closest to us, but death is also as far away as "being-possible." The animal world stands as an aporetic supplement to the possible. There is always an experience of being left out in relation to the animal life. As both unveiled and penetrated *as* impossibility, we can never quite "grasp" what the world of the animal is. Heidegger is, however, concerned with the question how the animal appears as both within and without human modes of accessibility. For Agamben, the animal is the *undisclosable* which man keeps and brings to light "as such." Animality is primary. Humanity is only accessed/ obtained through a (continuous) suspension of animality. It, therefore, must keep itself open to the closedness of animality, but as it ever forgets the primacy of the *animalitas* it closes itself to its own openness (Bhattacharjee). By taking stock of this "tiny secret" (Agamben 2004) and "monstrous coupling" (Derrida 1989) of the uncertain switching between man and animal, we would now turn to the question of "the lack of the world for the animal" implying a *difference of degree* or, in a heterogeneous order, to that of non-lack (*weltos* as "no world") or plenitude in terms of an otherwise relation to the human world.

In the *Mokshadharma Parva* of the Mahabharata, in the dialogue between the Brahmin Kashyapa and the Jackal, the Jackal contends that that all "inferior" creatures covet birth in the human race; humans are crowned with success that they have hands! For the non-human animals, there is no acquisition that is more valuable than the acquisition of hands – *na paani laabhaad adhiko laabhaḥ kash cana vidyate* (12.173.12). The animals covet hands as eagerly as men covet riches (*paanimadbhyaḥ spṛhaasmaakaṃ yathaa tava dhanasya vai*). In his book *What is Called Thinking* (1968), Heidegger famously hinges upon this question of "privation" [*Entbehrung*] and "poverty": "animals have no hand" [*er hat keine Hand*]; and, interestingly, Heidegger calls thinking "Handwerk," a work of the hand. Animalistic signs are foreclosed by their phenomenological impossibility of speaking; but this "lack" cannot be thought of in terms of pure nothingness; animal has its own world that takes on "meaning" only from a non-animal world "as such" (Derrida 1989). The Jackal expresses his sense of deprivation this way: "Behold, O Brahmana, I cannot extract this thorn that has entered my body, or crush these insects and worms that are biting and afflicting me greatly!" Humans that have bestowed upon them two hands with ten fingers succeed in constructing shelters for themselves from rain, cold, and heat. They succeed also in enjoying excellent clothes for themselves, good food, comfortable beds, and excellent habitations. Lying on this Earth, they that have hands enjoy kine and other animals and cause them to carry burdens or drag their vehicles, and by the aid of diverse means bring those animals under sway. The animals never *say* "ergo sum," and because of the "fault," man conceives animal as being inferior, prior to good and evil. The question of the pure sovereignty of the human being and "the reason of the strongest" is shattered by the notion of an "originary defect" (Derrida 2009) that allows *us* to be master over the animals. The *Mahabharata* episode makes us "confront" precisely the question of the undeniablity of animal privation and suffering. When exiled into the forest in the *Aranyak Parva*, Yudhisthira is approached by a lonely deer in a dream: "We are the deer of the forest; now only very few of us remain, like seeds, like broken words; if you do not leave us we shall all *perish* for your food." This "poverty" (*Ar-mut*), the animal feeling itself poor, implies a textual anachrony and is specifically concerned with the fissured relation between the everyday certainty of death and *Dasein*'s not-having-access to the "as such" of death. It is precisely the "originary fault" as conceived of *human finitude* that allows man to sacrifice animals.

The *Mahabharata* and the *Brahmana* stories foreground the fact that both humans and animals are "fit to be sacrificed" (Tull 1996). The difference between the eater and the eaten cannot be erased despite the promise of some kind of reciprocal justice in a future world (Das 1983, 2013). Again as "karma" in Brahmanism is nothing else but some regulated principles – no personal intention is involved – therefore, Manu's dictum, "killing in sacrifice is not killing... The violence sanctioned by the Vedas and regulated by official restraints is known as nonviolence" (*Manusamhita* V. 39), is placed on a surer footing (Bandyopadhyay 2010). The ritual of animal sacrifice in its classical form evokes a sense of non-injury and non-killing by way of advancing the idea of "healing" the victim and the sacrificial accoutrements. In the *Rg Veda* 1.162.21, the already dismembered sacrificial horse is told: "You do not really die here, nor are you hurt." In a similar vein, there is the well-known description, found in the *Satapatha Brahmana*, of the leading of the sacrificial victim to the place of its immolation or "ritual killing" in which the ritualist priests declare that "that which they lead to the sacrifice they do not lead to death" (*Satapatha Brahmana*, 3.8.1.10). The ritualist obscures and obfuscates the violent nature of the victim's death by declaring "lest we should become eyewitnesses" (*Satapatha Brahmana*, 3.8.1.15) and asserts that the process is not really a killing, but a "queting" of the animal: "One does not say: 'He strikes [the victim], he kills it ... but that (the animal) went away" (*Satapatha Brahmana*, 3.8.1.15). Interestingly, the name of the ritualist/liturgist priest in charge of performing the sacrifice is *adhvaryu*, derived from its Sanskrit root *a-dhvara* (Monier-Williams 1899), meaning "not injuring," and again, the term used for the slaughterer is *shamitra*, implying "the appeaser" (Malamoud 1998). On a different note, the eating and killing of animals in sacrifice are integrally linked with the violent preconditions of our life. The *Mahabharata* reckons the "state of violence" as an irremediable, unavoidable factor of "human condition" (Arendt 1998). Sacrifice is an animal action. Violence is not only inflicted on the animal, but it underlines that this *act* of violence itself is the performance of the animal other within the self. Our constant urge to "rationalize" the animal action – to fit it into the grammar of the *humanitas* – entails the question of ethics. Violence is intrinsic because the act of rationalizing attempts to construct the other as the object of knowledge. It is a violent interruption, an interruption of the epistemological (Bhattacharjee 2022). The question is: does the ritual of animal sacrifice make humans face alterity as death as he gathers the knowledge of his own death through the death of the other? This bond with the alterity of the animal and of the "as such" of death invariably pulls in the question of responsibility. I am responsible before the other for the other. I find myself in an ethical responsibility with the animal as alterity. And the question of ethical responsibility grows denser in my exposedness to exteriority (Bhattacharjee 2022). The *Mahabharata* text constantly grapples with the question in a series of *Upākhyān*-narratives, presenting a double challenge in its highlighting of what is seen and considered peripheral to the concerns and overall design of the putative core of the *Mahābhārata* and thereby un-grounds their (interpretative) dismissal as secondary to the epic (Hiltebeitel 2002).

In the *Shyena-Kapota Sambad* in the *Vana-Parva* of the *Mahabharata*, Indra disguises himself as a Hawk and Agni as a Dove to take a test of the King Ushinara, famously known as Sibi, if he might be "equal to gods" (3.31). Animals and birds, as they appear in the texts, act simply as means through which complex issues of dharma and ethics are delivered, ideologies advocated. The "animal forms" serve not only as tropes or figures to communicate human-god concerns, but they get inalienably linked to the matrix of moral dilemmas, provoking complex ethical questions on just treatment, protection, assurance, and charity. The double-edged dilemma that King Sibi faces in the dialogue is whether the king should protect the meagre Dove's life or the Hawk's right to consume the Dove. Violence is explicit in the Hawk's demand for sustenance, but it is, as he argues, the most primal and biological need that necessitates aggression and killing of creatures that complicates the dharmic (non-violent) interactions between beings. Again, the "voiceless" Dove's bodily proximity to the king, as it perches on his thigh, makes him concerned with the question of ethical care; conditional proximity goes beyond the ethics of a radical *ahimsa*. The Dove attains a privileged status as the text stages a "face-to-face" encounter between it and the king. Numerous pleas and offerings having been rejected, the righteous King finally surrenders to the Hawk's lethal demand: *yadaa samam kapotena tava maamsam bhavena nripa tadaa pradeyam tan mahyam saa me tushtir bhavisyati.* "If you love the love, overlord of kings, cut off a piece of flesh and weigh it against the dove. When your flesh balances the dove's, O King, you will give it to me, and I shall be satisfied" (3.131.20–25). The inclusion of the primal animalitas and biological continuism in the dharmic world of the *Mahabharata* disrupts the rigid code of ethical conduct. Radical sympathy requires bodily sacrifice. The Dove's being, "poor in world" (*weltarm*) (Heidegger 1995), reduced to pure materiality as consumable food, the Hawk makes the King the (experiencing) subject of suffering originally intended for the Dove. Hospitality is necessarily extended to the non-human beastly/aviary creatures and such a radical form of care leads to the annihilation of self. The "poverty" of the animal does not remain a mere negation or a lack, rather as "privation" that implies degrees or scales with a difference of alterity. The notion of the non-human animal world with its quantitative difference – "animal only perishes" (*verenden*) (Derrida 1989) – refers us back to the questioning "we" of *Dasein*. In each of the animal-*upakhyan*s in the *Mahabharata*, this denial is de-negated; the non-simultaneity of the human and the animal world is dismantled in the dialogues; the hierarchies between the animal and human appearance and speciesism are ruptured by the ethics of the situation and conditional proximity. The *Mahabharata* text never leaves the reader with the commandment of *ahimsa*, rather it opens up a pluralistic ethics of dharma and virtues of non-injury and non-cruelty, spotlighting inter-species care and radical openness to the other without waiting for reciprocity.

The *Kapot-upakhyana* in the *Santi Parva* of the *Mahabharata* brilliantly captures the law of (unlimited) hospitality and the virtue of hospitableness. A savage hunter wanders the earth, killing and selling birds in different quarters of the land, paying no heed to or in a way quite forgetful of his evil conduct. One day, a massive storm hits the forest where he has been in search of his prey. Unable to find a shelter, the hunter becomes terribly distressed by the violent gust of wind and the rain falling in torrents. Seeing a large tree, he sought shelter beneath its branches, in which there lives a dove-family. Induced by the virtues of hospitality the male bird prepares himself for honouring the hunter as his guest. When the hunter begs for relief from the cold, the dove kindles a fire with some dried leaves. But when asked for food, the dove, since being a forest-dweller, has nothing to offer; and cursing his lifestyle for leaving the hunter without food, the dove wonders how to satisfy the hunter's hunger. Kindling the fire's flames, the dove circumambulates it three times and enters it.

In the *Rg Veda* and in the *Upanishad*s, hospitality is considered one cardinal virtue (Doniger 1985: 111). For the *Mimamsaka*s, the ethics of being hospitable to the other (*Atithi Yajna*) is inalienably linked with the notion of the ritual living. As part of the ritualistic tradition, denial of hospitality wrought demerit upon the householder. *Rg Veda* says: "He is liberal who gives to the suppliant desiring food, wandering about distressed; to him there is an ample (recompense), and he contracts friendship with his adversaries" (*RV* 10.117.3, Doniger 2009). In certain passages of *Taittiriya-Upanishad*, a spirit of unconditional hospitality is ideationally visible (3.10.1). But in the *Mahabharata-upakhyan*, the act of giving yields an excess, hospitality beyond reciprocation (Bhattacharjee 2022). The bird-hunter, overwhelmed at seeing the dove enter the fire and offer his flesh as food, is stunned into re-evaluating his way of life. He resolves to renounce his occupation and depart for a final great journey (*mahaprasthana*). Meanwhile, the female dove starts grieving at the loss of her husband, remembering how good he was to her and how much she loved him! Despairing at the prospect of a widow's life, she follows her husband into the blazing fire. The male dove's act of reasoning and ratiocination inheres the *Shastrik* logic of reaping the Karmic merit by performing *Atithi Pujana*. The Sanskrit word for guest, *atithi*, is revealing in that it literally means the "one who comes without prior notice," without a set time, without appointment (George 31). The male and the female bird's onerous obligations towards their "guest" indicate that animals can productively engage with *dharma*. The animal's act of hospitality, the ample fecundity toward the infinitely inassimiliable other to whom the "I" owes an infinite debt of responsibility implies the excess of the ethical over the political. The act of giving lives in the blazing fire for the dove couple, in a way, radicalizes the notion of hospitality, engaging an undeclinable responsibility. The female dove's self-sacrifice not merely underlies the practice of *sahagamana* – going with the husband on to the funeral pyre, but also women's roles in ensuring that men pursue their proper *dharma*, the obligations to provide shelter to the *sharanagata*, even if he is an enemy (Jamison 1996). In her book, *Caring* (1986), Nel Noddings has argued that the "one-caring" has some form of obligation to the "cared-for" proximate humans and non-human animals to the extent that they are needy and able to respond to or reciprocate ethically with the offerings of care. Such an approach predicates care, an affective response, on the immediacy of the situation; and the ethic of care bases itself on the condition of proximity, a sense of shareability and interconnectedness; however, in Noddings' argument, it is impossible to care for all, especially the distant others. The Mahabharata episode stages a "face-to-face" encounter between the dove couple and the wildhunter; the "immediate" and the "proximate" here constitute the most primal ethical scene – "the face speaks to me and thereby invites me to relation" (Levinas 1985). The *dharma* of the protection and care for other beings requires a radical form of self-sacrifice, implicating the direct and inalienable connection between hospitality and ethics: "ethics is hospitality; ethics is so thoroughly coextensive with the experience of hospitality" (Derrida 2001). The *Mahabharata* narrative constantly employs fables involving birds, beasts, and fishes for conducting ethical discourse. The texts are sometimes overtly political as they articulate a hospitality that unconditionally opens the door of the home, the heart, and all that is "mine" to the stranger, the refugee, and the other.

Patrick Olivelle has argued that the "talking" animal narratives are pedagogical tools that "carry significant messages, sometimes explicit but more often implicit and below the surface – messages that may be religious, philosophical, or scientific" (Olivelle 2013). The article would, however, suggest that the animal-*upakhyan*s that open up *sites of contestation* where the complex and radical ethical issues are enacted in terms of metaphors or in metonyms, cannot solely be read as means for ideological or pedagogical ends, as they delimit and insinuate imaginative ways of understanding relations between lives through active, adaptive, and creative interactions that avoid claims to overarching moral structures. Animals are presented as sentient beings, which can experience pain, and have specific physical needs and emotions. Sometimes, the gods' choice of animal bodies is deliberate and purposive, demonstrating through narrative structures the "fluidity of birth" (Howard 2016) questioning the privileging of the "human" body and reconfiguring relation and ethical emergences of bodies beyond being represented and fictionalized (Maccormack 2012 1). In the dharmic world established in the Mahabharata, heterogeneity and different kinds of otherness exist within the fold of interiority – the "fold," which does not subsume difference/s into/within a homogenous whole, rather it includes and differentiates by "enfolding" and "unfolding" simultaneously, eliding the binary of multiplicity and unity, allowing each to co-exist (Deleuze 1992). The ethical erupts when the ordinary routines of life break down, the pulsing fibres of everyday get haphazard, the norms and ideals having sharp boundaries are at stake. The ethical breathes in the ability to counter the automation or mechanization of action by attentiveness to small details through which care is dispersed within habitual actions. The originary ethical bond of hospitality is posited as the base for conducting one's daily living by cordially taking the other into account. The unrestricted openness to the other as hospitality is the moment of the political.

The animal stays outside the torus of human thinking/reason, but the sheer alterity of the animal cannot be completely erased from human mode(s) of existence. It is ineluctably enmeshed with the totality of being. It is man's rationalizing capacity that disavows, denies and forecloses the question of the intelligibility of the actions of the animal. The "as such" of the "ungraspable" animal foregrounds the thinking (of) the animal as thinking death. We submit: the human reason, even in its transcendental architectonic, is intrinsically aligned with the experience of the primal *animalitas*; the nature of cognition is structurally incomplete without the recognition of the animal "as such."

Acknowledgements: Sibaji Banyopadhyay, Debashis Banerjee, Laura Dunn, Andre Buller, Christina do Santos. As I presented the draft paper in the Graduate Researchers' conference at IIT, Guwahati, in 2013, I would here take the opportunity to express my thankfulness to the organizers, chairs, and respondents for their acute comments and active encouragements.

Works Cited

Agamben, Giorgio. *The Open: Man and Animal*, Translated by Kevin Atell, Stanford University Press, 2004.

Ared017, Hannah. *The Human Condition*, University of Chicago Press, 1998.

Bandyopadhyay, Sibaji. "A Critique of Nonviolence", *Seminar*, 608, 2010.

Bhattacharjee, Anirban, "Reason, Death, and the Animal", *Journal of Dharma Studies*, 5 (1), March 2022.

Bowels, Adam. "Reflections on the Upakhyanas in the *Apaddharmaparvan* of the *Mahabharata*" in *Argument and Design: -The Unity of the Mahabharata*, ed. by Viswa Adluri, Joydeep Bagchee, Brill, 2016.

Das, Veena. 'The Language of Sacrifice', *Man, New Series*, 18 (3), 1983, 445–62.

———. "Being Together with Animals: Death, Violence and Noncruelty in Hindu Imagination", *Living Beings: Perspectives on Interspecies Engagements*, Ed. by Penelope Dransart, Routledge, 2013, pp. 17–30.

Deleuze, Gilles. *The Fold: Leibniz and the Baroque*, Trans: Conley, T. University of Minnesota Press, 1992.

Derrida, Jacques, *Of Spirit*, Tr. by Geoff Bennington and Rachel Bowlby, Chicago: University of Chicago Press, 1989.

Derrida, Jacques. *On Cosmopolitanism and Forgiveness*, Translated by Mark Dooley and Michael Hughes, Routledge, 2001.

———. "The Animal That Therefore I Am", Translated by David Wills, *Critical Inquiry*, 28(2), Winter, 2002, pp. 369–418, The University of Chicago Press, https://www.jstor.org/stable/1344276.

Doniger, Wendy. *Tales of Sex and Violence: Folklore, Sacrifice, and Danger in the Jaiminiya Brāhmaṇa*, University of Chicago Press, 1985.

———. "Zoomorphism in Ancient India: Human more Bestial than the Beasts", In L. Daston & G. Mitman (Eds.), *Thinking with Animals: New Perspectives on Anthropomorphism*, Columbia University Press, 2005, pp. 17–36.

———, *The Hindus: An Alternative History*, Cp. 5. "Humans, Animals, and Gods in the Rig Veda", Penguin Press, 2009.

George, Siby., "Hospitality as Openness to the Other", *Journal of Human Values*, 15(1), 2009, 29–47.

Heidegger, Martin, *The Fundamental Problems of Metaphysics: World, Finitude, Solitude*, Tr. by William McNeil and Nicholas Walker, Indiana University Press, 1995.

———. *What is Called Thinking?* Trans. J. Glenn Gray, Harper, 1968.

———. *The Thing*. In *Poetry, Language, Thought*. Harper, 2001. 161–184

Hermann W. Tull, "The Killing that is not Killing: Men, Cattle and the Origins of Non-violence (*Ahimsā*) in the Vedic Sacrifice", *Indo-Iranian Journal*, 39-, 1996, pp. 223–244, Kluwer Academic Publishers.

Hiltebeitel, Alf. 'Chapter Five: Don't Be Cruel', *Rethinking the Mahābhārata: A Reader's Guide to the Education of the Dharma King* (first published 2001), Oxford University Press, 2002.

Howard, Veena Rani. "Lessons from 'The Hawk and the Dove': Reflections on the *Mahābhārata*'s Animal Parables and Ethical Predicaments", Springer, September 2016, doi:10.1007/s11841-016-0538-9.

Jamison, Stephanie. *Sacrificed Wife/ Sacrificer's Wife: Women, Ritual and Hospitality in Ancient India,* Oxford University Press, 1996.

Nietzsche, Friedrich. *On the Genealogy of Morals*, Translated by Douglas Smith, Oxford University Press, 1996.

_____. *Beyond Good and Evil: Prelude to a Philosophy of the Future,* Ed. by Rolf-Peter Horstmann, Judith Norman, Tr. by Judith Norman. Cambridge University Press, 2002.

Levinas, Emanuel. *Ethics and Infinity,* Trans: Cohen, R. A.. Duquesne University Press, 1985.

_____. *Otherwise than Being, or Beyond Essence* (1974), Translated by Alphonso Lingis, Duquesne University Press, 1998.

Maccormack, Patricia. *Posthuman Ethics: Embodiment and Cultural Theory,* Routledge, 2012.

Mahabharata. The Mahabharata for the First Time Critically Edited. Edited by Vishnu S. Sukthankar, Shripad K. Belvalkar, Parashuram L. Vaidya, et al. 19 vols. Poona: Bhandarkar Oriental Research Institute, 1933–66.

Mahābhāratam, Translated and Edited by Haridas Bhattacharya Siddhantabagish, Viswabani Prakashani, Kolkata, 1336–45 (in Bengali).

Mahābhāratam (in English), Kisari Mohan Ganguli, *The Mahābhārata* (four volumes), Munshiram Manoharlal, 2004.

Malamoud, Charles. "Paths of the Knife, Carving up the Victim in Vedic Sacrifice", in R. Gombrich ed., *Indian Ritual and Its Exegesis*, Oxford University Papers on India, Vol. 2, Part 1, Oxford University Press, 1998.

Monier-Williams. A Sanskrit-English dictionary: Etymologically and philologically arranged with special reference to Cognate Indo-European languages. Oxford, The Clarendon Press, 1899.

Noddings, Nel. *Caring: A Relational Approach to Ethics & Moral Education*, University of California Press, 1986.

Olivelle, Patrick. "Talking Animals: Exploration in an Indian Literary Genre", *Religions of South Asia*, 7(1), 2013.

Satapatha Brahmana. Translated by Julius Eggeling, Book 1 & 2, Oxford Clarendon Press, 1882.

Sutherland, Gail Hinich. 1997. *Nonviolence Consumption and Community among Ancient Indian Ascetics*, Indian Institute of Advanced Study.

The Hymns of the RigVeda, Tr. By Ralph T. Griffith, Vol. I & II, Benares: E. J. Lazarus & Co., 1897.

The Laws of Manu, Tr. Wendy Doniger and Brian K. Smith, Penguin Books, 1991.

The Mahabharata, Translated literally from the original Sanskrit Text, Ed. and Tr. by Manmatha Nath Dutta, Elysium Press, 1895–1909.

Wilhelm, Friedrich. "Hospitality and the Caste System", *Studien zur Indologie und Iranistik*, 20, 1996.

14

THE MAHABHARATA WAR AND AMBEDKAR'S CRITIQUE OF VIOLENCE AND NATIONALISM

Kalyan Kumar Das

> *the responsibility for an intelligent control of force rests on us all. In short, the point is that to achieve anything we must use force: only we must use it constructively as energy and not destructively as violence.*

– Dr. B.R. Ambedkar, "Mr. Russell and the Reconstruction of Society" (1918)

In this chapter, I particularly focus upon the ancient war of Kurukshetra in the Indian epic or *mahakavya* – *Mahabharata*, especially its most "philosophically" famous component – *The Bhagavad Gita* which features dialogues between war hero Arjuna and his advisor Krishna and attempt to read it as a counter-revolutionary text along an Ambedkarite parlance.[1]Risking the nativist argument, let me in the beginning take a cue from Arindam Chakrabarty to point out the difference between Indian and Western epic traditions (Banerjee et al. 2016). Understanding this is important to realize why we need to blur the lines between "action" and "thought" especially in a context like Kurukshetra war. According to Chakrabarty, Indian verse narratives of epic length cannot be easily characterized as "epic" in the western sense of the term. The crucial difference is that western epics are centred on the grand moment of action in a time of war, while Indian epics are centred on dialogues. In the *Bhagavad Gita*, Lord Krishna and Arjuna are not directly engaged in fighting a battle. They are engaged in a philosophical conversation. Consequently, it would be foolhardy to think of such strict binarization of thought and action or "words about war" and "wars *as such*" in such a non-western context. To expand upon this, it is worthwhile to look to the work of philosophers – some of whom never participated in

DOI: 10.4324/9781003516408-17

the battlefield (unlike Sassoon or Orwell) and some who did and yet, all of them remained passionately engaged to philosophically preempt future possibilities of war – Bertrand Russell, John Dewey, and Leon Trotsky. For perspective, I invoke Dr. B.R. Ambedkar who brings Dewey, Russell, and Marxism together as interlocutors on issues like war, force, violence, and nationalism. Through this, I also reveal possible ways in which Ambedkar's ideas were shaped by their respective philosophies. While the context of the Kurukshetra war and its incessant invocation in the modern Indian political world serves my rationale as to why I put such widely disparate thinkers on the same platform, the textual connections I make here serve as my ultimate justification. I put these complex thinkers in conversation also because war and violence need not be thought through a single philosophical prism or ideological perspective. It requires, as Bertrand Russell suggests, a radical recuperation of "common sense" that cuts across "isms."

In the preface *to Common Sense and Nuclear Warfare*, Russell writes:

> What is needed is not an appeal to this or that –ism, but only to common sense. I do not see any reason why the kind of arguments which are put forward by those who think as I do should appeal more to one side than to the other or to Left-Wing opinion more than to that of men of conservative outlook. The appeal is to human beings as such and is made equally to all who hope for human survival.

Such a clarion call to "common sense" beyond strict ideological affiliations and the assemblage of these thinkers look especially relevant in discussing a thinker such as Bhimrao Ramji Ambedkar whose pragmatic concerns often speak to a broad spectrum of philosophical streams beyond the limits of the East and the West. Such scattershot critical cosmopolitanism in Ambedkar, however, is placed within the specific reference to the war of Kurukshetra.

The war of Kurukshetra or Krishna-Arjuna dialogues in particular or the Mahabharata, in general, can actually be considered as a rather anomalous illustrative example to cite in an essay on issues like violence or violence in war in particular. Just as it is difficult to define the most appropriate genre of the Mahabharata (*purana*/lore, *katha*/narrative, or *itihasa*/history?), it is almost impossible to resolve the tensions between the philosophic battle between "violence"/"himsa" and "non-violence"/"ahimsa" in a text that reaches its narrative apotheosis in the crisis of a war. For billions of modern readers of the *Gita* or the *Mahabharata*, the text(s) sends out a strong message against violence. That "ahimsa paramo dharma" or "non-violence is the highest principle" is a much-cherished maxim in these texts/text is sodominant in the aggregated "interpretive load" of these narratives that it might even seem strange as to why I choose such a text in the present context. Firstly, the "philosophic" issues that these narratives apparently espouse are almost always retrospectively cited in contemporary times in an inexhaustible fashion. In a sense, the Mahabharata is a text that brings the apparent extremities of the Indian political scenario closer than we can imagine and the *Gita* is hardly monopolized only by the Hindu right-wing to justify their political decisions or to reimagine themselves as rightful heirs of the morally superior brigade in that great war of Kurukshetra– Pandavas. While the former Indian foreign minister Ms. Sushma Swaraj was noticed to be distributing *the Gita* among foreign diplomats as the latest example of India's soft skill exercise, the President of Indian National Congress Mr. Rahul Gandhi recently reimagined his party as a team of Pandavas and his political opponents as Kauravas–the two belligerent parties in the Kurukshetra war. This suffices to conclude that the apparitions of the "literary unthing" or "literary monster" – the *Mahabharata* or the *Gita* are hardly exorcised from the political graffiti of present-day India.

Secondly, the text of Gita also creates possibilities of retrospective reading that foregrounds the emergence of a discourse of nationalism in India. This essay will keep engaging with the twin registers of violence in war and nationalism by taking the Gita as the textual hotbed where Ambedkar deployed several ideas of John Dewey, Russell, and Trotsky as well as commented on Indian texts like Jaimini's *Purba Mimamsa Sutra* or Badarayana's *Brahma Sutras*. As is evident from his short acerbic essay "Krishna and His Gita," for Dr. Ambedkar, the *Bhagavad Gita* is to be considered merely as a "philosophic defense of certain dogmas" and the text does not hold much importance beyond the status of a "counter-revolutionary text" that refuses to acknowledge its philosophical debt to the creditor – Buddhism. Despite the apparent celebration of the text as upholding "ahimsa" in modern times by his contemporaries like Gandhi or Tilak, Ambedkar mounts his attacks precisely because the text of *the Gita* defends and justifies violence in war and even validates a violent war against one's own kith and kin. This is, according to him, one of the "dogmas" on the basis of which he disqualifies it as a philosophic text.

Born as an untouchable Mahar and a son of an army person in the British Indian Army's Mahar Regiment, Ambedkar was certainly opposed to how the *Gita* legitimized the *varnashrama dharma* (that constitutes another "dogma" that the text defends). While criticizing the text of the *Gita* for upholding *varnashrama dharma* or denouncing it for legitimizing war is important for him, Ambedkar also attacks it on the basis of how the text inflates the meaning of key terms like "karma yoga" (by reading it as "action") or "jnana yoga" (by reading it as "wisdom") and paves the way for nationalist reconfiguration subsequently. Therefore, for Ambedkar, the *Gita* or the conversation between Arjuna and Krishna in Kurukshetra war constitutes a central concern for his moral as well as political philosophy. This essay is an attempt to engage with such a moral philosophy and to see how Dewey contributed to one of his illustrious student's understandings of war, violence, and force and how all these can figure in the "democratic ethos" of a polity that constituted a significant concern in their shared universe of moral philosophy.

Reading through Dewey, Trotsky, and Russell

In the July 1938 issue of the American journal *The New International*, Leon Trotsky wrote a lengthy essay titled "Their Morals and Ours." This text had a section completely dedicated to what Trotsky called "dialectics of means and ends." For Trotsky, morality was a contentious domain and there has to be some understanding of the "class nature of morality" instead of taking it at face value. In this text, Trotsky tries his best to differentiate his Marxist ethos from those of Jesuits, utilitarian philosophy of Bentham and Mill as well as the bureaucratic socialism of Stalin in the USSR. Against the backdrop of Dewey Commission's investigations into the allegations against Trotsky and his followers in Mexico City, Trotsky clarifies his stand on the philosophical conflicts between means and ends. For him, it is important to philosophically diffuse this by showing why means can use justifiable violence if the end is that of the dictatorship of the proletariat and focussing too much on the moral worth of means adopted to do it might actually become counter-productive for the revolution. Too much moralism on means might actually be a powerful method for destroying the revolutionary zeal of the proletariat. This is why Trotsky opines: "Morality is a function of the class struggle." For Trotsky, any generalizable moral value actually plays into the favours of the bourgeoisie. That is why he is immensely weary of the Kantian *categorical imperative*.

In the August issue of the same journal, John Dewey responds to Trotsky's concerns for the dialectics of means and ends in a short piece called "On *Their Morals and Ours*." Here, Dewey points out the problem of foreseeing the end that is supposed to justify the means. According to Dewey, the anticipation of an end might not meet the real end at the end of a social or political revolution and this "end-in-view" always differs from "end-in-reality." Moreover, there can be a multiplicity of ends, instead of one particular intended and anticipated end. There is always a possibility of also destroying other necessary ends in the process. The end-in-view, in this whole debate, must also be seen as a means in itself as it acts as an incentive for the end to be realized. While Trotsky does realize the dual nature of "ends-in-view," his perceptions are somewhat insensitive to dispositional changes that Dewey sees as necessary. Although Ambedkar does not mention this Dewey–Trotsky debate in particular, his criticism of Marxist methods that are likely to implement violence in bringing about a revolution is heavily based on Dewey's moral philosophy that did not foreclose the possibility of dispositional change in lieu of an unbridled usage of violence as a violation. A few months before his demise in 1956, this ardent Indian admirer of Dewey wrote a text called "Buddha or Karl Marx?" where he cites Dewey and raises the debates between means and ends. Ambedkar asks: "whose means are more efficacious?" (2014) while comparing Buddha with Marx. Commenting on the Buddhist understanding of Ahimsa, Ambedkar says that Buddha never deployed an absolutist understanding of ahimsa or nonviolence. According to Ambedkar, Buddha's pragmatic mindset allowed him to recognize how violence is an integral part of our existence and then refers to Dewey:

> There are of course other grounds against violence such as those urged by Prof. Dewey. In dealing with those who contend that the end justifies the means is morally depraved doctrine, Dewey has rightly asked what can justify the means if not the end? It is only the end that justifies the means.

A little later he says:

> As Prof. Dewey has pointed out that violence is only another name for the use of force and although force must be used for creative purposes a distinction between use of force as energy and use of force as violence needs to be made. The achievement of an end involves the destruction of many other ends which are integral with the one that is sought to be destroyed. Use of force must be so regulated that it should save as many ends as possible in destroying the evil one. Buddha's ahimsa was not absolute as the ahimsa preached by Mahavira, the founder of Jainism. He would have allowed force only as energy. The Communists preach ahimsa as an absolute principle. To this the Buddha was deadly opposed.

Such Deweyean understanding of violence, force, and energy is again cited by Ambedkar in another text. This time it is a longish review article that he wrote on Bertrand Russell's anti-war book *Principles of Social Reconstruction,* also known as *Why Men Fight?* In this 1918 essay "Mr. Russell and the Reconstruction of Society," published in the *Journal of the Indian Economic Society,* Ambedkar expresses his understanding of the dialectics of means and ends, force, and violence. This demands a quotation in extenso:

> The gist of it all is that activity is the condition of growth. Mr. Russell, it must be emphasized, is against war but is not for quietism; for, according to him activity leads to growth and quietism is but another name for death. To express it in the language of Professor Dewey he is only against

"force as violence" but is all for "force as energy." It must be remembered by those who are opposed to force that without the use of it all ideals will remain empty just as without some ideal or purpose (conscious or otherwise) all activity will be no more than mere fruitless fooling. Ends and means (= force in operation) are therefore concomitants and the common adage that "the end justifies the means" contains a profound truth which is perverted simply because it is misunderstood. For if the end does not justify the means, what else will? The difficulty is that we do not sufficiently control the operations of the means once employed for the achievement of some end. For a means when once employed liberates many ends – a fact scarcely recognized – and not the one only we wish it to produce. However, in our fanaticism for achievement we attach the article "the" to the end we cherish and pay no heed to the ends simultaneously liberated. Of course, for the exigencies of an eminently practical life we must set an absolute value on some one end. But in doing this we must take precaution that the other ends involved are not sacrificed. Thus, the problem is that if we are to use force, as we must, to achieve something, we must see that while working for one end we do not destroy, in the process, other ends equally worthy of maintenance. Applying this to the present war, no justification, I think, is needed, for the use of force. What needs to be justified is the destructive violence. The justification must satisfy the world the ends given prominence to by one or other of the combatants could not be achieved otherwise than by violence i.e., without involving the sacrifice of other ends equally valuable for the stability of the world. True enough that violence cannot always be avoided and non-resistance can be adopted only when it is a better way of resistance. But the responsibility for an intelligent control of force rests on us all. In short, the point is that to achieve anything we must use force; only we must use it constructively as energy and not destructively as violence.

Ambedkar's perceptions on the use of violence clearly imply that he considers force or even violence as an unavoidable part of our lives on earth. Referring to the British conservative political thinker Edmund Burke, Ambedkar in this review article reminds us that force and violence, even if it is deployed for a noble cause, might not sustain a revolutionary moment for long. Therefore, people need dispositional change through education and democracy. Here, Ambedkar is directly influenced by Dewey's idea of democracy that went beyond the usual definition of it in terms of universal adult franchise and he embraces Dewey's idea of democratic ethos and education as more efficacious ways of addressing inequality in human society. However, his understanding of violence or *himsa* follows his Buddhist comprehension of it in non-absolutist ways.

Ambedkar, a Modern Dharmavyadh?

In the *Aranyakparvan* (The Forest Chapter) of the Mahabharata,[2] one comes across an unusual term *anrisamsya* or "non-cruelty" as a substitute for *ahimsa*. In this chapter of the epic, the quintessential virtuous man, leader of Pandavas, and a prominent protagonist of the epic – Yudhisthira – is engaged in a conversation with Dharma, the incarnation of goodness. Dharma asks Yudhisthira: "What is the best principle in life?" To this Judhisthira answers: "Anrisamsya paromo dharmo" (non-cruelty is the highest principle). However, *anrisamsya* or non-cruelty, as a more practicable principle, is not philosophically presented by Yudhisthira. In Aranyakparvan, this maxim comes from Dharmavyadh of Mithila – a sudra – a man of low caste origin or a dalit in modern parlance. He is a fowler or a vyadh who sells meat in the market and in that sense, lives a life that depends on violence. Dharmavyadh, as Sibaji Bandyopadhyay shows, finds a more pragmatic solution to the philosophical rigmarole apropos of *ahimsa* (2016).

For Dharmavyadh, *ahimsa* or non-violence is, at best, an impossible ideal. Bandyopadhyay explains: Dharmavyadha reckons the "state of violence" to be an irremediable, unavoidable factor of the "human condition." In his system of ethics, ahimsa obtains the precarious status of an unrealizable ideal (Bandyopadhyay 2016). He, like Ambedkar, recognizes the presence of violence or force as energy and concludes that "ahimsa paromo dharma" must be supplanted with "anrisamsa paromo dharmo." *Anrisamsya*, Bandyopadhyay shows, can be understood as leniency or non-cruelty.

The fowler in this story recognizes non-cruelty as the more cherished path. Instead of dilly-dallying about an absolutist notion of non-violence, Ambedkar and Dharmavyadh both prescribe *anrisamsya*. In "Krishna and His Gita," Ambedkar's rejection of violence in the *Gita* is premised not on an absolute rejection of force. Rather, his path is a *majjhim pantha* (middle way) on the trajectory of Dharmavyadh's "non-cruelty." Such a path was only possible when Ambedkar recognized the distinction between "force as energy" and "force as violence or violation." In recognizing this distinction, Ambedkar acknowledges his intellectual debt to John Dewey. While it is important for Ambedkar to use some level of persuasive force either through his rhetorical schema or pedagogical deployment of the Deweyean idea of democracy as a social ethos, it is equally significant for him to perceive violence in a rather non-absolutist sense. But, in my opinion, this distinction between "force as violence" and "force as energy" does not fully exemplify Ambedkar's appropriation of Dewey's thoughts. Also, we need to ask why and how Ambedkar brings his criticism of Krishna and his rebuttal of Marxist thought together in the context of violence and means/ends debate. Is Ambedkar hinting at something more outrageous here? Is it possible to put Brahaminical delineations on violence and Marxist endorsement of violence as an inevitable means for revolutionary praxis together on the same philosophical footing? If Ambedkar's intellectual allegiances to Dewey is anything to go by, such speculations invariably find the basis in Dewey's moral philosophy.

While Scott Stroud has recently emphasized on the similarities between Ambedkar's interpretations of Buddhist idea of ahimsa/himsa and his appropriation of the pragmatist visions of violence, the philosophical basis of this apparent similarity between Ambedkar's critique of violence as legitimized by the *Gita* and his criticisms of the Marxist's deployment of violence is not underscored by Stroud. For Stroud, the only distinction that differentiates Marxists from Deweyean-Ambedkarite (read pragmatist-Buddhist) is the fine line between "force as energy" and "force as violence." In order to find such a deeper philosophical conflict between Dewey and Marxists, one needs to look at the last section of his response to Trotsky. In my opinion, such fundamental philosophical critique attempted by Dewey subsequently paved the way for Ambedkar's simultaneous debunking of Krishna's and Marxist legitimization of violence (in the form of violation). According to Dewey, there is, in Marxist orthodoxy, a solid, rooted perception that the means follow from *the* principle of class struggle. By saying that the means are deduced from the principle of class struggle, they foreclose the possibility of understanding human problems through other ways or negate the possibility of examining the means adopted to materialize Trotsky's noble goal/ end – "to liberate men from the control of other men and from the dominance of nature." Ambedkar shares a similar opinion about both Krishna and the Marxists. In "Krishna and His Gita," Ambedkar's primary concern about himsa does not come merely from a morality that rejects violence absolutely. His criticism of the Gita, in my opinion, comes from the fact that Krishna asks Arjuna to nullify his capacity to think and perform what varna system has assigned him to perform. Placing the onus on such a priori principle (varna or class struggle) is rejected by both Dewey and Ambedkar as they think it does not allow further examination of means adopted. This becomes clear from Dewey's closing statement in "On Their Morals and Ours" (1938): Orthodox Marxism shares with orthodox religionism and with traditional idealism the belief that human ends are interwoven into the very texture and structure of existence – a conception presumably from its Hegelian origin.

Towards a Critique of *Himsa* qua a Critique of Indian Nationalism: "Niskama Karma" in Context

Just as the maxim "ahimsa paromo dharma" is reimagined in our contemporary times as the seed message of the *Mahabharata* that helps Hindus to see themselves as a community of "non-violence," the seed *sloka* (verse) of the *Gita* is also thought to have supplied them with the most necessary philosophical lesson needed to survive in this modern world. The forty-seventh *sloka* of the second chapter (2:47) of the *Gita* is widely understood as the essence or kernel of the whole text and its philosophy: "karmanye ba dhikaraste ma phalesu kadachana." Simply translated this goes like: "You are supposed to perform your duties and not think of the fruits of your actions." This interpretation of the *sloka* has apparently given us the idea of "niskama karma" or "desireless action." But how is this oxymoron possible? In the pre-modern interpretations of the *Gita*, the notion of *karma* is very different from the idea of "worldly action" implied in this modern reading. The Indian non-dualist philosopher Adi Shankacharya's *Gita* commentary as well as all such pre-modern commentaries interpret *karma* as mere "ritual actions" (this meaning is also described in various other brahmanic texts). In this sense, the idea of "karma" could never be compatible with "jnana" or "wisdom."

However, in the era of Indian nationalist movement, this idea of petty ritual action got replaced with a new interpretation. The famous Bengali novelist and nationalist intellectual

Bankim Chandra Chatterjee, in his 1888 book *Dharmatattva*, gave us this modern interpretation of "karma" for the first time. This nationalist/ writer went on to explain that Indians needed to merge *karma* and *jnana* in order to sustain themselves in the modern times. Here we must note that the anti-colonial movement was based on the construction of a discursive space of "difference" as well as a construction of "modern self" among Indians. This paradoxical project, as Partha Chatterjee shows, could only be possible when Indians could convince themselves that the construction and articulation of difference in the domain of "spirituality" as something "essentially Indian" could be found compatible with a pursuit for worldly action. It is to make this project successful that they needed to inflate the meaning of these terms, especially "karma." In the nineteenth-century revival of non-dualist philosophy, Indian nationalist thinkers even went beyond the interpretive limits set by the founder of this school of Indian philosophy – Sankaracharya.

While for him, "jnana" and "karma" were like water and oil, for Bankim, these were intertwined and they implied "desire less action." The notion of *niskama karma* (desire less action) could then be extended to render this question asked by the Indian theosophist Annie Besant merely rhetorical – "Is spiritual Progress Inconsistent with Material Progress?" However, Ambedkar's "Krishna and His Gita," as Sibaji Bandyopadhyay shows, became an anomaly among this massive enthusiasm for neo-non-dualist *Gita* interpretations that fuelled the construction of the nationalist discourse (Bandyopadhyay 2011). Ambedkar, the leader of the untouchables and the primary architect of the Indian constitution, became almost the lone voice in saying that such a marriage of "jnana" and "karma" is impossible and to do so would mount to a deliberate act of misreading:

> Most translate the word *Karma Yoga* as "action" and the word *Jnana Yoga* as "knowledge" and proceed to discuss the *Bhagavad Gita* as though it was engaged in comparing and contrasting knowledge versus action in a generalized form. This is quite wrong. Ambedkar's observations, thus, not only attacked his contemporary celebration of the *Gita* through the registers of war, violence or *varnashrama dharma*/caste system, his inter- pretations questioned the very claims upon which the edifice of Indian nationalist discourse would be constructed. The notion of *karma* and how it is inflated to serve such purpose is an example among many similar instances. But such a reading does not immediately give us any concrete idea as to how Ambedkar himself thought of nationalism.

Out of the previous paragraph, it is evident that a committed reader like him could see through the implicit politics of such retrospective readings of the *Gita*. But how did he himself conceptualize the nation-state, especially when he put in such massive intellectual as well as political efforts to create the Constitution of the newly independent country? It is true that his contri- butions to the construction of the modern Indian nation-state can never be overestimated. It is now common knowledge that he was the principal archi- tect of the constitution, the first law minister of independent India, and he is also well known for giving us rigorous accounts of how the nation-state can have a stable life. But, contrary to the popular perception of Ambedkar as "a maker of modern India" (to borrow Ramachandra Guha's phrase), he was also a thinker who saw through the contradictions of the very idea of nation- state or nationalism. In articulating these thoughts about the inner contra- dictions of such a cherished idea, Ambedkar never explicitly quoted Dewey or cited him. But in his statements, he is unmistakably Deweyean. Let us compare their thoughts. Dewey, as Leonard J. Waks' essay "John Dewey on Nationalism" in *Dewey Studies* shows, did recognize how certain social contradictions in a given society can be overridden through the construction of a horizontal comradeship and yet, nationalism inculcates a strong sense of hatred among fellow nationalists against the citizens of another nation:

> Dewey grants that nationalism has been a "two-sided" ethical force, a "tangled mixture of good and bad." On the positive side, nationalism was a "movement away from obnoxious conditions": narrow parochial- ism and dynastic despotism… But on the negative side, nation states have been built up by and sustained through violent conflict. Internal unity and fellow feeling has been accompanied by hostility to the people of other nations.

It is this curious interplay of love and hatred that marks the paradoxical existence of nation-states. Dr. Ambedkar, in his book *Pakistan or the Partition of India* (2014), gives us a similar definition of nationalism: This national feeling is a double-edged feeling. It is at once a feeling of fellowship for one's own kith and kin and anti-fellowship for those who are not one's own kith and kin. At a time when nationalist jingoism is rising, hatred for other communities is equally strong both in India and the United States, the realization of duality in the very idea of nation-states or how nationalist claims of ancient origin are located not in remote unintelligible (yet "glorious") past but in recent, deliberately distorted readings of pre-modern texts or how war, violence, and nationalism can be subtly and intricately thought through are absolutely important. Both Dewey and Ambedkar can be our guide in helping us see through such intricacies. However, the fact that I have put Trotsky. Dewey, Ambedkar, and Russell in conversation with each other in this essay should not conveniently imply an easy subscription to any of their particular philosophical affiliations.[3] Rather, my concerns concerning war, violence, and nationalism in this essay reflect how all of them inhabited future points of criticism that their philosophical inclinations would encounter.

While Trotsky's thoughts might operate as much-needed correctives in negotiating with the hegemonic logic of global neoliberalism in our times, Dewey's "critical liberalism" or immanent critique of liberalism and critique of different hues of Marxist thoughts might help us see the limits of Left's multifaceted and wider political projects. As Chantal Mouffe and Ernesto Laclau suggest, Left does not necessarily have to see liberal democratic institutions as historically necessary obstacles that need to be overcome or toppled down through a radical revolutionary moment to envisage and politically realize the "end of politics" (somewhat analogous to Francis Fukuyama's "end of history"). Just as Dewey's moral philosophy comes as a required rupture to interrogate the validation of violence in both religious orthodoxy of the contemporary Right-wing populism and the revolutionary zeal of the non-electoral Left, one must recognize how Trotsky's insights help us see the persistent hegemonization of a neo-liberal market economy and "market society" (to borrow Michael Sandal's phrase). Neither of these two ends of the political spectrum (in India and in the United States) perhaps fully helps us to bargain and negotiate with the rising Right populism in global politics. In many ways, these thinkers anticipated these challenges that dalit activism in India and Leftist politics at a global scale have to negotiate with in constructing what Mouffe and Laclau call "hegemonic" and "contaminated" universality or a certain kind of particular universality that makes the contingent moment of politics happen. With his scathing criticism of the Marxist notion of violence as integral to revolution and the criticism of the deeply entrenched question of violence in the *Mahabharata* text as well,

I emphasize and conclude, Ambedkar's novel vision of morality that, while specific to the context of an Asian sub-continental cultural ethos, remains profoundly cosmopolitan in nature.

Notes

1 An earlier version of this paper was presented at the 2018 John Dewey Society annual meeting in New York (13–14 April 2018).
2 For a profound analysis of violence in the Mahabharata, see how its "Souptik Parvan" has been explored by Anirban Das. See Anirban Das (2014).
3 Richard Bernstein thinks that this particular attitude in itself is a fundamental characteristic of American Pragmatism of Charles Sanders Peirce, William James, and John Dewey. See Richard Bernstein, *The Pragmatic Turn* (Cambridge, Malden: Polity Press, 2010).

Works Cited

Ambedkar, Babasaheb. "Mr. Russell and the Reconstruction of the Society," 1918, in *Babasaheb Ambedkar Writings and Speeches (BAWS)*, ed. Vasant Moon (New Delhi, 2014), Vol. 1, 481–492.

_____. "Buddha or Karl Marx?" in *Babasaheb Ambedkar Writings and Speeches (BAWS)*, ed. Vasant Moon (New Delhi, 2014), Vol.3, 441–462.

_____. *Pakistan or the Partition of India,* in Babasaheb Ambedkar Writings and Speeches (BAWS) ed. Vasant Moon (New Delhi, 2014), Vol. 8, 1–482.

Bandopadhyay, Sibaji. "Non-Dualism and Nationalism: A Case Study-The Dawn Enterprise," *Sibaji Bandopadhyay Reader*. Worldview Publications, 2011. 38–104.

_____. "A Critique of Non-Violence," in *Three Essays in Mahabharata; Essays in Literary Hermeneutics*. Orient Blackswan, 2016.267–307.

Banerjee, Prathama. Aditya Nigam, Rakesh Pandey, "Work of Theory: Thinking Across Traditions," *Economic and Political Weekly*, Vol. 51, No. 37 (2016).

Chatterjee, Partha. *Nationalist Thought and the Colonial World: A Derivative Discourse?* University of Minnesota Press, 1993.

Das, Anirban. "Of Sleep and Violence: Reading the *Sauptikaparvan* in Times of Terror", in *Mahabharata Now and Then*, ed. by Arindam Chakrabarti and Sibaji Bandopadhyay. Routledge, 2014. 203–218.

Dewey, John. "On Their Morals and Ours," *The New International*, New York, 1938).

Laclau, Ernesto and Chantal Mouffe, *Hegemony and Socialist Strategy: Towards a Radical Democratic Politics*. Verso, 2014.

Russell, Bertrand. *Common Sense and Nuclear War*. Routledge, 2010.

Stroud, Scott R. "Pragmatism, Persuasion and Force in Bhimrao Ramji Ambedkar's Reconstruction of Buddhism," *Journal of Religion*, Vol. 97, No.2 (2017), 214–243.

Trotsky, Leon. "Their Morals and Ours," *The New International*, Vol. IV, No.6 (NewYork, 1938), 163–173.

Waks, Leonard J. "John Dewey on Nationalism," *Dewey Studies,* Vol.1, No. 2 (2017), 112–125.

AFTERTHOUGHTS

In Search of the Antecedents to the
Mahabharata Concept and Ideal of
Anrisamsya: Random Reflections

Ranabir Chakravarti

Afterthoughts to a scholarly edited volume such as this are perhaps akin to sundries accumulated to the score-card of a cricket match without adding to the credit of a batter or any discredit to a bowler. It only fattens the score-card with peripherals. The subject taken up here is lightyears away from the primary familiarity with the theme and professional ability of this contributor. The unique ideal of *anrisamsya* (non-cruelty) is a great gift of the Mahabharata; yet, this thought-provoking concept does not figure anywhere other than the Mahabharata. The concept of non-cruelty has been lauded as the highest virtue (*parama dharma*) in a text permeated with violence as a recurrent theme glorified as the salient marker of a hero of the kshatriya *varna*. This apparent contradiction naturally did not escape the attention and interrogation of engaged and celebrated scholars, consisting of Sanskritists, text-workers, philosophers, historians, and experts of cultural studies (Hiltebeitel 2001; Lath 2007; Bandyopadhyay 2016, 2023; Sinha 2019; Sinha 2021; Chakrabarti 2022; Bhattacharjee 2022). The Mahabharata, noted for its open-ended portrayals of human beings in multichromatic hues – deliberately refraining from a simplistic and simplified presentation of many of its characters in black and white – makes little attempt in ironing out contradictions and dichotomies in human nature. The text, therefore, always encourages new interpretations and novel insights into its contents which thus offers new vistas by revisiting the familiar storylines. This is a challenging and exciting task which renowned experts have often delved into to keep the Mahabharata alive and relevant in the current scenario.

DOI: 10.4324/9781003516408-18

Risking the obvious limitations to his intellectual wherewithal, the present essayist decided, rather foolishly, to revisit the concept of *anrisamsya*. The mainstay of this essay's arguments is the historical perspective and the contextual analyses of some of the utterances on *anrisamsya*. Needless to elaborate, this exercise will require restating some of the well-established views of experts on *anrisamsya*. The critical edition of the Mahabharata, with which all the preceding scholars are far more familiar than I could ever imagine, has enabled us to realize that the epic, now containing one hundred thousand verses, acquired its present shape over at least eight centuries (from c. 400 BCE to c. 400/500 CE) (Winternitz1987; Sukthankar 1936–1937, 1957). Taking the cue from Romila Thapar's innovative understanding that the Mahabharata is replete with an Indic historical tradition (*Itihasa-Purana*) (Thapar 2008 123–154, 173–191, 613–629; Thapar 2013) – distinct from what is History as an academic discipline emanating from European Enlightenment – Kanad Sinha demonstrates, by a masterly marshalling of a vast range Sanskrit textual sources, that the battle at Kurukshetra could have taken place in c. 900 BCE. He situates the account of the Kurukshetra battle in the context of the later Vedic society, culture and political processes (c. 1000–600 BCE) (Sinha 2021). The actual composition of the poem, according to him, began around 400 BCE and reached its culmination about 500 CE. The internal evidence from the text also bears testimony to it. The kernel of the narrative, attributed to Vyasa, consisted of 8,000 verses and was named the *Jayakavya*. Its first recitation goes to the credit of Suka Vaisampayana, Vyasa's disciple at the time of the snake sacrifice (*sarpasatra*) by Janamejaya (son of Parikshit, the grandson of the Pandavas), held at Takshasila. The purpose was to remember and narrate the feats of the ancestors of the ruler in the form of hero-stories (possibly a genre of poetic compositions descending from the Rigvedic narrative hymns in praise of men – *gathanarasamsi*). However, the oral narrative recited by Vaisampayana had increased to 24,000 verses (*slokas*). Having heard this recitation, Ugrasrava, a hereditary bard (*suta*, hence given the epithet Sauti), orally narrated the account to Saunaka and other Bhargava sages who had been engaged in the protracted performance of the Somayajna at Naimisha forest. The sages desired to listen to varied and entertaining narratives (*chitrahkathah*). The story told by the bard Ugrasrava Sauti contained 84,000 verses. Thus the Mahabharata was growing in size in terms of the number of verses, obviously by manifold additions to the core narrative of the Kurukshetra battle. Till this time, the composition was essentially oral and created by wandering minstrels or bards (*suta/magadha*), like Vaisampayana and Ugrasrava Sauti, whose position in the *varna-jati* norm of the Brahmanical system was being systematically degraded (Dayal 2009). It is no surprise that the robust and multi-faceted narratives of heroes and heroines (e.g. Draupadi, Kunti, Vidula, Damayanti, and suchlike) began to be taken over by orthodox Brahmanical socio-cultural and political norms and ideals. This is a process aptly labelled by Thapar as Bhargavization. The result is the addition of the massive didactic sections, like *Santiparvan, Anusasanaparvan,* and the *Srimadbhagavatgita.* The unmissable Vaishnava devotional (*Bhakti*) elements, superimposed on a primarily heroic tale, transformed it into a sacred *sastra.* An obvious exemplar of the process is the interpolation of an appendix-like (*khila*) *Harivamsa,* consisting of 16,000 verses, giving it the monumental size of a text containing one hundred thousand verses. A Sanskrit inscription from Khoh (in Madhya Pradesh), dated 533 CE, declared the text as a codified manual containing one hundred thousand verses (*satasahasri-samhita*).[1] It must be underlined that the particular expression figures in the very last section of the copper plate inscription to sanctify the royal grant of revenue-free landed property for ecclesiastical purposes and end. The transformation of a narrative heroic poem (*kavya*) orally narrated by wandering minstrels/bards (*suta/magadha*) into a Brahmanical didactic text (*Samhita*) can hardly escape our attention. This morphing is likely to have taken place sometime between 200 BCE and 400 CE.

II

In this context we propose to delve into the unique *Mahabharata* ideal of *anrisamsya,* denoting the ethical principle of the avoidance of cruelty. Thanks to Hiltebeitel, one can enlist nine occasions where *anrisamsya* as an ethical stand, promoting non-cruelty, was lauded as the ultimate ethics/ virtue (*parama dharma*) (Hiltebeitel 2001). Non-violence (*ahimsa*) figures in the Mahabharata four times also as the supreme virtue. The numerical superiority of the references to the former in comparison to the latter can logically be read as the Mahabharata's preference for embracing the ethical stand of minimum use of or the total absence of cruelty vis-á-vis the celebrated principle of non-violence (*ahimsa*). Although apparently near synonymous, the mention of both the terms in the Mahabharata clearly underlines the distinctiveness of the two concepts which were not identical. In view of the extant explanatory literature on this subject, it would be wise not to repeat the same. However certain remarks, which may or may not correspond to and/or overlap with the prevalent interpretations, will not be entirely irrelevant and/or out of order. First, the concept of non-cruelty (*anrisamsya*) is dovetailed with the ethical principle of literally crying after another's grief/ sorrow (*anukrosa*), denoting one's empathetic attachment to someone else's pain or grief. This concept of sharing someone else's grief emanates from and strengthens the notion of avoidance of cruelty. Both the terms, *anrisamsya* and *anukrosa,* are unique to the Mahabharata since these are not traceable anywhere outside the Mahabharata. There is a general agreement among several leading scholars that the concept of non-cruelty and/or the promotion of unavoidable cruelty (*anrisamsya*), in conjunction with sharing someone's grief with empathy (*anukrosa*), was an alternative to the ideal and principle of non-violence (*ahimsa*). Not only non-violence (*ahimsa*) is of foundational significance for the Sramanic tenets, best illustrated by Buddhist and Jaina ideologies, but also the ethical principle of non-violence sharply critiqued and rejected the cult of elaborate animal sacrifices (*yajna*) and the social and ritual primacy of brahmana priesthood as the sole repository of the sacred Vedic knowledge and ideology. In other words, the stress on the non-killing of living beings was the very cornerstone of the negation of the infallibility of the Vedic ideology (*nastika/Veda-apramanyavadi*), rooted in the cult of sacrifices (*yajna*) (Thapar 1984; Shrimali 2020; Singh 2008, 2017).

The renunciant philosophies totally rejected the criterion of the fourfold *varna* order and also the primacy of the brahmana as the highest *varna*. That the accident of birth could not determine one's social position, the principal plank on which stands the *varna-jati* system, was effectively challenged by the *nastika*/Sramana ideologies. Anyone from any *varna-jati* status could become a follower of the Buddha, Mahavira, and Makkhaliputta Gosala either as a lay follower (*upasaka*) or renounce the world. The idea of renouncing the world at any point of one's life stressed on the homelessness (*ageha*) of the wandering (*pavajja/pravrajya*) ascetic (*sramana*). Thus the ideal of the homeless, wandering ascetic stood directly in opposition to the householder (Sanskrit *grihastha*, literally one who stays at home/*gihi* or *gahattha* in Pali). It is around the fixed and permanent habitat that the stage of life (*asrama*) of the householder (*garhasthya*) attains the greatest and the most central status in the Brahmanical order of the four graduated stages (*asrama*) of life (Wagle 1966; Chakravarti 1987; Olivelle 2004). While the Brahmanical institution of *asramas* considered the final stage of *sannyasa* or *yati* (totally severing one's worldly ties) as preparatory to the attainment of emancipation (*moksha*), the maximum importance, on the other hand, was attached to the stage of the householder (*garhasthya*). *Garhasthya* enabled a man (literally a male) to marry a suitable wife (ideally from within the same *varna* but outside the *gotra*), to raise offsprings to continue the family line (and hence the inevitable preference for a son/sons, while the birth of a daughter is deplored – *krichchhramtuduhita*) and to perform domestic rituals every day (like the *panchamahayajna*). As the householder and in the capacity of the head of the extended family, a man was expected to earn his livelihood by following a prescribed and fixed profession/occupation, according to his *varna-jati* status. Put differently, the stage of the householder (*grihastha*) offered a man the avenues to attain three principal aims of one's life – righteous conduct (*dharma*), material matters/power (*artha*), and desire (*kama*), paving the way for his retirement to forest (*vanaprastha*) and to the ultimate stage of severing all worldly ties (*sannyasa*). In a way, therefore, the stage of the householder sustains the passages through and attainment of the other three graduated stages. The attainment of the four aims of life (*chaturvarga*), literally meant for and entitled to a male (*purushartha*), according to the Brahmanical ideology, rests on conscious efforts, and hence the relevance of the concept of *asrama*, which is derived from the root *sram*, standing for exertion. What can hardly escape one's notice is that the institution of *asrama* was inseparably associated with the *varna* order, the patriarchal society and family, and patrilineal descent (Jaiswal 1998). It is also plainly visible that the orthodox Brahmanical norms, drawing upon and sanctioned by the Vedic ideology, do not provide any scope for pursuing the four stages of life to the lower social orders and women (Roy 2010, Roy 2011).

Even at the risk of repeating it needs to be underlined here that the ideals of the homeless (*ageha*) wandering ascetic (*pravrajya*) emerged as a foundational challenge to the Vedic ideology and the socio-ritual primacy of the brahmana. Dwelling on the philosophical nuances of the principal tenets of Sramanic thoughts, several experts on the ethical issues in the *Mahabharata* and also Sanskritists have argued that the principle of non-violence (*ahimsa*), the very core of the Sramanic thoughts, is problematic since it is impossible to adhere to and practice perfect non-violence. Moreover, these scholars find in the Sramanic concept of *ahimsa* the elements of withdrawal and cessation from actions (*nivritti*) in opposition to engaged actions (*pravritti*). The more logical and practicable substitute for adherence to violence (*ahimsa*) – itself considered an elusive goal in life – was to practice minimum cruelty (*anrisamsya*). The essence of their arguments is that the Mahabharata creatively offered an alternative way (*marga*) to the widespread appeal of the Sramanic tenets, especially Buddhism and Jainism, which espoused the negative concept of withdrawal from life (Chakrabarti 2022; Lath 2007). The striking originality of this explanatory argument notwithstanding, the primacy of temporal sequencing, an inseparable prerequisite for historical studies, does not allow us to bring in the contrastive concepts of *nivritti* and *pravritti* paths (*margas*) to account for the championing of the ideal and practice of non-cruelty (and by extension, the unleashing of minimal and unavoidable violence). The binary opposition between *pravritti* and *nivritti* *margas* in the Brahmanical philosophical tenets is unlikely to have been coeval with the narrative elements (i.e. excluding the later didactic and prescriptive elements) in the Mahabharata. This, however, does not minimize the significance of the concept of non-cruelty, coupled with that of compassion and empathy (*anukrosa*), an undoubted gift of the Mahabharata.

III

Without repeating the nine well-known instances of *anrisamsya* in the Mahabharata, a selection of some exemplars may be taken up here for historical analysis. One of the most hallowed practitioners of non-cruelty is Yudhisthira who, as the very epitome of righteous conducts (*dharma*), was reluctant to engage in wars which is invariably lauded as the premier duty and function of a ruler, emblematic of an ideal kshatriya conduct. During his gripping conversation with the Yaksha (actually Dharma/Yama himself in disguise; also the progenitor of Yudhishthira as a *kshetraja* offspring of Kunti) in the *Aranyaparva*, Yudhisthira unhesitatingly stated that non-cruelty (*anrisamsya*) was the highest virtue (*para dharma*). Pleased with Yudhishthira's perfect answers, Dharma/Yaksha wished to give him a boon for bringing back only one of his four dead brothers. Yudhishthira opted for the gift of life for Nakula, though he was a step-brother. He justified this choice that at least one offspring of his deceased step-mother, Madri, should exist. This is indeed a shining example of the ideal of *anukrosa*, standing in tandem with *anrisamsya*. The Mahabharata, which does not erase unresolvable contradictions, also narrates that Yudhisthira was a party to and approver of the decision to surreptitiously get the five *nishada* sons and their *nishadi* mother burnt alive, asleep in the dead of night, in the house of wax (*jatugriha*) (Chakravarti 2022). No semblance of non-cruelty and empathetic sharing of another's grief can be invented by the most ardent supporter of Yudhisthira in the commission of this inhuman crime. Or, were the hallowed principles of *anrisamsya* and *anukrosa* irrelevant to persons of the *a-varna* groups, like the forest-dwelling and hunting communities like the *nishadas*?[2]

The other famous instance of clinging to the ethical stand of non-cruelty is the tale of the righteous meat-seller/butcher (*dharmavyadha*) at Mithila. A sage, deeply immersed in protracted meditation, was hugely infuriated by a bird's dropping excreta on his head. The enraged sage hurled a curse that killed the bird. The sage, in remorse on account of this terrible anger against the hapless creature, took to penance and began to live on alms. On one occasion, in the course of begging for alms, he reached a home where the wife of the householder delayed to offer him the alms, busy as she was in receiving her husband with the ritual oblations. The sage again uttered a terrible curse to the dutiful wife. She replied that the curse would do no harm to a devoted wife whose priority was to serve her husband first and then attend to the visitor. She pointed out the futility of the curse on a devoted wife and also pronounced the vacuity of the sage's morality and spirituality since the sage was given to vengeance. She advised the sage to learn non-cruelty from the righteous meat-seller/butcher (*dharmavyadha*). The sage went to Mithila and heard from the butcher the essence of non-cruelty. Though he was at the very margin of the *varna-jati* society and lived by selling the meat of buffaloes and pigs to varied customers, he himself never consumed meat and never killed the animals which he sold as per the desire of his customers. The butcher claimed perfect righteousness as he merely followed his profession and maintained his family and house-hold, as prescribed by the *varna-jati* norms – in other words, steadfast in discharging his duties and functions (*sva-dharma/sva-karma*), adhering to the *varna-jati* ideals. He never indulged in violence and, therefore, was upholding the ethical principle of non-cruelty (*anrisamsya*). The virtue of non-cruelty, not only by avoiding the killing of beasts but also by refraining from hurling verbal and mental violence was perceived as the highest ethics. Thus, an established brahmana sage was taught the principle of non-cruelty by a meat-seller/butcher who engaged, from the point of Brahmanical ide-als, in a heinous, deplorable, and impure profession. The meat-seller also emphatically pronounced the impossibility of perpetually pursuing perfect non-violence (*bahu sanchintyaiti…nastikaschidahimsakah*) (Chakrabarti 2022, 21). The ethical principle of non-cruelty thus was a viable alternative to non-violence (*ahimsa*). Moreover, it ensured the maintenance of the duties of a householder and furtherance of domesticity (*garhasthya*) by adopting non-cruelty and/or minimal violence.

While many experts highlighted the moral standpoint of non-cruelty in this tale of the righteous meat-seller, two crucial aspects of the fabular nar-rative remain understated and less discussed. First, the wife of the brahmana remained unaffected and unscathed by the sage's curse because she was a devoted and loyal wife (*pativrata*), steeped in domesticity.[3] The morality of being an ideal and devoted wife enabled her to advise the sage to learn the ethics of non-cruelty from a righteous meat-seller. The second point is that the meat-seller himself informed the visiting brahmana that the present meat-seller himself had been a brahmana in a former birth, but was con-demned to be reborn as a meat-seller/butcher in his subsequent birth because as a learnt brahmana he inadvertently killed another brahmana during a hunting expedition. The *dharmavyadha* accepted and justified his current low *varna-jati* status and the condemnable profession as an inevitable out-come of his killing a brahmana. So, his assiduous practice of *anrisamsya* is almost an act of penance and atonement of sin committed in a previ-ous birth. Both these aspects of the *dharmavyadha*-tale have an unmissable underpinning of the ideology of the *varna-jati* system which is inextricably tied also to patriarchy. The *varna-jati* system, in conjunction with the patri-archal setup of the family and overall society, is extremely oppressive (to say the least), institutionalizes interminable inequality in society and subjugates women. The harshness of the system is incongruent with the celebrations of non-cruelty (*anrisamsya*) and empathetic sharing of someone else's grief (*anukrosa*) as alternatives to the Sramanic ideal of non-violence (*ahimsa*).

Yudhisthira's avowed practice of *anrisamsya* finds almost total rejection by two leading and powerful female characters, Kunti and Draupadi. Kunti admonished Yudhishthira for his cowardice (*vaiklavya*) and being firmly set in the course of non-cruelty (*anrisamsyevyavasthita*); he was therefore

perceived as incapable of enjoying the fruits of due maintenance of his subjects (*prajapalanasambhutamkinchitpraptaphalamnripah*) (Sinha 2021).
Unable to arouse Yudhishthira to shed his stand on *anrisamsya*, Draupadi
tried to provoke Yudhishthira's anger by repeatedly pointing to the indig-
nity, dishonour, and distress of her two great warrior husbands, Bhima and
Arjuna, due to the machinations of the Kauravas. But her efforts were in
vain. The mocking of Yudhishthira's preference for non-cruelty by Kunti
and Draupadi probably fits in well with the heroic (kshatriya) tradition of
the narrative contents of the epic, as yet not coloured and taken over by
Brahmanical didactic superimpositions. The polarity between the two perceptions of *anrisamsya* coming respectively from powerful heroic women
(Kunti and Draupadi) and from a devoted and loyal wife is quite glaring.

One of the very best illustrations of Yudhishthira's unswerving commitment to the ethics of compassion and empathy (*anukrosa*) is his refusal to
enter the gate of heaven by leaving behind the accompanying dog (actually
Dharma). No less inspiring is his firm refusal to enjoy heaven since his four
brothers and his wife were condemned to punishments for the sins they had
committed in the mundane world. His singular choice was to share the grief,
pain, and torture, meted out to his brothers and wife in hell.

IV

Having delved into some of the stellar and celebrated instances of the ideals of non-cruelty (*anrisamsya*) and compassionately sharing others' grief
(*anukrosa*) – both being unique to the *Mahabharata* – we now propose to
take a close look at the principles of the Dhamma articulated by the greatest
Mauryan ruler Asoka (c. 272–233 BCE) (Thapar 1987, 1996). The ground
for my bringing in Asoka is that he is the lone ruler to have eschewed war
for good after a resounding military victory in c. 261 BCE. The other point
is to stress that Asoka's upholding of Dhamma is best read in the light of his
inscriptions and not in the legends about Asoka available in the Buddhist
Avadana tales (e.g. *Divyavadana* and *Asokavadana*). Written in hybrid
Buddhist Sanskrit these *Avadana* texts on Asoka, however important in the
history of Buddhism, were composed around second/third century CE –
thus much later than the actual reign-period of Asoka himself (Bhattacharji
2011). The primary object of these tales is to portray the transformative
power of Buddhism on Asoka who had initially been a fierce, blood-thirsty
ruler (Chandasoka) accused of killing many of his brothers to ascend the
throne, but whose embracing of Buddhism out of repentance made him an
ideal Buddhist ruler (*dhammika Dhammraja*), the pious and righteous Asoka
(Dharmasoka). Asoka's edicts, written in a conversational mode in Prakrit,
addressing to his functionaries and subjects in the first person singular (this
is unique in the entire range of Indic epigraphy), are doubtless coeval with

his reign and therefore, present a more reliable evidentiary corpus, strewn nearly all over the subcontinent and also in some parts of Afghanistan.[4]

Significantly enough, his Rock Edict (hereinafter RE) XIII narrates the terrible violence unleashed by the Maurya army during the conquest of Kalinga (no mention at all of Asoka's killing his brothers) when eight years had elapsed since his coronation (*abhisita*). In addition to the killing (*vadha*) of people on the battlefield, many died (*mute*-Skt*mrita*) as an aftermath of the war; even greater was the number of people who were taken away (*apa-vudhe*: probably as prisoners of war). The Maurya ruler categorically spoke about this bloodbath as deplorable and explicitly recorded his deep remorse (*tiveanusochaye*). This was followed by his embracing Buddhism as a lay follower (upasaka). He admitted that for some time he was not zealous as a lay follower but subsequently became active as an upasaka (Minor Rock Edict I). His personal leanings and deep attachment to Buddhism are writ large in his edicts carrying his own words. His visits to Lumbinigrama, the place of the Buddha's nativity (*hide Budhejate Sakyamuni*), to the site associated with the Buddha Kanakamuni (in Nepalese terrai), to Sambodhi (Bodhgaya, Bihar); his instructions for reading a few Buddhist canonical texts by the members of the Samgha (in Bairat Rock Edict) and his very firm admonition to those whose thoughts and actions could break up the Samgha (three Samghabheda/Schism edicts) (Tieken 2023) bear tell-tale marks of his ties to Buddhism. This, along with the portrayals of Asoka in later Buddhist legends, have resulted in the widely held, but erroneous, perception that he was a Buddhist ruler who made Buddhism the state religion.

That Asoka's Dhamma was not identical with his personal leanings to Buddhism is best evident from the seven Greek and Aramaic edicts found from Taxila (Pakistan) and Shar-i-kuna, Kandahar, Pul-i-Darunta and Laghman (in Afghanistan) (Mukherjee 1984). These Greek and Aramaic edicts contain translations, transliterations, summaries, adaptations and elucidations of his utterances engraved in his Prakrit edicts. The Prakrit term Dhamma, the central theme of his edicts, is translated in Greek as *Eusebia* which means Piety. The corresponding Aramaic words for Prakrit Dhamma are *Data*, meaning Law and *Qsyt*, denoting Truth. It is quite palpable through these translations that Asoka's Dhamma was never synonymous with Buddhism. In fact, his Prakrit edicts are silent on some of the fundamental tenets of Buddhism. Thus, he never pronounced anything on the Four Noble Truths (*Chaturaryasatyas*), the Eightfold Path (*Ashtangika-marga*) and even *Nirvana* (the highest goal in Buddhism). His personal leanings to Buddhism cannot be equated with Dhamma which therefore is not rendered into English as Buddhism, but translated as the Law of Piety.

Asoka did not exactly define what he meant by Dhamma. But he was eloquent on the salient features of Dhamma and some of the foundational principles of his Dhamma. Of immense importance was the principles of the non-killing of living beings (*anarambhoprananam; avihisabhutanam*). Yet, he was frank enough to have conceded that a couple of deer and a peacock were still being killed in the royal kitchen, though he had already drastically reduced the vast number of animals meant for slaughtering (RE I). This was perhaps not imposed as a blanket ban on animal slaughter at a single stroke, but given effect to in phases. Thus the two Aramaic edicts from Laghman, issued when sixteen years had elapsed since his coronation, announced that the ruler had banished from his realm those who were excessively fond of hunting and fishing. This was followed by a longer list of animals which were not to be killed on certain auspicious days and also a list of animals which were pronounced as inviolate (Pillar Edict V; hereinafter PE). The same principle of avoidance of violence led to the banning of royal hunting expeditions (*viharayata*), which were replaced with the tours of Piety (*Dhammayata*). It is only natural that the Maurya polity had no known association with elaborate Vedic sacrificial rituals (e.g. Asvamedha sacrifice), prescribed for claiming and achieving the status of a super-ordinate ruler Chakravarti (Chakravarti 2016). At the core of this ideology and programme was his conviction that a living being should not be sustained by another living being (*jivena jive no pusitaviye*, PE V). His compassion and empathy for human beings and non-human animals are captured by his arrangements for the medical treatments of both humans and beasts (*manusa-chikichha* and *pasuchikichha*) which were included within the Dhamma programme.

The abstention from violence and the promotion of compassion were not confined to the battlefield, hunting expedition and animal welfare only. The negation of verbal one-upmanship, denouncement and violence was also a major component of Asoka's Dhamma. Of great value to Asoka was

The promotion of the essentials of all sects (*saravadhi*). A promotion of the essentials (is possible) in many ways. But its root is this, viz. guarding one's speech that neither praising own sect nor blaming other sects should take place...; it should be moderate in every case. ... For whoever praises his own sect or blames other sects, all (this) out of devotion to his own sect with the view to glorifying his own sect,... he rather injures his own sect very severely (RE XII). (Hultzsch 1925: 23)

Asoka therefore repeatedly asks for seemly behaviour to the brahmana and the sramana alike and on equal footing as an essential element of his Dhamma ideology. Also included in this ideology was courteous behaviour to slaves (*dasa*) and servants (*bhataka*), reverence to parents and elders (REs IV, XII and XIII) and liberality to friends, acquaintances, and relatives (RE XII). With this end in view, Asoka created a new administrative position, viz, the officers in charge of the propagation of the Law of Piety (*Dhamma-mahamatra*). Among their various functions was the welfare of servants and masters and brahmanas and the well off (*ibhyas*), the destitute, and the aged. Asoka's ideals of Dhamma were inclusive enough to accommodate the Jainas (Nirgranthas) and the Ajivikas, the two Sramnic groups which had sharp differences from the Buddhists. A shining example of this broad accommodative ideology is available in the donation of cave shelters for the Ajivikas by Asoka and his grandson at Nagarjuna hills near Gaya, which was very much within the metropolitan Magadhan zone of the Mauryan empire.[5]

Asoka's ideals of Dhamma are totally bereft of any association with or reference to the *varna-jati* institution. On the contrary, he enjoins the inculcation of some virtues and avoidance of vices, cutting across social hierarchies and sectarian differences. The promotion of little sin (*apasinave*), many meritorious deeds (*bahukayane*), kindness (*daya*), gift-giving (*dane*), truthfulness (*sache*) and purity (*sochaye*) marks the virtuous practices (PE II). The vices to be shunned are, according to the PE III, fierceness (*chamdiye*), cruelty (*nithuliye*), anger (*kodhe*), pride (*mane*) and jealousy (*issya*). The list of vices to be avoided or at least controlled was presented almost in an unstated chain of cause and effect. The first two vices are actually expressions and manifestations of the last three. The promotion of the virtues and the negation of the vices, engraved in Asokan edicts, have nothing to do with Buddhism per se. In fact, it is too broad-based to be ascribed to any particular ecclesiastical orientation. Dhamma was actually a code of ethical conducts. However, by his steadfast following of the ethics of non-killing of living beings, Asoka certainly drew the inspiration from Sramanic tenets.

His Greek edict from Kandahar on *Eusebia* speaks of the familiar ideas of Dhamma found in Asoka's Prakrit edicts, particularly the contents of Res VII, XII, and XIII. Of the virtues to be promoted for the sustenance of *Eusebia* (i.e., Dhamma) was the firm devotion to the king's interests (*ta touBasileossumpherontanoi*) – implying, in other words, the subjects' firm devotion to the king. This explicit statement in the Greek edict is an elucidation, elaboration, and explanation (through translation) of the Prakrit expression *didhabhatita* (firm devotion). While the Prakrit text did not elaborate the nature of the devotion, the translation in Greek did that. Firm devotion to the king cannot but imply that the explicit articulation of the subjects' allegiance to the ruler was one of the components of Asoka's Dhamma.[6] The Dhamma of Asoka was, therefore, not merely a very broad-based socio-ethical principle/code of conduct but also had in it a distinct political element. Asoka would treat his subjects with paternal care but also demanded their allegiance.

At this juncture, we once again take up the RE XIII that graphically records the terrible violence during the Kalinga war and the resultant remorse of Asoka. The same edict also unequivocally states that he would pardon a wrong-doer only up to the pardonable limit. His stern threat uttered against the forest-dwellers (*atavis*) in RE XIII cannot escape one's notice. The very last portion of RE XIII is striking. "The inscription of Dhamma has been engraved so that any sons or great grandsons that I may have, should not think of gaining new conquests (*navamvijayam*), and in whatever victories they may gain should be satisfied with patience and light punishments (*lahu-damdata;* Skt*laghu-danda*)" (Hultzsch 1925). Thus, Asoka did not rule out violence and even military campaign(s). The term *danda* (the rod of chastisement) manifests the coercive authority of the ruler and also stands for the army.[7] The insistence on the application of light or minimal chastisement and also war-like mobilization was an option of governance available to Asoka who also accorded unprecedented salience to the ideology and the practice of non-violence and non-injury to living beings in the statecraft (Visvanathan 2011).

V

A few points may emerge from the foregoing discussions. First, the contributions of the *Mahabharata* to the coining of the two unique vocabularies, viz. *anrisamsya* (non-cruelty) and *anukrosa* (sharing the grief of another with empathy), as socio-political and moral maxims, are well recognized. Second, the propositions and possibilities of qualified violence and chastisement by Asoka in the third century BCE as a component of his Dhamma ideology – which is otherwise permeated with non-violence, non-injury, accommodation of diverse (and in fact, competing) faith-based traditions – has no known historical precedence in South Asia. This is particularly evident from his explicit approval of the minimal and limited application of the unavoidable coercive authority, chastisement and even future conquests (all collapsed in the advocacy of *laghu-danda* in RE XIII). The first two points lead to the third: the uniqueness of the two complementary Mahabharata terms *anrisamsya* and *anukrosa* notwithstanding, the originary and genealogy of these two concepts are traceable to Asoka's Dhamma ideology. Contrary to the common view that Asoka – under the spell and influence of Sramanic ideals in general and Buddhism in particular – was a votary of pristine non-violence, Asoka's stated approval of the minimal and unavoidable violence and chastisement calls for serious attention, introspection and a revision. What was explicitly mentioned in Asoka's RE XIII as light and minimal degree of chastisement, coercion and even a military mobilization (*laghu-danda*) seems to have been taken up in the *Mahabharata* and given a new labelling, *anrisamsya* (non-cruelty). One may also cogently argue that the *Mahabharata* concept of non-cruelty has its clear antecedent in the Asokan principle on the cessation of fierceness and cruelty (*chamdiye* and *nithuliye*). Similarly, the two Sramanic ideals of compassion (*karuna*) and kindness (*daya*) are likely to have been at the root of the *Mahabharata* concept of *anukrosa*. These are perhaps not instances of an innocent borrowing of concepts between two diametrically contesting ideologies – the

Brahmanical and the Sramanic – based on some affinity of principles. The immense popularity of Buddhism and Jainism on a subcontinental scale from c. 600 BCE to 300 CE, palpable in textual, epigraphic and visual testimonies, appear to have also generated considerable contestations from the Brahmanical ideologies. Patanjali in his *Mahabhashya* (the great commentary on Panini's grammar), ascribed to c. second century BCE – perhaps immediately post-Mauryan in date – aptly observed that the irreconciliation between the brahmana and the sramana was comparable with that between a snake and a mongoose (*ahinakula*). The creation and the exposition of the concepts/ideals of *anrisamsya* and *anukrosa* in the *Mahabharata* are possibly symptomatic of the Brahmanical process of appropriation. The process and method of appropriation cannot obfuscate the asymmetry between the appropriator and the appropriated. The appropriating ideology often takes over the salient features of competing and contesting ideologies without any semblance of acknowledgement of the actual source of an ideology which is presented as the appropriator's own creation. The process is neither innocuous nor innocent and involves subordination and marginalization – social and political as well – of the appropriated ideologies and their respective ideologues. Appropriation is a marker of Brahmanical ideology and often thrives on it. Appropriation is thus distinct from absorption, assimilation and co-option of thoughts/ideologies, otherwise incompatible with and contested by Brahmanical ideology which would claim its originary by an erasure of its demonstrable antecedents and genealogy. Of the readings on the utterances on *anrisamsya* in the Mahabharata, Bandyopadhyay's is perhaps the sole voice to have pronounced that the notion of *anrisamsya* was largely a Brahmanical one and it was a reaction to the Sramanic ideal of non-violence (Bandyopadhyay 2016, 2022). His hints at the possibility of tracing the roots of the concept of non-cruelty (*anrisamsya*) to the Sramanic thoughts have provided the platform for this present enquiry.

Moreover, the problem of perspective in arguing that the Sramanic ideologies were rooted to the path of cessation and inaction (*nivritti-marga*) can be diagnosed when one looks at a statement of Asoka engraved in his MRE I. People of Jambudvipa, who had previously not been mixed with gods, have now been mingled with gods (*amisa deva husutedanimisa kata*); this was the outcome, according to the record, of his zealous exertions (*pakamasaesa hi phale*; pakama= Skt. *prakrama*, i.e. effort, exertion).[8] Finally, the twin concepts of *anrisamsya* and *anukrosa* in the *Mahabharata* are embedded to the institutions of *varna-jati* and patriarchy, while Asoka's Dhamma was formulated and applied as an ideology to weld a subcontinental society (Thapar 2002 200–204).

The multiple layers and contents discernible in the *Mahabharata* do not allow its readers to treat and revere this epic in a hegemonic and monolithic manner as a normative treatise (*Samhita*). The openness and the polyphonic nature of the *Mahabharata* underscore the inherent fluidity of both its narrative and didactic contents, which when historically contextualized, continue to offer new insights into the situations of remote pasts. Revisiting the pasts not for the glorification of bygone times, with a revivalist agenda, but for explaining the past in relation to lived experiences is crucial to appreciating the appeals of the *Mahabharata* to its innumerable readers and listeners right up to the current moment.

Notes

1 Fleet 1888: 135–39, line 19. The mention of the Hunas (the Central Asian nomadic Huns) among the list of people engaged in the Kurukshetra war is another clear instance of the interpolations into the text as late as the late fifth and early sixth century CE, since the warlike activities of the Hunas in South Asia cannot be dated prior to the mid-fifth century CE.
2 The assignment of hierarchic *jati* status to a large number of forest-dwelling communities and occupational/professional groups by the orthodox Brahmanical normative treatises as results of the admixture of unequal *varnas* through marriage (*varnasamkara*), which is as presented as social chaos, reads almost like a legal fiction (Yamazaki 2005).
3 See: Bhattacharji (1992) on the ideal of a devoted and loyal wife (*pativrata*) who must be subordinate to her husband; she must follow her husband like a shadow (*chhayevanugata*).
4 For the texts and translations of Asoka's edicts (14 Rock Edicts, two Separate Rock Edicts, seven Pillar Edicts, two Minor Rock Edicts, three Schism Edicts, three Minor Pillar Inscriptions and 7 edicts in Greek and Aramaic) may be consulted Fleet 1888, Hultzsch 1925; Basak, 1959; Sircar 1965, Sircar 1972, Sircar 1979; Mukherjee 1984; Tieken 2023.
5 On the three territorial components (the metropolitan state of Magadha; the core territories and the peripheral tracts) of the Maurya empire, vide Thapar 1987.
6 Mukherjee 1984; excerpts of the English translation by Schlumberger are available in Ray, Chattopadhyaya, Mani, and Chakravarti 2000: 593.
7 Ghoshal 1966; *danda* is the sixth of the seven elements (*sapta-prakriti*) of the state, according to the *Arthasastra*, denoting the army. For a broad overview of the political culture related to violence in early India, see Singh 2017.
8 Sircar 1965: 48–49. The term Jambudvipa that was affected by Asoka's exertions (*pakama/prakrama*) signifies the Maurya realm under his jurisdiction. This is the earliest known use of the term Jambudvipa as a geo-political entity, distinct from the mythical idea of Jambudvipa in the Puranas. Raychaudhuri 1957; Chakravarti 2016 and Chattopadhyaya 2017.

Works Cited

Bandyopadhyay, Sibaji 2016 *Three Essays on the Mahabharata*, Hyderabad: Orient Blackswan.
_____ 2022 *Bharate Mahabharate*, Kolkata: Charbak (in Bangla).
Basak, R.G. 1959 *Asokan Inscriptions*, Calcutta: Firma K.L. Mukhopdhayay.
Chakrabarti, Arindam 2022 'Himsa, Ahimsa, Anrisamsya: DvaipayanerDvanda', in Anirban Bhattacharjee ed., *Mahabharate Himsa*, Kolkata: Alochanachakra: 17–49 (in Bangla).

Bhattacharjee, Anirban ed. 2022, *Mahabharate Himsa*, Kolkata: Alochanachakra (in Bangla).

Bhattacharji, Sukumari 1992 *Women and Society in Ancient India*, Calcutta: Basumati Publications.

———— 2011 *Buddhist Hybrid Sanskrit Literature*, Kolkata: The Asiatic Society.

Chakravarti, Ranabir 2016 *Exploring Early India up to c. AD 1300*, New Delhi: Primus Books (third edition).

———— 2023 'Kathamukh', in Sibaji Bandyopadhyay, *Bharate Mahabaharate*: 11–31, Kolkata: Charvak and Ranaghat: Harappa.

Chakravarti, Uma 1987 *Social Dimensions of Early Buddhism*, New Delhi: Oxford University Press.

Chattopadhyaya, B.D. 2017 *The Concept of Bharatavarsha and Other Essays*, Ranikhet: Permanent Black.

Dayal, Naina 2009 *Tellers of Tales: Pauranikas, Sutas, Kusilavas, Vyasa and Valmiki*, unpublished Ph. D. thesis, New Delhi: Jawaharlal Nehru University.

Fleet, J.F. 1888 *Corpus Inscriptionum Indicarum*, vol. III, Calcutta: Government Press: 135–39.

Ghoshal, U.N. 1966 *A History of Indian Public Life*, vol. II, London: Oxford University Press.

Hiltebeitel, Alf 2001 *Rethinking the Mahabharata: A Readers' Guide to the Education of the Dharma King*, Chicago: University of Chicago Press.

Hultzsch, Eugen 1925 *Inscriptions of Asoka, Corpus Inscriptionum Indicarum*, vol. I. Oxford: Clarendon Press.

Jaiswal, Suvira 1998 *Caste: Origin, Function and Dimension of Change*, New Delhi: Manohar.

Lath, Mukunda 2007 'The Concept of *Anrisamsya* in the *Mahabharata*, in T.R.S. Sharma ed., *Reflections and Variations on the Mahabharata*, New Delhi: Sahitya Akademi: 82–88.

Mukherjee, B.N. 1984 *Studies in the Aramaic Edicts of Asoka*, Calcutta: Indian Museum.

Olivelle, Patrick 2004 *The Asrama System: History and Hermeneutics of a Religious Institution*, Chicago: University of Chicago Press.

Ray, Niharranjan, B.D. Chattopadhyaya, V.R. Mani and Ranabir Chakravarti 2000 *A Sourcebook of Indian Civilization*, Hyderabad: Orient Longman.

Raychaudhuri, H.C. 1957 *Studies in Indian Antiquities*, Calcutta: University of Calcutta.

Roy, Kumkum 2010 *The Power of Gender and the Gender of Power*, New Delhi: Oxford University Press.

———— ed. 2011 *Women in Early Indian Societies*, New Delhi: Manohar (paperback edition).

Singh, Upinder 2008 *History of Ancient and Early Medieval India*, New Delhi: Pearson.

———— 2017 *Political Violence in Ancient India*, Cambridge (Masachusetts): Harvard University Press.

Sinha, Kanad 2019 'Rethinking Dharma in a Time of Transition: Anrisamsya in the Mahabharata as an Alternative End of Human Life, *Studies in History*, XXXV: 147–61.

———— 2021 *From Dasarajna to Kuruksetra, Making of a Historical Tradition*, New Delhi: Oxford University Press.

Shrimali, K.M. 2020 *The Age of Iron and Religious Revolution*, New Delhi: Tulika (paperback edition).

Sircar, D.C. 1965 *Select inscriptions Bearing on Indian History and Civilization*, vol. 1, Calcutta: University of Calcutta: 15–78.

_____ 1972 *Asokan Edicts*, New Delhi: Publication Division.

_____ 1979 *Asokan Studies*, Calcutta: Indian Museum.

Sukthankar, V.S. 1936–37 'The Bhrigus and the Bharatas: A Text Historical Study', *Annals of the Bhandarkar Oriental Research Institute*, XVIII: 1–76.

_____ 1957 *On the Meaning of the Mahabharata*, Bombay: The Asiatic Society of Bombay.

Thapar, Romila 1984 *From Lineage to State*, Bombay: Oxford University Press.

_____ 1987 *The Mauryas Revisited*, Calcutta: Centre for Studies in Social Sciences.

_____ 1996 *Asoka and the Decline of the Mauryas*, New Delhi: Oxford University Press (second edition).

_____ 2002 *Early India from the Origins to c. AD 1300*, London: Allen Lane.

_____ 2008 *Cultural Pasts*, New Delhi: Oxford University Press.

_____ 2013 *The Past before Us: Historical Traditions of Early North India*, Cambridge (Masachusetts): Harvard University Press.

Tieken, Herman 2023 *The Asoka Inscriptions, Analysing a Corpus*, New Delhi: Primus Books.

Visvanathan, Meera 2011 'Asoka's Dhamma', in Upinder Singh ed., *Online Lectures on the History of Ancient India*, Delhi: University of Delhi.

Wagle, N. 1966 *Society at the Time of the Buddha*, Bombay: Asia Publishing House.

Winternitz, Maurice, 1987 *History of Sanskrit Literature* vol I (trn. by Srinivas Sarma), New Delhi: Motilal Banarasidass.

Yamazaki, G. 2005 *The Structure of Ancient Indian Society: Theory and Reality of the Varna System*, Tokyo: The Toyo Bunko.

INDEX

Abhiram 27
Abdullah ibn Muqaffa 48
Abdul Rahim 61
Abul Fazal/Fazl 28, 51–53, 56–59, 62
abuse 44, 89, 105, 162; verbal 69
accretion xii, 95, 188
Achilles 183
Adbhutaramayana 19
Adi Shankacharya 220
admonition xx, 60, 232
Advaita 41–42
Advaitin see Advaita
Aegisthus 183
Afghan 94, 170
Afghanistan 232
Agamemnon 183
ageha 227, 228
agency 5; human 102; political 9
Ahmad, Fakhruddin Ali 125
Ahmadnagar 38
Ahura (Asura) 189
Ajivika xix, 234
Akbar 28–29, 45, 49–63
Alberuni 25
Alexander (the Great) 186
Alkazi, Ebrahim 99
Al-Mamun 48
anachronism 38
anachrony 2, 205
anachronistic 10, 38, 40, 118
Anandatirtha 25
Anandavardhana 39

Andhra [Pradesh] 18, 27, 104
Anglo-Indian 89
animosity: Hindu-Muslim 58; Kaurava-
    Pandava 174; Naga-Kuru 187
Aniruddha see Ramasarasvati
anrisamsa/anrisamsya/anrsamsa/
    anrsamsya 199, 218, 224–31,
    235–36
antagonistic compound xx
anukrosa/anukrosh xxi, 196, 226–31,
    235–36
Anupasimha, Maharaja of Bikaner 38
Anwar-i Suhaili 48
aporia xvii
ascetic 6, 21, 92, 227–28
Asoka 231–37
asrama/ashrama 23, 214, 227–28
Assamese Mahabharata 28
Asvalayana 194
Atharva/Atharvan/Atharva Veda/
    Atharvaveda 18, 50, 184–94
autobiography/autobiographical 11, 156
auto-critique 3
avatara 73–79, 116

Babur 49–50
Baburnama 50, 62
Bachchan, Amitabh 184
Badauni/Badayuni, Abdul Qadir 28,
    50, 171
Bakhtinian 163
Ballalasena 25

Banaras/Benares 38, 40–42, 90
Bangabasi (publishing) 89–91
Bangadarshan 87
Bangla (language) xviii, 84, 89–91, 96
bard xiv, 22, 138, 141, 173, 179, 187, 225, 226
bardic 141, 155, 187
Baroda 18
Basawan 52
Basu, Rajnarain 88–89
Batman 184–85
Baudhayana 186
Bayqara, Muhammad Hussayn 48
Bengali/Bengalee (language/people) 9, 26, 49, 66–80, 84–87, 89, 92, 94–97, 114, 165, 172, 220; *see also* Bangla
Bentham [Jeremy] 215
Besant, Annie 220
bhadralok 85, 91, 97, 114, 119
bhakti 34, 42, 67, 78, 80, 122, 226
Bhakti, the movement 122
Bhanubhakta 28
Bharatiya Janata Party (BJP) 4, 13–15, 17
Bharati, Subramania 166
Bhardwaj, Nitish 133
Bhargavayana xiv
Bhargavization 187, 190, 225; *see also* Bhargavayana
Bhasa 6, 165
Bhavabhuti 32, 33
Bhavan, Shaykh 50, 52, 53
Bheel Bharath 7
Bhriguramadasa 66
Bhyrappa [S.L.] 7
Bikramjit, Raja of Malwa 50
bildungsroman 156
biological continuism 207
Bodhgaya 232
Bollywood 131, 132, 184
Bombay 19, 28
Bombay Plan 107
Brahmanic 3, 4, 220
Brahmanical/Brahminical xiv, xv, xix, 111, 190, 192, 194, 225–31, 236, 237
Brahmo [Samaj, a member of] 85, 89–90
Brihadaranyaka Upanishad 145, 194
Buddha [Siddhartha Gautama] 92, 216, 227, 232

Buddhism 4, 214, 228, 231–32, 235, 236
butterfly-effect 177

Calcutta 89, 90, 114
camera 170
capitalist 104–7
Carvaka xix
caste xiv, xvii, 4, 6, 104, 118, 122, 128, 148, 191, 196, 198, 218, 221
Categorical Imperative xvi, 215
celibacy 7, 143
celibate xvii
Chadar-Badar 175
Chaitanya movement 75
Chandragupta II 186
Chandrahasakhyana 28
chaos theory 177
Chattagram 26, 27
Chattopadhyay, Bhudhar 91
Chaturbhuj/a 28, 52
chaturvarga 228
Chauhan, Gajendra 133
Chishti, Abdur Rahman 57
Christ 61, 92
Christian: eschatology 116; missionary 85, 86, 89
chronology 88, 95, 145
Clytemnestra 183
comics 172–76, 184
Communist 216; Party 104
compassion xxi, 60, 111, 228, 231, 233, 235
composite text 144
Congress, Indian National 107, 122, 124, 133, 135, 214
court-epic 6
cosmic 6, 68, 69, 71–73, 77
cosmogony 80
cosmological 2, 58, 147
counter-history 125
criminal xxi, xxii, 184
cruelty 12, 175, 199, 226, 234, 235

Dacca [Dhaka] 90
Dakshineswar 85, 86
dalit 218, 222
Dara Shukoh 57
Das, Nilambara 28
Dasein 205, 207
daya 234, 235

deification 149, 157, 166
democracy 103, 121, 126–29, 133, 217, 218
devotion/al 72, 87, 97, 117, 121–23, 133, 226, 233–34; *see also* bhakti
Dhamma 231–36
dharmavyadh/dharmavyadha/dharma-vyadha 12, 218, 229–30
dharmic/dharmika/dharmikah 166, 190, 198, 206, 207, 209
dialogism 163
dileptus 170
domesticity 230
Doordarshan 121, 130, 145, 146
Doyle, Arthur Conan 183
dutiful 192, 229
Dutta, Akshay Kumar 96
Dutta, Narendranath *see* Swami Vivekananda
duty xvii, 104, 106, 194, 220, 229, 230
Dvija Abhiram *see* Abhiram

ecclesiastical 226, 234
e/Enlightenment 42, 112, 225
empathy 183, 196, 199, 227, 228, 231, 233, 235; *see also* anukrosa
Entbehrung 204
entropy 89, 143
epistemological 206
epistolary 86; novel 156
erasure 3, 85, 236
ethical care 206
ethical Responsibility 206
everydayness 4, 5
evil xv, xxi, 72–74, 149, 193, 196, 198, 203, 207, 216

faith 78, 96, 111, 117, 123, 235
Faizi/Fayzi 50–52, 57
Fatehpur Sikri 49
femininity 129
feminist politics 157
fetishization of the mythic past 126
flashback 143–45, 147–48
forest xix, xx, 2, 6, 21, 22, 69, 101, 104, 117, 141, 167, 172, 179, 186–87, 198, 203, 205, 207, 225, 227, 229, 234, 237
forgiveness 68, 102, 163, 195–96, 199
freedom 101, 104, 127, 159, 161
friendship 102, 127, 160, 184, 185, 202

gallery 170
Gandhi, Indira 124, 125, 128, 129, 135
Gandhi [M.K.] 99, 103, 126, 214
Gandhi, Rahul 214
Gandhian 45
garhasthya 227, 230
Gaza xxi
gaze 152, 170
gender battle 157
genocidal 6, 186, 194
genocide 7, 103
Ghosh, Aurobindo 84
Ghosh/Ghosha, Nityananda 27, 66
Godavari 38, 45
grihastha 227
Gupta, Annada Prasad 90
Gupta, Mahendranath 85

habitus 5
Hafiz 59
Halebidu 171
Hamza, Amir 50; Hamzanama 50, 56
Handwerk 204
Haribara Bipra 28
Harivamsa/Harivamsha 19, 24–25, 38, 51, 92, 93, 96, 226
Hasan al Jili, Abul 49
Hastie, William 86–87
Hastings, Warren 146
hatred 194, 221, 222
hegemonic 3, 10, 123, 222, 236
Helen 183
Herat 48
Herodotus 94
heterodoxy 101
heterogeneity 209
heterogeneous 204
heteroglossia 163
heterotopic 99
Himachal Pradesh 29
himsa xix, xxi, 213, 217, 219
Hindavi/Hindvi 52, 53
historia xviii
historicity 3, 9, 94
Hitler, Adolf xx
Homelessness *see ageha*
hospitality 23, 207–9
household 117, 230
householder xix, 4, 73, 207, 227, 229–30
Humanism 112
Humanities 112

Hussain Shah 26, 27
hyper-sexuality 158

inaction 151, 236
interconnectedness 164, 208
interlocutor 54, 213
Iran 58, 189
Islamic 28, 48, 52–63
itihasa xii–xxii, 3, 83, 94, 138, 140, 142, 187, 213, 225

Jainism 4, 216, 228, 236
Jain/Jaina xix, 33, 52, 62, 107, 227, 234
Jaipur 29, 61
jatra 32
jealousy 160, 167, 234
jingoism 222
Jivanmukta 42
jyotisa 38

Kaal/Kala 71, 79, 147; kala–narrator 148; *see also* time
kabya/kavya 87, 142, 226
Kalhana 24, 26
Kalidasa 6, 26, 32, 90, 165
Kalinga 172, 232; Kalinga war 234
Kaliyuga/kali era/Kali Yuga 6, 7, 95, 102, 116, 156, 177
Kama 100, 227
Kamasutra 24
Kandahar 232, 234
Kannada 7, 10, 27, 32, 35, 99, 149, 165
Karma Yoga 214, 221
Karpuragrama or Kopargaon 38
karuna see compassion
karuna-rasa 113
Kashifi, Husain Waiz 48
Kashmir 24, 39, 103
Kashmiri Ramayana 28
Kathakali 172, 175
Kathasaritsagara 23–27, 33, 34
Kavi Karnapura 52
Kerala 7, 18, 124, 172
Khan, Chhuti 27
Khan, Dvija Ramchandra 27
Khan, Paragal 26, 27, 75
Khoh (in Madhya Pradesh) 226
Khosrow Anushirvan 48
kindness 197, 234, 235; *see also daya*
kingship 6, 50, 58–61, 106, 190
Kiratarjuniyam 6
Kitab al Hind 49

Kolkata 97, 111, 114; *see also* Calcutta
Krishnadasa 52
Kshatriya xvi, 4, 34, 40, 41, 160, 185, 189–94, 198, 224, 229, 231
Kudiattam 172
Kushan period 173

Lalitaditya Muktapida 24
liberation 44, 162
lila 76–78, 117, 118
linear 8, 117, 147
linearity 143, 145
lisible 1
literary unthing 214
literate 62, 91, 141, 145
Livy 94
Lokayata xix
lore xii, 141, 213
Lumbinigrama 232

Madhvacarya/Madhvacharya/Madhva 25, 40, 41
Magadha 225, 226, 237
Magadhan 234
Magdhi (people) 173
Magha 6
Mahabhashya/Mahabhasya xx, 236
mahakavya 6, 172, 212
Maharashtra 38, 122
Maharashtrian Prakrit 33
Mahasweta Devi 165
Mahatma Gandhi *see* Gandhi [M.K.]
Mahavira 216, 227
Majma ul Tawarikh 49
Makkhaliputta Gosala 227
maktab khana 49
Maladhar/Maladhara 74, 75, 77
Malayalam 32
Malayali 124
Malla, Kalyana 49
Mandela, Nelson 171
Mannerist School of painting 41
Marathi 22, 28, 165
Markandeya Purana 17, 34
Marxism 213, 219
Marxist 85, 215, 219
masculinity 105, 175
materiality 5, 207
maternal instinct 167
matrilineal 186
Maulana Imamuddin 50
Maurya/Mauryan 173, 190, 231–37
Maus 174

maya 40, 75, 106, 189
Mexico City 215
Midnapore 84
minstrel xii, xiv, 225, 226; *see also* bard
mise-en-scène 131
Mishra, Ananta 27
Miskina 54
Misra, Debi 28
Misra, Madhusudana 28
misreading 117, 221
Modernism 10, 113, 114, 116
Modernist 10, 111, 113–18
Modi, Narendra 133
Moily, M. Veerappa 166
moksa/moksha 162, 227; *see also* liberation
Mughal Court 38, 49, 52, 65
Mukammal Khan Gujarati 52
multicultural 45
Muntakhab ul Tawarikh 51
Mustafa Khaliqdad Abbasi 50

Nagarjuna hills near Gaya 234
Nair, M.T. Vasudevan 167
Nandarama 66
Nandi, Rameshvar 27
Nandi, Shrikara/Srikaran 26–27, 74
nastika 227
nationalism xxiv, 85, 87, 121–36, 185, 212–14, 221–22
nationalist discourse 9, 12, 124, 219, 221
Nehru, Jawaharlal 10, 45, 99–101, 104–7, 125–28
neoliberalism 222
niskama karma 195, 219, 220
nivritti 228, 236
Nolan, Christopher 185
non-cruelty 196, 199, 207, 210, 218, 224, 226, 228–31, 235–36; *see also* anrisamsa
non-dualism 40–42, 220; *see also* Advaita
non-injury 205, 207, 235
non-killing 205, 227, 233, 234
non-violence xix, 205, 210, 218, 219, 221, 222, 226–28, 230, 235
Nowness xvii, 4, 5, 12
nrsamsa 199

objectification 140
Odisha 172

Odiya/Oriya (sic) Mahabharata 20, 28, 66, 81, 165
Odyssey 183
Onesikritas 186
ontological 202, 203
ontology 3
Orientalist 96, 112
Orwell, George xxi, 213

Padma Purana 33
Padmacharitra 33
Pahlavi 48
Panchatantra 18, 25, 48, 50, 60
Pandavapratapa 22
Pandavavijaya 27
pandemic (COVID19) 150
Panjab/Punjab 114, 189
paramecium 170
Parmenides 4
Patel, Vallabhbhai 104
Patroclus 183
Paumacariyam 33
performative 2, 5, 113, 123, 138, 144–45, 154
Persian 9, 28, 40, 48–64, 172
Pillalmarri Pinaveerabhadriah 27
pity 111, 118, 196, 197
Plato 117
plenitude 204
plurality 12, 140–41, 148
polyphonic 2, 4, 163, 236
postcolonial 6, 10, 130, 135
pragmatic 213, 216, 218, 223
pravritti 228
purusartha/purushartha 39, 228
Purva Mimamsa 17–18, 23, 25, 26, 34, 214

Qasimbazar 90; *see also* Gupta, Annada Prasad
quietism 216
Quranic 52, 56

race 93, 179, 192, 204
Raghunatha 66
Raghuvamsham 26, 32
Rahim *see* Abdul Rahim
Rajavinoda 49
Rajatarangini 24
Ramanuja 25, 41
Ramasarasvati 28
Ramayan, TV show 130, 131, 133, 135
Randamoozam 167

Rangpur 84
Rankean 3
Rashid, Harun al 48
Ravisena 33
recollection 4, 140, 143
religion 3, 4, 54, 57, 61, 63, 97, 104,
    117, 128, 189, 190, 194, 219, 232
religiosity 146, 150
repetition 4, 7, 113, 125, 140, 144
rhizomic 2
righteous xvi, xvii, 7, 105, 149, 183,
    206, 227, 229, 230, 232
righteousness xvii, 149, 151, 229
right-wing 135, 214, 222
ritualistic 18, 74, 77, 86, 90, 154, 207
Roman 48
Romanticism 114
RSS 135
Russia xxii
Rustam and Sohrab 55

sacred xiii, 58, 127, 162, 226, 227
sacrifice xv, 2, 3, 8, 17, 19, 22, 30, 33,
    54, 70, 76, 84, 122, 127, 174–75,
    178, 185–87, 194–95, 199, 205–8,
    217, 227
Sagar, Ramanand 130
Sahu, Indramani 28
Sakyamuni *see* Buddha
salvation 73; *see also* liberation and
    moksa
Samashrami, Satyabrata 96
Sanjoy's Mahabharata 27
sannyasa 227
Saraladasa 66, 81
Sarasvati, Madhusudana 42
Sarkar, Akshay Chandra 87, 91
Satrapi, Marjane 174
secular 122, 128, 131, 135
secularism 45
self-affirmation 159
semiosis 149
Sen, Adhar 86
Sen, Keshub Chunder 88
Sen, Shashthibar 27
Sen/a, Gangadas/a 27, 28, 66
sexuality 158, 161, 167
Shahnama 55, 58, 62
Shastri, Ramadhar Shukla 28
Shaykh Faizi *see* Faizi
Shivaji 46
Shramanic *see* Sramanic
Shrikrishnavijaya 74, 79, 80

Shrimadbhagavatam 71–77, 79
simultaneity 1, 5; non-simultaneity 207
Sitaramayya, Pattavi 104
socialism 215
Somadeva 23, 26, 33
Spiegelman, Art 174
spiritual 41, 156, 157, 160, 161, 220
spiritual writing 159
spirituality 220, 229
Sramana xix, xx, 175, 227, 233, 236
Sramanic xix, xx, xxi, 3, 227–28, 230,
    234–36
Sridhara 22
Sriramulu, Patti 104
Stalin [Joseph] 215
storytelling/story-telling 99, 141, 157,
    159, 164, 172, 175
St. Augustine 117
subjectivity 10, 11, 143, 154, 158, 163
Sufi 61
Sufism 59
Sulaimaccarita 49
supplement 88, 124, 131, 204
surveillance 170
swadharma 60
Swami Vivekananda 86
Swaraj, Sushma 214

tabaqat 58
Tabrizi, Sayyid Ali 52
Tagore, Abanindranath 84
Tagore, Rabindranath 9, 83, 97
Tamil 36, 149, 165
Tamil Nadu 19, 122
Tantric 43
Tanvir, Habib 99
tarikh 58
Tarikh i Khandan i Timuriyya 58
tarjuma 51
Tarkachudamani, Sasadhar 89, 90, 96
tawarikh 58
teleological 116, 117
televisual 132, 146, 148, 150
Telugu 20, 27, 32, 104, 165
Thanesari/Thanessari/Thanisari,
    Shaikh Sultan (Haji) 28, 51
theological 44, 52, 57, 59, 76
theology 9, 40, 42, 43, 188
Theosophist 90, 220
Theyyam 175
Thiruvananthapuram 124
time, Hindu *vs.* Christian conceptions
    of 116

time-entropy 143
time-loop 5, 154
Timurid 48, 61, 62
transcreation 10, 110, 113, 115
Troy 183
Tulsidas 28

Udayraja 49
undisclosable 204
Upadesasutra/Upadesha Sutras 18, 20
USSR 215
*Uttararamacharita/Uttara
    Ramcharitam* 32, 34

Vacaspatimisra/Vachaspati Mishra
    34, 41
Vaishnava/Vaisnava 34, 41, 43–46, 66,
    67, 71, 76, 77, 80, 190, 226
Vaishnavism 75, 80
Vaishnavite/Vaisnavite 40, 150
Vaisnavization 190
Varaha-Mihira 24
Varanasi 104; *see also* Banaras
varna xvi, 194, 196, 219, 224, 225,
    227–30, 234, 236
varna-based xix, 190
varna-ordered 190
varnasamkara 237
varnashrama 214, 221
Vatsyayana 24
vegetarianism xix
Veronese [painter] 41

Vibhatsya Rasa 116
Vidyaranya 41
Villipputturar 149
Vimalasuri 33
violence xxi, xxiv, 6, 11, 12, 132, 185,
    158, 161, 162, 167, 132, 187, 195,
    199, 206, 212–18, 230, 232–36,
    228, 230, 232–33, 235–36, 238;
    legitimization of violence 219
virtue 57, 60, 127, 144, 196, 198, 207,
    224, 226, 229, 230, 234
virtuous 155, 218, 234
Vishnu Purana 18, 26, 71–73
Vishnuvarman 48
Vishvaroop/vishvarupa/Vishwarupa
    76, 146, 151
Vivekananda *see* Swami Vivekananda

War poetry in English 115–16
war reportage 143, 148
weltanschauung 114
West Bengal 122, 174
Wordsworth, William 86
worldview 93, 123; *see also*
    weltanschauung

Yakshagana 29, 32
Yama-pata 174
Yarlagadda, Lakshmi Prasad 166
yati 227
yoga 26, 68, 79, 214, 221
yuga 115, 116

For Product Safety Concerns and Information please contact our EU
representative GPSR@taylorandfrancis.com
Taylor & Francis Verlag GmbH, Kaufingerstraße 24, 80331 München, Germany